Praise for Jill McGown's
Inspector Lloyd and Judy Hill Mysteries

"A plot that Dame Agatha Christie would have much admired . . . An ingenious puzzle . . . A smashing finale with a solution that is both right and inevitable."
The Washington Post

"Low-key and engrossing, and pleasantly English."
Chicago Tribune

"A murder so baffling it might even have stumped Agatha Christie's Miss Marple . . . A lively, entertaining mystery."
The Philadelphia Inquirer

"McGown uses all the situations of the classic locked-room mystery but revitalizes them with very modern personal predicaments."
Houston Chronicle

"Ingenious, stylish, and distinguished . . . A fine introduction to a talented new author."
Mystery News

Also by Jill McGown:

A PERFECT MATCH*
MURDER AT THE OLD VICARAGE*
AN EVIL HOUR
THE STALKING HORSE
GONE TO HER DEATH*

*Published by Fawcett Books

MURDER MOVIE

Jill McGown

FAWCETT CREST • NEW YORK

A Fawcett Crest Book
Published by Ballantine Books
Copyright © 1990 by Jill McGown

All rights reserved under International and Pan-American Copyright Conventions. Published in the United States by Ballantine Books, a division of Random House, Inc., New York, and simultaneously in Canada by Random House of Canada Limited, Toronto. Originally published in Great Britain by Macmillan London Limited in 1990. First published in the U.S. by St. Martin's Press, Inc., in 1991.

Library of Congress Catalog Card Number: 90-49302

ISBN 0-449-22070-2

This edition published by arrangement with St. Martin's Press, Inc.

Manufactured in the United States of America

First Ballantine Books Edition: January 1993

FOREWORD

Should anyone involved in film-making read this novel, please forgive my trespasses. I have played fast and loose with your craft (not to mention the morals of its practitioners) in order to accommodate mine, and I can only hope that you will accept the book in the spirit in which it has been written . . . as a thank you to your magical profession.

I am well aware that the process of producing the magic is much more time-consuming, complex and frustrating than the impression given here, but perhaps you can take consolation in the fact that it is also (I trust) much less *dangerous*.

JM

CHAPTER ONE

". . . AS ONCE AGAIN MR. INGRAM DISPATCHES ALL the bad guys and wins through. It's nonsense, of course, but it's fun. Mark Ingram's next film role, however, is a quite different proposition, and we will be hearing more about that and other matters after the break, when Gussie Christiansen, our spy in the Hollywood camp—take that how you will— keeps us abreast of the doings of our compatriots in the Dream Factory. See you in a couple of minutes."

An advertisement for toothpaste carried over the calls of the gulls circling the beach. The woman turned from the steep drop down to the ebbing tide, walking back up the long, neat kitchen-garden into the house which sat virtually on the edge of the cliffs. She was around forty, blonde, blue-eyed, and by any standards beautiful.

She turned the TV sound back to its normal level, and heard the doorbell for the first time. Impatient ringing—she opened the door with an apology.

"Where were you?" he asked, removing a cigar from his mouth. He had fair wavy hair, and a boyish look despite a slight tendency to middle-aged spread.

"Looking at the view," she said.

"Can't fault Ardcraig for its views." His Cockney accent was still there, but it had been modified. He rubbed his hands together as he followed her into the sitting room. "Bloody cold for April, though," he said.

1

"Gussie Christiansen," she said, nodding at the TV as the programme came back on.

"Good God, do they get her on this side of the Atlantic too?" he said, as she started to speak.

"Oh, yes. I fed her some news about the book before we left, so hush—I want to hear what she's saying."

The man shrugged.

". . . is Frank Derwent's new film, Three Clear Sundays. It's another of F.D.'s excursions into more serious film, and is an adaptation of a novel by Simon Waterford. All the expat Brits you can shake a stick at will be in it, I'm told . . . all being shipped over the pond to Scotland, where the film is to be shot . . ."

"She makes it sound like Quo Vadis," he said with a smile, and was hushed again.

". . . meanwhile, F.D. himself has, we understand, completed shooting what were called 'essential scenes' in Florida—doubling as a South Sea island—which essential scenes of course include his latest protégée, Barbara Slaney . . ."

The woman tensed up a little, the man shook his head and knocked ash from his cigar. "You didn't give her that bit of news," he said.

"Slaney is a nineteen-year-old blonde, blue-eyed—what else?—British actress whom F.D.'s assistant director, R. Howard Maxwell—another Brit—you do believe in sticking together, don't you?—'discovered' on a field trip earlier this year, as he has done so often before . . . The Dodgers should have such a talent scout! It seems F.D. and Slaney have got stuck in London, for reasons that remain a little unclear, because everyone else is in Scotland, raring to go. Well—I guess they must be taking the high road . . ."

He crushed the cigar out, his back to the screen.

". . . and no one is saying where either of them is, least of all R. Howard Maxwell. The 'R' stands for Ron, by the way, but Mr. Maxwell seems to think that Howard is more distinguished . . ."

The man's attention also turned to the screen, eyebrows raised.

2

"Howard's reputation as the most discreet man in Hollywood has not been earned lightly. Howard has lots to be discreet about . . ."

He smiled at the woman, holding it until she turned to look at him.

". . . and we hear that F.D.'s wife Wanda has been picking his brains for her long-awaited, much-hyped exposé of the English in Hollywood. Trying to do me out of a job, Wanda? Well, with two husbands from that neck of the woods, the Anglophile Wanda would seem to have all the qualifications . . ."

She did look at him then, and returned a brittle, almost nervous, smile before turning back to the TV.

". . . and the book, from what we hear, is going to leave more than one person in Tinsel Town hopping mad. Watch out for low-flying law suits is the word . . . One of the publishers—yes, there are several, what with hardback, paperback and magazine rights, not to mention the British tabloids—said the book should carry a health warning, it will induce so many heart attacks. Don't get mad, Wanda, get a six-figure publishing contract?"

The man chuckled.

". . . and what has all of this got to do with F.D.'s latest movie? I'll tell you. Seems it's to star Susan Quentin from Stones—*the diamond-studded soap that's been pure gold for its producers—and none other than action man heart-throb Mark Ingram . . . Mark, those of you over thirty-five may recall, was married to Wanda Derwent—until F.D. came on the scene, that is. But over twenty years have passed since then, and I guess the wounds have healed . . ."*

"Do you?" murmured the woman to the screen, and the man looked a little concerned.

". . . Well, let's hope they have, because apparently Wanda still has some 'vital' background research to do on her book—and guess where that has to be done? Yes, Wanda's going with her ever-loving—both of them—to Scotland . . . So watch out for sparks flying, with all those ex-husbands and current protégées in the same small Scot-

tish town. Are you Brits really ready for the return of these particular natives, do you think?''

The screen went dark, and she laid down the remote control, turning to her visitor.

"Don't you want to hear the rest?" he asked.

"She'd finished. You can tell—she closes her eyes. When she opens them, she's on to another item."

He smiled, and picked up the remote control, bringing the TV to life again.

". . . has been called the Divorce of the Decade, and the court-room drama would make a feature film all on its own . . ."

"I'd never noticed that," he said. "I'll have to watch her more closely." He smiled. "You don't want to waste a minute of your time, do you, Wanda?"

". . . and in this Land of the Rising Divorce Settlement Elise Wyatt is all set to pick up what will amount to the largest payout yet . . ."

"How does Gussie know that my first name's Ron?" he asked.

"I told her." Wanda looked penitent. "Shouldn't I?"

He smiled. "But how do you know?"

"Ah—you slipped up."

The smile remained; his eyes looked just a touch wary. "Slipped up?" he repeated.

"You let me borrow that lovely old book of yours," she said. "Inside, it said 'To Ron, from Mum, Christmas 1949.' "

Howard nodded slowly. "Well," he said, "that's what sentiment does for you. My secret is out."

She smiled her brittle smile again. "And you're so good at keeping other people's," she said. "Why *is* F.D. in London?"

He shook his head.

". . . all that for four years of marriage? Hey, for that sort of loot, I'd marry Freddy Krueger . . ."

Gussie was cut off again.

Wanda went to the drinks table and poured herself a Perrier. "Can I get you something?" she asked, waving the whisky bottle at him.

4

"Of course," he said, and smiled. "That's what I like about you, Wanda. You might drink bottled water and eat raw vegetables and run a hundred miles a day, but you let the rest of us go happily into cardiac arrest without preaching." He joined her at the table, taking a fistful of ice and dropping it into the glass.

"What you do with your body is no concern of mine," said Wanda.

"Pity," said Howard, with a grin.

"Why is he in London in the first place? I got a flight straight to Glasgow. So did you."

"I don't know. Maybe you have to fly to London from Miami."

"And there's a three-day wait at Customs is there? Where *is* he, Howard?"

He shrugged. "I don't know," he said. "And I wouldn't tell you if I did."

She just looked at him.

"So he likes blue-eyed blondes," he said, into the silence. "So did Hitchcock. It didn't mean he was sleeping with them."

She splashed whisky on to the ice. "Howard," she said patiently. "As soon as I hit twenty-five, F.D. jumped into bed with a bimbo clone. He's been doing it ever since, and you find them for him." She pushed the cork home. "If it makes you feel less like a pimp to believe that he's giving her extra coaching, fine." She prodded his chest with the neck of the bottle. "Just don't expect me to."

He feigned pain, then grinned again, picking up his glass. He flopped down on the long sofa, looking up at her. "Listen, girl, if I thought it would keep F.D. churning out box-office hits, I'd sleep with him myself."

She looked at him for a moment. "I believe you would," she said seriously.

The pub was beginning to empty. A couple sat in the corner, their meal finished, their faces strained. She was blonde, blue-eyed, young. He was late fifties, with a strong, sun-tanned face and grey hair.

"*. . . and that's about it for* Matinee Performance *this week. Join us next Thursday afternoon, when we'll be reviewing, amongst others, the latest . . .*"

"She wanted to come," he said, his voice low, as another group of departing customers passed their table. "I couldn't stop her. That's why I arranged for us to be in London for a couple of days."

"But why does she want to be here?"

"She says it's to do some research."

"That woman doesn't believe that," she said, nodding at the TV.

"Neither do I," he said grimly. "Which is why we will have to cool it for a while."

She finished her drink and stood up. "Where have I heard that before?" she said. "Oh—I know. It's the line that comes just after 'I'd marry you if I were free.' Right?" She turned and walked to the door.

He sighed, knocked back his own drink and followed her out, blinking as he went from the dim interior into the bright, cold air.

He tutted at her. "Such cynicism in one so young," he said, and smiled.

"Why don't you divorce her?" she asked.

"On what grounds? Wanda is a model wife, and has been for twenty years."

"Leave her."

"You're joking."

They walked slowly through the unglamorous streets of London, past graffiti-covered walls.

"I thought you wanted to be free."

Her heel caught in a crack in the pavement; she leant on him as she put on her shoe.

"Freedom isn't free," he said. "You heard what that woman's screwing out of Wyatt. And we are going to be as good as strangers in Scotland—no sparks are going to fly."

6

"Are you sure?" Barbara let her body rub against his before she moved away, walking a little way ahead of him.

He stood still, watching her, his eyes narrowing a little. Then he smiled and caught her up.

Howard sipped his drink. "It's like caddying," he said.

Wanda frowned.

"Golf caddies. If their man's winning, they're winning. They're on a percentage, and so am I. And a percentage of F.D. is worth being on. If talent-scouting is part of the job, that's fine by me. My job is to make his path as smooth as possible, and that's what I do."

"This one isn't box office," said Wanda. "It's a neo-Victorian melodrama, for God's sake."

Howard smiled. "F.D.'s going for Oscars," he said. "Oscars are box office."

"Oscars? With a soap star, a swimmer and a bimbo?"

"They can act." He grinned lazily. "Well—they can take direction, and they're not likely to have ideas of their own. That's the way F.D. likes it. He's after Best Picture, Best Director. He can get a performance out of a tin of baked beans when he's on song, and we both know what F.D. needs to stay on song."

"This one wasn't even born when F.D. and I were married," she said. "He's thirty-seven years older than her, Howard—don't you have any principles?"

"What are they?" He put down his drink and took out a cigar case. "Have you ever been unfaithful to him?" he asked.

She shook her head.

"If it's principles that make you play the dutiful wife all the time, forget them. Throw them away." The match flared, and lit his face with little spurts of flame as he puffed. "You must be a bit lonely," he added, as the cigar end glowed red.

"Why?"

"You just said it. F.D. isn't getting any younger. If he's giving his all to the bimbos, there can't be much left over for you."

7

"There's nothing left over for me."

"Well, then."

"You think if you're not having sex you must be lonely?"

He smiled. "That's how it is with me," he said with a wistful shrug.

They walked out of the afternoon sunshine into a tall, dilapidated block of flats. F.D. punched the broken button beside the graffiti-covered doors, and the lift opened.

"At least the lift's working now," he said, pushing Barbara into it.

It took a moment after the doors had closed to begin its airless, noisy way to the top of the building. Her neck glistened with perspiration, as she stood a little in front of him, her eyes fixed on the light as the car climbed.

He touched her shoulder. "The lift bothers you, doesn't it?" he said.

She didn't reply, as she followed the light's progress through the floors, relaxing only when the doors, with a moment's indecision, slid open at the top floor.

She got out, licking dry lips, and took a breath. "I don't understand why we can't just use my flat," she said.

"Because, my love, the tabloids will be keeping a very close eye on your flat."

"Why are you so afraid she'll find out?" she asked. "Everyone obviously knows anyway."

"Knowing and proving are two different things. She doesn't know where we are, so she can't prove a thing."

"No," said Barbara, as she stopped at the shabby door. "And she's not likely to guess."

"That's the idea." He took the key from his shirt pocket and unlocked the door. "In Scotland, she'll know exactly where we are." He locked the door behind them.

She looked round at the flaking paint, the dingy walls, and slipped off her jacket. "Did you bring the others to this grotty flat?"

"What others?"

8

"The ones that woman was talking about," she said. "The other girls Howard found for you. Did you bring them here?"

"Are you jealous?"

"Who knows about this place? Does Howard?"

"No. And don't try it. Don't even think about it."

"Think about what?"

"Blackmail, my sweet." He took off his coat. "Wasn't that what you had in mind? Threatening to tell Wanda about what the gutter press would call my love-nest? It would do you no good. I have no connection with this place. I cover my tracks much too well."

"I just don't want to carry on like this," she said. She crossed to the window, looking down at the paved square with its carousels of washing drying in the early spring sunshine. "I want to have you to myself."

"You've got me to yourself now."

"For a day or two." She pulled the shade on the bright sun. "In a high-rise bedsit, with pub lunches thrown in."

"Make the most of it," he said. "Wanda's given me a lot of rope, and now she wants to watch me hang myself. That's why she's here."

"You mean she's already in Britain?"

"She's already in Ardcraig," said F.D. "To keep an eye on me. She thinks I won't be able to keep my hands off you."

Barbara turned from the window and began to undress slowly, never taking her eyes from his. "And will you?" she asked, her naked body silhouetted against the light.

A slight frown creased his brow as he watched her cross to the bed, and sit, drawing up one leg, her elbow resting on her knee as the other leg dangled over the edge. He smiled, and began to remove his own clothes, just as slowly as she had. Then he moved towards the bed.

"No hands," he said, kneeling on the floor in front of her.

A ribbon of sunlight streamed through a tear in the blind, across the bed, accepting the open invitation of the carelessly spread legs. His shadow took its place; she caught her breath, then smiled, her fingers tracing the strip of light as it lay across his bowed head.

9

". . . and if you and I could have fun with one another, why shouldn't we?" Howard concluded. "You could get your own back on F.D."

She finished her drink. "If I wanted to get my own back, I'd have a twenty-five-year-old stud, not a middle-aged gopher."

Howard smiled, not at all put out. "Assistant," he said.

"Glorified foreman," said Wanda.

"A very well rewarded glorified foreman."

"And we know why that is, don't we?" said Wanda. "Why don't you just get yourself a bimbo while you're about it?"

"I can't give them speaking parts, can I? Nineteen-year-old girls don't exactly throw themselves at me."

"But what you've got will be all right for me?"

"Yes." He smiled and got up, walking to the window, looking out at the hills rising beyond the woods. "Nice place," he said, and turned to her. "And it wouldn't cost half what F.D. paid for just one of your houses, girl." He smiled. "You've got what F.D. really has to offer, and you want to hang on to it." The ice rattled in his glass as he tossed back the whisky. "And I'm the most discreet man in Hollywood—Gussie Christiansen says so. What she omitted to mention," he said, leaning across her to put his glass down, "is that I am also a very kind and considerate lover."

She smiled. "I don't imagine you actually came here to seduce me," she said.

"No. I came on business." He straightened up. "You said you wanted somewhere to work?"

"Yes, if possible."

"I can't see what's wrong with this place. It's huge—there must be dozens of rooms."

She shook her head. "I want somewhere private," she said. "I don't want anyone having access to my papers."

"Not even F.D.?"

"Especially not F.D.—if he ever bothers to join me."

"Have you been to the Lodge? Where the rest of us are?"

She shook her head.

"We've got the place to ourselves. There are spare rooms there, but I imagine that you won't want that either. In view of who else will be there."

"Correct."

Howard smiled. "And you ask me if *I've* got principles?"

She looked slightly offended. "I can back up every single word of this book," she said.

"I know, I know." He sat down again. "But you can't say you've got some highly principled reason for writing it."

"Oh, I learned the only principle that really matters six months after I arrived in LA," she said.

"Which is?"

"Screw them before they screw you."

Howard smiled. "And are they going to screw you?" he asked.

"Two of them already have." Her voice was hard.

Howard held up his hands in surrender. "I've found a sort of a cottage. Well—it's one room, really. It's the one they haven't been able to con anyone into having as a holiday cottage. But it's wind- and weatherproof, with the usual amenities, if somewhat cramped. Its main drawback is that it's only a few minutes along the cliff road from the location. Is that too close for comfort?"

"Does it have a lock and key?"

He nodded. "It doesn't have a phone, but there's a pay phone right outside—and a post box just along the road. It's about a ten-minute drive along the coast from here—do you want to come and have a look at it?"

"Sure," she said. "Would I be able to jog there and back along the shore? You can get right down on to it from the back here. There are steps."

He looked pained. "Yes—well, there are steps at the other end too. But it's miles," he said. "And this isn't LA, girl. It's cold."

She ran her hands from a slim waist to trim hips. "I'll jog," she said, decidedly. "And I'm from Minnesota." She

11

smiled. "But you can drive me over there this time—if you don't drink any more," she added.

"You think it might be OK?"

"It sounds fine."

"See? We gophers have our uses."

"How close are we to London?" she asked.

He raised his eyes to heaven. "We're on the west coast of Scotland, Wanda," he said. "We are not close to London."

She reacted to the scathing tone. "It's such a small island," she said. "How would I know?"

"We're a long way away from London," said Howard.

She frowned. "Does the hotel get much business?" she asked. "The Lodge, or whatever it's called?"

"It's not a hotel. Not really. It used to be someone's Scottish residence for the shooting season—that's why it's called the Lodge. Now it holds business seminars. Self-awareness, that sort of stuff. Freebies for executives. So the poor overstressed businessman can get away from it all for a week."

She frowned thoughtfully.

"Don't panic, Wanda. It's got bars, and a sauna, and a swimming pool. Tennis courts . . ." He poured himself another drink. "And you're not so far from the town, which manages to supply most people's needs. I think you'll be able to survive."

"I don't need Bond Street to survive, Howard," she said, sharply.

"What then? Thinking of popping down and surprising F.D.?"

"No," she said. "I may have some business in London, if one of the contacts comes through."

He hesitated before he spoke. "The one I put you on to?" he asked.

"Well—a friend of a friend of his. He was going to meet me in Glasgow, but now it might be London."

"Oh? Well, don't worry, girl. I believe there's some sort of primitive transport system rigged up."

She handed him her empty glass. "You're very sensitive all of a sudden," she said.

12

He shrugged. "I feel like a foreigner here. Everything's changed."

"Things do."

He handed her her drink and sat down. "When I left," he said, "the Earl of Somewhere owned that house, not some business psychology outfit. Britain didn't have hypermarkets and drive-in McDonalds. We had department stores and Lyons Corner Houses. Shipyards and steelworks—not marinas and theme parks. Railway stations, not shopping malls."

Her eyes rested on him for a moment. "Poor Howard," she said, smiling at him. "You've just lost the Empire."

F.D. lay half on top of her, asleep. She waited for a few moments before easing her body out from under his; the movement made him roll on to his back. She looked at him as he slept, smiling a little.

Shivering, she stood up, and felt the radiator on the wall. She frowned, running her hand down to the bottom, and sighing. She turned the knob at the side, but nothing happened. She tapped it lightly, then sharply. Somewhere in the plumbing a knocking began, growing louder.

"Sorry," said F.D.

She turned, startled. "*I'm* sorry," she said. "I didn't mean to wake you." She felt the radiator again. "It's getting warm," she said, triumphantly. "What are you sorry about?"

"I didn't mean to fall asleep."

She smiled. "You always do. I don't mind." She sat on the bed, curling her legs under her. "Isn't it all biological or something? It winds women up and it makes men sleep?"

"Is it?" He ran his fingers down her arm. "I don't know much about the theory," he said. "Are you wound up?"

She shook her head. "I feel very peaceful."

"And cold," he said, apologetically, putting his arms round her. "That's another thing I'm sorry about. I'm sorry about the heating, and the grotty flat. And I'm sorry about Scotland. It's not exactly what I had in mind either."

13

She smiled. "She'll have to leave the hotel sometimes," she said.

"Ah, well . . ." He looked a little sheepish. "Wanda and I won't be staying at the hotel," he said.

"What?"

"Phil Sumner's lending us his house. Restless Bodies are doing a tour of North America, so . . ."

"But I'll never see you! And we'll be there for weeks!"

"You'll see me every day. We'll be working, for God's sake."

"You know what I mean!"

He kissed her. "We might work something out," he said. "We'll see how the land lies when we get there."

"I don't *want* to see how the land lies! I want to be with you." Her eyes held his for a moment. "I love you," she said.

He let her go and got off the bed. "Get up," he said grimly, holding out his hand to her.

Puzzled, she took it, and unfolded her long limbs, rising from the bed. He grabbed at the blind as they passed the window, sending it running up, filling the room with the hard afternoon light, and she automatically folded her arms, covering her breasts.

"We're twelve floors up," he said, angrily pulling her towards the mirror, where he pointed at their naked bodies side by side. "What do you see?" he asked.

"Us."

"You see a girl of nineteen," he said. "Firm-bodied, clear-skinned, healthy and beautiful. And you see an old man with a thick waist and sagging muscles."

She shrugged a little, and went back to the bed, sitting down on the edge. "I see us," she repeated obstinately. "You and me."

He went over to her and crouched down. "You need to get a couple of things straight," he said, tapping her knee. "You want me because I'm wealthy and influential and I can make your career take off."

"I don't want you just because you—"

14

He put a finger to her lips, silencing her protests. "And as long as you . . ." He searched for the right word. ". . . excite me," he said, after a moment's thought, "you can have anything you like. Jewelry, cars, clothes . . . maybe even stardom."

She drew her legs up, like a child, her hands clasped round her ankles.

He stood up, both hands on her knees. "That's why you let me grunt and groan and sweat all over you," he said. "That's why you pretend that you're enjoying it." His hands moved from her knees to her thighs as he spoke. He barely touched her, and the youthful, eager body reacted. "And that's why I want you," he said. "It's a bargain, pure and simple."

He took his hand away, and slapped her knee hard. "Don't ever try to manipulate me again," he said mildly.

CHAPTER TWO

THE HILLS, MISTY BROWNS AND GREENS AS THE
rain threatened again, nestling white-painted clusters of
houses at their feet, swept down to the craggy coastline,
where the long grass suddenly gave way to steep barren rock
and white sand. A small cove had been bitten out of the land,
its semi-circle of sand surrounded by sheer rocks on one side
and a gentler, grassy slope on the other.

Scaffolding had been erected on the beach, on which were
perched powerful lights. Up on the high ground trailers were
scattered across the grass, and a generator throbbed. A large
group of people milled around the slope, then took up their
various positions, leaving just two in the centre of a cluster
of lights and microphone booms and trailing cables.

"Roll," said Howard.

"*Three Clear Sundays*, scene thirty-two, take seven." The
clapper-board snapped.

"Action," said F.D.

Barbara Slaney pushed off the young man's restraining
hands, and got to her feet, her long dress covered in mud.
She ran down the slope to the beach, along the edge of the
water, disappearing into a small cave entrance in the rocks.

"Cut," said F.D.

Barbara came out of the cave, and joined F.D. and the
young man as swarms of people began to move cameras and
equipment to the cave entrance.

F.D. strode over to where Barbara stood, and looked up at the sky. "Wouldn't you know the rain would finally hold off when we're filming inside a bloody cave?" he said.

Barbara didn't answer; she looked nervous.

"Is it going to work?" asked Howard.

"Of course it's going to work! We've got so much lighting equipment in there, there's hardly room for the actors. We're having to do them one at a time." He smiled. "No room for you, I'm afraid."

"I'd have thought a mock-up in a studio would have been easier," said Howard.

"Yes, Howard, it would have been easier—and everyone would have known it was a mock-up in a studio. Right," he said, as he arrived amidst the crew. "Stella—where is that girl?"

"Here, Mr. Derwent." Stella Swift was a girl no longer, and was totally unimpressed by F.D.'s continuing bad humour.

At last, they were ready.

Barbara licked her lips slightly, and took a deep breath.

"Right," said F.D. "We'll do Sophia's point of view first, so we just need Landers for this."

"Mr. Derwent?" Landers said mildly. "You did say you would do Samuel's POV first."

F.D.'s eyes narrowed. "Did I?" he said.

"Yes—well, Barbara wanted to get it over with. Filming inside the cave, I mean."

"Then let's stop wasting time," said F.D. "You first."

"But Mr. Derwent, you really shouldn't make her wait—she's psyched herself up for it, and she's . . . she's been having *nightmares* about it."

"You'd know," said F.D.

"What?" Landers made a move towards him.

"Forget it, John," said Barbara.

"She's had to take sleeping pills, she's been so worried about doing this scene!" Landers shouted.

F.D. strode up to him. "You heard what the lady said. Forget it. But try, this time, not to forget your lines. We don't want to be stuck in there any longer than we can help." He smiled coldly at Barbara. "And I think we'll call it a day when we've finished with John," he said. "We won't be needing you until tomorrow now."

Howard Maxwell raised his eyebrows at Barbara as she passed.

"Did you want something?" F.D. demanded.

Howard bowed slightly, and sauntered away.

F.D. was alone in his trailer when Barbara found him. She stood in the doorway looking at him for some moments before she came in.

"You are a bastard," she said, sitting beside him.

F.D. looked enquiringly at her.

"You know how I feel about that cave! Why did you make me wait until tomorrow to do it?"

"I know how you feel about Landers," he said. "Draping yourself round him every chance you get."

"Are you jealous?" Barbara asked, amused.

"No," he said.

"It's not my fault your wife's here, is it?" She smiled. "You get rid of her, and you can have sole rights," she said.

"Forget it, my love," he said.

"I seem to remember marriage being mentioned once," Barbara went on. "Only once, and only to indicate that it was out of the question, of course, but it was mentioned."

He picked up his unfinished coffee and pulled a face as he drank it. "Barbara, my dear," he said quietly, opening a cupboard and taking out a bottle of brandy, "if I were ever foolish enough to contemplate marriage to you, it would be with a pre-nuptial agreement so firm you could build a skyscraper on it." He made his coffee more agreeable with a shot of brandy, and put the bottle back.

"I might sign it," she said. "If the terms were good enough."

He laughed. "Do you know why I want you?" he asked.

"For sex. You told me."

"No. For excitement, I said. You're on the make, Barbara,

and that excites me. But I can't have you. So I'm bored, and frustrated. Not jealous—merely envious.''

"Is that why you're not keeping your end of the bargain?''

He shrugged. "You're in the film,'' he said.

"And no one's going to notice,'' said Barbara. "It's a lousy part. She's only there to die.''

"If you can work out some way to keep *your* end of the bargain, I'll work out how to keep mine,'' he said.

"There's always my car,'' she said.

He shook his head. "I left the back seats of cars behind forty years ago. And you and I are not disappearing off the set for any length of time, with Wanda just down the road.''

"Then it's impossible!''

"I know.'' He shrugged. *"C'est la vie,''* he said.

Barbara went silent for a few moments. "What does she *do* in that cottage all day?'' she asked, looking malevolently out of the open door in its general direction.

"She works.''

"How do you know?''

"I know my wife. And besides, I've been snooping. Seeing what she's up to with this book.''

Barbara frowned. "How?'' she asked.

"I pay the rent,'' he said. "Howard got me a key. And, every time I've looked, there are a great many more scurrilous things on her files about people who think she's a friend of theirs than there were the last time.''

"She could do that at the house. Why does she need a cottage? How do you know she isn't seeing someone?''

"Wanda isn't being unfaithful to me,'' said F.D. "Or why come here? She would have stayed in California.''

Barbara reluctantly acknowledged the logic of that, as Howard came in.

"The thing about Sophia,'' F.D. said, his voice at a normal pitch, "is that she has been betrayed. Samuel is giving her nothing, nothing at all. Because he's seen something he wants, and that he can't have. And she can never give him what he wants. She knows that. She is offering water when he craves wine.''

19

"Thank you," said Barbara. "That's very helpful." She dropped her voice. "And it's where Sophia and I differ," she said.

That night the rain came again, sweeping off the hillside and battering against the window of the Lodge, where a TV flickered in the subdued lighting. The staff worked late, keeping the film people well supplied with drinks as they watched the late-night chat show.

"I didn't think there was a problem, until the media kept insisting that there was." Mark Ingram smiled the smile that crinkled the skin around his eyes, and had made women's hearts beat faster ever since his first film.

"You can see why they might be intrigued," said the host. *"After all, it was something of a* cause célèbre *at the time."*

There was a pause as the words caught up with the satellite's time delay, and Mark shook his head. The hair was greying a little at the temples, and it only made him more handsome, contrasting with his Californian tan. *"Wanda and I married over twenty years ago,"* he said. *"I think we both knew we had made a mistake, straight away. She was much too young—she was twenty years old. Come to that, perhaps I was too young at twenty-five. What did we know? Besides, you can't hold a grudge for ever."*

The audience gave him a warm round of applause.

"But you've not taken the plunge again," said the host. *"Though your name has been linked, as they say, with some of the most attractive women in the world."*

Mark Ingram laughed, after a moment. *"And the British tabloids have decided that I must be carrying a torch for Wanda,"* he said. *"I've seen the English newpapers."* Then his face grew serious. *"I admit that my experience of marriage made me very wary of commitment. But there are no loose ends, and no hard feelings. I'm sorry to disappoint everyone."*

"He's going to be *here*," said the older of the two women working behind the bar.

The other one nodded, her eyes firmly fixed on John Landers, who sat at the bar, engrossed in something that Barbara Slaney was whispering to him.

"It's a bit of an improvement on all those wimps on the self-assertiveness," said the first, and they both laughed.

"Of course, everyone is more used to seeing you as Barry Strong, soldier turned spy—this part is a bit of a change from playing an ex-SAS man, isn't it?"

Mark frowned a little and adjusted his earpiece. *"It certainly is."* He looked a little apprehensive. *"It's a long time since I had to do anything much more subtle than refusing to flinch."*

More laughter, as he demonstrated.

"Well, let's have a look at you in action," said the host. *"In a clip from* Strong Medicine, *the film which started it all. It should be coming up just about . . ."*

"I bet she still fancies him," said the first woman. "Her husband made sure they weren't staying here, you'll notice."

The sound of automatic weaponry filled the air, and the audience clapped.

"Leo March isn't a lot like Barry Strong," said Mark.

"Do you see this part as a challenge, then?" asked the host.

"Yes, to some extent. But there was life before Barry Strong, and I think it's time I did something completely different, as they say. I'm not knocking the Strong films—they are first-class escapist entertainment, and they've been very good to me, but a film like Three Clear Sundays *makes different demands, and I'm looking forward to that, especially since . . ."*

"Do you think she's his girlfriend?" asked the younger woman, inclining her head slightly towards the couple at the bar.

The older woman shrugged.

". . . Simon Waterford's novel?" said the host. *"I've heard it described as a murder mystery, and a love story, and an indictment of the 'return to Victorian values' ethic. Which is it?"*

"All three. The title refers to the length of time which had

21

to elapse between sentence of death and the punishment being carried out. And on each of those Sundays, Leo, my character, learns more about the events leading up to the murder trial—the action takes place in flashback." He smiled. *"It's a very clever book, and I think it will make a stunning film. Of course, Simon Waterford himself has written the screenplay with Frank Derwent . . ."*

"Nice plug, Simon," said one of the men.

Simon Waterford smiled a little shyly.

"Well," said the host, *"we look forward very much to seeing it, and to seeing you back on these shores once more. Meanwhile, Mark Ingram, thank you very much."* He swivelled back to the camera, as the applause died away, and the screen behind him turned into a swirling haze of moving colours. *"Mark Ingram, ladies and gentlemen, live from Los Angeles. Join* Trade Secrets *after the break, when Wanda Derwent will be in our Glasgow studio to give us her side of the story, and tell us a little about* her *book, also tipped to become a best-seller . . ."*

Barbara let a couple of ads go by, then smiled at John, and finished her drink. "I think I'll go up," she said.

There was a hint of relief on John Landers' face as she slid off the barstool and left.

And he may have assumed that she turned right in the hallway, and went upstairs to her room. But she didn't.

". . . I think we all accepted the situation at the time. And I have been married to Frank now for nineteen years—I guess we're all quite used to the idea by now."

"I'm sure you are. Now then, this book of yours is causing almost as much fuss. We keep hearing about all these scandalous things you're going to tell us—is that just hype?"

Wanda laughed. *"It isn't all scandal,"* she said. *"But it isn't all hype, either."*

F.D. turned down the sound, and plugged headphones into the hi-fi, selecting a record and turning the sound up almost as high as it would go. He picked up the morning paper, turning to the sports pages, and the reports of rain washing out the racing. The music rose in his ears, then fell; through the softer passage he heard the urgent, quiet knocking at the door.

She stood coatless in the rain, on the doorstep. Behind her sat a shocking pink car, beaded by the saturating rain. His eyes widened slightly. "What the hell are you doing here?" he asked. "And what in God's name is that?"

"Keeping my end of the bargain," she said. "And that's my new car. I told you I'd got one."

"Are you crazy?"

"She's in Glasgow. And you didn't even tell me."

"Go away. And get that thing out of the driveway."

"Who's going to see it? There isn't anyone for miles."

"Just get it out of here."

She stood there, and he took a step towards her.

"All right," she said quickly, backing off.

He watched as she drove away, then closed the door and went back into the sitting room, where Wanda mouthed at the viewers. He turned the sound up.

"*. . . enjoying the beautiful scenery—when it isn't raining . . .*"

Another knock. He muted the sound and strode to the door.

"It's out of sight," she said. "In the woods."

"Go away."

"You don't want me?"

"Not here! Not in this house!" He turned and walked back into the room, leaving the front door open.

The music could still be heard, a small and delicate *pas de deux* from the headphones lying over the arm of the sofa.

Barbara smiled and closed the door. She went up to him, standing behind him, her arms round his waist, her head on his shoulder. "You don't need me?" she asked.

He turned to face her, disengaging himself from her. "You're wet though," he said. Her blouse clung to her; the music spiralled up towards them. "No," he said firmly. "I don't need you."

"That's why you're making everyone's life hell? That's

23

why you're making John Landers forget what he could do perfectly well in Florida?''

''He needs taking down a peg or two.''

''John?'' She laughed. ''John Landers is a nice, well-mannered all-American boy. He calls you 'Mr. Derwent' even behind your back. That's not what the rest of us call you.'' She moved closer to him. ''He believes in motherhood and pumpkin pie,'' she said, her lips on his mouth, her tongue teasing his. ''And he's not sleeping with me, so you can stop being jealous.''

''If he isn't, it's not for the want of trying on your part.''

''No,'' she agreed readily. ''You might want to be celibate for as long as this thing lasts, but I don't. And now we've got some time, at last.''

The music played on, an elfin orchestra on the sofa. ''I said it had to be somewhere *safe*,'' he said.

''This is safe,'' said Barbara. ''She's in Glasgow.''

F.D. looked over his shoulder at his wife, and looked back at Barbara. The miniature music rose, its rhythm insistent, like a heart-beat.

''Glasgow's not that far away,'' said F.D.

Barbara laughed. ''My God, F.D., how many men can actually *see* that their wives are a hundred miles away?''

''Eighty,'' he corrected her. ''And anyone could come here.''

''At this time of night?''

''Yes,'' he said, but he pulled her down on to the sofa.

The slow passage again; they kissed, just once, and the music faded to silence. They drew apart, holding eye contact. She smiled.

Sudden, dramatic chords issued thinly from the headset: definite, decisive, arrogantly rising only to fall away again. Taking their time, holding back until they had to let go, moving faster, faster, until the whispered dance furiously ripped along, frantically making up for lost time.

Her flailing foot caught the cable, and the music, freed at last from its tiny cage, wildly and deafeningly swirled around

24

them as they rolled together in noisy, gleeful ecstasy until the final, climactic chord died away.

"Frank! What's going *on*?" Wanda's muffled voice, raised against the music, echoed through the silence.

"Jesus Christ!" F.D. looked helplessly at the TV, where Wanda still discussed her book, at Barbara, at the front door, where the handle was turning. Then he jumped to his feet, dragging Barbara from the sofa. He pushed her towards the kitchen with one hand, picking up discarded clothing with the other. "Get out," he whispered, pushing her through the swing door as Wanda's key turned in the lock. He shoved her underwear into her hands and opened the back door. "Get *out*!" he repeated, slamming shut the serving-hatch doors.

Barbara stood at the back door. "What if I don't?" she said.

F.D. paused for the tiniest moment in his frantic pulling on of trousers. "Out," he said, once his dignity had been restored, and took a threatening step forward. This time she didn't move.

"How much is it worth to you?" she asked.

"*What?*"

The wet blouse, still unbuttoned, clung to her naked breasts; she still held her knickers in her hand, and the front door was opening.

"All right!" he whispered fiercely. "What the hell do you want?"

"If you agree to get someone to watch her, I'll leave. Otherwise I stay. All right?" she said, extending her hand.

"F.D.? Are you in the kitchen?"

Desperately, ridiculously, he shook on it.

"A bargain," she whispered. "Pure and simple." She smiled. "But I'm neither, F.D. Don't forget that."

He closed the back door as Wanda came into the kitchen. She frowned. "Is something wrong?" she asked.

"I . . . er . . . I thought I heard something outside," he said. "It must have been some country noise. Or you, I suppose. But—it seemed to be at the back."

25

"Oh? I'm surprised you could hear anything with the music that loud." She made a move towards the back door.

"I've checked," he said. "Anyway—how come you're in two places at once? I thought that show was live?" He blew out his cheeks as Wanda turned and went back into the other room.

"It used to be," she said. "But they got one drunk too many. It's recorded a few hours before transmission." She turned up the sound.

"Wanda Derwent, thank you very much." He turned. *"Next week on* Trade Secrets, *the show that looks behind the scenes of showbiz, guests will include . . ."*

"Damn," she said. "I've missed it all."

"Until then, this is Charlie S. Hall saying see you next time."

She switched it off.

F.D. poured himself a drink, which he drank in one gulp. "I think I'll have a shower and go to bed," he said. "I've got another hot sweaty scene inside that bloody cave tomorrow."

Inside, the essential crew members crowded into the narrow mouth of the cave. Barbara pushed through them, squeezing past the camera dolly, to where the cave widened slightly into a small chamber. She swallowed, took a deep breath, and planted her feet in the mud.

The clapper-board clicked down. "Action," said F.D. quietly, but his voice echoed. "He's coming in after you."

Barbara looked into the camera, her eyes gradually focusing on her imagined husband, growing afraid as he came closer.

"Sophia, I will not tolerate this disobedience," said Stella, in a monotone.

"I'm . . . I'm stuck, Samuel." Barbara's eyes pleaded with the camera not to be angry with her.

"Stuck?"

"My boots are stuck in the mud. I can't move. I can't reach the laces to get them off."

"Perhaps this is God's punishment."

"Look," she said, desperately, pulling up her heavy skirts to show the camera her predicament.

"Sophia, do not add immodesty to your list of sins."

She dropped the skirt, and put a hand to her face to smooth back her hair, smearing it with mud.

"Cut."

Make-up removed the mud, endless adjustments were made to lighting and camera angles, and the scene was done again, the mud going on and coming off; the wait for more adjustments. Make-up removed perspiration from Barbara's forehead, and touched up the mud a little.

"OK. 'You came here without assistance.' And remember, Barbara, this is one long take. The camera is closing in all the time. Action."

"You came here without assistance, you can leave without it."

"I can't!" Barbara looked stricken, holding out her hand.

"You must seek God's help."

"It isn't God's help I need, it's yours!"

"Blasphemy. Blasphemy too. This is all a direct result of association with that woman," droned Stella.

"She's our neighbour, Samuel." There were tears in her eyes as she implored the camera to understand. "She's been very kind to me, Samuel—Samuel, help me!"

"You will have no further communication with Mrs. Lovelace. I will speak to her myself after church. You will pray for forgiveness here where God has led you," said Stella, boredly.

"He's turned his back, he's walking off. You're watching him," said F.D.

Dismay, as her eyes went beyond the camera. Her eyes closed against what they were seeing, and the tears trickled down her face, through the mud. Then she wiped them away defiantly, and stepped with ease to freedom, as the camera held her in shot.

"Cut." F.D. didn't try to hide his satisfaction with her performance. But they needed another take.

"OK," said F.D. "Let's go again."

The camera was moved back, and make-up repaired the smudge of mud.

"Action."

"You came here without assistance, you can leave without it."

"I can't!"

F.D. watched as she did it all again, as perfectly as the first time, until a jet overflew the coastline, the noise of the engines reverberating through the cave. Take three. This time, her foot slipped in the mud, her head ducking out of shot. The stiff-backed fear of the confined space was beginning to show between shots, but only between shots. Take four, and she was Sophia to whom the cave was a refuge, not a threat. A bulb blew. Five, and she dried. Six. The smudge was forgotten. Seven. The sound man was getting interference from somewhere.

"Go again," said F.D., wearily. "Take eight."

Make-up removed the smudge, covered with pale powder the red mark that had appeared on Barbara's face with the putting on and taking off of mud, and dusted away the beads of sweat.

"It'll be all right this time," the girl said. "Don't worry, love."

Barbara licked her lips, breathing slowly, deeply, keeping control.

"Action."

"You came here without assistance, you can leave without it."

"I can't!" said Barbara, Sophia's defiance back in her eyes. And this time she made it to the end. Nothing went wrong. She closed her eyes, and let out a shuddering sigh. "Oh, thank God," she said, almost sobbing with relief.

F.D. looked through the script for some moments before he looked up. "Let's do one for luck," he said, his voice soft, his eyes hard.

* * *

"How much?" The young man had attempted designer stubble which merely looked as though he had mislaid his razor. He stared at F.D., and waited for confirmation.

"If that's not enough, just name your terms," said F.D. "I'm out of touch with the cost of living here."

They were sitting—F.D., Barbara and the private detective—in the corner of the empty lounge bar of the Lodge, but they were none the less conversing in near whispers.

"Oh, it's enough," he said. "But you're not expecting *me* to jog there and back, I hope?"

F.D. raised his eyebrows at Barbara.

"No," she said. "She uses the beach—you can see her from the cliff road. Follow her there, wait until she leaves again, and follow her home."

"You'll do it, I take it?" said F.D.

"Oh, I'll do it." He looked a little puzzled. "Do you think she's carrying on with someone, Mr. Derwent?"

"That really doesn't concern you, Mr. Anderson," said F.D. "Keep at a very discreet distance."

"I'll park where I showed you," he said. "No one'll see the car, not even in daylight—I guarantee it." He took a stick of gum from his pocket, unwrapping it and folding it into his mouth.

F.D. watched with distaste.

"When she leaves," Barbara said, "ring here. Ask for Miss Slaney."

The young man looked uncertainly at F.D., who shrugged. "Do as she says," he said.

"Right, Mr. Derwent. You're the boss." He winked at Barbara and sauntered out.

F.D. sat back. "And that, I believe, makes us quits," he said. "Though what you hope to discover, I can't imagine."

Barbara raised her eyebrows. "The price went up this afternoon," she said. "I want your key to the cottage."

He frowned. "You're not standing half-naked in the kitchen any more," he said. "You have nothing to bargain with." He shook his head. "But I'm intrigued." He took

29

out his keys, removing the cottage key from the ring, handing it to her. "Why on earth do you want it?"

"You'll find out," she said. She put the key in her bag, without explanation. "And no more forms of torture," she said.

"If there are no more forms of blackmail," he replied pleasantly.

The bleak coast road was still. In a clearing in the bracken, almost completely hidden by the branches, a car could just be glimpsed; Wanda might have seen, if she had been looking, the gleam of chromium through the spiky foliage; she might have noticed the sun, out again at last, glint on the wing-mirror. But Wanda wasn't looking. She was jogging along the sand, the picture of health and vitality, up the steps in the sea wall, and along the row of cottages to the one furthest from the shore.

She changed out of the jogging suit and slid open the door of a cubicle which contained a washbasin, a toilet and a shower in what seemed like an impossibly small space. She showered, then slipped on jeans and a sweatshirt, and came back in to start her day's work. The Spartan little room was furnished with a desk, a chair, and a goatskin rug that had seen better days. Behind the desk was a cupboard, on the door of which was hung a heavy, old-fashioned mirror, in what seemed like a vain attempt to make the room seem larger.

Two touches of luxury; a coffee-maker sat on the tiny worktop, alongside a two-ring hotplate, and a twin cassette recorder sat on the desk with the microphone already set up. She made coffee first, but didn't have any straight away. She sat at the desk, pressed the record button, and started speaking as she sorted through the papers in her briefcase.

"I was young," she said. "And shattered. Lost, lonely—I felt dirty, I felt used . . ." She paused, and looked into space for a moment. "But I have forgiven him," she said. "You may sneer at that when you read these words—you may think that I have written this as an act of revenge. But if I had wanted revenge, how much sweeter it would have been at the time. No—this is not being written for revenge, but rather out of a sense of injustice. I was seen as the villain of the piece, and I want to set the record straight. This is my story; I have the right to tell it.''

She switched off the tape and rewound it, listening to the piece she had just added. Now and then she would make a note on the typewritten page in front of her. Then she rewound the whole tape, removed it, and put it in the other deck. She put a new tape in the recording deck, pressed a button, and the tape began to jabber at double speed as the second recording was made. She turned off the sound and went back to the manuscript on the desk, making a final note, then returning it to her briefcase. She pulled out a thin file, and laid it on the desk.

SUSAN QUENTIN, the label read. Inside were letters, scraps of paper, copies of birth and marriage certificates, and a publicity photograph of a good-looking, dark-haired woman in her mid-forties. A confident, smiling woman, posing in front of Cartier, with diamonds dripping from every inch of her body not covered in mink. Underneath, the text read:

Two security men stood guard as Susan Quentin posed for this publicity photograph for *Stones*, in which she plays a diamond merchant of dastardly deeds and duplicitous dealing. Of course, the security guards were part of the hype, as the lady wore rhinestones. Not that she couldn't flash a few rocks of her own . . .

Wanda pulled the little portable typewriter towards her, and inserted a sheet of paper.

"Dear Colin," she wrote. "I do hope you meant what you said about having something for me, because I am in Scotland now, and I'll be glad to meet you anywhere you say . . .''

The long, thin cigarette burned in the ashtray; spirals of smoke rose and hung in the air. Susan Quentin had arrived at the Lodge.

"Howard, darling, I'm hearing terrible things about this

31

movie—tell me they're not true." They were the clipped tones of an acquired standard English accent defending itself against American inflections.

"What have you heard?" Howard settled himself down with his drink, and smiled across the table at her.

"That F.D. is making everyone's life an absolute hell, that he couldn't direct traffic—that he's doing so many takes and retakes and reshooting so much footage that he will probably have to end up cutting his losses—I don't want to be associated with a flop, Howard."

The waitress brought the menus.

"It won't flop, Sue." He put on his glasses to read the menu. "Well—who can tell? But it won't fold—and Ingram tells me that the product isn't suffering. Just the cast and crew."

"All because he can't bed whichever child you've lined up for him this time?"

Howard smiled comfortably. "I'll have the pâté, I think," he said. "Are you having a starter?"

"I'll have the pâté too. Howard—I thought it was your job to make F.D.'s life run smoothly?"

"I'm doing my job. I'm telling you that your first scenes are being shot tomorrow."

"I'm not going to have him try to make a fool of me in front of everyone. I know him, Howard. So, you let me know when it's safe, and that's the day I'll recover from this mild but debilitating illness that I'm about to have. All right?"

"Done. I'll have the trout to follow. How about you?"

"The steak. Before I'm confined to my room."

The sun shone, and the Victorian clothes were actually proving too warm for the actors.

"Yes," said F.D., as Barbara got to her feet again and sat down, her skirts giving her trouble. "Yes, good." He looked at John Landers. "Good," he said absently. "But . . . well, I'd like to try something. If you feel comfortable with it fine, if not, we'll talk about it."

Simon Waterford, watching, looked startled, but Landers didn't seem at all surprised at F.D.'s manner.

F.D. paced up and down the grass as he spoke. "You've got this man," he said. "I mean, you've got the pomposity, and the rigidity . . . but . . ." He turned. "When you push her to her knees, and tell her to pray for forgiveness—you're thinking of how this Victorian, Bostonian ex-missionary would treat his wife."

Landers nodded.

"I want you to try thinking of how he would treat his dog. I think you're showing too much respect for Sophia. Think of her as a puppy. A puppy who has just done a mess on the carpet, and you are going to rub her nose in it. There's no respect. There is total dominance."

Simon Waterford blinked a little, and looked round at the various people who milled about the set. He saw Mark Ingram talking to some of the crew, and made as if to move towards him, but checked his stride, and looked back at F.D.

"And Barbara. Remember—this is the scene just before the one in the cave. She runs because she's bewildered by his reaction to what she's just said. So, do you think perhaps she *shouldn't* be embarrassed while she's saying it?"

Simon frowned, and walked a little way away, still within earshot.

Mark detached himself from the group. "You must be Simon Waterford," he said, hand outstretched. "I think I just missed your last visit to us."

"But she's talking about sex," said Barbara. "Isn't she bound to be embarrassed?"

"She should be," said F.D. "But what if she isn't? What if she is a total innocent? There are things she enjoys—the garden, playing the piano, embroidery, and sex. And she has no idea that any one of them is any less acceptable than another. Sex is something she knew nothing about until she was married—he introduced her to it, so there can't be anything wrong with it. She explains what she enjoyed about it—if you take away the embarrassment, it's really very explicit."

Simon dragged his attention away, and turned to Mark Ingram. "I suppose I must," he said. "What's happened to him?'' he asked. ''Last time I was here he was biting every-one's head off.''

''I think he's . . .'' Mark thought. ''Happier in *himself*,'' he said, with a grin. ''He's been a teddy bear all week. Something's put him in a good mood.''

Simon shook his head slightly. ''He's changing it all,'' he said. ''I think I preferred him in a bad mood.''

''I thought you'd got an agreement that the script wouldn't be altered?''

''He *isn't* altering it,'' said Simon, in a defeated voice.

''He wants to give her a showcase. At least she can act.''

''But *why*? The whole point is that Sophia's incidental to the plot—Samuel regards her as a chattel—that's what she's supposed to be.''

''Well,'' said Mark with a slow smile, ''I imagine that acting isn't the only thing Ms. Slaney is good at.''

''Quiet! We're going for a take!''

Simon watched from F.D.'s trailer as the scene was filmed. He couldn't hear, but it wasn't necessary. He saw Sophia's earnest, innocent face as she uttered the now devastating words, saw Samuel's horror and rage. Watched him drag Sophia to her feet and force her to her knees in the muddy grass. Saw Sophia run from this terrible, violent, bewildering reaction. Even in the short, disjointed bursts of action, even through the takes and retakes and the sudden laughter when things went wrong, the scene was powerful.

And he watched the actors leave, their job done for the day; watched Barbara Slaney as she backed her pink car out of its parking space, opening the doors for Mark Ingram and John Landers to get in. He watched the crew begin to pack away equipment. But he didn't move.

Eddie Anderson removed his chewing gum as the cottage door opened. Wanda Derwent came out, locked the door, and walked along to the post box, before jogging down the steps to the beach, and away. Eddie started the car and backed out of the clearing. He left the engine running, went to the pay phone, and made a quick call. Then he returned to his car, turned it round, and drove off slowly, keeping his eye on the bright yellow figure jogging along the sand.

"Still here, Simon?" said F.D.'s voice. "Exercising your right to ensure that I'm not buggering up your script?"

He turned from the window. "Yes," he said. "That isn't the Sophia that I created."

F.D. smiled. "Film's like that," he said. "You have flesh and blood people playing the parts—the parts become flesh and blood." He came in and sat down. "And that girl's good," he said. "We're lucky to have her." He sat back. "You don't like what I'm doing?"

"I'm not sure," said Simon. "Sophia's part seems to be being beefed up."

"Her part?" queried F.D., a note of irritation in his voice. "You wrote the part—I haven't altered or added a word. I'm not allowed to, am I?"

"All right, you're switching the emphasis, then, if you prefer."

"And that's bad?"

Simon shook his head. "If they played that scene the way you suggested," he said, "it'll be wonderful." He looked away. "But it won't be mine."

"Nor mine," said F.D. "How many people were on the set? That scene will be the lighting cameraman's, Barbara's, John's . . ." He smiled. "It doesn't even end there. It'll be the composer's, and the editor's—maybe the editor's most of all. She decides what it all looks like. The cutting can make all the difference, and Fiona Egerton's good—I give her a lot of autonomy."

"You don't believe in the auteur theory?"

"Of course not! Hundreds of people make a movie. You and I are just two of them."

"Aren't we the most important?"

F.D. shook his head. "In the literary world, this is a Simon Waterford novel. In LA, it's a Frank Derwent project, and nobody gives a damn who wrote it. And to the public it's a Mark Ingram or a John Landers movie, depending on

35

age, and they couldn't care less about either of us. Samuel has got to be more sympathetic than he is in the book, or we'll alienate the kids. The audience has got to understand why he reacts so violently, even if they don't entirely approve.''

"They'll understand that all right," said Simon. "What they won't understand is why the hell he doesn't *sleep* with her! If you take away the embarrassment, you're losing the difference between her and the native girl!''

"Yes, I'm blurring it.''

"Why?''

"Because the difference isn't between the two girls, but in Samuel's perception of them. What he lusts after in the native girl disgusts him in his wife. *That's* why he won't sleep with her, why he tries to murder her—that's why he rapes Mrs. Lovelace . . .''

"But that isn't my novel.''

"No. It's my film. It's all illusion, Simon. And illusions depend on where you're standing.''

The phone rang. F.D. answered, muttered something, and hung up. "We'll talk," he said. "Come to the dailies tomorrow—see what you think when it's on the screen.''

Simon nodded, and went out into the evening sunshine.

"Well, I think the audience will know—do you know, kids?"
The youthful audience shouted out.
"That's it! You see—easy, isn't it, when you . . ."
"Know How!" yelled the kids.
"And tune in next week, when who knows, someone you know might show how on . . ."
"Know How!"
Susan Quentin hurriedly switched off the TV when she heard the knock, and went back to looking pale and wan.
"Who is it?" she said.
"Sue, my love, it's your personal physician.''
She smiled. "Come in, Howard, darling.''
He came in, and smiled. "I think the crisis is over, and

you should be feeling strong enough to undertake light duties.''

"Are you sure?"

"I am. Life is much more tranquil now—if life is ever tranquil on location. He wants you there at nine.''

"You have arranged for me to have my own trailer, haven't you, Howard? I'm not sharing with F.D.'s latest.''

He gave a little bow. "It's ready and waiting,'' he said. "Of course, it does mean that she's got *her* own trailer, too . . .''

"I don't crave status, Howard," she said. "I want privacy. And I don't want to feel I'm playing gooseberry.''

Howard smiled. "Your wish is my command, Sue.''

"Thank you, darling. You may tell F.D. that I will be with him tomorrow. At nine.''

"Good girl." He winked, and left.

Susan Quentin picked up the phone. "Room one-oh-nine," she said. "Could you cancel my order for dinner in my room? I think I feel well enough to come down tonight.''

The bleak coast road was still. In a clearing in the bracken, almost completely hidden by the branches, a car could just be glimpsed, flashes of shocking pink showing through the spiky foliage as the low sun caught the shiny surfaces. One of the cottages was inhabited; outside the window, from behind the slats of the half-closed Venetian blind, muted, vague sounds could be heard.

Inside, there was nothing muted or vague about it as F.D. and Barbara lay sprawled on the goatskin rug in strips of light and shade, her cries of abandoned pleasure rewarding his loud grunts of effort until they drew apart.

"You're fantastic," she said, when she had got her breath back.

"And you're a good actress," he said, as she kissed him. He looked at his watch. "I have to go.''

They dressed quickly, and F.D. looked at himself in the mirror, smoothing down his hair.

37

"Why would I fake it?" she asked.

He smiled. "Don't try too hard, Barbara," he said to her reflection. "I'm in trouble with Waterford as it is. I can't turn you into the star of this movie, however much you massage my ego."

"We're good together. It's got nothing to do with the film. Wouldn't you like to have that all the time?"

He turned, smiling. "My dear girl, I don't think I'd have the strength."

"You know what I mean." She kissed him, a long, lingering kiss. "Don't you think I'd be worth it?" she asked, turning away to the window.

"You're worth taking a risk for," he said. "For as long as we're filming together."

A small frown came and went on Barbara's brow with his words. She opened the blind, and the dark slashes of shadow disappeared. The frown had gone when she turned round.

"But not even you are worth what it would cost me to divorce Wanda," he continued. "And Wanda persists in being entirely faithful, as your useful private detective has been proving for the last ten days." He smiled. "We are talking tens of millions of dollars, my love."

She nodded. "It was a brilliant idea," she said, as he opened the door. "Admit it."

"Yes, it was a brilliant idea. Don't forget to tidy up."

He walked quickly back to where the trailers were being made secure for the night. Somewhere a radio was playing pop music; the singer was explaining that there could be desire and need without love. He wandered round, making himself available to answer questions about costume and props and make-up before getting into his car and driving away with two blasts of his horn.

He was in the house, sipping a martini, when Wanda came jogging up the back path, and in through the kitchen. "Hello," he said. "I had almost given up on you. Would you like a drink before we eat?"

* * *

38

The church hall provided a makeshift viewing room. Thick curtains blocked the light from outside as they watched the rushes of the previous day's filming.

"We got a lot done yesterday," F.D. said to Simon, in the lull before it started. "Don't think we're always that lucky. Sometimes we cheer if we get a minute's worth in the can."

The clapper-board showed scene forty-one, and crane shots of a naked John Landers walking up the slope from the beach towards a woman who stood high above him, over a steep, rocky drop. She didn't move as he pushed her to the ground; he tore at her clothing as she tried to push his hands away. The struggling stopped; he raped her, the waves rolling on to the beach below.

"This is the master shot. We'll intercut with close-ups," F.D. explained to Simon. "But Sue Quentin's come down with something, so they're having to wait. And there will be shots of water going into the cave, of course," he continued. "We can't film that yet, because the tide doesn't come in that far until before dawn and after dark at the moment. According to the experts, the tide and the time of day and everything should be right in a few weeks. Keep your fingers crossed for the weather, because we're going to have to wait until we've practically finished filming before we can do the stunt. And the high-tide shots are important. He thinks Sophia is trapped in there while he's forcing himself on Letitia."

"I know the story," said Simon, a touch sourly.

F.D. smiled, and looked round as Mark Ingram came in and sat beside him on the only vacant seat.

The screen went blank.

"We didn't shoot any of your scenes yesterday, did we?" F.D. asked Mark.

"No," he said. "Just curious to see how the praying scene turned out."

"Oh." F.D. turned his attention to the screen once more, where the second take of scene forty-one was just beginning. He watched it, and nodded thoughtfully. "I prefer take two," he said.

Another crane shot. John Landers running towards the

sea, scattering his clothing. A long shot over the shoulder of the woman who watched as he split the waters with a fast, streamlined crawl, turned, and smoothly breast-stroked back, unaware of her scrutiny.

"Is that John himself?" asked Mark.

F.D. raised his eyebrows. "You're out of touch, Mark old son," he said. "Young Landers did that TV series about the life guard. He swims. That's why I wanted him."

"Isn't he here?" Mark twisted round.

"No," said F.D. "He doesn't like watching the rushes."

In amongst the so-so medium shots were some beauties. The sun caught the water, shimmering over Landers' naked body as he moved like a dolphin, diving down and out of sight; emerging, hair sleek and shining; turning into a lazy backstroke, then making fast for the shore.

Mark Ingram watched; F.D. glanced at him, then looked back at the screen.

Rivulets of water on the muscles of his back; his arms stroking through the water; a sudden shaft of lucky sunlight catching him as he swam against the tide, through a haze of sparkling spray, then turned back. Looking up, seeing something; standing still in the breast-high sea, his body nudged by the waves, his face beaded with water.

"Great stuff, Len," said F.D.

"We were lucky with the weather," said Leonard Charles. "And the camera likes him. He's a good-looking boy."

Landers powering through the waves, submerging, rising in a shower of froth; on his back, then twisting, diving, his submerged form skimming under the surface. Standing, his eyes staring blankly, the sea dropping slowly from chest to waist level as he moved towards a static camera. The camera had continued to film as he emerged, strong legs striding through the waves, in a full-frontal advance as inevitable, as irresistible, as the tide rushing between his legs, around his knees, racing ahead of him, preparing his way. He looked like a god.

"Shit," said F.D. "The best shot we get, and we can't use it."

"We might get away with it if we do a quick cut away," said the editor.

"Won't be as good as staying on him like that," said F.D.

"If you want art, F.D.," said Len, "you get an eighteen certificate."

"No fear," said F.D. "Art isn't worth losing half his public at the box office."

Scene Thirty-one. John and Barbara, walking along the promenade, medium close.

"Here's the praying scene, Mark," said F.D.

But Mark had gone.

CHAPTER THREE

HOWARD LEFT THE CLIFF EDGE, AND WALKED OVER
to the trailers. "Gil!" he called to one of the crew. "Is F.D.
around?"

"Yes," he shouted back. "He was on the phone a minute
ago."

Howard looked into the trailer. "He's not now," he said,
as Kevin Gilbert came up to him. He craned his neck to see
the smattering of cars still in the makeshift car park. "But
his car's still here," he said. "He must be around somewhere."

"Do you want me to find him?"

"No," said Howard. "He's probably with Len. I won't
bother him if he's busy." He yawned and said, "I'm packing
it in. I'm not staying here all night just because he's a work-
aholic. Tell him I'll see him tomorrow."

Barbara heard F.D.'s feet on the path, and opened the cottage
door. He kissed her as soon as the door was closed again; a
long, luxurious kiss from which she had to come up for air.

"God," he said. "I thought she was always going to leave
early." He was undoing her blouse as he spoke. "I think if
she had beaten us to it again, I'd have gone mad."

She kissed him. "Well," she said, "she's safely on her
way back to the house now."

42

F.D. smiled back. "Thank the Lord," he said, turning his attention to his own clothes.

Barbara picked up the chair, bringing it round to the front of the desk, setting it down. She smiled at him. "Make yourself comfortable," she said.

F.D. raised interested eyebrows.

"You don't want to get bored, do you?" she said, as he sat down, facing away from the mirror.

Which was important because, behind his back, inching across the full reflection of the painted surface of Wanda's desk, her hand was reaching for the cassette recorder.

And Barbara knew which buttons to press.

Mark Ingram rang the bell for service, got up from the bar, and joined John Landers, the only other customer in the lounge. He smiled. "Have you been deserted, or is Barbara coming back?" he asked.

Landers smiled back. "She had to go into the town for something," he said. "She said she'd be about a half-hour."

"What are you drinking?"

"Coke. Thank you."

Mark got a Coke and a double whisky. He sat down, taking out cigarettes. "Smoke?"

"No, thanks."

"No wonder you're in such good shape," said Mark. "You don't smoke, you don't drink . . ." He left a pause.

"I like to take care of myself."

Mark nodded. "You . . ." He hesitated a little, then went on. "You don't seem to go out much," he said.

Landers laughed. "There aren't a whole lot of places to go," he said. "Not unless you're mobile."

"No, I suppose not. But Barbara's got a car."

"Barbara?" he said.

"Oh, I'm sorry. I thought you and she were . . ."

"No," said Landers. "Nothing like that. She's been real friendly, and helpful—but nothing like that."

Mark knocked back his drink, and signalled to the girl as she looked into the bar again; he didn't have to give her his

43

order. He caught the fleeting look of concern on the younger man's face. "I drink too much," he said.

"Oh, I didn't mean to imply—"

"I've drunk too much already, and I'm having another."

"Well," said Landers. "Why shouldn't you? I guess I just never got the taste for it myself."

Mark took the drink from the girl, who managed to hand it to him without taking her eyes off Landers.

"Now, she's a pretty girl," said Mark, quietly, as the girl went back through to the reception, walking on air. "Don't you think?"

"Sure is," said Landers.

"You don't seem to be making the most of your opportunities," said Mark. "I mean, she would go to bed with you right now if you asked her to."

"I know," said Landers.

Mark looked at him over the rim of the glass. "But . . . ?" He shook his head a little.

"I'm not interested," he said.

Mark smiled. "I've never met an actor who didn't have any vices," he said.

Landers shrugged. "I never meant to be an actor," he said.

Mark swallowed what was left in his glass. "I don't suppose any of us meant to be what we are," he said.

Her hands gripped the chair-back, her breath coming faster and faster as she spurred F.D. on to ever louder appreciation of her efforts.

Beyond her hands, on the desk, coloured lights rose and fell; pushing up into orange, falling back to yellow, green . . . up again to orange, back down. Charging up, peaking on red, again and again. Staying in red as he fairly roared with pleasure; red, red, red . . . down through orange, yellow, green . . . his long groan of satisfaction died away, and the display went dark.

Barbara lay against him for some moments until she caught her breath; then she slipped off his knee, her skirt falling

44

back down of its own accord, buttoned her blouse, tucked it in, and smiled at him.

He lay back on the chair, exhausted, his eyes closed; she walked behind him, stopped the tape, and pressed the rewind button.

F.D. made a little puzzled sound as the tape spun back to the beginning. "What are you doing?" he asked, without opening his eyes.

"Copying a tape," she said, removing it, putting it in the other deck; she put in a second tape, slid down the volume control to zero, and pressed the high-speed dub.

"What?"

"Copying a tape," she repeated.

He frowned, still not opening his eyes. "What time is it?" he asked.

She reached across for his hand and looked at his wrist-watch. "You've got a few minutes before you have to go," she said.

He sat up, and pushed himself off the chair, frowning at her as she stood behind the desk. He picked up his trousers. "What are you copying?" he asked. "You're not messing about with Wanda's tapes, are you? She'll know how she left them."

Barbara smiled. "*I* know how she left them," she said. "Don't worry, I'll put everything back the way it was."

F.D. began to dress in puzzled silence. "What tape is it?" he asked. "What do you want with her tapes?"

"It isn't hers. It's one of mine. I wanted a copy."

He carried on dressing, still bothered. "Have I been asleep?" he asked.

"No," she said.

"Well, now I know what you think about," he said, his voice huffy. "What you're going to do as soon as I finish."

"Don't be silly," she said.

"Well, my God, you didn't need much recovery time, did you? Anyway, I don't want you hanging about here copying a tape."

"It's on double speed," she said.

45

"Even so—a whole tape still takes—"

"A whole tape?" she said, and shook her head, smiling. "Not even you, F.D."

He frowned. "What's going on?" he asked, baffled, coming over to her as he tightened his tie round his collar. "What tape *is* it?"

"Turn the sound up," she said. "And you'll hear."

F.D. examined the cassette player. A little tentatively, he pushed up the volume.

The mouse-like squeals and squeaks meant nothing to him for a moment; when they did, his mouth fell open, and his face grew red. Barbara smiled.

"Jesus Christ!" he said, pushing down the eject button, pulling out the cassette. "What in God's name are you *doing*?" His words echoed round the little room. "What the hell are you playing at?"

Barbara still smiled, as she switched off the other tape and took it out, putting it in an envelope.

Then she moved quickly. Darting to the door, running fast when she got outside, her heels ringing along the empty road. A glance over her shoulder, and she could see him come after her; she ran faster still.

He caught up as she dropped the envelope in the post box, and pulled her round to face him.

"I did warn you that I wasn't simple, F.D.," she said.

He stared at her. "What the hell is this about?" he demanded.

"Us," she said. "You and me." She smiled. "Oh, you do like it noisy, don't you, F.D.? I'm sure none of your partners would have any trouble identifying you."

He stood, appalled, beside her, trying to catch his breath. "Where?" he gasped, when he could speak. "Where have you sent it?"

She smiled. "Not to Wanda," she said. "It's got nothing to do with her. It's a love-token, F.D. Like in *Half a Sixpence*, you know? You have yours, I have mine—and they are reunited in a luxury apartment in Bel Air." Her voice

46

was hard. "Tens of millions of dollars?" She smiled. "It won't cost you that much," she said.

F.D.'s face grew pale and angry as he looked at her. "Where have you sent it?" he asked again.

"To myself," she said. "Well? What's it to be, F.D.?"

He nodded. "Get that place straight before you leave here," he said, walking away.

Barbara went back to the cottage, and put things back the way she had found them, opening the slats of the blind again, letting in the evening sunshine; she locked the door, and got into her car. Suddenly, her hair was caught from behind, her head jerked back.

"I warned you, too, Barbara, remember?"

His lips almost touched her ear as he spoke; she was speechless, stiff with fear.

"You'll regret this," he said. He let go of her hair, got out of the car and strode away.

It was some time before she moved off.

"You should have a drink," said Mark, stumbling over these simple words. He smiled. "Funny thing," he said. "Booze makes me want to talk, and then doesn't let me say the words. Anyway, you should have a drink. You should smoke—you should ruin your body. That's what women go for. No need for you to work out in the gym, not if you're doing it for their benefit. They don't appreciate it, you know. Look at F.D. That's the sort of man women go for."

"Rich," said Landers.

Mark conceded that with a wave of his glass. "But they like them like that anyway," he said. "Lived in. Frayed round the edges." He looked a little unsteadily at Landers. "You are wasted on a woman," he said.

Landers looked uncertainly at him, then smiled.

Mark stubbed out his cigarette, and lit another. "I am doing my very best to ruin my looks," he said, and grinned.

Landers laughed.

"Mark! What are you having? A fruit juice, as usual?"

Mark twisted round to see Howard Maxwell, and raised a

less than sober hand in salute. "He is a case in point," he said to Landers, pointing at Howard. "Look at him. Overweight, running to seed. Has to wear glasses to see where he's going. And not *even* rich—but women think he's lovely—that's the word they use. Lovely." He smiled at Howard. "Just telling John it's pointless his looking after his body," he said.

Howard ordered another round as Barbara arrived back; she sat at the table with them, smiling at Landers. Howard joined them, taking part in the inconsequential conversation, as Mark became more and more drunk and less and less circumspect. Landers ordered the next round, and sat down as Mark fixed Barbara with a glazed eye.

"What do you think of Howard, Barbara?" he asked, downing his previous drink, and accepting the next from the girl who brought the order.

Barbara looked at Howard, a little surprised at the question, and smiled. "I think he's lovely," she said, taking her lager from the tray. "Aren't you, Howard?"

Wanda Derwent, unnoticed by the people at the table, came into the lounge and stood at the bar, listening to the conversation.

"What did I tell you?" Mark almost knocked over John's drink as his hand swept the air expansively, hitting the girl's as she reached across the table. "I do beg your pardon," he said, then looked unsteadily at Landers. "What did I tell you?" he repeated.

He looked back at Barbara. "And F.D.?" he asked. "What do you think of F.D.? He's middle-aged, carrying a bit too much weight round the waist, and let's face it, he is a complete bastard, isn't he? Is it worth going to bed with him just to get special attention on the set?"

He became aware of John Landers' unhappy eyes looking beyond him, and the silence into which his words had fallen. He turned to see Wanda.

Barbara smiled, looking at Wanda as she spoke. "I wouldn't know, Mark," she said. "But you could try."

Mark's eyes held Wanda's for a moment before he looked

back at Barbara, and crushed out his cigarette. "Barbara, my love," he said, "never try to kid a kidder."

Wanda turned and went out.

"Good going, Mark," Howard muttered sourly, going after her.

By the time he had walked through reception and out into the courtyard, the aquamarine of Wanda's jogging suit was bobbing down the driveway.

Howard sighed, and went to where his car was parked. He drove slowly down until he was moving along beside her, the window wound down. They were well out of sight of the building before she even acknowledged his presence.

"Don't try telling me there's nothing in it," she said.

"I wasn't going to," he said. "I've had a phone call about your contact in London. I got a friend of mine to do a bit of digging."

"Oh," she said, and gave him a little smile. "Good. What did he say?"

"Why don't you let me take you back?" He looked at her, then back at the road ahead. "You've done your fitness quota." He let her get ahead of him, and took off his glasses, slipping them into their case. He accelerated gently until he was beside her again. "What happened? Did you take the wrong turning?"

"What did he say?" Wanda asked again.

"He said to forget it, in a nutshell."

"No," she said.

"Yes, well . . . you're going to have to be careful." He crawled along beside her. "These people aren't amateurs, Wanda. And they don't make the sort of blue movie you can pick up in a video shop, either. They do real hard-core stuff— the sort of thing Mrs. Whitehouse couldn't even imagine. Christ, some things *I* couldn't even imagine."

"Who's Mrs. Whitehouse?" asked Wanda.

"If you'll stop jogging and get into the bloody car, I'll tell you!"

She stopped, and took deep breaths. "All right," she said, walking round.

He leant over and opened the door. "She complains about sex on TV," he said. He drove the car off the road, and took out his cigars. "Wanda, they've got a set-up to protect."

She laughed. "I'm not going to tell the cops."

"They don't know that." The flaring match lit the gathering gloom. "And think about it—he reckons he can get you a copy of a movie that was made . . . when? Mid-sixties? It isn't MGM, girl. They don't keep archive material. But someone's hung on to that one. Was getting it transferred to video. That has to be because she's on it, and they want to distribute it."

"So?"

He shook his head. "Your friend Colin's going in for a spot of private enterprise, like everyone else in this country." He puffed at his cigar. "I got you into this, and I don't want you going any further in with your eyes shut. The set-up's in Glasgow, and it's run by a couple of crooks who've been peddling porn for over twenty years. Magazines, strip joints, films, videos—you name it. They're into some very murky stuff indeed these days, and friend Colin isn't one of them. He's someone who makes pirate videos for them.'

She shrugged.

"Think about it, Wanda! He said he'd meet you in Glasgow. Now it's London. He's on the run, girl. He's stolen that film instead of making the video. They're none too happy—and he's way out of his league."

"Are you saying I shouldn't meet him?"

He sighed. "Is it that important to you?" he asked.

"You're the one who told me there was dirt to be found if I dug around in her background."

He nodded. "I wish I hadn't bothered," he said. "Don't you have enough startling revelations without this one?"

Wanda smiled. "You're telling me that she made a hard-core pornographic movie, and I should just forget it?"

"Yes," he said. "All right, the British aren't very high in your esteem, but what harm's she ever done you?"

"None." She smiled her brittle smile. "But she might be going to do me a lot of good."

"And you might end up with your face slashed!"

"I want that movie, Howard. I want to know exactly what she did on it."

"It's probably unwatchable by now!"

"People pay thousands of dollars for undrinkable wine," she said.

"Christ," said Howard. "All right, so she let someone screw her on celluloid. So what? She's not Mother Teresa, for God's sake."

"So *what*? Do you know how many countries are showing *Stones*? Do you know what her fan-mail is like? Are you telling me that all these people wouldn't be very interested to know what sort of thing she did before?"

"No. They'll be interested, all right. But you could be walking into trouble. And I'm not talking about law suits."

"I'm not leaving this country empty-handed," she said. "If I have that film, I've got proof, and that's what the publishers want." Her eyes were bright. "I'm *sick* of being F.D.'s wife, Mark Ingram's ex-wife—I'm having to put up with all of that shit again and I'm at least going to get what I came for!" She looked down. "Everyone else has," she muttered.

He ducked his head to look at her properly. "What's up, girl?" he asked.

Her eyes rose to his. "F.D. is screwing that little bitch," she said. "I don't know where, and I don't know when, but he is, and he's making a fool of me."

Howard nodded. "Probably," he said. "Is that why you were at the hotel? Trying to catch him out?"

She didn't answer.

"Come on, girl, that's beneath you. Why's it bothering you now? Why this one?"

She sighed. "Because it's going on right under my nose," she said. "I know it is. And . . ." She paused. "Maybe you made me restless," she said.

"Me?" Howard looked utterly innocent. "What did I do?"

"Told me I was lonely."

51

Howard smiled. "The offer's still open," he said.

She smiled back, shaking her head.

He put his arm round her shoulders. "When was the last time you got a proper kiss?" he asked.

"I don't recall," she said.

Howard took her in his arms, his mouth on hers, his tongue gently seeking and finding a response. "That was nice," he said with a broad smile, as they drew apart.

She looked a little uncertainly at him, and he let her go.

"I won't push it," he said, reaching into his pocket for his glasses.

"Thank you."

He started the engine and pulled the car back on to the road. "I think maybe you could use some company when you meet this bloke," he said.

"Yours?" Wanda asked.

"No, though you're welcome to it if you want it. But I meant minders. Heavies."

"A bodyguard? You don't think that'll put him off?"

"They'll keep out of sight. But they'll be there, if needed. I think these lads are on to him, and they'll want their film back."

Wanda shrugged. "OK," she said. "If it makes you feel better."

"It does." His headlights swept the bend in the road, and he gave a little sigh of achievement. "I'll let you know what I've arranged," he said.

A car followed them round the bend half a minute later; it followed them back to Phil Sumner's house, and drove on past.

F.D. had eaten alone. He looked up from the breakfast bar as Wanda came in. "Working late?" he asked.

"I had to see Howard about something," she said. "He brought me back."

He nodded.

"I'm going up," she said.

"Aren't you well?" he asked.

52

"I'm very well, thank you, F.D. I've got some work to do."

She went upstairs; after a few moments, F.D. followed her. He knocked on the door, and found her sitting at the table in the bedroom, writing.

"You don't usually work here," he said.

"Oh, this isn't the book. This is my next project—you might like to direct it. It's called *The Casting Couch*—set in thirties and forties Hollywood—full of directors and producers getting laid by hopeful starlets. Doesn't happen now, of course," she said, and looked up. "Shouldn't you get two, if you're a producer-director?"

F.D. sat on the bed. "What's that supposed to mean?" he asked.

"Whatever you want it to mean."

He shook his head. "Have you ever thought that you might be paranoid?" he asked.

"No. I've thought that you might be oversexed, but if you are, I don't get the benefit. And you know," she said, her voice concerned, "you *are* looking tired. Perhaps you should slow down, F.D. It can't be easy keeping up with them—especially since they get younger as you get older."

"Oh, for . . ." He sighed. "I'm not bedding starlets," he said. "Ask, if you don't believe me. Ask anyone you like."

"I have. And there is no funny business on the set, and Barbara Slaney leaves when filming's over, and gives Mark and John Landers a ride back to the hotel. And you wait until everything's all safe and sound for the night before you leave, and you come straight home like a good boy. I've tried coming back here at odd times of the day—I've gone to the hotel instead of coming here, and you are always here or she is always there. I know."

"Well, then." He smiled and spread his hands. "I'm not having an affair with Barbara Slaney, am I?"

"I know that! An affair means romance, love, caring for someone—you only understand that if it's on a cinema screen. But you and she are copulating. I know that, too."

53

"If you think that, you have my permission to have me followed—night and day, if you like."

"No," she said. "That's so undignified, don't you think? I'm just warning you to be very careful, Frank. Because if I catch you at it, I will take every penny I can from you. And if I don't, she might—because from what I've seen of Miss Slaney, she isn't like the others. She doesn't keep her brains exclusively between her legs." She picked up her pen. "Now, if you don't mind—and on the assumption that there is no other business—I'd like to get on."

F.D. went to his own room and worked on the shooting schedule until the small hours, before finally getting into bed and putting out the light. He lay awake; he tried listening to the radio, but it was someone mournful who seemed to think he'd missed out on love. He switched it off, and tried to sleep.

There was a tape. A big, old-fashioned tape. It was Elvis Presley declaring his monogamy, and pleading for kindness, and it proved that F.D. was guilty and should be hanged. They were going to use the tape to hang him; he was surprised about that. Surprised, and interested. He had always thought that they used rope, but—ah, yes. It turned *into* rope, of course it did. He remembered now, remembered how annoying it was when you were listening to Elvis, and the tape turned into rope. Wanda stripped him naked, ready for the hangman.

He woke up, sweating. And he stayed awake well into the night—so well into it that the sky held the glow of dawn before he lay back and closed his eyes with the deep sigh of a man who had done some hard thinking, and had come to a decision.

"Howard Maxwell!" Susan Quentin's imperious call echoed over the empty sands.

Howard, sitting on a rock, turned to see her negotiate the grassy, sandy slope to the beach, her high heels making the task virtually impossible. He smiled broadly as she lost her footing, and made the rest of the journey with her shoes in her hand.

"Howard Maxwell, you lied to me!" she said, as she came up to him.

"Would I do that?" said Howard, with a grin. "What about?"

"This film!" She defiantly put her shoes on again only to sink into the sand, losing some dignity. "Oh, to hell," she said, taking them off again. "You told me everything was fine—it was safe for me to recover!"

"It *was*," protested Howard, warily eyeing the four-inch heels. "I wish you'd put them down while you're yelling at me," he said. "I think they constitute an offensive weapon."

"It *was* all right. It isn't now! This week I've had more insults from that man than I've had from all the creeps I've ever known put together!"

Howard grinned. "But it was fine up until Tuesday," he said. "You can't deny that."

"*Do* something!"

He held out his hands in a helpless gesture. "What can I do? I've done my bit."

"I'm seriously considering a relapse," she said.

"I think F.D. might not fall for it twice," said Howard.

"I don't care! I'd sooner be sued than work for him in this mood." She looked at him, her famous green eyes bright with anger. "You've seen him! Telling me how to play the love scene! How dare he?"

Howard sat down again. "F.D. always tells people how to act," he said.

"That has some merit in Mr. Landers' case," she said archly. "I'm told he can swim."

"Well, cheer up," he said. "We've got tomorrow off, thank God."

"Yes. So you can treat me to whatever a Saturday night in Ardcraig has to offer."

"Sorry," said Howard. "I've got a date in a local pub that no woman has ever set foot in."

SUNDAY LUNCH: ROAST BEEF, ROAST POTATOES, NEW POTATOES, PEAS, GRAVY, read the blackboard. Inside the café,

F.D. sat with Eddie Anderson, who seemed to be enjoying his.

"I wouldn't swear to it, mind," said Eddie. "It was getting dark. But they sat in the car talking for about ten minutes, and he might have kissed her."

F.D. nodded. "Right," he said. "Carry on. But from now on you will ring me, at this number." F.D. wrote the number down and handed it to Anderson.

In the little café, Eddie pocketed the piece of paper, and had a visible argument with himself before he spoke.

"Mr. Derwent, I've been doing this for almost a month. And that's the closest she's got to doing anything that you might not like. I sit there all day every day, and me and the postman are the only people who ever go there."

F.D. stiffened slightly.

"I don't think anything's going on, Mr. Derwent," said Eddie earnestly. "She does the same things every day. She gets there at nine, she goes for her dinner at one, and she always has it here. She always has salad, and she's always alone. She goes back after an hour, and then she leaves again, at five. Now and again it's been earlier, but she still just goes home or to the hotel, and she doesn't see a soul, not to talk to, except for that one time. And if he did kiss her, it wasn't what you'd call passionate. If you want my opinion—"

"I'll ask for it," said F.D. brusquely. "You don't object to earning money, do you?"

"No," said Eddie. "I get through a lot of paperbacks, though. Maybe I should be putting them on expenses."

"You do that," said F.D. "You see, Mr. Anderson, I like knowing where my wife is. It gives me a distinct advantage."

Eddie looked a bit disapproving. "Oh, I see. Right," he said. "You're the boss." He left.

F.D. nodded slowly in agreement with Eddie's final statement and left a note to cover the bill. He drove straight to the Lodge and went up to Howard's room, where a bleary-eyed Howard opened the door, pulling a robe round himself.

"Howard," said F.D. briskly, "you look bloody awful."

Howard sat gingerly on the edge of the bed. "What do

56

you want?'' he asked hoarsely. He groaned. ''It's Sunday morning, I've got a hangover, and I did not expect a visit from you before sodding dawn.''

''I've had lunch, Howard. A very nice little café in town.''

''Christ.'' Howard picked up his watch from the dressing table and fumbled for his glasses. ''Christ,'' he said, again, when he finally read the time.

F.D. smiled. ''You still have underworld connections, don't you, Howard?'' he asked.

Howard looked up. ''Very droll, F.D.,'' he said. ''Why do you ask?''

''I might want to make use of them,'' he said. ''A little job I might want to have done.''

''You don't need to rob a bank, F.D. Your investments are sound, your tax dodges are legitimate, you're making a bomb.''

''If I wanted a couple of hard men, you'd know how to go about acquiring their services?''

''As it happens, I've already got a couple,'' said Howard. ''Who do you need protection from, F.D.?''

F.D. raised his eyebrows. ''I could ask you the same question,'' he said. ''But I don't want the protective kind. I want someone taught a very hard lesson.''

''Who?''

''Miss Slaney.''

Howard's mouth opened. ''She's just a kid, F.D.!''

''She's playing dangerous games—that's how kids get hurt.''

Howard looked away.

''Are you refusing?''

There was a long moment before Howard answered. When he did, it was with a sigh. ''I can get you a couple of psychopaths, if that's what you want,'' he muttered.

F.D. smiled. ''Good,'' he said. ''Then get them. I'll let you know if they're going to be needed.''

He closed the door on Howard's defeated expression, and walked quickly down the corridor, knocking on the door two down from Howard's.

Barbara's eyes widened as she opened the door. "What do you want?" she asked.

"A chat." He pushed his way in, knocking her off balance, and went into the room. "In private," he added, locking the door and putting the key in his inside pocket.

She backed off a little. "What do you *want*?" she asked again.

"The tape, Barbara—what do you suppose I want?"

"It isn't here."

He shook his head. "It must be," he said. "Even with the noticeable lowering of the Post Office's standards while I have been out of the country, they must have delivered it to you by now."

She swallowed. "I haven't got it," she said.

He took a step towards her. "I want the tape," he said.

She looked at him defiantly.

"There's no need for you to get hurt," he said. "But you will, if I don't get that tape."

She drew away as he got closer. "It's not here," she said, backing towards the bed, sitting down suddenly as she hit it.

He stood over her, turning his head as he checked the room, his eyes resting on the radio and lamp by the bedside, the china ornaments on the dressing table, the coffee and tea kit on the deep windowsill, the half-open wardrobe with the suitcases on top, the chest of drawers, with a small pile of magazines, and a Walkman. He smiled.

"It isn't there," she said.

He went over to the Walkman and picked up the handful of cassettes. He listened to a few moments of every one, then shook his head, frowning slightly. His eyes went to the radio by her bed, and she tensed up.

He raised his eyebrows and bent down towards it. "It plays cassettes," he said. "Well, well." He smiled, as he took it out, turned it to side one. "Hidden in plain sight?" He pressed the play button.

". . . *last Sunday in April. Spring is just around the corner—maybe someone should tell this guy. It might cheer him up.*" Someone bitterly regretted his jealousy.

58

She made to turn it off, but he caught her hand, tightening his grip as she tried to pull away from him.

"I'm going to find that tape," he said softly, as he slowly turned up the volume.

The staccato violin theme-tune to a TV serial accompanied the meal, as the dining room filled up with hungry members of the film crew looking for Sunday lunch.

"Do you think Barbara's OK?" asked John Landers as the waitress brought him his meal. "I know she comes down late on Sundays, but she's usually here by now."

"I'm sure she's quite all right, darling," said Sue Quentin. She buttered a roll and started on the soup.

Mark Ingram smiled. "F.D.'s visiting," he said. "I saw him as I came in—I think I'll have traditional roast beef and Yorkshire pudding, if I may, Winnie," he said to the woman, who visibly wilted as he smiled at her. "And melon to start."

"In full view?" said Sue Quentin, when the waitress had gone.

"Well, no. He did shut the door."

She laughed. "But you *saw* him! He *is* desperate."

Mark laughed at Landers' shocked face. "You're not still defending her honour, are you, John?" he asked.

"It's Sunday," he said.

Mark shook his head. "You really were the perfect choice for Samuel, weren't you?"

Landers went slightly red. "I'm no bible-thumper," he said. "I just . . . well, I just don't think that sort of thing is right on a Sunday. I mean, well, it is adultery."

Mark glanced at Sue, who was trying to keep a straight face.

"Is adultery all right during the rest of the week?" Mark asked, as not one but two slices of melon arrived. He asked the waitress if her daughter had had the baby yet; she could hardly speak.

Landers waited until she had gone. "Of course not," he said. "But it's worse on a Sunday."

"I don't think that Lord's Day Observance is uppermost in their minds at the moment," said Sue.

"But it's a sign from God, none the less," Mark said, in Martin Luther King's voice. "He is delivering us from evil, and putting F.D. in a good mood at last."

Even Landers smiled.

The knife tore through the lining of her suitcase. Barbara sat hunched on the bed, her knees drawn up to her chest, half-hidden by the mattress which lay against it, surrounded by rumpled sheets and pillowcases.

"Don't we all feel like running away sometimes?" said the DJ. *"But things aren't always as bad as they seem . . ."*

The loud, jolly music that followed assured her that life went on as he searched through her stuff, pulling out and upturning every drawer, ransacking every cupboard. He went into the bathroom, picking up the dirty linen basket, scattering its contents. She could hear him pull things out of the cabinet, hear them rattling into the basin. She covered her ears as he smashed any jar large enough to conceal a cassette.

He came back out, crossing the devastated room towards her, standing at the end of the bed. He shook his head, then slowly, deliberately, he put on driving gloves, and walked to the dressing table. He picked up one china figure, and snapped it in two. "Where is it?" he asked.

There were tears in her eyes as she shook her head. "I don't have it," she whispered. "Please—leave them. They're good luck."

"That's what you think."

One by one, they were broken in two, until they all lay in pieces. Barbara had turned her head away; F.D. stood and looked at her until she turned back.

"You think that as long as you have the tape, you have the upper hand," he said quietly.

Barbara looked at him, shaking her head.

"But it'll do you no good," he went on. "You don't want Wanda to hear it any more than I do. Because once she has, it's of no value to you."

60

The soft, mellow sounds of a guitar were trying to emulate a soaring, diving seabird as he moved closer, his feet trampling her clothes.

"All it can do is harm me," he said. "It won't benefit you at all." He shook his head at her. "Is it worth getting hurt just so as you can hang on to it?" he asked. "Because that's what's going to happen."

She shrank away as he bent down towards her.

"Oh, *I'm* not going to hurt you," he whispered. "I don't have to. Because money buys violence. Real violence—impersonal and vicious." He smiled grimly. "And if you don't give me that tape now, you're going to be on the receiving end of it."

"No," she said, tears running down her face.

"It will have nothing to do with me," he went on. "I don't know who they are, and they don't know who I am. I don't know where it's going to happen, or when." He crouched down, his face close to hers. "And neither do you." He touched her face, wiping a tear. "I'm sure they'll take full advantage of the situation," he said.

"No," she whispered.

"If you want to keep the tape, that's the price you pay," he said. "A bargain, pure and simple." He stood up.

"No, please, no!" She caught his hand. "I can't, I *can't* give you the tape. I don't have it!"

"Then you've nothing to bargain with," he said, picking his way through the debris to the door, unlocking it.

"F.D., for God's sake!"

The seabird glided on the wind, and Barbara inclined her head towards the sound.

"*That's* the tape!" she sobbed. "I taped over it. I didn't want it. You scared me in the car—I didn't want it! I put it in and taped the radio over it!"

He looked at her for a moment, then came back, and switched off the music, removing the tape and putting it in his pocket. He looked amused. "Stick to being an easy lay," he said. "You're not cut out for blackmail." He straightened up. "I'll call them off," he said.

She sighed with relief, and watched through the tears as he left, closing the door. Whereupon her composure returned instantly, and she smiled a small, self-congratulatory smile.

CHAPTER FOUR

THE SUN HAD ALREADY RISEN BEYOND THE WINDOW, and now it was doing it all over again in F.D.'s headphones. The low, rumbling C major, almost inaudible at first, grew in strength, in suspense, until the trumpets heralded the glimmering of light. He closed his eyes as the brass soared and the timpani pounded, oblivious to everything but the majesty of the music until dawn broke over the horizon in triumph. He smiled with satisfaction, and switched off the record.

He had just put the coffee on when he caught a glimpse of Wanda through the serving hatch, and frowned as she pulled one of the pictures away from the wall and opened the safe. His eyebrows rose as she took out bundles of notes and began packing them into a document case. Then she put the whole lot back in, locking the safe again.

"Coffee?" he called, after a moment, making her jump.

"I didn't know you were still here," she said, and picked up her weekend bag, already packed.

"Late start today. I thought you weren't going until this evening," he said.

"I'm not."

"Why are you all packed now?"

"Because I've got a lot of work to get through, and I can't get away before three. I want to have everything ready." She

63

went out into the fresh breeze, and put the weekend bag in the boot of the dark grey Mercedes that sat at the door.

"What *is* this business you've got in London?" he asked, leaning on the hatch as she came back in and went into the kitchen.

"Buy the book. Find out."

Framed by the picture window, the climbing sun lit the tops of the hills, dramatic black and white.

"Do you think I should have made this movie in monochrome?" he asked.

"I think you should have made it in the south of France," she said.

He smiled. "I thought you didn't mind the cold?" He pushed open the door and joined her in the kitchen.

"I don't really," she said. "I mind the natives telling me that this is warm." She picked up the jacket that lay over the chair, folded it and put it in the tote bag in which she carried her office clothes.

He poured two mugs of coffee, and regarded her for a moment as she broke eggs into the pan. "Where did we go wrong?" he asked.

"I grew up. You don't like grown-ups, Frank. You like actors. You don't even like real actors. You like ones who'll do things your way."

He turned. "So I should have married an actress?"

"No," she said. "You shouldn't have married anyone. But you did, and you're stuck with it." She scrambled the eggs. "*We* didn't go wrong, Frank—you did. Because all your emotion ends up on the screen. You just use people like tissues—and you want them to be just as disposable. But they're not."

He gave a little laugh. "Sounds as if you rehearsed that," he said.

"Maybe I did."

"Any special reason?"

She shook her head. "I'm not leaving you, if that's what you're hoping," she said. "When I leave, Frank, I'll take a lot more money with me than that."

She finished her coffee, put her handbag into the other bag, put it over her shoulder, and went off.

F.D. watched her as she jogged away, a splash of blue against the browns and greens.

"You can keep your pants on from now on, John!" shouted F.D. "No need to show off—we won't be shooting below the waist."

Sue Quentin fanned herself with her hand as she sat in the spring sunshine, decked out in over-the-top Victorian finery. "What's that poor boy ever done to F.D.?" she asked.

Barbara, wearing fetching and modest Victorian underwear, her shoulders bare, shivered a little in the wind. "He thinks John's sleeping with me," she said.

"And is he?"

Barbara laughed. "John has a sweetheart back home in Iowa or wherever it is he comes from. The girl next door."

"That wouldn't stop most men sleeping with you," said Sue.

"No," agreed Barbara. "Stops him, though." She watched as he walked up and down the cliff top, talking to Len. "It's a shame," she said. "But there it is." She looked at Sue for a moment, smiling. "Actually . . ." she said, then stopped.

"What?" said Sue.

"Oh, nothing."

They both laughed as someone went in pursuit of the hat that had been blown off his head.

"Go for it, Steve!" shouted Howard, as the cap bowled along the grass.

"A flying tackle," advised Len Charles, as it came to rest on the edge of the cliff.

Steve Ellis made a rude gesture, then stalked it, planting his foot on it just as it made to lift into the air again, and put it firmly back on his head to a round of applause.

"Was it as windy as this when they did the long shots?" Sue asked.

"Just about. It's always windy up here."

Sue lit a long cigarette with considerable difficulty, shielding the lighter with her hand. "Is that why F.D.'s in such a foul mood all the time?" she asked, when she had succeeded. "Because he thinks you and John are an item?"

"Could be."

"Look, darling, as long as I get paid, I don't give a damn how much screen time he gives you, so couldn't you try worming your way back into his affections?"

"That might not be too easy," said Barbara. "But believe me, I intend to try."

"I think I might have a relapse," said Sue. "Do you want to catch it? Perhaps everyone could come down with it, and let F.D. rant and rave at himself for a few days."

Barbara smiled, and looked thoughtfully at her. "Do you know anything about this book his wife is writing?" she asked.

"No," said Sue. "But I can guess what she's simply dying to tell the world."

"Are you sure?" asked Barbara, as Howard called them on to the set.

Sue frowned a little, and watched John and Barbara being drenched.

John shivered. "I hope this doesn't take too long," he said.

"Darling, if you were wearing this lot, you'd be glad of it," said Sue.

"Right, places."

Sue arranged herself on the grass by the edge of the cliff, and John knelt over her. Barbara walked down the grassy slope a few yards.

"Quiet!"

The clapper-board snapped. "Action," said F.D.

John pushed her down on the ground.

"Cut." F.D. sighed. "You're raping her, for Christ's sake! Put a bit of force into it!"

This time, he pushed her down with enough force to bang her head, and apologised.

"Oh, cut, for God's sake! That was good! Why did you

66

have to—? We can use it, I suppose. OK. Let's have the rape. But you're too dry, John."

He was drenched again, and shook with cold as he knelt down beside Sue.

"Mr. Derwent?" he said. "Could you remember that I'm getting married in the fall?"

Sue laughed, but F.D. didn't find it amusing. He stopped the first take before it had been going ten seconds.

"You're supposed to be *raping* her, John, not fitting her for a corset!"

"Mr. Derwent, I don't know if you have ever *tried* raping someone in full Victorian—"

"Just pull! It'll rip. Costumes spent hours making sure it would. It doesn't matter if it seems too easy—we're not close enough to see what's happening, until we move in, and you start to *help* him, Sue. Then just get on with it. All right?"

He stopped take two. "You're not doing press-ups, John," he said. "And you're getting too dry again, I fancy."

John submitted himself once more to the water treatment, by now angry enough to give a convincing performance.

"Cut. Fine."

The camera was moved to a different set-up, and John had water thrown over his back again.

"Now we'll be in close on your hands and arms, John, as you pull at the skirts. Then your hand comes into shot, Sue, and you aren't pushing him away, you're helping him get the material out of the way. OK?"

It was OK, much to the participants' surprise. Another long wait, while the next shot was set up.

"This is head and shoulders—close in. Don't forget to act, John."

John knelt beside Sue again, and anxiously watched F.D.

"Action."

His lips on Sue's partially exposed breast, John began to move up and down, eyes closed, breath rasping. It made Sue laugh.

"Cut."

"Sorry," she said.

"It might help, John," said F.D., "if you could look a little more as though you were having an orgasm, and less as though you were having an asthma attack." He sighed loudly, and take two began.

Sue giggled.

"Cut."

Take three, and she tried hard, but her efforts not to laugh were too evident.

"Cut. Try kissing her on the mouth, John. It might stop you making that very peculiar noise, and it might prevent her from laughing."

Sue sat up on one elbow. "He's raping me," she said. "Kissing doesn't seem appropriate. I mean—she's decided to take the line of least resistance, but kissing's too romantic."

Landers looked at her, and at F.D., and resignedly reached for his blanket.

"You know the sort of kiss I mean! He's forcing himself on you. You're letting him do it, but you're not responding. It's no different!"

"But if he's kissing me, how can I see Barbara?" she asked.

F.D. thought for a moment. "Kiss her on the mouth, then move to her breast," he said. "He moves from your mouth to your breast, and you turn your head away. That's when you see Barbara. Barbara!"

Barbara's head popped up over the edge of the cliff, and Sue went into another fit of laughter.

"Barbara, you come up when he moves to her breast."

"How will I know?"

A signalling device was worked out, and take four was working, until Barbara came up. Sue was in stitches.

"For God's sake!" F.D. roared.

"She *can't* do that!" said Sue, through almost helpless laughter, which was transferring itself inexorably to John and Barbara, and members of the crew, especially Howard, who was enjoying it all hugely.

It had not transferred itself to F.D.

"She'll have to come up before I look—I can't watch her suddenly pop up like . . ." Sue dissolved.

"That might be better," said F.D. "If you're in shot all the time, Barbara. We're in close on them until Sue turns her head, then pull the focus to you. And you're watching." He nodded. "Will that solve your problem?" he asked the recovering Sue.

"Yes," she said, pulling herself together. "Yes, I'll be all right."

Take five was giggle-free, but F.D. stopped it.

"Cut." He looked at Barbara.

"What?" she said.

"You have been left to drown by your husband. You wait, wanting to teach him a lesson, then swim against the tide to get out, climb up the rocks to safety, and come face to face with your said husband, stark naked, screwing the woman you regarded as your friend and confidante, in broad daylight on the top of a cliff, *and you look as if you'd found there was no milk in the fridge*!" he roared.

Barbara glared at him. "You do it, F.D.," she said. "Show me."

"She's horrified!" he said. "She's—" He broke it off. "I'm sure you can remember an instance in your life when you were appalled," he said. "By something that happened. Or something that was *going* to happen? Can't you?"

Barbara's eyes blazed. "Yes," she said.

They were drenched again, having dried out too much, and take six was fine.

"Can I get dry now?" asked John.

"Not much point. We're setting up Sophia's point of view—you'll have to be wet for that."

He sat huddled in a blanket, as Barbara went to get dry. Sue went and sat beside him.

"I don't get it," he said. "Sometimes he's as nice as pie, and sometimes . . ."

"You could always catch my infectious disease," said Sue.

"I'll be lucky if I don't catch pneumonia."

They did it in one take, and escaped at last from F.D.

Sue found Barbara having coffee and a sandwich. "What did you mean?" she asked. "About Wanda's book?"

Howard rounded everyone up after they had been dried off, and the next scene had been set up.

F.D. squinted up into the sun, then looked through the camera. "Sorry, John," he said, as he climbed up the slope towards him. "You'll have to take your clothes off again, after all."

John sighed. "I'm not in this shot, am I?"

"Yes, you are. You see, the camera will be here, this time." F.D. went down to the bottom of the slope, and paced out on to the sand. "Barbara will be there," he said, pointing to the rocks still covered with sea water. "And she won't be able to see, because she's at the bottom of the slope, but the *camera* will be seeing Samuel on top of the cliff, walking towards Letitia up above." He smiled. "It's too good to lose," he said.

John sighed.

Howard watched F.D. play with Landers like a cat with a mouse, and glanced down the road towards Wanda's cottage. He waved as Mark arrived.

"Mark?" said F.D. "We don't need you till Monday."

"I like to watch," said Mark. "I like not being the one who's being yelled at," he said, *sotto voce*, and Howard smiled.

A car pulled into the car park, and Simon Waterford came across the sandy grass towards them.

"Simon," said F.D. "It must be Friday again."

"It is," said Simon.

"This is the man who has you running about wet and naked all the time, John," said F.D. "Blame him."

"The scene only lasts three minutes," said Simon.

"Trouble is," said John, "it takes two days to shoot, what with the stunt and all."

"Oh," said Simon. "Well, I'm sorry. You could have got a worse day," he added encouragingly, nodding to the sun. "Why the lights?" he asked.

Howard smiled. "The sun's the problem," he said. "We're shooting Barbara at eleven o'clock in the morning, and the stunt-woman at eight o'clock in the morning. We don't want shadows. But is it overcast today? Is it hell. It's sod's law."

"Why don't you do them both at the same time in the morning?" asked Simon.

"Because even if we were prepared to risk Barbara when the tide was coming in, it doesn't come in at the same time every morning like a train," said Howard.

"Which train would that be?" asked Simon.

Howard smiled. "High tides are about twelve and a half hours apart," he said. "It gets about an hour or so later each morning. But it would be too dangerous for Barbara if the tide really was coming in, anyway," he added. He stepped forward. "Right! Clear the set, please!"

Barbara appeared in her long, bedraggled dress, and Howard winced as she paddled into the cold sea, and lay down on the still-submerged rock. John was saturated again, and they were ready, except that F.D. had disappeared. He came running back from the direction of the Portaloo, strategically hidden behind the trailers.

"Sorry," he said. "It must be all this water. Right, let's go. And remember, the sooner we get it over with, the sooner we can all go home."

The clapper-board clicked. "Action," said F.D.

John strode towards Sue, as Barbara picked herself up from the rock and began divesting herself of her dress. Its heavy folds made the job difficult, but she finally freed herself from it, and made to move towards the steep rock face.

"Cut," said F.D..

"Was that OK?" John called from the cliff. "Can we all go and get dry now?"

"Sorry," F.D. called back. "Not quite."

"Oh, what now?" Landers reached for the blanket.

F.D. turned to Barbara. "You moved off the rock too soon," he said.

"No," she said, puzzled.

"You're supposed to take your clothes off, my love."

71

"Just the dress!"

F.D. frowned, and looked at his script. "No," he said. " 'Sophia removes her sodden clothes,' it says here."

"But it is just the dress," said Simon, helpfully.

" 'Her sodden clothes,' " repeated F.D. "Is or is not your underwear sodden, Barbara?"

"I'm not taking it off," she said.

"I should think she isn't!" said Simon. "Why would she? She can move perfectly freely."

"She would take it off because I'm telling her to take it off," said F.D.

"But that would be all wrong!" Simon said angrily.

"Can we get this sorted out?" Landers shouted. "Quickly?"

"Yes!" Barbara shouted back. "We can." She turned back. "I was wearing underwear in the other shot, F.D." She shivered as the wind blew in off the sea.

"Only because you didn't have to take it off," said F.D. "We could only see your shoulders."

"It's perfectly clear in the novel," Simon began.

"The novel?" said F.D. "The novel?"

Howard sucked in his breath, and glanced at Mark. "Poor little sod," he said.

F.D. walked towards Simon. "I read all the reviews of your novel, Simon. I read all the crap about whether or not the whole thing was just a fantasy in Leo's mind, and how it was really an illustration of how spurious feminism is, and all the rest of the hogwash."

Simon looked a little helpless.

"Your novel is nothing more than a ludicrous story with generous helpings of sex and sadism, dressed up as art so that everyone can enjoy it with a clear conscience. So I'm giving the filmgoer the same chance as the literary crowd to enjoy a bit of titillation."

Simon looked shocked. "But that's not what—"

"Of course it is! Why do you think I wanted to do it? It's got sex, violence—Christ, it's got a willing rape victim! Do you know how long it is since we've been allowed to get away with that? But this is art, and anything goes. And the nude female is art—everyone knows that.''

Simon turned and walked away.

''I'm not taking my clothes off!'' Barbara shouted.

''Oh come on, love,'' said F.D. as she stormed past him, and up to the trailers. ''We're going for a fifteen,'' he called after her.

''What the hell does that mean?'' roared Landers.

Mark Ingram smiled serenely up at him. ''No genitals, I understand,'' he said.

''You soon won't have to worry about that as far as I'm concerned!'' Landers yelled. ''I'll be in my trailer!'' He strode off, wrapping the blanket round himself like a toga.

Mark Ingram strolled away.

F.D. groaned. ''Go after them, Howard,'' he said. ''Before Ingram jumps him.''

Howard looked exasperated. ''Landers can take care of himself,'' he said.

''I understood, Howard, that it was your job to maintain order and discipline on the set,'' said F.D. ''Go *after* them. And take them back to the Lodge, if they're going. Miss Slaney won't be able to chauffeur them.''

Howard frowned. ''What about the scene?''

''We'll go with what we've got.''

''What the hell are you up to now, F.D.?''

''Just do it, Howard. I don't know what's bringing out the Galahad in you, but if it's Miss Slaney, don't waste your time.'' He looked round at the crew. ''OK!'' he shouted. ''Call it a day!'' He looked back at Howard. ''Go,'' he said, and turned away. ''Len!'' he called. ''We need to talk about the stunt—I'll see you at the Lodge after lunch.''

Howard sighed, and walked towards the trailers.

Mark rubbed John's back vigorously as John towelled his legs, and pulled on his jeans.

''I guess I'm dry now, thanks,'' John said, reaching for his shirt.

Mark handed it to him, smiling. "You really are a very beautiful specimen," he said.

John pulled on his shirt. "Like I said," he replied a little warily, "I keep in shape."

Mark nodded. "What is it?" he asked. "Am I too old for you?"

Landers frowned a little, then his eyes slowly widened, and he understood. "Oh," he said, keeping his voice low. "No—no, you've got me wrong."

Mark looked crestfallen. "But in the bar—you said you weren't interested in women."

"I meant I wasn't interested in fooling around. I've got a girl at home. We're getting married in the fall." He smiled a little apology as he spoke. "I'm not gay," he said, and shook his head a little. "I—I didn't know until that time in the bar that you were."

"I'm not," said Mark, miserably. "I'm terminally pissed off."

Landers smiled.

Mark looked sadly at him, shaking his head. "Wasting all that beauty on a woman," he said. "I tell you, they don't appreciate it. They don't understand male beauty." He smiled. "You're not threatening to punch me," he added.

"Should I be?"

"A lot of people do, if you make a mistake."

Landers sat down, relaxed. "Maybe that's when you haven't really made a mistake," he said.

Mark nodded. "You said you didn't mean to become an actor," he said. "What did you mean to be?"

"I never got the chance to find out. I was a swimmer. I would have been in the team for the Moscow Olympics, but . . ." He gave a little smile. "The USA pulled out. The local TV station did a piece on me because I couldn't go, and someone called next day."

There was a pause while Mark looked at him with frank appreciation, and smiled. "I'll bet it wasn't a woman," he said.

Landers grinned. "It wasn't," he said.

74

Mark pressed on. "All right," he said. "You hadn't thought of being an actor, but you discovered you were one."

Landers laughed, unconvinced. "I say the words and don't bump into the furniture," he said. "*You're* an actor."

"Have you ever had a drink? Other than Coca-Cola, I mean?"

"Sure. I have a beer occasionally. But like I said, I never really got the taste for it."

"Drugs?"

He shrugged. "Joints, once or twice. Coke once. Not my thing."

"You didn't get the taste for them either?"

Landers shook his head, smiling.

Mark leant forward. "But you tried them before you made up your mind," he said. "Didn't you?"

Howard pushed open the door of the trailer.

"I hope I'm not interrupting," he said.

"Just trying to persuade John to sample a little alternative lust," Mark said. "Before he hitches himself for life to a female."

Howard grinned. "Sorry, Mark. Some of us are glad to be straight."

"I wasn't offering myself to you, Howard. Heaven knows, I have my pride." He frowned at the smiling Howard. "What the hell is wrong with F.D.?"

"Why does everyone blame me? I don't know what's wrong with him. I know Barbara's upset him somehow, that's all. I'm getting away from it all for the weekend."

"He complains about sadism," said Mark. "He's destroying Simon Waterford, distressing Barbara, and . . . well . . ." He looked at John, who laughed.

"I'll survive," he said, then looked worried. "Will Barbara be OK?" he asked. "He seems to get pretty mean when he's angry."

"Oh, I think she knows what she's doing," said Mark.

"Does she?" said Howard. "Anyway, Mark, do you promise not to make any more passes at John if I take you two back to the Lodge?"

Mark laughed. "John is pass-proof," he said. "Male or female. I don't know how he does it."

John smiled. "Getting freezing water thrown over you six times a day helps," he said.

Barbara sat in the trailer, trembling with cold, the Victorian underwear lying in a wet, discarded heap on the floor.

"Where the hell are my clothes?" she demanded, as F.D. came into the trailer, leaving the door open. "Where are the towels?"

"I have them," he said.

"You set this whole thing up," she said, stammering slightly as she shivered.

He smiled, and sat down. "Well, my love, you are very predictable, in some ways."

"I've been stuck in here f—" Her breath failed her. "For twenty minutes," she continued, as she fought to get the words out. "I'm . . . I'm freezing."

"I know."

She nodded. "All right," she said. "S-so now where are my clothes?"

"Not yet. I have a few things to say to you, and I want your undivided attention."

The wind whistled into the trailer. "Can we c-close the door?" she asked.

He shook his head. "What *would* people think?" he said archly.

"Get on with it then!"

He waited for a moment before he spoke. "There are a dozen actresses out there," he said in a quiet voice, "just as young as you, just as beautiful as you, who could act you off the screen. I know. We auditioned them. But I hired you instead. And you know why."

"And now you're f-firing me," said Barbara, wrapping her arms round herself. "Good." She shuddered. "J-just do it, for God's sake!"

"I could. We've all but finished your scenes—the ones that are left could be got round. But I'm not firing you."

76

"Oh, for—! What's all this about?" She couldn't stop shivering. "D-don't you understand how cold the water was?"

He smiled again. "Yes," he said.

"Then what . . ." It was too much of an effort. She gave up as the draught from the door chilled her even more.

"You tried to blackmail me," he said. "You didn't think you were going to get off scot-free, did you?"

"I'm sorry," she said, trembling violently as she spoke, the words barely whispered. "I never m-meant to blackmail you. That's why I t—" Her teeth chattered. "Taped over it," she said determinedly.

"I thought it was because I scared you," he said.

"Please," she said. "I'm t-too cold." She got up. "I'm closing the door."

He pushed her down again. "You're not," he said.

Her legs began to shake. "Please," she said. "I won't try any . . ." Her whole body was trembling. *"Please,"* she said again.

He went to the open door, but he didn't close it. He looked out, not speaking. Gulls called over the ever-present sound of the sea; the doorway framed misty hills and grey sky with fast-moving clouds.

"Y-you said you needed me," she said, desperately.

He turned to look at her, and raised his eyebrows.

"We . . . we c-could go back to our . . ." She took a moment to frame the vowel. "Original bargain," she finished.

"Oh, I think that was too many bargains ago," said F.D. He sighed, and looked at her again. "I think you've had enough," he said. "I'll get your clothes."

He went out; Barbara stumbled to the door, closing it, leaning against it, shuddering with cold.

A few minutes later he was back, pushing the door against her. She could hardly move to let him in.

"Here." He thrust them into her trembling hands, and she managed to pull on the sweater, but the skirt fastening defeated her. He did it up for her, and she sat down.

77

He had brought a bottle of brandy, and a paper cup with coffee in it. "Drink this," he ordered.

Barbara drank, and coughed, and drank some more.

He smiled, and poured more brandy into it. "Sip it," he said.

Barbara did as she was told.

"You want to go back to the original bargain?"

She nodded, still trembling, and drank more.

"We can, as long as you understand that I am the boss, as our friend Mr. Anderson would have it."

The shivers were subsiding. She nodded. "You're the boss," she said, and even smiled a little. "I suppose I deserved it," she added, pouring more brandy into the empty cup.

"You did," he said. "Try blackmail a third time, and I promise you will really regret it."

"Yes." She finished the brandy. "I'll have another one of these," she said. "I feel better already."

"I think you've had enough," he said. "It's all psychological anyway. It doesn't really make you warmer. In fact, they say it makes you colder."

"It makes me *feel* warmer," she said, reaching for the bottle. "It's stopping the shivering."

He took the bottle away. "What did you just agree?" he asked.

She shrugged. "You're the boss," she said.

"Good. You're learning." He put the cork in the bottle. "What I say goes," he said. "On or off the set." He held out his hand. "Bargain?" he said.

"Bargain." She smiled, extending a hand that no longer shook.

Wanda looked up, startled, as she heard the knock at the door. She smiled as Howard came in.

"I thought I'd come to see the author at work," he said. "You don't go in much for luxury, do you?"

"It's easier to keep it tidy like this," she said. "Shouldn't you be working?"

78

"Filming's finished for today."

She came out from behind the desk. "I've imported some creature comforts," she said. "I can offer you a cup of coffee."

"Oh, well, yes. Thanks."

She picked up the mug. "You'll have to have mine."

He smiled. "Suits me," he said. "Look, I've finalised the arrangements for tonight. Two guys will meet you at the airport. They'll travel on the same flight, but once you're on the plane, you don't know them. OK? Their names are Mo and Harry, and they look Neanderthal, but you listen to them, all right?"

She poured his coffee.

"And do as they tell you," he said. "They know what they're doing."

He touched her arm, and she turned to face him.

"And if they say run," he said seriously, "you run like *hell*."

She was smiling as he spoke; when he had finished, she pressed her lips to his, and they stood together in the middle of the room, exchanging small, intense kisses.

"Don't go," he said, breaking away.

"I want that film," she said.

"Then let me go instead."

She looked surprised, and pleased. Then she shook her head. "He said he wouldn't deal with anyone but me," she said.

"Oh, that's bullshit. He'll deal with anyone who's waving readies at him."

"But I'm all packed," she said.

"Christ, you can unpack! Let me go instead, Wanda. It makes sense."

She smiled. "Does it?"

"I know these people. I grew up with their kind. I might not be at my fighting weight, but I can take care of myself. I don't want you getting hurt." He suddenly hugged her fiercely, holding her close to him, his eyes screwed shut. "For God's sake, I *love* you, girl!" he said.

79

She gently pushed him away, until she could see his face, and she smiled, almost laughed.

"Is it funny?" he asked.

She shook her head. "No," she said, taking him in her arms.

CHAPTER FIVE

A HORSE REARING UP, FROZEN IN MID-GALLOP AS it thundered across the range, its rider twisted round in the saddle, gun blazing at his pursuers, muscles taut . . .

The Polson Bunch lay discarded on the passenger seat of the car as Eddie watched the door of the cottage.

It opened, and Howard Maxwell stood for a moment in conversation with Mrs. Derwent, before bending to kiss her. It could have been a kiss between two old friends, if they had left it at that, but they didn't.

Eddie's eyes widened as he watched them embrace; each time one tried to draw away, the other would begin again, as though they couldn't bear to let go. At last, they parted, and the door closed.

Eddie watched Maxwell walking away, checked his watch, and picked up his notebook, his finger running over what he had previously written, his lips moving slightly as he read.

May 4th, 12:15 P.M. Man, medium height, fair hair, glasses (which he removed before going in), dark suit. No vehicle. Same man as subject met at Lodge.

Neatly, underneath, Eddie wrote this next piece of information.

Departed 12:55 P.M. Embraced subject passionately for some minutes before leaving.

He put the notebook down with a smile of accomplishment, and watched the door again.

Moments later, Wanda Derwent came out and started walking down to the town. Eddie kept her in sight, and waited until she was some distance away before reversing out of the clearing.

His car had barely disappeared round the bend in the road when Barbara's car arrived, and nosed carefully into the little clump of bushes.

She got out, catching her sweater on the thorns; she extricated herself with some difficulty and walked slowly to the cottage. F.D. arrived on foot before she had got there; he waved the brandy bottle and two paper cups at her, smiling as she joined him, putting his arm round her as they walked up the path, her head resting on his shoulder.

Mark sat with Sue Quentin, and watched through the Lodge window as Landers, his shirt clinging to him in the wind, stood outside talking to Len Charles. He sighed wistfully, and looked at Sue.

"I sighed wistfully," he said.

"What?"

"I was setting myself up for some homophobic joke," he said. "I go to all that trouble, and you don't even notice, never mind make a wisecrack."

Her eyes seemed to focus on him for the first time. "Sorry, Mark," she said. "What?"

He frowned. "Is everything all right?" he said.

"Yes," she said. "It's just this film, it . . . ."

"Well, this bit's over," said Mark. "F.D.'s conceded the point about the underwear, stopped throwing water all over poor John, and gone to have a long heart to heart with his *ingénue*." He smiled. "I expect she'll be playing all the parts by Monday, but who cares? We've got the weekend off."

Sue smiled weakly.

"Hey, what is it? You're not letting that get you down, are you? So, he takes three hours lighting her shots and stands the rest of us under a bare light bulb—forget it."

She shook her head.

"Do you feel ill? Do you think you're coming down with whatever it was again?"

"No, I'm fine, honestly." She sighed. "This bit's over for you," she said. "*I* don't have the weekend off. On Sunday morning, I've got to go and get raped by John again."

Mark grinned. "Oh, no. You wouldn't do my joke. I'm not doing yours."

The mirror reflected the shaded window, the far edge of the desk, a scrap of rug, and a corner of the little room. The brandy bottle, caught by Barbara's outstretched arm as she gripped the desk, rolled into view and spun round slowly, falling with a quiet thud on the goatskin rug.

The rug rumpled up under their feet, nudging the bottle on its way again; it rolled gently into the mirrored corner of the room, bumping up against the three-pin plug which lay harmlessly by the skirting board, ensuring that this time Barbara's tipsy giggles and F.D.'s loud grunts of effort were not recorded for posterity.

"And this is Sir Alistair's wife, Lady Duncan," said Mark, passing the woman on to John Landers, who poured out all his downhome American charm, leaving Mark free to slope off back to the bar and his drink.

"Sorry, darling, but there's hours of this to go," said Sue. "You can't off-load them all."

"I don't really mind," he said, settling himself comfortably on his barstool. "I feel very much at home here."

"F.D. isn't here yet, I see," she said.

"Oh yes he is," said his voice behind her, making her jump.

"Well?" said Mark. "Shouldn't you be circulating? It's your party."

F.D. smiled. "I'll circulate," he said. "But it's the stars

these people are coming to see, not me.'' He shook his head at Mark's whisky. ''Do you think you could try to stay sober?'' he asked.

''I'm going to have to pop out later,'' warned Sue.

''Oh, don't run out on me, Sue,'' said F.D. ''You're the one they *all* want to see.''

''I won't be gone for long, F.D.,'' she said. ''I'll be back.''

From his new vantage point, Eddie watched as Susan Quentin arrived. She leant back into the taxi and spoke to the driver before going up the path and knocking. After a moment, she was admitted.

''Susan Quentin arrived 2:20 P.M.,'' he wrote, smiling happily. He didn't read his book; he watched the door.

''Mr. Derwent, if I have to smile and nod to one more female this afternoon I'll—'' Landers foundered.

''Sorry,'' said F.D. ''But Barbara hasn't put in an appearance at all yet, Sue has drifted off somewhere, and Mark's as drunk as a skunk. I have to introduce them to you.''

Landers sat down. ''Just give me a break, will you? Let my face muscles relax for ten minutes. Mark can handle them even if he's drunk.''

F.D. looked over at the bar, with considerable doubt, then sighed. ''All right, John,'' he said. ''I'll round up a few matrons who won't care whether Mark's drunk or sober, as long as he smiles at them.''

Mark had managed to acquire another drink before F.D. had crossed the room.

''Go easy on that stuff, Mark—this little do is going to go on into the evening, you know.''

''Get lost,'' said Mark. ''It was your idea—you talk to them, F.D.''

F.D. sighed. ''Have you seen Barbara?'' he asked.

Mark frowned. ''No. I rather thought you had.''

''She was supposed to be coming back here,'' he said, not denying it. ''It really is too bad, you know. I invite these people here to meet the stars and suddenly the entire cast has better things to do."

"Not better," muttered Mark. "More important."

"Getting drunk is more important than meeting the people who pay your rent?" asked F.D.

"I'm here," said Mark. "I don't think you can ask much more than that."

Eddie's pen once again moved over the notebook.

2:55 P.M. Susan Quentin departed. Looked upset.

Eddie frowned, and watched Susan Quentin as she went back to the waiting taxi, walking slowly, almost as though she was in a daze.

Almost as soon as the taxi drove off, the door opened again, and Eddie reached once more for the notebook.

Subject left 3:00 P.M.

He had to duck down as she passed the car on her way to the steps in the sea wall; he could see her as she jogged down to the shore, while he made his phone call. He crossed the road back to his car, his eye still on the bright blue jogging suit bobbing along the sand.

"Oh, they're not really violent," said Mark. "It's fantasy violence. All explosions and bursts of gunfire—but I guarantee, Mrs. Gillies, not one drop of blood. It's escapism."

She smiled. "I'm a bit squeamish about that sort of thing," she said. "That's why I was so pleased when I heard you were doing a real—" She broke off, embarrassed. "Well, you know—a film about real people. Like the ones you used to make."

Mark smiled, and her eyes positively misted over.

"Do you think . . . ?" She rummaged in a handbag large enough to convey a small atom bomb. "Do you think I could have your autograph?" she said, producing an old, battered autograph book.

Mark smiled again; a genuine smile. "I haven't seen one of these since I was at school," he said. "Everyone wrote rotten rhymes in them."

"I got it when I was leaving school," she said. "All my school friends signed it. Then years after that I began to meet some celebrities—with my husband being the entertainments manager for the arts centre—so I dug it out. He couldn't come today," she said. "He's working. He hopes he can pop in this evening." She handed the little book to Mark. "Could you make it out to Rose, please? That's my first name."

He wrote in it. "Rose," he said, giving it back with a smile. "What a lovely name."

She blushed like her namesake, and went off, her trophy consigned once more to the enormous handbag.

"What did you write?" Sue stood by his elbow, her face unnaturally bright, her eyes heavy with too much make-up.

"To Rose, who brought back memories," he said.

"Well," she said. "She'd like that."

Mark shrugged. "I hope so," he said. "It's true."

"Yes," she said, her eyes sad. "I had an autograph book like that." She sighed. "I don't know what happened to it. I didn't hang on to it like Rose."

"What's wrong?" asked Mark.

"Nothing," she said briskly. "But F.D.'s run out on us," she said. "I met him as I came in. He sets this thing up and then doesn't even stay. Are you sticking it out until the bitter end?"

He nodded. "This is where I live," he said. "This stool and I are old friends. I'm here now, and I'm not moving." He frowned at her. "Something's up," he said.

She nodded briefly, then took a breath. "Mark, you know about Wanda's book, I take it?" she asked.

He smiled. "Oh, yes," he said.

"Doesn't it bother you? What she's going to say?"

"She'll draw a veil over that," he said, confidently.

Sue sighed. "Who told you that?" she asked.

He looked quickly at her. "Well, no one," he said. "But she always has. She's never told anyone—" He stared at Sue. "She wouldn't," he said. "Not with the *Strong Medicine* contract and everything—she wouldn't."

Sue looked unhappily at her feet.

Mark licked his lips. "What—what exactly has she written?" he asked nervously.

"Exactly everything," said Sue bitterly. "About everyone she could think of."

Howard looked round anxiously as the London flight was called, walking slowly to the gate.

He made an inward sigh of relief as he saw the beetle-browed man who came towards him.

"Is she not coming?" the man asked, as he pushed past Howard into the crowd.

"It's me now," muttered Howard, apparently to himself, as Mo went on his way.

A huge bare forearm hoisted a suitcase over the heads of some children, and Harry nodded briefly as he passed.

Howard smiled, and sighed aloud.

The quiet, soulful voice had never seen her look as lovely; Sue Quentin sat alone at a table in the bar, her drink barely touched.

John Landers, still manfully on duty as the clock moved towards nine o'clock, said goodnight to the last of the evening guests, and got himself a beer from a tray that was passing. He looked round the more popular of the two bars, and went back through to the lounge.

Singing the words absent-mindedly under his breath, holding his glass of beer, he hovered uncertainly between the bar and her table; at the bar, Mark Ingram was drinking steadily and seriously, and Simon Waterford was almost in tears. He tried Sue.

"You haven't seen Barbara, have you, Sue?" he asked.

She shook her head.

"Do you want company?" he asked. "I could do with some."

"Not really." She drew on the cigarette, without its usual holder. "Len and some of the others are in the other bar," she said.

John smiled. "I don't really know them."

87

"You don't really know me," she said, then relented. "Sorry, yes, I think I would like company."

He nodded a little, and sat down. He held up the glass. "This is the warm beer I was told to expect," he said. "I think I like it."

"Why do you need company?" she asked.

He sipped the froth. "Doesn't everyone?" he asked, wiping it from his lips.

"I suppose."

But that was the extent of her conversation. Soon, all he could do was listen to the discussion at the bar.

"I thought he understood the novel," Simon said. "He seemed to, when we were working on the script."

Mark pushed his empty glass across the bar, and the girl refilled it, automatically making it a double.

"I thought he understood that the sex was allegorical," Simon went on. "Sophia—she wants to be a part of his life, but he just shoves her in a cave and leaves her there. And she says she's trapped, but she isn't. And then she comes *out*—she takes the dress off so that she can move *freely*, and then all she does with her freedom is go back into the cave!"

Mark waved a hand. "He does understand," he said. "He's conceded that."

"Only because of Barbara! Not because of what it all means! The willing rape victim—I thought he understood that, at least. Letitia seems to be more independent than Sophia, but she's gained her independence by giving men what they want. That's why both things are happening at once! Sophia gets all the way to the top just to see that Letitia is even more submissive than she is—however much freedom she seems to have. Women *are* willing rape victims."

"Bugger women," said Mark.

"Thank God he left that bit out," said Simon.

Mark actually laughed at his morose joke, and Simon smiled. "Sex is basic to it," he said. "Sexual taboos, sexual freedom, sexual attitudes—but the erotic content is about five minutes of the whole script! He's making it—"

"He's going for a fifteen," Mark said, the words slurring

slightly. "It'll all be very tastefully done. You'll see—after it's been edited, it'll all be suggestion and lighting and fuzzy shots, and the odd groan." He almost fell forward on to his elbows. "Ten feet of film get shot for every one that gets shown. In the end, there'll be nothing on the screen that you couldn't show your granny. It's all illusion, Simon."

Simon sipped his drink; someone was taking the singer's breath away. "That's what F.D. said," he muttered.

"He's right. Look—your book is set in high summer, right? I mean, that's why they're not averse to all this nude swimming and al fresco sex. And we're here in early spring. Because the light's better. It *looks* more like high summer, especially if you find a place with coniferous trees. Blossom being a dead giveaway."

He was getting expansive, his hands waving about. Simon rescued his drink before it went flying.

"Have you watched Len Charles working? Helping nature out so that the lighting's just the way he wants it? It'll be lyrical when he wants it to be, and harsh when he wants it to be. And someone will dub on all the sounds of people running through long grass or walking on the edge of the sea. Because the real sounds aren't convincing."

Simon laughed.

"And there will be dissolves and fade-outs, quick cuts and long shots . . . The film gets made in post-production. You might not like the finished product, but don't judge it by what you're seeing here, because this doesn't bear any relation to the actual film. It's all illusion."

"Yes," sighed Simon.

"*I'm* an illusion." Mark got to his feet. "And I'm pissed," he said, with a concluding, charming smile.

"Are you going to your room?" Simon asked, in a worried voice.

"I thought I might, I thought I might." He laughed, without humour. "Go to my room, and consider my future," he said.

"I'll give you a hand," said Simon.

Into the silence, a hard clear voice sang from the speaker

above their heads. Mark listened for a moment. "So should I," he said. "I should have known better."

Simon supported Mark as he stumbled across the room, almost falling himself as Mark swivelled round towards Sue and John, who each looked as miserable as Mark.

"What's she done to you, Sue? It's her, isn't it?"

Sue didn't turn round, John looked bewildered, and Simon had a permanently puzzled expression, as he tried to stop his charge from falling flat on his face.

"It's the legs," Mark assured him. "The legs go. I'm fine." He looked sadly at his legs. "But the legs go," he said.

A light was on in the house, visible through the windscreen as the wiper passed over, fragmenting into unidentifiable streaks as the rain streamed down again.

"At least he's still up," said the man in the passenger seat.

The radio bleeped monotonously as the car negotiated the flooding road.

"Thank you, Yankee Papa. Maintain watch . . ."

The car pulled into the driveway, two beams of light sweeping through the horizontal rain, picking out the lit window, the front door. The man and his uniformed driver got out, and trudged wearily up the steps.

The music was loud. The man knocked, but no one came to the door. He waited for the sturdy, busy violins to fall silent before he knocked again.

The sweet, sad chords of the next movement were turned down; the door was opened, F.D. looking angry for an instant; then he smiled. "Oh—sorry. I thought you might be someone else," he said.

The man seemed a little surprised. "Mr. Derwent?" he asked, uncertainly.

"Yes. Won't you come in? You're getting a bit wet out there." He frowned as the uniformed man stepped into the light. "Police?" he said. "Was I playing the music too loud? I didn't think anyone would mind, not—"

"No, sir," said his visitor, removing the cap he was wearing to reveal a balding head, fringed with grey hair. He was tall, well built, and wore a short, greying beard. "I'm Detective Superintendent Patterson—this is Constable Baxter."

Baxter was average height, tending to plump, with a round, earnest face.

"I'm afraid we have some bad news for you, Mr. Derwent," said Patterson.

"The plane," said F.D., looking alarmed. "Has something happened to the plane? No—no, she must have been in London for hours—what, what bad news?"

"There's been a car accident, sir. The car involved is on hire to your wife, we understand."

"Car?" said F.D., uncomprehendingly. "You mean she's—?" He broke off, shaking his head, and looked from one face to the other. "She's dead, isn't she?" he said quickly.

Patterson nodded. "I'm sorry, Mr. Derwent." He motioned to the sofa. "Perhaps you'd like to sit down?"

"No—no, tell me. Tell me what happened."

Patterson glanced at the other man. "It seems that the car swerved off the cliff road," he said. "The sea's very deep at that point when the tide's in." He shrugged slightly. "The car wasn't discovered until the tide went out again," he said.

Cellos answered agitated violins as F.D. sank down on to the sofa.

"Is there someone you'd like to have here?" asked Patterson. "Or somewhere we could take you?" He looked round at the big, opulent, empty house. "I don't think you should be here alone," he added.

F.D. looked up. "Everyone else is at the Lodge," he said.

"Oh, yes, of course. We can take you there. Maybe you'd like to get a few things."

F.D. looked at him blankly. "Yes," he said. "Yes." He got up. "I don't know what happens," he said, helplessly. "What do you do?"

"There are formalities, sir, but they can wait till morning."

F.D. went upstairs to get his things, and Patterson tapped

his foot as he listened to the minuet. "So this is whatsisname's house," he said, glancing round.

"Phil Sumner," supplied Baxter. "I came up here when he moved in. Said I was the local bobby, and welcome to Ardcraig and all that." He looked round at the polished wood and soft leather, the original paintings. "It was really just to get a look," he admitted. "It's very posh, isn't it?"

Patterson didn't agree or disagree. He walked to the rear of the room, pulling aside the curtain, able to see nothing but the rain-washed window and the reflection of the room. "Do you think if we looked we'd find funny wee plants out there?" he asked.

"I did have a look, sir."

Patterson let the curtain fall back with a smile. "Did you now?" he said.

"It was just cabbages and stuff. He's married to Thelma Wilson—the cook on the telly? She's into organic vegetables."

"So the wild man of rock's a pillar of the community now?"

"Looks like it, sir."

"Well, first pop stars, now film folk. We'll have them queuing up for your job when you move on, Baxter." Patterson wandered round the room, glancing at the odd letter, casting his eye over the shooting script on which F.D. had apparently been working.

"I told you Mr. Derwent was an awful lot older than his wife, sir," said Baxter.

"Like I said, Baxter," Patterson murmured absently. "Film folk." He picked up the script. "Fascinating," he said. "All the different camera angles, different shots. 'Setups,' they seem to be called." He looked up. "Set-ups," he repeated. "Do you think there's any significance in that?"

Baxter looked a little confused.

Patterson glanced back at the sheets of paper. "Hard work, just so that someone can go to the pictures and say it wasn't bad." He put the script back where he had found it. "Do you go to the pictures much, Baxter?"

"No, not much, sir. I watch the Spaghetti Westerns when they're on the telly."

Patterson nodded. "The Wild West," he said. "Men getting shot to pieces before your eyes."

Baxter looked a bit sheepish. "They're just a bit of fun," he said.

"But it wasn't the Wild West, was it? It was nineteen-sixties Spain. And they weren't shot to pieces. They got up and walked away."

"I don't think Mrs. Derwent will be getting up and walking away, sir," said Baxter.

Patterson's tough, handsome face broke into a broad smile. "No, that she won't," he said.

"Sir?" Baxter checked to make sure that F.D. was still upstairs, and lowered his voice below the level of the bright, cheerful finale. "Why do you think it wasn't just an accident?"

"The firm said she was going to the airport, and they had to pick the car up there."

Baxter nodded.

"And the luggage in the boot confirmed that. And her husband has just confirmed it."

"Yes, sir."

"So where's her handbag, Baxter?" He shook his head. "My wife can hardly bear to go into the next room without hers," he said. "It's got everything in it. Money, credit cards, hankies, make-up, keys, and, if she was going to the airport, her ticket would be in there too. So where's Mrs. Derwent's handbag, Baxter? Where's her ticket?"

He switched off the hi-fi as F.D. came back downstairs. "Right, Mr. Derwent," he said. "Let's get you to the Lodge."

"I wonder . . . ?" said F.D., hesitantly.

"Yes, sir?" said Patterson.

"I wonder if it might be possible to get these . . . formalities over tonight?"

"Yes, of course, Mr. Derwent," said Patterson. "If you prefer."

93

Mark was getting more and more talkative, and ever more unsteady on his feet. He swayed, and Simon braced himself to catch him if he fell.

"You'd better get him to bed, Simon," said Sue.

"That's what I'm trying to do."

"Right. Right. Lead on. Wanda's Revenge. That's what I'm suffering from."

He tried variations on the theme of Wanda's Revenge during the journey to his room, stopping anyone they met to give them his diagnosis. It was with great relief that Simon finally off-loaded him on to the bed.

"Will you be all right?" he asked.

"Oh, yes. Now that I'm lying down from choice." He laughed. "I always know when I've had enough. I fall over."

Simon smiled. "I'll let you sleep it off," he said, turning.

"Goodnight Barry Strong. Whoever heard of a gay SAS man?"

Simon stopped, and turned. "I expect there are some," he said, after a moment.

"Are you shocked, Simon?" he asked, indistinctly.

"I just didn't realise," he said.

"No one does. No one ever realises." He half sat up. "I hardly ever get propositioned in gents' toilets. And once in a club someone was convinced I was an undercover police-man. Wouldn't have anything to do with me." He flopped back down again. "Can you believe that bitch? She's written about me. Everything. After all these years, she's—"

Simon sat on the edge of the bed. "Perhaps she's done you a good turn," he said.

Mark snorted.

"It can't have been easy," he persisted. "Pretending you're something you're not all the time."

Mark sat up, with some difficulty. "But that's my stock-in-trade," he said.

Simon smiled. "Other actors get time off," he said.

"For good behaviour? I'm well-behaved. These days. Can't do what I used to do. What Wanda's going to tell the world I used to do. It's too risky.'' He laughed. ''One way I risk my health, the other way I risk my career. I spend all my life being careful. I've been a bloody monk for three years, Simon.'' He laughed. ''It's true! Frightened I'll catch something, frightened people will find out, and I'd lose Barry Strong. Frightened—'' He fell back. ''Frightened,'' he said.

''It doesn't have to be one-night stands and gay clubs or celibacy,'' said Simon, tentatively putting his hand on Mark's. ''There is another alternative.''

Mark's eyes opened a little. ''You can only have two alternatives,'' he said decidedly, and closed them again.

''It's better once everyone knows,'' said Simon. ''They don't take that long to get used to it.''

''No?'' Mark shook his head. ''You haven't seen the letters I get from women.''

''It won't put them off,'' said Simon. ''They'll all think that *they'd* change your mind.''

''Thanks,'' mumbled Mark. ''But that's not how the *Strong Medicine* producers will see it.''

''No,'' conceded Simon. There was a silence. ''But Barry Strong *is* crap,'' he added.

''It's lucrative.''

''You've made money—how much money do you need?''

Mark looked up at him, his eyes barely focusing. ''It's not just money,'' he said. ''It's continuity.'' He stumbled a little over the word. ''Security.''

''You can have that.'' Simon's hand tightened on Mark's.

Mark looked at him bleakly. ''Do you?'' he asked. ''If you're so secure, why are you here?''

''I did have security. Thought I did.'' He looked down. ''It lasted longer than some straight marriages,'' he said defensively.

''I'm sorry. Sorry. I didn't mean to . . .'' Mark's eyes were closing again.

Simon let go of his hand and made to rise.

''Don't go,'' said Mark, and promptly fell asleep.

* * *

F.D. took a breath as they took him into the bare, clinical room, and over to where the sheet-covered body lay.

Patterson nodded to the attendant, who drew back the sheet, and F.D. took a step forward. He looked at the body, and frowned, looking up at Patterson.

"But—but that's not Wanda," he said.

Patterson's eyes widened, and he looked down at the body. "Are you sure, Mr. Derwent?" he asked.

"Quite sure. That's not Wanda. But I know who it is," he added.

And he looked again at the pale, dead face of Barbara Slaney.

CHAPTER SIX

MARK OPENED HIS EYES AS PALE LIGHT FILTERED through the rain battering at the window. It was a moment or two before he became aware of the arm that lay flung out across his. Slowly, nervously, he turned his head.

Simon lay still asleep, his fair hair tousled, his face almost angelic in repose. Mark nodded slowly, carefully, and lay back again, taking stock of the situation.

His own clothes were neatly draped across the chair; Simon's were folded in a little pile on the floor beside it. Mark took that in. Then he closed his eyes, and massaged his temples; he opened his eyes again, and drew his hands down his stubbled face. Gently, he removed Simon's arm, and slid out of bed.

The bathroom door opened when he was in the shower. Simon, dressed, stood in the doorway.

Mark switched off the shower. "I . . . I don't remember," he said.

"I'm not surprised," Simon said, smiling. "Do you remember anything?"

Mark frowned. "You," he said. "You were upset with F.D."

"You made me feel better about that," Simon said.

Mark's frown grew deeper. "Did I?" He thought. "You— we . . . we were in the bar."

"I helped you up to bed," said Simon.

97

"Did anybody see us? I mean, other than . . . Did any of the staff see us?"

"Yes. You tried to tell most of them. I don't think anyone knew what you were talking about. I didn't, come to that."

Mark's face coloured. He took a breath, and closed his eyes for a second before he spoke. "Did we . . . ?"

Simon shook his head, and caught the hastily cancelled look of relief on Mark's face. "Well," he said briskly. "I won't stay."

Mark watched as he walked quickly through the room, and out, and closed his eyes with a deep sigh.

The window framed the loch, the dark hills with their white, huddled houses, and the dark green sea, heaving today as the wind and the rain swept the coast. F.D. looked out worriedly at the weather, as Patterson came in, apologising for keeping him waiting.

He hung up his raincoat and his cap, taking a small boxlike object from the pocket of his coat before sitting down. He looked out of the window for a moment. "Yesterday, that was like a millpond," he said, and turned to face F.D. "It must make your job difficult."

F.D. agreed.

"I've borrowed this office from Constable Baxter," he said. "I'm based in the town itself. He's the local bobby."

F.D. smiled politely.

"You see, I got involved in this when we thought it was your wife in the car. No handbag. It bothered me."

F.D. frowned. "No handbag?" he said.

"No." Patterson set the little box down on its side.

F.D. looked at it. Cog-wheels, a little drum, something like a fine-tooth comb, a metal thing like a propeller, going round in what seemed like slow-motion.

"It still bothers me," he said. "Where's Miss Slaney's handbag?" He tapped the blotter in front of him. "There was a big carry-all canvas bag in the car," he said. "Empty."

F.D. frowned. "Wanda uses a bag like that," he said.

"She takes files and things in it. I think she usually puts her handbag in it too."

"Nothing was in it," said Patterson.

The box suddenly pinged. F.D. jumped slightly.

"Now, you said that Mr. Maxwell might know where your wife was staying in London," said Patterson. "But . . . well, Mr. Maxwell isn't here either."

"Howard?" F.D. looked surprised. "Isn't he?"

"It seems he told the staff at the Lodge that he would also be in London for the weekend."

"Really?" F.D. frowned. "He'd better be back for tomorrow," he said, to himself rather than the Superintendent.

The box pinged again.

"Is it likely that Mr. Maxwell would have offered your wife a lift to the airport?"

"Yes," said F.D. "Perfectly possible."

"So if we can get hold of Mr. Maxwell, he might know where your wife is?"

"I expect he might." He sighed, and looked over the Superintendent's shoulder at the rain streaking the window, and the low, grey clouds.

"Naturally, you're worried about your wife, Mr. Derwent, but I'm assured that there is no possibility that she was in the car."

F.D. looked back at him. "I have a complicated stunt sequence to film tomorrow morning," he said. "It has to be filmed in a very narrow time corridor, it has to be right first time, it has to match as closely as possible the shots we took yesterday, and as you have remarked, the weather has taken a distinct turn for the worse. That's what I'm worried about, Superintendent."

Patterson made a silent O with his lips, and swivelled round to look out of the window. "It's clearing up," he said. "Just an April shower, Mr. Derwent."

"It's May," said F.D.

"Ah, yes, but we're a wee bit behind the times up here," said Patterson. He swung back. "So you're not worried about your wife?"

99

"You tell me she wasn't in the car," said F.D. "If she had been, she'd be beyond worry. But as she wasn't, I expect she is doing whatever she intended doing."

"Would you have any idea what that was?"

"Only that it involved a fairly large cash sum. She had what looked like a couple of thousand pounds in the safe, in an old document case. It was gone last night when I got home."

"Cash?" Patterson drew in his breath. "And you've no idea what she needed it for?"

"None."

"What does this document case look like?"

F.D. blew out his cheeks. "A document case," he said. "Burgundy." He shrugged. "I didn't get that good a look at it."

"We didn't find it in your wife's car," said Patterson.

"Well you wouldn't," said F.D. "Not if she went to London with Howard. She would take it with her."

"Uh-huh." Patterson managed to look as though he was looking over his glasses, despite not wearing any. "But not her luggage? It was still in the car." He sat back. "Still, I'm sure your wife can clear all this up. Perhaps she lent the car to Barbara Slaney, if she didn't need it herself."

"I don't think that's very likely," said F.D. He stood up. "Now, if you don't mind, Superintendent, I really do have to get to work."

"And you can't tell us any more than you have about Barbara Slaney?"

"I know nothing about her, Superintendent. The LA office will be closed today, but you can get the Personnel Manager on the number I gave you."

"Well," said Patterson. "It's two o'clock in the morning in Los Angeles. I thought someone might know something about her here."

"Howard might—I don't. I don't get involved in that sort of area."

"It's her parents, you see," said Patterson. "I want to make sure they know before this gets out. Obviously, it's the sort of story the newspapers will want. I just wondered if she had spoken about her family . . ."

"Not to me! I really do have to go, Superintendent. I have a great deal to do."

"Perhaps someone else knew her a bit better than you?"

"Quite possibly. Try Landers."

"Oh, right. Thank you," He picked up a pen and touched the little propeller blade, which resumed its slow-motion turning.

F.D. watched, despite himself.

"Musical box," said Patterson. "It used to be inside a trinket box, but that fell apart in the end. It was my daughter's—she kept the movement. She gave it to my granddaughter to play with, and it got overwound."

"Oh," said F.D.

"But you can persuade it to unwind," he said, touching the blade with the pen again. "With a bit of perseverance."

It pinged as a tooth was caught by a spike on the drum, and the Superintendent smiled.

"Plays a nice wee tune," he said. "Once it's going."

The empty brandy glass went down on the bar, and Landers shuddered.

"It'll help," said Mark Ingram. "You were fond of her, weren't you?"

John Landers nodded, his face pale. His hand shook as it left the glass. "She was so full of *life*," he said.

"Yes." Mark picked up his own drink. "They thought it was Wanda at first," he said, and knocked it back. "It should have been."

"Don't *say* things like that!"

"No," said Mark. "Sorry." He signalled to the girl.

"Is that another brandy as well?" she asked.

Landers shook his head, and got up. "I'm going for a walk," he said.

"Why was she in Wanda's car?" asked Mark. "Do you know?"

Landers shrugged. "I didn't see her after the row on the set," he said.

"Neither did I," said Mark, taking his drink.

"I don't know what to think," said Landers. "I can't believe it's happened." He left.

"Will he be all right?" asked the girl.

"Yes," said Mark, taking a gulp of whisky. "He's just had a shock. He knew her better than the rest of us."

"You didn't know her, then, Mr. Ingram?" said a deep voice.

Mark turned to see Superintendent Patterson behind him. "I'm sorry," he said. "I don't think—"

"Patterson. Detective Superintendent. Young man said I'd find you here."

Mark turned back to the bar. "If you want to know anything about Barbara, you'd be better asking him," he said.

"I will," said Patterson. "But he didn't seem to be in the mood to answer questions." He sat down. "I'll let him sort himself out for a wee while," he said. "Was he her boyfriend, do you know? One of the staff here said she thought he might have been."

"I don't think so," said Mark. "But he was working very closely with her. That's why it's shocked him so much."

"Mm." Patterson nodded. "How well did you know her, Mr. Ingram?"

"I didn't know her at all," Mark said.

"But you've been working with her too, haven't you?"

"Working on the same film," said Mark. "Not together. I mean, we didn't have any scenes together or anything. And I didn't really see much of her socially." He drained his glass.

"Another for Mr. Ingram, and a small one for me," said Patterson. "Can you bring them over to the table?"

Mark looked a little uncertainly at him, then followed him to the table furthest from the bar.

"So you'd have no idea why she was in Mrs. Derwent's car?"

"None. I just asked John if he knew."

102

The drinks came, and Patterson dug in his pocket for the money.

Mark smiled. "Put them on my bill," he said.

"That's very kind of you, Mr. Ingram. You were once married to Mrs. Derwent, I believe?"

"Over twenty years ago, Superintendent. She doesn't check with me before she lends her car to someone."

"So you think that's what she did?"

"Well, to be honest, no. I don't. But what other explanation is there?"

Patterson sniffed the bouquet of the whisky. "I heard—correct me if this is wrong—that you accused Barbara Slaney of having an affair with Mr. Derwent."

Mark laughed. "What?" he said.

"You didn't accuse her?"

"It isn't the word I'd use," he said. "I didn't *accuse* her, Superintendent, I asked her if it was worth it. F.D. isn't at all a nice man, you know, and I've known him a long time. It was in a spirit of enquiry."

"Are you saying that you *know* that she was having an affair with him?" asked Patterson.

"Let's put it this way, Superintendent. If she wasn't, she was the first blonde blue-eyed nobody that Howard has produced who didn't regard sleeping with F.D. as part of her contract."

"Are you serious?"

Mark shrugged. "It's an open secret," he said. "F.D.'s blonde bimbos." He backtracked. "But to be fair to her, I don't think Barbara quite came into that category. Bimbo, I mean. I think she came into the other category without question."

Patterson sat back, his head to one side like a bird. It had a comic effect on so large a frame, and Mark smiled.

"You called her a nobody," he said. "So the fact that I've never heard of her isn't just because I'm out of touch?"

"No one's heard of her," said Mark. "Unless you were a devotee of a short-lived, low-budget lunchtime soap the name of which escapes me."

"No," said Patterson. "I'm not much of a man for soap operas." He finished his whisky. "Could she act?" he asked.

"Yes," said Mark. "She seemed pretty good. I don't think she would have had any formal training, but she was a good, natural actor."

"I'm trying to find out where her parents live," he said. "Do you remember which TV company did the soap opera?"

"No, sorry. I don't know anything about it. Howard would know, of course, but I think he's gone somewhere for the weekend."

"What exactly is Howard Maxwell's function?" asked Patterson.

"Well, F.D. calls him assistant director on the credits, and he more or less performs that function on the set. It's an admin job, really. But basically he's . . ." He smiled. "F.D.'s John the Baptist," he said. "He . . ." Mark made a smoothing motion with his hands. "He prepares the way. Makes sure F.D. has everything he needs. Keeps him happy." He shrugged. "He's got some sort of stake in F.D.'s production company, but as to his exact function . . ." He shrugged.

Patterson smiled. "Thank you," he said.

"I don't think I quite understand why you're here," Mark said. "Do you get involved in all fatal accidents?"

"No," said Patterson. "Just the odd ones."

"Odd?"

"Well . . ." Patterson lowered his voice a shade. "We can't find anything mechanically wrong with the car. It wasn't going that fast. It was raining—the windscreen wipers were on. But that first lot of rain wasn't all that heavy. Not like later on."

"It happened on the cliff road?"

Patterson nodded. "Up by the holiday cottages," he said. "It seems to have been going towards them from further up the coast—presumably from the Sumner house."

"It's windy up there—could it have been a freak gust or something?"

"Wind lifts cars, Mr. Ingram. It doesn't happen often,

104

thank God, but it lifts them. They topple over. They don't leave skid marks.''

"Maybe she braked for something. Or someone.''

"Most people would surely turn the wheel inland rather than towards the cliff edge, don't you think?''

"I suppose so. So—what do *you* think?''

"I think it's odd, Mr. Ingram. But I'll keep speculation to myself until we get the forensic reports and the post-mortem results.'' He rose. "And until Mrs. Derwent tells us why Barbara Slaney was using her car in the first place,'' he added.

"Haven't you found her yet?''

"Not yet,'' said the Superintendent.

"Doesn't F.D. know where she is?''

"London. But he doesn't know specifically where.''

"London's a big place,'' said Mark, helpfully.

"Quite. Thank you, Mr. Ingram.'' Patterson rose from the table. "Oh, and thank you for the dram.''

A jaunty hand slammed down on the bell, and the girl appeared in reception.

"Mr. Maxwell! We weren't expecting you back so soon.''

"I got the first flight back up to see you, darling,'' he said, taking off his glasses and wiping the mist of rain from them. "That's better,'' he said. "I can see you properly now. Gorgeous as ever.''

"Mr. Maxwell—''

"Howard, sweetheart,'' he said, smiling. "Howard.''

"There's been an accident.''

Howard's grin vanished. "On the set?''

"No,'' she said. "A car accident. Barbara Slaney. She was killed, Mr. Maxwell.''

"Christ Almighty,'' said Howard.

"The police have been here all morning,'' she said, reaching behind her for Howard's key.

Howard took the key. "Police?'' he said. "Why?''

"Well, it's all a bit strange. They thought it was Mrs. Derwent at first, because she was in her car.''

"What? Was Wanda involved?''

105

"No, but—"

"No, Mr. Maxwell," said Patterson, cutting the girl off as he came out into the foyer. "Mrs. Derwent wasn't in the car." He introduced himself. "I'd like a word in private, if I could."

"Yeah, sure." He motioned with his key, and they went upstairs. "Poor kid," he said.

"Did you know her well?"

"No, not especially. Had a drink with her, that sort of thing. She was a friendly kid."

"That's twice you've called her a kid, Mr. Maxwell."

"Well, she was. Just turned nineteen."

Patterson nodded. "I've been told to ask you how Mr. Derwent came by her for this film," he said.

"Oh, yes. I met her at a party, knew she was F.D.'s type, scouted round for some of her work that I could show him. Found a video of a soap opera she'd had a part in—showed him it." He shrugged. "That's that, really." He showed the Superintendent in. "He liked it."

"His type?" queried Patterson.

"Yes. Cool, blonde—you know."

"I want to contact her next of kin. Would you be able to help?"

"Yes—she would have filled all that in for insurance," said Howard. "I'll get someone to ring you with the details."

"Thank you." He paused. "I've also been told Mr. Derwent was having an affair with her," he said, his voice light.

"Wouldn't know." Howard threw his bag down on the bed, and sank down after it.

"But it wouldn't surprise you?"

"Nothing much surprises me any more."

"I take it," said Patterson, leaning down to examine himself in the mirror, "from your reaction downstairs, that Mrs. Derwent didn't travel to London with you?"

"I went instead of her," said Howard.

"To do what?"

"I'm sorry. I was just acting as her agent. You'll have to ask her."

"I can't."

Howard's face grew worried. "What do you mean, you can't? Where is she?"

Patterson looked out of the mirror at him, his face a blank. "You mean you don't know where she is?" Howard jumped up. "How do you know she wasn't in the car?"

"Both doors were locked. One body. The body of a very young woman. A girl." He turned. "A kid, Mr. Maxwell. Was she having an affair with Frank Derwent?"

"Look—I don't know! I'm sure she was, but I couldn't swear to it, and neither could anyone else."

"But Mrs. Derwent could have believed that she was?"

Howard looked a little wary. "What are you suggesting?" he asked.

"I'm asking if Mrs. Derwent could have believed that her husband was having an affair with a girl of nineteen."

"Of course she could. What's that got to do with the accident?"

"It could have quite a lot to do with it. You see, I don't think this accident is entirely . . . kosher, shall we say?"

"And you think Wanda had something to do with it?" asked Howard, incredulously.

"It happened in her car."

"Look, F.D. has girls—Wanda's known for years. She thinks he's looking for a younger version of her, but that's not how it is. He's always done it. He only married Wanda because of all the fuss."

"Fuss?"

"Golden Boy Ingram's twenty-year-old bride stolen by a man sixteen years older than her, all that. But it made no difference." He shook his head. "Wanda still doesn't know that she wasn't even a comma—he just carried right on."

"Aided and abetted by you?"

"Since the Californian community property acts," said Howard. "Since he realised that Wanda would get at least half of everything he's got, if not more. He runs his extra-marital affairs like an MI5 operation.''

"And you're part of it?''

"It worked out that way. The assistant director on a movie hires the extras. I know F.D.'s tastes. I just introduce them, that's all. In the normal run of films, I'll take on anything upwards from twenty extras. And there's always a kid who's quite happy to be nice to F.D. for the chance of saying a couple of lines. Gets them an Equity card, for a start.''

"So they're always kids, are they? His type?''

Howard grinned. "Over the age of consent,'' he said. "I don't sacrifice virgins to him, Superintendent. Barbara had been around, believe me. His type is young, blonde, sexy and available.'' He grinned. "And they can always say no,'' he said. "One or two of them do.''

"But Barbara Slaney wasn't an extra.''

"No, she just happened along. F.D. wanted to cast an unknown. He was auditioning, and I happened to meet Barbara. So I made sure she could act, and sent her along to see him. But whether anything developed from there, I wouldn't know.'' He smiled grimly. "F.D. would make sure of that,'' he said.

"I take it you've known Mr. Derwent a long time?''

"Best part of thirty years,'' said Howard. "He gave me a part in a play he was putting on, would you believe?''

"Oh, I'd believe, Mr. Maxwell. One of the more difficult aspects of this is that everyone I've had to interview is an actor. And actors can make you believe anything.'' He smiled. "Can't they?''

"Well, I couldn't,'' said Howard. "That's why I'm in administration.''

"Is that what you call it?''

Howard shook his head, smiling. "Wanda called me a pimp,'' he said. "Pusher would be more accurate.'' He gave a little sigh. "Do you have a hobby, Superintendent?''

"I have a passion,'' said Patterson, dramatically.

"Don't tell me, let me guess. Golf.''

"Right first time, Mr. Maxwell.''

108

"Well, F.D.'s passion is making films. He makes big extravagant blockbusters that break box-office records and make him so many millions that your eyes would pop out of your head. And when he's got some time to himself, he treks all the way over here and makes one like this with his own money."

"Highly commendable," said Patterson.

"No, that's not what I'm saying. It's an obsession. But film-making is painstaking work. You can spend all morning shooting the same thirty-second piece of action, and then when you see the rushes next day, you find you've got to do it all again. F.D. can't spend half a day walking a golf course, or all evening sticking stamps in an album—he has to do something fast and exhilarating, and free-fall parachuting's too dangerous."

"Are you defending him?"

"I'm just stating facts. It's how he is. Wanda knows that— and she couldn't give a damn. So if you're thinking that she had something to do with this iffy accident, forget it." He got up and opened the fridge. "Drink?" he said.

"Yes, I'll have one with you," said Patterson.

"Good," he said, opening two miniatures.

"So don't you think you'd better tell me what you were doing in London?"

"Why?"

"Think about it, Mr. Maxwell. Mrs. Derwent's car was found smashed on the rocks when the tide went out. Barbara Slaney was tall, blonde—very like Mrs. Derwent, in fact. Mr. Derwent's type. Someone may have mistaken her for Mrs. Derwent. And she isn't around."

Howard was reaching for the glasses; he stopped, and turned to face Patterson.

"She could be in trouble, Mr. Maxwell."

Howard stared at him. "But they—" he began, then shook his head. "No," he said. "That's crazy."

"What's crazy?"

"It's got nothing to do with—" He shook his head again. "I don't think you're very sure of that," said Patterson.

"Did your business in London involve a cash sum of about two thousand pounds?"

"Two and a half," muttered Howard, his mind far away.

"And what was she buying for two and a half thousand pounds in cash?"

Howard looked torn. "An old film," he said, eventually.

"Really? Woolworth's could have sold her an awful lot of old films for two and a half grand."

"Not this one, they couldn't."

"What was so special about this one?"

"Collector's item," said Howard.

"Why did you go instead?"

Howard hesitated. "I . . . I know the market better than she does," he said.

"You anticipated trouble, in other words."

Howard didn't answer.

"Why does the police being here bother you?"

"It doesn't."

"You seemed startled, when the receptionist told you," said Patterson. "Aren't the police usually involved with motor accidents?"

"Yes, I suppose so. I don't know how I seemed."

"Was there trouble?" Patterson asked.

"What?" Howard was distracted.

"Were you right to go instead?"

"Yes," he said, then gave a little, grim smile. "Mo and Harry said run, so I ran," he said. "And I didn't stop running till I got back here."

"You went instead because you thought Mrs. Derwent might get hurt," said Patterson.

"Yes," said Howard. "She might have got hurt! She might have got thumped, and the film taken off her. But you're saying someone tried to kill her!"

"I'm saying that it's a possibility which has to be considered."

"Look—some people might have got a bit miffed about it, but Christ, no one was going to get killed over it!"

110

"All the same," said Patterson. "You're worried about her."

"She wanted to get hold of this film," Howard said. "Yes—I'm worried. Why isn't she here? Why doesn't she want to know if I got it?"

"Her husband isn't worried," said Patterson.

"No. Well, that's F.D. for you."

"How would you describe Mr. Derwent?" asked Patterson.

"Rich," said Howard.

"All right, I'll rephrase it. What's your opinion of him?"

Howard emptied the bottles into glasses, and handed Patterson his.

"If the bastards had a kingdom," he said, "F.D. would be king."

Sue Quentin looked into the bar, checking round. Only Mark sat there, quite alone, and becoming rather drunk. She went in, wearing her very best smile.

"Mark, you shouldn't drink alone, you know. It makes you morose."

"Is that just me, or are you using 'you' in its general sense?"

She perched on the barstool. "Buy a girl a drink, then," she said.

He hit the bell. The barmaid appeared immediately, and he pushed his glass over the counter. "Another one in there, and whatever the lady is having," he said.

Sue looked round. "Well, the lady seems to have gone, so I'll have a gin and tonic," she said.

Mark looked at her. "Why the act, Sue?" he asked.

She poured tonic into the gin. "What act, darling?" she said as the girl vanished into reception again.

"Yesterday, *you* were morose without drinking a drop. Now you want me to believe that everything's all right. But it isn't." He poured what was left of his previous drink into the new one. "Barbara's dead, Wanda's missing, her car was involved—and now F.D. has just issued an edict that he expects filming to continue at seven o'clock tomorrow morning despite 'the unfortunate incident.' "

"Yes, well, I think he's probably right. Does no good to sit around feeling gloomy."

"Something was wrong with you before any of this happened. Now, I don't believe this has made you feel better, therefore it must have made you feel worse." He paused, going through the sentence again under his breath to make sure it had come out the right way. "Yes," he said. "Worse. So bad that you feel obliged to put on your soap-opera persona."

"Don't be silly, Mark, dear. Don't you think you had better start sobering up? It's only eleven o'clock. Go on at this rate, and you'll still be unconscious by seven o'clock tomorrow morning."

Mark dropped his head in his hands, and muttered an obscenity about tomorrow morning. He raised his head enough to get the glass to his lips. "I'm not needed," he said, after a deep swallow. "Remember? And I doubt very much if John will be going. So if you are, you'll—"

He turned to look at her; she was shaking with helpless, silent sobs.

His shoulders drooped, and he turned back to the empty bar. "Why me?" he said aloud to his reflection in the mirrored wall. "Why do they wait till I'm drunk?" He looked back at Sue. "Do you want to take me to bed too?" he asked.

Then he slid off the stool, and took her in his arms, where she at least sobbed aloud. He supported her with one arm while he searched his pockets, and found, rather to his surprise, a handkerchief.

"Here," he said, when she seemed to be stopping. He aimed it at her nose. "Blow."

Patterson came in, and looked at the tableau with interest. Mark glanced at him over his shoulder. "Oh," he said. "Hello, Superintendent." He looked helplessly at Sue. "She's a bit upset," he said.

"Yes," said Patterson, concernedly. "I can see that. Come

112

on," he said, relieving Mark of her. "You come and sit down over here, and Mr. Ingram will find you a nice cup of tea."

Mr. Ingram did as he was told, and went off.

"What's making you cry?" he asked.

She shook her head.

"The wee girl that got killed?"

She looked up, sniffing back the tears. "No," she said. "Not really. Oh, it was a terrible thing to happen, but I didn't really know her at all. But I suppose it was just the last straw."

"Is it me?" he asked.

She frowned. "You?" she said, wiping her eyes with Mark's handkerchief.

Patterson smiled. "You don't recognise me, do you?" he said.

"I don't understand," she began. "I've only just—" She broke off, and stared at him. "Hugh?" she said, her voice almost a whisper. She looked away, almost as though she were looking for somewhere to run. Then she turned, and looked at him again, trying to smile. "Where's your hair?" she asked, and there were tears in her eyes.

"Gone."

"It was so dark." She gave a little sigh. "You were so handsome." She smiled. "You still are. I should have recognised you." The last word was almost a sob.

Patterson frowned. "I'm not that bad, am I?" he asked.

She put her hand to her mouth, and determinedly held back the tears. "I'm sorry," she said. "I can't believe I didn't recognise you. When—when I knew I was coming here, I thought I would go to Glasgow, see if I could find you. But I couldn't go. I *couldn't.*"

"Just as well you didn't, since I'm not there any more," he said, with a smile. "Anyway, you wouldn't recognise the place." He frowned. "What happened?" he asked gently. "Why did you leave me?"

She shook her head.

"Don't you think I have the right to know?"

"Yes," she said, still tearful. "But I couldn't tell you then,

113

and I still can't." She went into her bag for cigarettes. "I'm so sorry," she said.

Patterson took out his pipe. "Can you imagine what it was like?" he asked. "A note, anything—anything would have been better."

She nodded. "I'd know better now," she said, and looked at him, smiling through the tears. "I can't believe I didn't recognise you. It's the beard. Very distinguished. When did it arrive?"

He smiled. "When my hair left," he said, lighting his pipe. "Well, you've done all right for yourself."

"Yes. What about you? What have you done?"

"Got a promotion," he said.

"I'd gathered that, Sergeant Patterson."

"Got married. Twenty-three years ago."

"Are you happy?"

"Very. One daughter, one grand-daughter."

"Good."

"What about you?" he asked, as the pipe smoke drifted round them.

She sniffed it in. "I always loved that smell," she said. "Once, I went into a room and smelt it, and . . . I cried."

"Are you married?" he asked again, not letting her change the subject.

She smiled ruefully. "Now and again," she said. "Not at the moment."

"Do you think," he asked, "if we had married, we would still be together?"

"No," she said.

"No." He sighed. "Do you want to tell me what upset you so much just now?"

She shook her head, still sniffing. "I . . . I trusted someone," she said. "And I shouldn't have." Her voice shook. "And then this morning they said Wanda was dead, and then they said she wasn't, and then they said it was Barbara, and . . ." She blew her nose. "So I went to my room, and I thought, all right, be as hard as nails. Everyone thinks you are anyway." Her breath came in little sobs, and she pressed

114

the hankie to her nose. "So I slapped on make-up and tried to pretend everything was all right, and Mark saw right through it."

Sue smiled tearfully at Mark as he appeared with a tray, on which were three cups, and a silver tea service.

"I thought I'd do it in style," he said.

"I understand," said Patterson, "that there was a bit of a barney when you were filming yesterday?"

"Storm in a teacup," said Mark, as he picked up the teapot.

"But it did involve Barbara Slaney?"

Mark shrugged. "She wouldn't take her clothes off, and in the end F.D. agreed that she needn't," he said. "It was nothing."

Patterson nodded. "But did you see her *after* that?" he asked.

"No," said Mark, slowly. "Neither did John. And F.D. was looking for her at the reception."

Sue Quentin shook her head. "I didn't either. John was asking where she was last night," she said, remembering. "She wasn't here then."

Patterson puffed his pipe, his face giving nothing away.

"What are you thinking?" asked Sue.

"I was just wondering if she told you anything about herself."

"Not really."

He smiled. "Not really means that she did," he said.

"Well, I doubt if it meant anything. I said something about F.D. being old enough to be her father, and she said maybe she was looking for a father. But it was all said in fun. It was just that I thought . . . well, I thought she might have meant it."

"Half in fun and whole in earnest?" he said. "Well, it's more than she seems to have said to anyone else." He paused. "I gather from that that you also believe she was having an affair with Mr. Derwent."

"She more or less told me she was," said Sue. "Not in so many words, but she said she thought F.D. was jeal-

115

ous of John Landers. I advised her to steer clear of F.D., but . . .'' She shrugged.

Patterson accepted his tea from Mark. ''John Landers,'' he said. ''The young man who was so upset this morning?''

''Yes. And . . .'' Sue was clearly in two minds about whether to impart the next piece of information. She took a deep breath. ''And she had access to Wanda Derwent's papers,'' she said.

''Her papers?''

''For her book,'' said Sue, her voice bitter. ''She told me about . . . some correspondence which concerned me. She thought I ought to know. She was trying to help, I think.''

Patterson nodded, and sipped his tea. ''So you think she was entertained at the Sumner residence?'' he asked.

''Well, either that or the cottage.''

''What cottage?''

''Wanda rented a cottage to work in,'' said Mark. ''One of the cottages near where her car was found. Sorry, I thought you would know that.''

''Did she now?'' Patterson finished his tea. ''Well, I'll take my leave,'' he said, setting down his cup. ''Nice to have met you, Miss Quentin.''

Sue smiled gratefully.

''Lovely tea, Mr. Ingram,'' he said, as he stood up. ''Did you make it yourself?''

Mark laughed.

F.D. opened the door to Howard's room.

Howard swung round, his face falling. ''Oh,'' he said. ''It's you.''

''What the hell's going on, Howard?'' asked F.D.

Howard stared at him. ''What? Why ask me? I've not even been here.''

F.D. closed the door and walked up to him. ''I told you to call your goons off,'' he said.

Howard's mouth opened slightly. ''So that's it,'' he said. ''You think your hired hands dumped poor little Barbara into the sea.''

"And did they?"

Howard shook his head in disbelief. "No they did not, F.D. And I didn't call them off, because I didn't have to. I never got them for you in the first place."

F.D.'s face went blank, and then a tiny frown appeared. "What did you say?" he asked.

Howard sat on the bed and kicked off his shoes. "You heard. There's a limit, F.D."

"Is there?" said F.D. slowly.

"Yes!" shouted Howard. "You've spent the last twenty-seven years finding out just what it is—well, now you know."

F.D. nodded slowly, and smiled. "You're tired, Howard," he said. "All this travelling. Why were you in London?"

"None of your business."

"Were you with Wanda?"

"No, I wasn't."

"Do you know where she is?"

"No, I don't! Now piss off, F.D.! I've had more than enough."

F.D. opened the door again. "I didn't need the services of your friends, as it happened," he said. "But don't let me down again, Howard, or you'll be sorry."

CHAPTER SEVEN

A HAND SHIELDED THE MATCH AS THE FLAME WAS sucked down into the bowl of the pipe, and the tobacco glowed. Hugh Patterson stood on the cliff, drew on the pipe, and shook his head. A huge van housing a mobile generator vibrated and hummed beside him; he stepped closer to its warmth as he watched. A crowd of sightseers, kept well back, was also there; his ID had got him a grandstand view, unobserved by the participants.

Water lapped the rocks as a young woman in a long Victorian dress waded into the cave mouth. Bobbing up and down, out of sight of the camera, was a rescue dinghy, with a life-jacketed seaman on board. On the cliff top, John Landers shivered in a blanket, wet, and naked to the waist. Sue Quentin sat on the ground beside him.

High above, a helicopter circled. All around, on safer ground, were crew members, a medical team, cameras, lights on scaffolding. Big reflector screens enhanced the artificial sunlight being produced, and another camera towered overhead, on a bright orange crane.

"All right?" called F.D. into the cave. "Shout when you're ready."

The tide rushed in, swirling round the rocks, bubbling into the cave. F.D. kept up a conversation with the girl above the sound of the waves, while his assistant director organised the set.

"Ready when you are," came the echoing voice from the cave.

"OK, Howard?" asked F.D.

Howard picked up a microphone, and his voice boomed out over the rocks. "We have ten minutes from when the stunt starts to get this," he said. "After that the tide will be running too fast for the swimmer. So let's get it right. Good luck, Sheila."

The cameras rolled, and F.D. called for action, running out of shot as the swimmer emerged, getting knocked back as often as she made progress, from the cave mouth. At last, she caught the edge of the high, flat rock, and dragged herself on to it as water covered it completely.

"Cut!"

People in boots waded out to help her get out of the dress, but it still took valuable minutes. They left her, and she waded through the water to the base of the cliff face.

This time, the crane swooped lower, its shadow getting into the ground camera's shot. It was sorted out, and the girl began to climb the steep rock face, slowly, hesitantly, looking for handholds in the rock, almost missing her footing. F.D. signalled to Landers and Sue Quentin, and once again Sue Quentin was raped. At last, the girl reached the top and made to pull herself over, but stopped when she saw the couple. Then she began her descent, with an apparent disregard for her safety, clambering down as fast as she could into the ragged water. There, she turned and waded back to the flat rock, which was still just discernible as the waves withdrew. They crashed over it again as soon as she was on it; she stepped off the edge, up to her waist in the rushing water, and allowed herself to be swept back into the cave.

Patterson watched, his mouth open.

"Cut!"

F.D. gestured to the sky, and the helicopter's rotors grew louder, thundering overhead as it came down, and lowered a winch. It seemed like a long, long time before the girl emerged, swimming out of the cave much more strongly than before, but in the face of a deeper, faster tide. She struck out across the flow of water towards the dinghy, which was paddling towards her. The man on board leaned out to her, dragging her aboard, where he fastened on a life belt, caught the winch, and sent her up to the cheers of the crew and the crowd.

The helicopter hovered overhead like an over-protective mother as the dinghy was paddled with considerable difficulty into safer waters and ashore. Then the helicopter lifted and banked, landing a few hundred yards from where Patterson stood. The wind from its rotors caught his coat, making it flap, as he watched its passenger run, head bowed beneath the whirling blades, to a nearby trailer.

The crowd wandered off as the film crew continued to film the in-rushing tide itself, though this was no less spectacular: breakers pounded the rocks, and spray was thrown in the air, slapping against the waterproofed cameras and men. The cave entrance disappeared so quickly that the enormous consequences of failure to do the stunt properly were hideously obvious. Patterson watched it all, watched the yellow-coated F.D. as he got the shots he wanted, and called it a day.

"Great stuff, Len!" he shouted, as he turned to climb up the grassy slope which still projected well above the water level.

"Congratulate me when you see the results," said Len. "Not before."

"Thank you, everyone," said F.D. "Thanks, John!" he called to Landers, who had now reappeared fully dressed, his face pale and grim. "Sue! Wonderful—thank you."

Neither Landers nor Sue Quentin acknowledged him, but he didn't seem to notice.

"Thank you, Clive," he said, slapping a plump, balding man on the back. "They'll be signing you up for the lifeboat!"

Clive Oliver grunted, and went on his way.

"Went like a dream," he said to Howard Maxwell, as he got to the top of the cliff.

"It had to be done," said Howard. "I suppose."

"What?"

"Some of us found it a bit upsetting," said Howard.

"Don't blame me," said F.D. "Anyway—she'd do, wouldn't she?"

"Sorry?"

"For the remaining scenes with Sophia. Long-shot, shoot them silent, use Sue's voice-over. She's perfect. I mean, that could have *been* Barbara down there."

"Christ," said Howard. "You're unbelievable."

"Talk to her. See if she's free."

"Now?"

"Now."

"No room for sentiment in film-making, Mr. Derwent?" asked Patterson, as Howard Maxwell walked quickly away.

"Where the hell did you spring from?"

"I was watching the stunt," said Patterson. "Very, very impressive. But I was wondering what makes a young woman prepared to risk her life in the cause of an illusion."

"It has a very strong pull on some of us, Mr. Patterson. And, as you saw, we do keep the risk to an absolute minimum. We were even quite prepared to lose the dinghy rather than a life, believe it or not."

"People do lose their lives though," said Patterson. "From time to time."

"It has been known. Not on one of my films. And this time, as it happens, it all went according to plan."

Patterson nodded. "But that," he said, pointing to what was now nothing but choppy sea, "that was where Barbara Slaney did the scene yesterday?"

"Yes. And we didn't put her in danger at all. We did it when the tide was going out. All she got was very wet and cold."

"You miss my point," said Patterson. "I meant, didn't it bother you at all? It seemed to bother Mr. Maxwell, and Mr. Landers."

"They're too sensitive," said F.D. "No, it didn't bother me. That was Sophia down there. It doesn't matter who's playing her. It's just Sophia. Can you understand that?"

"No," said Patterson. "I'd be lying if I said I did." He

sucked his pipe, which had long since gone out. "I believe you're paying for all this yourself, Mr. Derwent?"

F.D. smiled. "My production company is financing it, yes. But it's fairly low-budget, for a costume drama. Four people in the cast—no sets, no interiors. And it doesn't usually involve three cameras and an air-sea rescue crew, I assure you." He smiled. "And perhaps the stunt wasn't just as dangerous as all that," he said. "It's all good publicity."

"You don't always finance your own pictures, do you?"

"Good God, no. But I wanted to do this one, and it isn't the sort of project that investors are too keen on. They prefer car chases and shoot-outs—one-man armies, like Mr. Ingram's character. I make that kind of movie too."

"But you do want it to make money?"

"I want to prove the investors wrong," said F.D. "I believe if you have a strong story, a great cameraman like Len, and a cast who are known to millions, you've got a winner. We'll have to wait and see."

"So the casting was important?"

"Yes. Ingram and Landers to bring in the full age-range of cinemagoers, and Quentin to bring in the TV audience. They are all international names, Mr. Patterson. That's what I needed."

"Yet you cast an unknown in the fourth role?"

"It had to be an unknown. Sophia is . . . everywoman, if you like. It couldn't be anyone with an identifiable screen persona. It's the only role we auditioned."

"But Miss Slaney didn't attend the auditions, did she?"

"No. Howard found her. He's got a good eye for talent."

Patterson tapped out his pipe on the side of the wheel. "I've been hearing rumours, Mr. Derwent," he said. "About you and Barbara Slaney."

"Oh, not that old chestnut," he said.

The wind whipped along the cliff edge, as the water rose.

"Old chestnut?"

"I have had an affair with the youngest female member of every cast I have ever assembled," said F.D. "If you listen to the showbiz gossip columnists, that is. It's a legend—like

122

Jack Benny hanging on to his money, or Bing Crosby and Bob Hope hating one another's guts. These things gather their own momentum.'' He shrugged. ''If I sued everyone who ever said it, I'd never be out of court. It's a sort of standing joke—no one takes it seriously.''

''Not too many people are joking this morning,'' said Patterson.

''Then they are gullible.'' F.D. smiled. ''Do you think I'd have hung on to a lovely girl like Wanda for twenty years if I played around like that?'' He pushed himself away from the van, and walked into the wind, towards the trailers. ''Is that why you came to see me?'' he asked.

''Yes,'' said Patterson. ''Partly.''

''Partly?'' shouted F.D., above the howl.

''Well, you see, Mr. Derwent,'' Patterson went on, raising his voice again, ''according to the pathologist, young Barbara had taken barbiturates and a considerable amount of alcohol. He was surprised that she could drive a car at all, even if it was just over a cliff.''

F.D. stopped walking and turned, with the attitude of a man who knew the answer to be simple. ''Suicide,'' he said.

''Pills and booze?'' said Patterson. ''It's a classic method, I'll give you that. But its adherents very rarely get into cars and drive away, never mind other people's cars.''

''She probably didn't know what she was doing,'' said F.D.

''Maybe not,'' said Patterson, putting the pipe in his pocket, and walking after F.D., who was striding ahead once more, waving to Howard, who was making for F.D.'s trailer. ''But if she got into your wife's car, that would suggest that she was at your house, don't you think?''

''If she was, I've no idea why,'' said F.D.

Patterson looked at him. ''She was nineteen years old, Mr. Derwent,'' he said.

''I know she was nineteen years old, Mr. Patterson.''

The wind gusted and blustered round them as they walked.

''Were you having an affair with her?'' asked Patterson.

"No, I was not. You'll have to find some other reason for her killing herself."

Patterson raised his eyebrows. "Oh, I've not ruled out foul play yet, Mr. Derwent," he said. "For one thing, there are some bruises that the pathologist can't account for."

F.D. looked puzzled. "She was in a car that went over a cliff," he said. "Wouldn't you expect some bruises?"

"Her injuries are—in the main—consistent with the accident," said Patterson. "But there is some minor bruising—to her upper arms, and her neck. They don't fit, Mr. Derwent."

Derwent shrugged, stopping at the door of his trailer.

"I'd like to know where your wife is," said Patterson, his voice raised. "She didn't go with Mr. Maxwell to London."

The wind suddenly dropped. "I know," said F.D. "I've spoken to him."

"And you're still not worried about her?" asked Patterson, at a more normal level.

"I don't see that worrying gets you anywhere."

"No, that's true enough, Mr. Derwent. But I'm afraid I have to worry. I have to ask myself questions that I'd rather ask your wife." He stepped closer to F.D. "Why was Barbara Slaney in her car, for instance? Did Mrs. Derwent fail to see the standing joke too, do you think?"

F.D.'s mouth fell open. "You're not suggesting that Wanda *killed* Barbara, are you?" He gasped in disbelief. "Because she thought I was having an affair with her?"

"I'm suggesting nothing, Mr. Derwent. But I'm told that these sleeping pills are not ones that would ever have been prescribed for a healthy nineteen-year-old. So it's hard to see where she would get hold of them."

Derwent threw back his head and laughed. "You think Wanda stuffed her full of pills and booze?"

He pushed open the door of the trailer to reveal Howard, sitting at a table, looking pale and tired, trying too late to conceal the worried expression on his face.

"Do you hear that, Howard?" he said. "Can you imagine Wanda exacting vengeance on a supposed mistress?"

F.D. was amused; Howard wasn't. "No," he said. "I can't."

F.D. smiled.

"Oh, neither can I, Mr. Derwent," said Patterson.

F.D. frowned. "Who, then?" he said. "Oh! Me?" He smiled. "Sorry, Superintendent. I know things must get boring round here, but I'm afraid that this was probably just an accident, however hard you try to make it seem more mysterious." He looked back at Howard. "You look as though you could do with a drink," he said. "Will you join us, Superintendent?" He stood aside to let Patterson into the trailer.

"No, thank you," said Patterson, stiffly.

"Well, I'm having one," said F.D., climbing up into the trailer.

"Would she be at the cottage, do you think?" asked Patterson, before the door closed.

"No, of course not. It isn't for living in—at least, not the way Wanda's got it."

The wind blustered, almost pushing Patterson off balance; he held on to the door. "You didn't tell me she had a cottage, Mr. Derwent."

"You didn't ask! It's got nothing to do with this." He poured two large brandies for himself and Howard. "Down the hatch, Howard," he said. "We did well this morning."

Patterson frowned. "Does Barbara Slaney's death affect you at all, Mr. Derwent?" he asked.

"Yes," said F.D. "We still have a couple of Sophia's scenes to shoot." He turned to Howard. "How's Sheila Drage fixed?" he asked.

"She'll do it," said Howard, his voice flat.

"In that case, Superintendent, the answer is that I am covered for the delay in shooting, and I have a stand-in for the remaining scenes. Barbara Slaney's death is therefore of no further consequence to me."

Patterson nodded, and left.

* * *

125

John sat up straight as he saw the Superintendent come into the station, and talk to the young policeman at the desk.

Patterson glanced round at him. "Mr. Landers, would you like to come into my office?"

John was shown in, and sat down, frowning a little at the musical box.

Patterson took off his coat and hat. "What can I do for you?" he said.

"Well, sir, I owe you an apology for my bad manners when you came to the Lodge yesterday."

Patterson's mouth opened slightly, and he sat down with a bump. "In the first place," he said, "you weren't ill-mannered. You were upset, and I could see that. In the second place, I call you 'sir.' You call me 'Superintendent' with a supercilious air. You must get these things right."

John smiled a little.

"But I did want to see you," said Patterson. "You were friendly with Barbara Slaney, I'm told."

"Yes. She was a very friendly girl. She was helpful. I liked her. I can't believe this has happened."

Patterson nodded. "I'm not prying, Mr. Landers, but were you romantically involved with Barbara at all?"

"No, sir." He smiled a little. "Superintendent," he amended.

"Did she talk to you about herself? Where she came from, that sort of thing?"

"Not much. She said London, when I asked, but then she said not originally. And she got kind of cagey when I asked her about school and stuff like that."

"We've been given an address in London," said Patterson. "But there's no one there, according to the neighbours. And she gave her next of kin as . . ." He glanced down at the note on his desk. "Jerry Bryce," he said. "Did she ever mention him to you?"

Landers shook his head. "No, sir." He hesitated for a moment. "She did mention some guy once, but that wasn't his name."

Patterson leant forward, interested. "What was his name?" he asked.

"I can't . . ." Landers frowned as he tried to remember. "It began with a J too," he said. "I'm sure it did. Or maybe a G, I suppose. But it wasn't a name I was familiar with. It wasn't Jerry."

"What did she tell you about that one?"

"Not much. She said he was in some sort of trouble—well, what she said was that he was always in trouble, but that this time it was bad. I think maybe he went to jail. And I think it might have been drugs."

"Oh?"

"Well, I . . . that is, she had to do a scene in the cave. The one at the beach where we're filming? She was scared. She hated to be closed up. And I found her one night taking some sort of pills. I asked what they were, and she said she wasn't sure, but she was panicking about doing this scene and if she took one it helped her to sleep."

Patterson frowned.

"I told her she shouldn't take pills if she didn't know what they were, and she said they worked, and that was all that she cared about. I asked where she had got them, and she said she got them from a friend of . . . Jez. That was it. Jez."

Patterson nodded. "Jerry," he said. "It's short for Jerry."

"Oh! So she *was* talking about this guy that you—"

Patterson picked up the phone. "See what the Met have got on Bryce," he said. "He might be doing time." He hung up. "Go on, Mr. Landers," he said.

"She said it was on account of this other guy that Jez was in trouble. She knew he would go to jail, and that panicked her—because of how she felt about being enclosed herself, I guess. Anyway she went to this other man for something to help her sleep, because she was working on this soap every day, and she wasn't getting enough rest. So I figured that this other guy was some sort of dealer."

Patterson nodded, looking almost disappointed. "Barbara

127

did have sleeping pills, then,'' he said, almost to himself. ''What did they look like?'' he asked Landers.

''Capsules, sir.''

The silence which fell was interrupted only by a small, flat ting from the musical box.

''Sir?'' said Landers. ''Mr. Derwent might know more about her. She . . . I think she was . . .''

''Yes?'' said Patterson.

''I think she was seeing him,'' Landers said. ''I mean, I didn't believe it at first. She was only nineteen, and he . . .'' He cleared his throat. ''But—well, Mr. Derwent came to the Lodge last Sunday lunchtime, and . . .''

Patterson touched the fly of the musical box, and it rotated slowly.

''He was with her in her room,'' said Landers. ''I went up to my own room after lunch, and I could hear this music—real loud, you know? But I could hear noises.''

''Noises?''

''Like a fight, maybe.'' Landers' worried frown deepened. ''Things getting knocked around. I tried to go in, but the door was locked. Then it went quiet, and I heard him unlock the door, so I went back into my room and watched. He came out. I didn't like the way he . . . well, the way he looked. He was wearing *gloves*,'' he said. ''That seemed a bit strange. So I went to see if Barbara was OK.''

Patterson's eyebrows rose slowly. ''And was she?'' he asked.

''Well, he hadn't hurt her—not physically, anyway. But I've never seen anything like it. He had ripped the room apart. She said he was looking for something, but all her little china animals were broken. Snapped in two. You don't—'' He broke off, shaking his head. ''Well, you don't have to do that to look for something, do you? I told her that she should get the police—that was against the law, what he'd done. But she . . .'' He shrugged. ''She said they were playing a game I wouldn't understand.''

''Rough game,'' said Patterson.

"That's what I thought. I didn't want to understand it. And then Howard said on Friday that she had upset him, and I wondered if she'd be OK, but I didn't *do* anything, and now she's . . ." His voice trailed off. "I shouldn't have said that," he said.

"Oh, but you should. What you shouldn't do is blame yourself. Even if it was something to do with this business. What was he looking for in her room? Did she say?"

"She wouldn't say. But she said he wouldn't be bothering her again," said Landers. "I helped her get the place straight—you should have seen it. The tub was full of broken jars and bottles—I cleared it all up for her before she saw it. But there was hardly anything left whole."

The musical box uttered.

"Thank you, Mr. Landers," said Patterson.

"And—sir?" said Landers.

Patterson smiled. "Yes, son?" he said.

Landers indicated the musical box. "It'll work better if you put it on its back," he said. "I think."

Patterson looked at it. "Will it?"

"Yes. Suspend it between two books or something—so the key can still turn. You see, if you look at the little brake thing—you know, the thing that stopped it when the lid was closed? Well, that means its lid went on here." He indicated the open side. "So I think if you have that at the top, it'll work better that way."

Patterson nodded. "Thank you, son," he said, lining up his tobacco tin and a notepad, and suspending the box as instructed. The fly turned quite enthusiastically all by itself, and the teeth produced an almost recognisable, if deathly slow, sequence of notes.

He beamed. "Thank you for coming in, Mr. Landers," he said.

"There's one other thing," said Landers. "I don't mean to . . . but I think you . . . have you looked for *her* car, sir?"

"What car?" roared Patterson.

* * *

129

"A shocking pink Austin Maxi, registration number . . ."

Eddie, his radio tuned to the police waveband, jumped up from his large, late Sunday breakfast.

"What?" said his mother. "What's wrong with you now?"

"That car!" he spluttered, his mouth still full of toast. "I know where it is! I've known since Friday!"

"Well, don't burst a blood-vessel, son," she said comfortably. "Finish your breakfast."

"No! I've got to tell them. It's got to do with that accident at the cliff."

"How do you know?"

"I just know. I'm away."

"Do you not think you'd be better getting dressed first?" asked his mother.

Eddie looked down at his pyjamas in near despair, and raced upstairs to change.

"A Mr. Anderson's here to see you, sir," said the young policeman.

"Wee Eddie?" sighed Patterson. "What does he want?"

"Wouldn't tell anybody but you, he said, but Baxter's seeing if he won't do, sir."

Patterson smiled. "Eddie plagued me for years, Constable. I thought I'd shaken him off." He sighed. "I'll see what the wee man has to say. Tell Baxter to bring him in."

Baxter came in with Eddie; Baxter looked amused, and Eddie looked important. Patterson looked up from the note he was making, and put down his pen. "Eddie," he said.

"You're looking for a pink Austin Maxi," said Eddie before Patterson had time to ask him to sit down.

Patterson nodded, and indicated the chair.

"I know where it is." Eddie sat on the edge of the seat, bristling with excitement and pride.

"Good work, Eddie," said Patterson.

Eddie's face lit up.

"Where is it?" Patterson asked, gently, when it became obvious that Eddie had forgotten the bit about actually telling them.

"Oh! Sorry," Eddie said sheepishly. "Up by the holiday cottages. I checked before I came. It's still there. The key's in the ignition."

Patterson's eyebrows lifted a shade. "*Still* there?" he queried. "How long's it been there?"

"Since . . ." Eddie took a Filofax from his inside pocket and consulted it. "Since some time between twelve fifty-five and one P.M. on Friday afternoon," he said. "At least, that's when it arrived there. And it's there now. But I wouldn't know if it's been there all the time, of course."

Patterson looked over his non-existent glasses at the notebook. "You were watching this car, were you, Eddie?"

"No," said Eddie guardedly. "But I noted its presence at the scene."

Baxter, standing behind Eddie, bit his lip.

"The scene of what?" asked Patterson.

"I'm afraid I can't tell you that, Mr. Patterson. Client confidentiality."

"Uh-huh," said Patterson. "Baxter, get a message out about the car—I don't want anyone at all touching it until Forensic get there. You go and make sure everything's done right."

"Yes, sir," said Baxter.

Patterson leant his elbows on the desk. "Is there anything you can tell me that won't jeopardise client confidentiality?" he asked.

"Well," said Eddie. "I think it's got something to do with that accident." He sat forward a little. "You see . . . the Mercedes involved in the accident was . . . well, I saw it too, during the course of my investigation."

"The same investigation in which you noted the presence of the pink car at the scene of whatever it was?"

"Yes. And since there was never anyone at the . . . scene . . . who wasn't directly involved with my investigation, I think the pink car must be involved too. That was why I noted its presence."

"You're quite right, Eddie," said Patterson. "It is involved with the accident."

Eddie smiled happily.

"Did Mrs. Derwent hire you to watch her husband?" asked Patterson.

Eddie looked startled. "No," he said. "Just the—" He stopped. "I'm sorry, Mr. Patterson," he said. "I can't give you that information."

Patterson stood up and looked out at the loch. The grey sea moved restlessly in the wind, the hills on the other side of the harbour were shrouded in a veil of misty rain. "Eddie," he said, "would you like to work with the police on this one?"

He didn't turn round; if he had, he would have seen Eddie look as though he was about to burst.

"But no," he carried on. "I can't ask you to do that."

Eddie looked panic-stricken.

"And we really would have valued your help," he said. He flexed his back. "You see," he said, turning, "I think we have a very serious crime on our hands, Eddie. But if you can't see your way clear to breaking your code of client confidentiality . . ." He sat on the desk, on Eddie's side, and looked at the consternation on Eddie's face.

"It would mean working together," he went on. "That is—I would release information to you which has not been made public, but you would have to sacrifice client confidentiality. And I couldn't promise not to make that known to your client, in the course of the investigation."

"Honestly, Mr. Patterson? You'll let me work with you?" Eddie's eyes were shining with excitement. "Really and truly?"

"I would be grateful," said Patterson, seriously. "You obviously have information on certain aspects of this case to which I am not yet privy."

"If it's a serious crime, I think it's my duty," said Eddie. "I'll work with you, Mr. Patterson."

Patterson smiled. "In that case, I'll tell you that the accident victim was a girl called Barbara Slaney." He got off the desk. "Does her name mean anything to you?"

Eddie was nodding. "Yes," he said. "I had to ring her."

Patterson went back behind the desk and sat down. "I'll tell you what, Eddie," he said. "You begin at the beginning." He reached across and removed the Filofax from Eddie's hand. "And while you're doing that, we'll have your notes photocopied. All right?"

The blue and orange flashes lit the white fronts of the cottages in the grey morning light. Baxter's car was parked at an angle, preventing access to the clearing in the gorse bushes in which Barbara Slaney's car sat, virtually hidden from view. On the road stood the breakdown truck. Baxter stood beside it as the clamp was fitted to the steering wheel of the pink car, enabling it to be driven without disturbing fingerprints.

"Right!" shouted the boiler-suited man now inside the car. "You can move your car now!"

Baxter backed away, and watched as the bright pink car was backed slowly out, then turned in the road. With great care, it was driven on to the breakdown truck.

Patterson's car drew up, bumping on to the pavement to make room, as the diesel engine of the breakdown truck shuddered into action, pumping out clouds of exhaust fumes as it manoeuvred with its cargo.

Patterson got out of the car, and waved off the truck. "Right," he said to Baxter. "Let's take a gander inside this cottage."

They walked towards the row of white-painted houses as rain, drifting on the wind, hit their faces.

"Wee Eddie turned up trumps," said Patterson. "I think he'd be quite happy to die now."

"Who *is* wee Eddie, sir?" asked Baxter, mystified.

Patterson smiled. "I'm surprised you haven't come across him, Baxter," he said. "You obviously haven't been here long enough for Eddie to trust you yet."

Baxter looked interested.

"Wee Eddie had one ambition in life, Baxter. Well—two. One was to be a cowboy, and the other—more realistic, he thought—was to be a policeman. But fate dealt him a cruel blow."

133

"He's only five foot two," said Baxter.

"He is only five foot two," repeated Patterson. "So Eddie went into private investigation. He makes a reasonable living at it, mind you."

They turned up the path, and out of the drizzle.

"Serving summonses, chasing debts, minding the valuables when they have exhibitions at the Lodge. He's quite bright, you know." He tried the door, without hope. "But he has an emotional age of about fourteen," he said. "A bit of a mammy's boy." He grinned as he stepped off the path, and walked with Baxter to the window. "Wouldn't have done for the rough, tough world of Ardcraig policing even if he'd been six foot two, eh?"

The slats of the blind were slightly open. The two men peered into the shaded room, then looked at one another rather than at what was inside.

"It's getting rough and tough enough for me," said Baxter.

CHAPTER EIGHT

IN THE VIEWFINDER, THE SMASHED MIRROR RE-flected the camera itself; the photographer shifted his position, and pressed the shutter on the shattered glass.

"Look at it this way," said Patterson to Baxter, as they picked their way carefully from the door to the desk. "Excuse us, Mr. Philips," he said, as they got between the camera and its subject.

"Chris." Baxter nodded to the photographer.

"Other people have to get up on Monday mornings and go into boring offices," Patterson went on. "You get to come to scenes of crime."

Baxter looked at the blood-stained goatskin rug, and grunted.

"Right," said Patterson. "According to the pathologist, she was almost certainly hit from behind with the mirror, and strangled, also from behind, as she lay on the rug." He frowned. "With the belt of her jacket, which she was wearing. What does that tell us, Baxter?"

"She had just walked in," said Baxter. "She was taken by surprise."

Patterson nodded.

The fingerprint man was working on the inside of the broom cupboard door, which had been standing open when she was found. Patterson moved slowly round the little room, over to the kitchen area, with its sink and its hotplate.

"According to Eddie," he said, "she left here at three o'clock and went home. According to the pathologist, she had been dead for thirty-six to forty-eight hours. So it happened on Friday. And she was last seen at four o'clock, when Eddie saw her go into the Sumner house. So what brought her back?" he mused.

"Maybe something she'd forgotten?" suggested Baxter.

"There's a bag in here, Mr. Patterson," said the fingerprint man.

"Right, Masson." Patterson looked into the dark recess, where a leather shoulder bag lay, then glanced back at the desk on which sat a bag like a large wallet. "Two," he said to Baxter. "First none, now two." He shook his head. "Even Mrs. Patterson doesn't use two at once," he said.

"Three," said Baxter. "If you count the canvas bag."

Patterson smiled. "Three," he said. "One for her money and her make-up and all the other stuff women cart round with them, and one, according to her husband, for her clothes and files and things." He pushed open a door with the toe of his shoe, to reveal a tiny shower compartment and a toilet. "She jogged down here from the Sumner place, showered, and changed into her day clothes," he said. "Then she would change back and jog home. You know what, Baxter?"

"What, sir?"

"I don't think both these handbags are hers," he said, in the manner of one who had made a great and useful discovery.

Baxter smiled. "No, sir," he said.

"So—did she come back to meet someone, do you think?"

"And got knocked out with the mirror when she walked to the desk?" Baxter was beginning to get enthusiastic.

Patterson nodded, then noticed the cassette player. "Oh that's one of these . . ." He made a twirling movement with his hand.

"Twin cassettes, sir. You can record one from another."

"Is that not against the law, Baxter?"

Baxter smiled again. "I think Mrs. Derwent used them

136

for her work," he said. "She would just be copying her own stuff."

"That's all right, then. I wouldn't want to think she was a double-dyed villain." Patterson looked at the neatly stacked cassettes, labelled, dated. "I think we should have these," he said, then bent down to take a closer look at the cassette player. "That microphone's plugged in," he said. He straightened up. "Has this been done, Masson?"

"Yes, Mr. Patterson."

"So who was she meeting?" asked Patterson, rubbing his hands together as he addressed himself to the intricacies of the cassette player. "Maybe this wee box of tricks will tell us."

Baxter's eyes lit up. "You think she recorded her interviews and things?" he said.

"Journalists do." Patterson frowned at the row of buttons. "If she *was* recording . . ." He peered at the tape, and rewound it, then pressed the play button.

At first, it was a jumble of confusing noises. The scrape of a chair, rustles. No conversation. There never was conversation, but the indeterminate sounds resolved themselves into something that they all recognised.

Patterson frowned, Baxter went bright red, and Fergus Masson smiled to himself. "It takes all sorts," the photographer observed, as the passionate goings-on grew ever more intense.

"Well, well," said Patterson. "Comments, Baxter."

"If Eddie's right about this Howard Maxwell . . ." He didn't finish the sentence; as he spoke, the tape suddenly turned into fifties pop, a whistled middle eight. The singer came back in; he wanted to run away, but felt there would be no point.

The basic rock and roll rhythms played in the little room; it was some moments before Patterson switched off the tape.

"Right," he said, briskly. "So she's meeting Maxwell. For some reason, their liaison was recorded?"

"Sounds like it, sir," muttered Baxter.

Patterson was shaking his head. "Who switched it off?"

he asked. "Neither of them. Not at that point in the proceedings."

Baxter looked perplexed.

"It's all supposition, Baxter," said Patterson. "I want that tape tested for prints," he said to Fergus. "And I want a copy of it." He turned back to Baxter. "We don't know who's on that tape. We don't know it's any of them. But someone switched it off, and right now my money's on Derwent. If wee Eddie couldn't turn up any hard and fast evidence, then he'd do it himself."

"And they had a fight that got out of hand," said Baxter. "She put on her jacket to leave, and . . ." He was getting positively enthusiastic.

"It could explain Maxwell's sudden decision to go to London," said Patterson. "Staying out of it."

Baxter frowned. "Where does Barbara Slaney fit in, sir?"

"Well, if she was involved, it could answer a lot of questions. Derwent's killed his wife; he needs help. Turns to her. Maybe to help him cover up his tracks. That could explain why she was driving Mrs. Derwent's car, don't you think?"

Baxter nodded, his face clearing as the scenario began to present itself.

"Oh, don't think it's solved, Baxter," warned Patterson. "Because there are an awful *lot* of questions, and this doesn't answer them all. Why did she take Mrs. Derwent's canvas bag? Why was the car on its way to the cottages, not from them?" He smiled. "Why were the proceedings being recorded in the first place? How come it gets switched off without their apparently being disturbed?"

"Some people video themselves," said Baxter. "I understand. Maybe some people do sound recordings. Perhaps they got a kick out of it."

"Oh, you're too worldly for me," said Patterson, with a twinkle.

Baxter smiled a little shyly.

"And that still doesn't explain how it got switched off," said Patterson. "Someone came in, walked across the room, switched off the recorder, and they're too carried away to notice?'' He looked sceptical. ''I can't believe that.''

''Maybe he *didn't* switch it off,'' said Baxter. ''And maybe the murder was recorded too. So he wiped that bit of the tape.''

''But it hasn't been wiped,'' Patterson pointed out. ''It was being recorded over some pop music, and the recording just stops.''

''Oh.'' Baxter looked crestfallen.

''But I think you're right, all the same,'' said Patterson cheerfully. ''We'll get to the whys and wherefores in the end. Right now, Mr. Derwent has some questions to answer.''

F.D. walked slowly up the drive to the Lodge, passing the police car which sat outside. He walked into the foyer where two members of the staff stood talking. As he passed them, they went quiet; he climbed the stairs, and heard their voices begin again, in whispers.

''His *wife*—are they sure this time?''

He raised his eyebrows slightly, and carried on up, to where the police were working in Barbara's room. He watched for a few moments until someone closed the door. He took a deep breath, and went back down to the dining room.

Mark Ingram, Sue Quentin and John Landers were lunching together; they too fell silent as he approached.

''Do you mind if I join you?'' he asked.

''Of course not,'' said Landers. The other two didn't speak.

F.D. sat down and cleared his throat. ''I want to say something,'' he said, and they looked at him.

''So say it,'' said Mark.

''I don't want people to stop speaking because I have come into the room,'' he began. ''Wanda is dead. She has been murdered. It's a ludicrous, theatrical situation about which we can do nothing.''

Landers' mouth was slightly open.

''And I won't pretend to be broken-hearted by her death

to you or anyone else," F.D. went on. "I have been told twice in two days that she was dead, and both times it shocked me, but neither time did it particularly sadden me."

"But she was your wife, Mr. Derwent," said Landers, horrified.

"Yes," said F.D. "She was my wife. I take it you are not married?"

"No," said Landers defensively.

F.D. held up a hand. "Then you will discover, young man, when you do marry, that the bloom wears off. Isn't that right, Mark?"

Mark had dark shadows under his eyes; he looked with undisguised loathing at F.D. "Wanda found me in bed with someone I picked up in a bar," he said. "It isn't quite the same thing. I wouldn't know."

"Sue!" said F.D., his voice loud enough to make people turn their heads. "You're the expert—what advice would you give our young friend?"

"To keep well away from you, F.D.," she said quietly. "But then, that's advice I'd give everyone."

F.D. sat back. "The fact is," he said to Landers, "that between them Mark and Sue have had four unsuccessful marriages, which barely add up to fifteen years altogether. I, on the other hand, am now a widower after twenty years, and you can take it from me. The bloom wears off."

"Even so," protested Landers.

"Sometimes it turns to hostility, and sometimes to mere indifference. The latter is true in my case."

"How can you be indifferent about someone being *murdered*, for God's sake?" shouted Mark.

Sue put her hand on his. "Don't, Mark," she said. "It isn't worth it."

"Oh, it bothers you does it, Mark?" asked F.D. "That someone murdered Wanda?"

"Of *course* it—"

"But you aren't asking *why*, are you?" said F.D. "You aren't asking who would do such a dreadful thing to Wanda, are you? Because there are a lot of people who would be

140

happy to do such a dreadful thing to Wanda. You're one of them." His eyes went to Sue Quentin. "And you're another," he said, standing up. "She was going to do dreadful things to both of you."

Mark jumped to his feet. "Are you suggesting that one of us murdered her?" he demanded.

"I'm saying that I could do without displays of grief," said F.D.

Mark tensed up; Landers watched him, and rose from the table, walking slowly round to where he stood.

"Mark—don't!" said Sue, as Mark made to strike F.D.

"Leave it, Mark," said Landers, catching his arm as he raised it. "He's not worth it."

F.D. smiled, and walked back out into the foyer, where two uniformed policemen stood.

"Mr. Derwent? Superintendent Patterson would like to ask you a few questions at the police station."

The fly turned at a uniform, if desperately slow, rate. It caught a tiny cog-wheel which turned a larger one. It in its turn moved the largest cog, attached to the cylinder, which moved a fraction of an inch, releasing three steel tongues which were caught on the raised pins. A musical chord sounded.

"Uh-huh," said Patterson, into the phone, making a note on his pad. "Uh-huh. Yes. Right. Well, we thought as much. That's why I asked you to check." He laughed. "No," he said, picking up the cassette from his desk. "No keen detection. Sheer luck. Well, as soon as you can, doctor." He smiled. "Just as well we caught you," he said. "But I'll make it up to you. Another couple of nights in Ardcraig needn't be that dreadful a prospect." He laughed again. "We'll have a drink tonight—no, I'll tell you what. You come to dinner this evening. No, no. She won't mind. She likes showing off her cooking. One of my wife's dinners will make up for any number of missed planes back to civilisation. I take it you're at the Hamilton? Right. I'll pick you up at half past eight. I'll see you then."

141

Patterson went to the door, and looked out to where Derwent sat. "Good of you to come in, Mr. Derwent," he said.

F.D. came into the office. "I wasn't aware that I had a choice," he said.

"What?" Patterson looked shocked. "If we gave you that impression, I can only apologise, Mr. Derwent. You've been asked here to help with our enquiries—nothing more. Do have a seat."

F.D. smiled grimly as he sat down, and didn't acknowledge Baxter's presence. "Helping with enquiries?" he said. "As I recall, that's when everyone sits back and relaxes in the knowledge that the miscreant has been apprehended."

Patterson shook his head. "No, no," he said. "We need everyone to help with enquiries. My men are questioning other people at the Lodge right now. But I thought you would rather have a bit more privacy. And I know this must be upsetting for you, but I'm afraid I have to ask you some questions concerning your wife. I'm sure you understand."

F.D. indicated that he did.

"Perhaps you wouldn't mind telling me your movements on Friday afternoon," said Patterson.

"My 'movements,' Superintendent?" F.D. smiled. "Why?"

"Well, obviously we don't yet have the full post mortem report on your wife, Mr. Derwent, but the doctor has made a preliminary examination. I am told that she died roughly between one o'clock in the afternoon and seven o'clock in the evening on Friday, and that the full post mortem is unlikely to narrow this down. So, naturally, I'm interested to know where everyone was on Friday."

"I was at the Lodge," said F.D. "Most of us were there all afternoon and evening. Except Sue—she left for a few minutes. And young Landers felt he was being overworked, so I don't know if he was there the whole time. And Barbara, of course, didn't turn up at all. We were holding a sort of reception for local dignitaries—as a thank you for letting us commandeer the beach."

"And when did that finish?"

142

"I'm not sure. I left just after three o'clock."

Ping.

"So *you* weren't there all the time, were you?"

F.D. smiled.

"You left after three," said Patterson. "Where did you go?"

"Why do you want to know?"

Ping. Baxter smiled quietly to himself.

"I've explained why, Mr. Derwent. Did you go home?"

F.D. shook his head.

The sky grew dark as the weather closed in on the loch. The hills loomed in the distance, the white houses barely discernible.

"You took a phone call at about three o'clock, I understand."

The agonisingly slow turning produced a single note, as F.D. confirmed that with a slight smile.

"I know who the call was from, Mr. Derwent. It was from a private detective that you have had watching your wife for several weeks." Patterson opened the file. "Subject left home eight A.M.," he read. "Jogged along beach to Headland Cottages. Arrived . . ." He looked up. "You suspected your wife of infidelity, Mr. Derwent?"

"No," said F.D.

"No? Why the private detective?"

"I really don't think that that's any of your business, Superintendent."

"Oh, maybe not, maybe not," Patterson said affably. "But her lover could be my business, don't you think?"

F.D. smiled. "My wife didn't have a lover," he said.

"Why did you ask the private detective to telephone you when your wife left the cottage?"

F.D. sighed. "There's nothing very private about the detectives round these parts, is there?" he said.

"There's nothing very private about murder, Mr. Derwent."

"*Touché*, Superintendent. But you are on entirely the wrong track, I assure you. My wife did not have a lover."

143

Patterson pushed a Walkman over the desk. "It's not mine," he said. "I've borrowed it from Baxter. But I want you to listen to this tape. It was found on your wife's cassette player."

F.D. put on the headphones and pressed the play button. He stiffened as he listened, and switched it off.

"I'd like you to listen to a bit more," said Patterson. "It turns into pop music—I'd like you to listen until it does. I've run it almost to that point—it won't be long."

F.D. took a deep breath, and pressed the play button. After a moment, he switched it off.

"It ends rather abruptly, doesn't it?" Patterson peered over invisible specs. "Someone switched the tape off, by the sound of it."

F.D. didn't speak.

"I think it was you who switched it off, Mr. Derwent. I think you knew about your wife's lover, and you set a trap for her. I think you interrupted them, and her lover ran away. I think you lost control when your wife tried to go after him. I think you killed your wife, Mr. Derwent. I think you involved Barbara Slaney in some sort of cover-up, and she died trying to help you."

F.D. was shaking his head, almost smiling. "This is 'helping with enquiries'?" he said.

"Your wife got home at four o'clock, according to your private detective," Patterson went on. "You left the reception at three. You refuse to tell me what you were doing."

F.D. looked a little wary. "I just don't like my privacy being invaded," he said. "I got home some time after seven."

Patterson looked interested. "Were you surprised not to find your wife there?" he asked.

"No. I didn't expect her to be there. I thought she had gone to London."

The musical box made a strange metallic thud.

"You left the Lodge at three, but you didn't get home until seven," said Patterson, making a note on the sheet of paper in front of him. "What were you doing in that time?"

144

F.D. shook his head. "I don't have to tell you," he said. "But if you must know, I went to the location, to sort out the best positions for the cameras for the stunt on Sunday."

"And you didn't leave until seven?" Patterson looked sceptical. "It's a bit dark by then, isn't it?"

Baxter leant forward, trying to catch his superior's eye, without success.

"I think you went to the cottage. I think you set up the tape to catch your wife out. I think she came back to meet her lover."

"I presume this is some sort of psychology you're practising," said F.D. "But I went to the location and did some work in my trailer. I left at—" He turned to Baxter. "What time would you say it was, Constable Baxter?" he asked.

Patterson glared at Baxter, who looked apologetic.

"About seven-thirty, I think," he said to F.D. "I saw the light on in the caravan," he explained to the less than happy Patterson. "I went to investigate. Mr. Derwent was just leaving."

Patterson nodded, and turned back to Derwent. "You still had plenty of time," he said. "I still think you wanted to catch your wife with her lover."

"Oh, for God's sake! How many times? I didn't suspect my wife of infidelity, Superintendent. She didn't *have* a lover!"

"Oh, but she did. She had been with someone shortly before she died, Mr. Derwent. The pathologist has just confirmed that."

F.D.'s face was a complete blank.

Patterson smiled a little, nodded. "It's a fact, Mr. Derwent," he said.

"Wanda?" he said. "But that's—" He shook his head.

The rain began, splashing against the window, hard sudden rain, obscuring the loch.

Patterson frowned a little. "Are you still saying you didn't know?" he asked. "Why the private detective?"

F.D. watched the fly turn and turn and turn without producing a single note, and regained his composure. "My business," he said. He looked at the musical box. "It was going faster than that a while ago," he observed.

Patterson nodded. "It does that," he said. "That wee thing like a propeller. It's a speed regulator. It's called a fly—you get them on weaving shuttles and things like that. It's having to sort itself out."

"You make it sound as if it ought to be seeing a psychoanalyst," said F.D.

Patterson smiled. "Well, it is a wee bit uptight," he said.

"Jokes," said F.D. "Very good, Superintendent."

The rain lashed the window.

"The tape," said Patterson, bringing the conversation firmly back to the subject. "Don't pretend it means nothing to you, Mr. Derwent."

"It does," he said. "But it isn't Wanda and some lover."

"Oh? Who is it, then?"

"It's . . . it's Barbara Slaney and myself," said F.D. "If you must know."

Patterson took out the cassette and looked at it. "You and Miss Slaney?" he said. "Are you now admitting that you *were* having an affair with her?"

"No," said F.D. "It wasn't an affair, Superintendent. It was Wanda who pointed that out to me, as it happens. She said we were copulating—a much more appropriate description of our activities."

Patterson's lower lip jutted out. "Uh-huh," he said. "So there was no emotional involvement on your part?"

"None whatsoever."

"And the wee lassie?"

F.D. sighed extravagantly.

"Did she ever indicate to you that the attraction was more than physical?"

"I doubt very much that I attracted her physically, Superintendent," said F.D. "Financially, professionally. She tried to say she loved me once—I set her straight." He nodded towards the Walkman. "That's why I wanted her. I made that very clear right from the start."

Patterson glanced at Baxter. "And you made a habit of recording the proceedings, did you?"

"No, of course I didn't!" shouted F.D. "Your wee lassie was trying to blackmail me, Superintendent!"

"Is that right?" said Patterson, totally unconvinced. "So who switched off the tape?"

"I did!"

"Oh, come on, Mr. Derwent. You were otherwise engaged at the time."

"Not *then*! I . . ." He sighed. "It's a long story," he said.

The cog-wheels turned; two notes sounded, like a two-tone doorbell. Patterson smiled comfortably, and put the Walkman in his desk drawer. "I've got time," he said.

Sue Quentin nodded her head tiredly. In another corner of the empty bar, another young man spoke to Mark; she looked at the one who was asking her questions.

"And what sort of mood would you say she was in?" he asked.

Sue shrugged, and looked towards the open door as a small commotion could be heard in the foyer. Police were everywhere; a few more materialised as someone tried to gain entry.

The detective looked over his shoulder, and turned back to her. "Did she seem frightened at all? Did she think she was in danger?"

"Not as far as I could tell."

"Did she mention London?"

She stiffened. "Yes," she said.

"Did she say whether or not she was going there?"

She shook her head again.

"In what connection did London crop up, can you tell me?"

Sue looked a little desperate. She glanced at Mark. His young man was tougher than hers. Sharp clothes, slicked-back hair. Hers wore a pullover.

"She . . . she mentioned a mutual acquaintance there," said Sue.

147

"Did she indicate to you that she intended returning to the cottage later in the afternoon?"

"No."

"What did you do when you left her cottage?" He glanced over his shoulder again as the protests grew louder, and shook his head. "Press," he said. "They're all over the place."

"So when exactly was it that Miss Slaney recorded the proceedings?" Patterson asked.

"Two weeks ago today."

"That would be the . . ." Patterson looked at the wall calendar. "The twenty-third of April," he said.

F.D. smiled. "St. George's Day," he said.

"You were at the Lodge the following Sunday, I believe," said Patterson. "Sunday the twenty-ninth. Was that what you were looking for when you turned her room upside down?"

F.D. looked a little surprised. "Yes," he said. He sat back. "How do you know that?"

Patterson didn't enlighten him. "Why were you wearing gloves?" he asked.

"You're good, Superintendent. I wouldn't have expected such efficiency in a one-horse town like this."

"You still have to answer the question."

"I thought I might just be a little clumsy with her things," said F.D. "I didn't want to get cut on anything that I might accidentally break. She convinced me that she had destroyed it. Taped over it. I believed her." F.D. shook his head. "I thought I had frightened her into telling the truth. She must have been a better actress than I thought."

Patterson raised his eyebrows. "Frightened her? How?"

"I was going to let some hired muscle loose on her, since you ask."

"That, Mr. Derwent, is a criminal offence."

"I thought she had destroyed the tape. I didn't engage their services."

"Threatening to do so is an offence."

F.D. smiled. "So charge me," he said. "If I'd realised she was lying, I'd have gone through with it. I don't make

148

empty threats, Superintendent. People know exactly where they stand with me. And blackmail was very naughty.''

"Barbara died between six and nine on Friday evening. Where were you after half past seven, when the constable here saw you, Mr. Derwent? Just for the record?''

"Sorry, Superintendent, but you're off on the wrong road, if you imagine I took retribution to these lengths. Barbara and I had resumed our relationship by lunchtime that day.''

"Resumed your relationship? Why would you want to resume a relationship with someone who had tried to blackmail you?''

"She requested a return to the status quo, as I knew she would if it got a bit rough the other way. It suited me. It was resumed on my terms.''

Patterson frowned. "I'd heard that you and she were still far from friendly on Friday morning,'' he said. "Wasn't there some sort of row during filming?''

F.D. smiled. "I engineered that, Superintendent. I knew she wouldn't do a nude scene. As I told you—she was very wet and very cold when she walked off. I just made sure she stayed that way for long enough to convince her that crossing me wasn't a good idea. That was when she asked if we couldn't go back to the way we'd been.''

Patterson's eyes widened a little and he looked across at Baxter.

"There was no duress. It was a bargain,'' said F.D. "She understood that. I thought she'd learned her lesson. I certainly didn't kill her because of a spot of amateur blackmail, I do assure you.''

"Nevertheless, I'd like to know where you were between seven-thirty and nine o'clock on Friday evening.''

"I was at home. I went home after the constable and I spoke, and I stayed there. I ate, and then I worked on the shooting script for Sunday's stunt. Which I was still doing when you called on me.''

Patterson nodded. "So . . . let me get this straight. You and Miss Slaney used the cottage whenever it was possible to do so without other people noticing your joint absence.''

149

A nod confirmed this.

"This was always immediately after your wife left the cottage, of which circumstance you were notified by wee Eddie." He was speaking slowly, as though he were trying to get to grips with a particularly tricky scientific theory. "You and she would meet at the cottage while your wife was jogging back to the Sumner place—that gave you the best part of an hour. You would be home by the time your wife got there, and she was none the wiser."

"Correct," said F.D.

"Why the elaborate arrangements, if your wife knew?"

"Knowing and proving are two different things," said F.D.

"There was a period of . . . what?" Patterson did a mental calculation. "About ten days when the relationship was off?"

"Yes."

"So why did Eddie still have to ring?"

"Because I liked knowing where my wife was."

The cogs were moving more quickly; the box emitted pings more often.

Patterson watched the musical box for a moment. "Young Mr. Landers advised me to do that," he said, indicating the two books between which the box was now suspended. "It seems to be working." He smiled at F.D. "I think it's unwinding itself, slowly but surely," he said.

"I'm pleased to hear it," said F.D.

Patterson sat up. "But on Friday the fourth of May, you had made it up, and you left just after Mr. Anderson rang you, as usual. I take it that you didn't really go to the location to look at camera angles?"

F.D. looked a shade uncomfortable. "Not at first," he said. "I went to meet Barbara. But it was all a bit up in the air."

"Oh?"

"She was supposed to have been at the reception," F.D. said. "We were going to leave at different times after Anderson's call, but she wasn't there. So I went to the cottage,

150

just in case. Her car was there, so I waited, but she didn't turn up. That's when I went to the location."

"Did you go into the cottage?"

"No, I've told you. Anyway, I don't have the key."

"But we found Barbara Slaney's fingerprints," said Patterson. "In the cottage. Fresh prints. On the desk, on the cupboard door, on the windowsill. And we found her shoulder bag in the cupboard. She was there, Mr. Derwent. Would you be prepared to let us have your fingerprints to confirm that you weren't?"

"I was there," said F.D. "But not in the afternoon. I was with Barbara at lunchtime."

A trill was heard from the musical box. Patterson sat up straight, his eyebrows raised.

"Oh?" he said. "Was that usual?"

"No. But Barbara was . . . keen," said F.D. "Keen to re-establish the relationship before I changed my mind."

Patterson frowned slightly. "And you were intending seeing her again just a couple of hours later?" He glanced again at Baxter, his eyebrows raised.

"Yes. Is there some sort of law round here about how often you can—"

"No, no, no," murmured Patterson. "But . . . well, Miss Slaney—she was agreeable to this?"

"She seemed to be," said F.D.

"But she died because she drove a car over a cliff after taking an overdose of barbiturates and alcohol," said Patterson.

F.D. shrugged. "So?"

"According to the pathologist, the drugs and alcohol had been in Miss Slaney's system for some hours before she died. Moreover, there was no trace of the capsules themselves. The contents had been emptied out of them and taken neat."

F.D. frowned, politely puzzled.

"The capsule acts as a regulator," said Patterson. He touched the fly with his pen, and it resumed its slow spinning. "A bit like my wee friend here," he said. "As it dissolves, it releases the drug slowly—the effect is reasonably gradual. Take the drug out of the capsule, and it takes effect much more quickly. She might have thought she could kill herself that way. You yourself thought that it sounded like a suicide attempt.''

"So?'' said Derwent again.

"As I said, she died between about six and nine on Friday evening, so she must have taken this stuff between about two and five. A funny time to take sleeping pills, don't you think? Especially since she wasn't even at the Lodge.''

F.D. shrugged again.

"And just after you had been with her, Mr. Derwent. With the promise—if that's the right word—of another meeting that afternoon. Are you so certain that she understood about this bargain?''

"She was in no doubt about where she stood with me, I can assure you,'' said F.D.

"What exactly were your terms for the resumption of the relationship?''

F.D. took a breath. "I was the boss,'' he said simply.

"Can you account for these bruises that she had?''

"I didn't have to beat her into submission, if that's what you think,'' laughed F.D. "Barbara was a very enthusiastic partner, Superintendent. I quite often had bruises too.'' He leant forward. "Look—she had tried blackmail, and I had convinced her, I thought, that that wasn't a clever idea. She seemed only too eager to go back to the previous arrangement.'' He sat back. "Perhaps I should have smelt a rat,'' he said. "Because if you found that tape on Wanda's cassette player, then Barbara obviously carried out her threat.''

"And wouldn't that mean that you would carry out yours?'' murmured Patterson, still apparently engrossed in the workings of the musical box.

"Certainly, if I'd known, but I didn't. Perhaps Wanda's reaction wasn't all Barbara hoped for, and she became violent.''

"You think that *she* killed your wife?''

"It's a possibility.''

152

"You think she murdered your wife, then killed herself. This is the girl who wasn't emotionally involved with you?"

"Isn't that what you think?" asked F.D.

"It's what you want me to think," said Patterson. "But I've got a few more questions for you, Mr. Derwent."

"Were you on friendly terms with your ex-wife?"

Mark drew in his breath. "I wasn't on unfriendly terms," he said, after some consideration.

The noise in the foyer grew louder, and Mark looked over, nodding at one of the men who stood arguing with the police. "I see the fourth estate is with us in force," he said.

"Pardon?"

He smiled. "The tabloids," he said. "Gathering like vultures over the corpse."

"They seem to think you still fancied your wife," said the young man. "From what I've read."

Mark didn't speak.

"Do you have anything to say about that?" persisted the sharp youth.

"Yes," said Mark. "I suggest you start taking a newspaper instead."

He didn't seem at all put out. "They say there's no smoke without fire," he said.

"If there is any smoke," said Mark, "then it has been produced by these so-called journalists themselves. Fumes, I'd say, rather than smoke. The foul-smelling exhaust gases produced by burnt-out talent."

"They're wrong, then?"

"They're wrong." He smiled. "And soon, everyone will know that they are wrong. But they won't mind that one bit."

The young man's brow furrowed, but he decided on a change of subject. "Where were you on Friday afternoon?" he asked.

"Here. Howard Maxwell drove me and John back from the location, and I didn't leave again."

* * *

"Where did Miss Slaney go after you left the cottage at lunchtime?"

"I've no idea. I left first. I always did—Barbara stayed and did the tidying up. We always left separately—it was safer."

The musical box produced a little flurry of notes.

Patterson tapped his fingertips together. "And she had the key," he said. "That would be one of the keys found in the car?"

"Were they in her car? I needn't have waited outside like a lemon then, need I?"

"Why do you suppose she left her keys in the ignition?" asked Patterson. "Why do you think she left the car at the cottage, come to that? Why did she leave her bag there, if she was supposed to be tidying up?"

"I'd taken the rest of the brandy—she drank most of it."

"The rest of the brandy?"

"I'd given her some in her trailer to warm her up."

Patterson looked at him unblinkingly. "Brandy?" he said. "After freezing her half to death? How magnanimous, Mr. Derwent."

"She was a bit tipsy even before she left the location," F.D. said, ignoring him. "And then she drank more at the cottage. She must have forgotten her bag. And she must have been way over the limit. She probably didn't want to drive. I expect she walked." He smiled.

"Where?"

"How should I know?" F.D. shrugged. "Not to the Lodge, which is where she was supposed to be."

"So you never saw her again after you left her at the cottage?"

"Correct."

"Nobody did, Mr. Derwent. Nobody that we can find, anyway. But she was found in your wife's car—are you not even a wee bit curious about that?"

"Not really."

"Your wife left the cottage at three," he said. "Eddie followed her home. But she came *back*, Mr. Derwent. To meet someone." He swivelled round, his back to F.D., and looked out at the rain. "I think you knew that, Mr. Derwent. I think you set this whole thing up."

Outside the window, a TV news team drew up. Sue Quentin watched worriedly.

The detective smiled. "Don't worry, we'll get you past them," he said. "Where did you go when you left Mrs. Derwent?"

"I came back here. There was a reception for the locals. I had put in an appearance, but I felt I ought to do a bit more than that."

They had quietened the reporters down, apparently by doing some deal. They stood in the foyer, cameras and recorders at the ready.

"What time did you get back here?"

"At about ten past three, I think." She glanced a little nervously at the knot of pressmen.

"Did you see Mr. Derwent?"

"Yes. He was leaving just as I came in."

"And you stayed until the party was over?"

"Yes."

"Who else was here?"

"Mark," she said. "And John. Len Charles, Clive Oliver, Stella, Marcia . . . everyone, really."

"Was Barbara Slaney here?"

"Apparently not. F.D. was furious because she hadn't turned up."

"I left the cottage on Friday at about one forty-five, and I haven't been back since," said F.D.

"I think you went back at three o'clock," said Patterson. "I think you knew your wife would be coming back to meet her lover—you knew she had a lover, or why the private detective in the first place? I think you had a fight, and you killed her. You involved Miss Slaney in whatever set-up you hoped to produce, but she had already taken the pills on top of all the alcohol she had consumed, and she was good for nothing. Nothing except a fall-guy. I think you killed her, and you planted your own copy of that tape to incriminate her.''

F.D. stared at him. "Now, why would you think that?" he asked.

"Why wouldn't I? On the one hand you were scared to death your wife was going to grab at least half of your God knows how many millions of dollars and on the other that a nineteen-year-old chit of a girl was going to blackmail you out of them. If she could blackmail you about sex, what couldn't she do with murder? So she had to go too.''

F.D. shook his head in disbelief. "When am I supposed to have accomplished all this?" he asked.

"As far as I can see, you are the only person with any sort of reason to murder your wife who could have accomplished it," said Patterson. "You had from three o'clock in the afternoon to do it.''

"Except that I still have my copy of the tape," said F.D. "Which rather stumps your theory."

Patterson looked surprised. "You didn't destroy it?" he asked. "I'm sure I would have.''

"I was going to. But then I kept it to remind me how vulnerable one can be.''

"And you can produce it to me? Now?''

"You can come home with me and pick it up.''

"I will,'' said Patterson, standing up. "Let's go, Mr. Derwent.''

"Someone said your ex-wife had upset you. How?''

Mark didn't answer. Sue had been released; her interrogator was now seeing her through the gaggle of reporters. He took a deep breath, then visibly changed his mind. "No,'' he said, "I am entitled to my privacy for as long as I can hang on to it. Do you actually suspect me of murdering Wanda?''

"That depends on whether anyone can confirm that you were here all the time.''

The flashes of the cameras were like bursts of gunfire; not

pointed at Mark yet. They were pointed at Sue, cameras held high above their heads by the people at the back of the crush.

Mark smiled. "The staff," he said. "They'll confirm that I was here." He pointed to the bar. "There, to be precise. Getting drunk, and pretending to be sober when F.D. brought people to talk to me."

"And you didn't leave here?"

"I can't, when I get drunk." Mark smiled at him. "My legs cease to function. I was here until I went to bed—and I even have a witness for that."

The detective smiled. "And she would come forward, would she?"

Mark just smiled back.

The drawer was pulled open, and the shirts removed. Underneath lay a cassette.

"There it is," said F.D., and he held his hands up. "Nothing up my sleeve, no sleight of hand—you may remove it yourself, Superintendent."

Patterson looked at the tape. "I must admit," he said, "I thought it would have been stolen, or lost. I was calling what I thought was your bluff, Mr. Derwent."

"You still are," said F.D. "You think it'll have nothing on it, and I'll say it must have got wiped by mistake. But it hasn't. It's all there, Superintendent."

"And it doesn't suddenly get switched off?"

"No, of course it doesn't. It is the original. The full, unexpurgated version. And it's followed by some other pop song—don't ask me which." He smiled. "I wasn't even worth a couple of new tapes," he said.

"You know we have experts," said Patterson. "They'll know if it's been tampered with in any way, whatever sophisticated equipment you have at your disposal."

F.D. smiled broadly. "What sophisticated equipment?" he said. "I didn't need any. That is the original, recorded over some programme that plays old hits—Barbara seems to have become a fan of one Duncan Jameson on the local radio station during her stay north of the border. She had half a dozen cassettes with his programme on them. She obviously reused two that she had grown tired of," he said, with a shrug.

"I'll have a copy made," Patterson said, picking it up with his handkerchief and putting it in a plastic bag. "If it proves to have no connection with the investigation, this will be returned to you."

"No need." He closed the drawer. "I'll show you out."

Patterson stopped as he passed the open door to the sitting room, looking at the expensive hi-fi. "Was Barbara Slaney ever in this house?" he asked.

F.D. took a breath. "Yes," he said. "She turned up uninvited one night. In fact, that was her first attempt at blackmail." He smiled. "She stood half-naked in the kitchen, with my wife's key turning in the lock, refusing to leave until I agreed to hire a private detective to watch Wanda."

Patterson raised a disbelieving eyebrow.

F.D. shrugged. "It's true," he said. "You wanted to know why I'd hired a detective? Well, that's why. And I thought it was her again, the night you came to tell me about the accident. I thought she had come with her excuses for not showing up at the reception."

"I remember," said Patterson. "You seemed none too pleased when you opened the door."

"I would have been very angry. But that young woman enjoyed playing with fire, Superintendent."

He watched as Patterson drove away into the dusk, and closed the door. After a moment's thought, he picked up the phone.

"Howard Maxwell," he said.

"Mr. Maxwell has asked not to be disturbed," said the girl.

"Tell him that F.D.'s on the phone."

"I'm sorry, he's asked—"

"Tell him!"

The phone clicked.

"F.D.?"

"Howard, get over here. I want to talk to you."

158

"What about?"

"Wanda."

"I don't want to talk about her," Howard said, after a moment.

"I don't care what you want. I think, my friend, that you have abused your position with me by bedding my wife."

"Yes, I abused my position. And you want to know something, F.D.? That was the one and only time Wanda was ever unfaithful to you, though Christ knows why."

"Get over here, Howard. Now."

There was an unamused laugh from the other end. "Are you pretending to *care*, F.D.?"

"Someone murdered her! You were with her just before that!"

"Jesus, you don't think I—"

"I want to know what was going on. If you're not here in twenty minutes, I guarantee you'll have the police questioning you instead."

There was a silence.

"Twenty minutes, Howard."

"All right, all right!" His voice was muffled when he spoke again. "Wait a minute! I'm on the phone." He spoke to F.D. again. "Look, someone's at the door. I might be held up—I'll get there as soon as I can."

"You'll be here for half past seven, Howard. Twenty minutes—not a second longer. I don't fall for the old ones that easily."

"Someone's at the sodding door, I tell you!"

"Twenty minutes." F.D. paused for a moment. "Or you know what's going to happen."

"And you saw it in the woods near to Mr. Sumner's house?"

"Yes," he said. "On Friday evening. I was taking the dog for a walk and I saw this car. He started barking, so I didn't get too close—you never know these days, do you? I'm not as young as I was. But they're saying it's a Mercedes you took out of the sea—there's not many of them in Ardcraig."

"No," said Patterson.

159

"So I thought aye-aye, you know. Then I thought it would belong to that Phil Sumner, though you see him in a Range Rover, don't you? But that's what I thought. It's his land, you see. But then I wondered why he'd have it parked there instead of in his garage."

"What time was this?"

"Oh—when, now. Six. Sixish. Say half past. It was gloaming. Half past six, say." He paused. "It was when I was walking the dog just now that I remembered it."

"But it's—" Patterson looked at the clock, and sighed. "It's almost eight," he said. "You don't take the dog out at the same time every evening?"

"Oh, no. No. I'm like you, I work till the job's done. I was late taking him out tonight."

"Well, thank you very much," said Patterson, looking more puzzled than pleased. "If you could see the officer on the desk, he'll take your statement. Very good of you to come in."

The door opened. "Someone brought this for you, sir," said the young policeman, handing Patterson a cassette.

"Oh, good, son. Could you take Mr. . . . er . . . ?" He looked enquiringly at the man.

"Tommy Watson," he said.

"Mr. Watson. Sorry. Yes, could you take Mr. Watson's statement, please?"

"Yes, sir."

They left the room, and Patterson smiled broadly. "The copy of Derwent's tape," he said to Baxter, and reached into the drawer for the Walkman. He took one tape out, and put the other in, pressed fast forward, and listened. He raised his eyebrows, and pressed fast forward again, leaving it for longer. He played it, and his eyes widened a little. Fast forward, listened, and stopped the tape. He took off the headphones and looked at Baxter. "He's older than me," he said with grudging admiration.

Baxter grinned.

"I'll wait for the experts," Patterson said. "But I'm beginning to think that he must be telling the truth."

"And Barbara Slaney really did leave that other tape on the machine?" asked Baxter.

"The lab tells me that only her prints are on it." He rubbed his eyes. "And on the car. Steering wheel, gear lever, hand brake, door. No other prints—that's odd, don't you think?"

"I don't know," said Baxter. "If you were hiring a car to a multi-millionaire's wife, would you not make sure it was spotless, sir? If whoever delivered it wore gloves, maybe Barbara's the only one who's driven it since."

Patterson nodded. "True," he said. His pen nudged the fly into reluctant action. It turned twice, and stopped. "Why the hell was she driving it?" he asked. "And what was it doing in the woods? I don't like mysteries, Baxter. Everything has an explanation."

"Do you think . . . ?" Baxter began, then looked down. "Sorry, sir," he said.

"No, Baxter, you go ahead. It's your beat. I'm just here to assist you."

Baxter took that with the pinch of salt it deserved, but carried on. "Do you think it's possible that the Barbara Slaney thing isn't connected?" he said.

Patterson looked interested. "Go on," he said.

"Well, sir, suppose she got Mrs. Derwent to go to the cottage and listen to the tape, but she didn't want to know. I mean, if she'd got something going with Maxwell, maybe she didn't care what her husband was doing."

Patterson began filling his pipe as Baxter spoke.

"And Barbara Slaney deliberately killed herself in Mrs. Derwent's car," said Baxter. "You know. Because it was a sort of a . . . well, symbol, of what she couldn't have."

Patterson puffed serenely at his pipe. "I never suspected a romantic streak, Baxter," he said.

"Girls that age," said Baxter, not to be put off. "They've got romantic streaks. And with her background . . ."

"And meanwhile, back at the ranch?"

"Mrs. Derwent's meeting Maxwell. They fall out about something, and it gets violent. He kills her, and goes to London to get out of the way. But then he thinks that his absence would be suspicious, so he comes back to brazen it out.''

The phone rang, and Patterson picked it up, pulling a face at Baxter's theory. "I think it's time you went home to your bed, Baxter," he said. "You're getting fanciful."

"Mr. Frank Derwent for you, sir."

"Put him on."

"Mr. Patterson? Derwent. It might interest you to know that Reginald Howard Maxwell died in the Blitz, at the age of five, along with the rest of his family. The man calling himself by that name is known to the Metropolitan Police as Ronald Neve."

Patterson took that in. "You didn't mention this before, Mr. Derwent," he said.

"Maxwell hadn't crossed me before," said F.D., and hung up.

Patterson shivered a little, and replaced the receiver.

"I hope I never have to cross Mr. Derwent," he said to Baxter, picking it up again. "Scotland Yard," he said. "Urgent."

CHAPTER NINE

"I'VE ALWAYS KNOWN HE HAD A RECORD," SAID F.D.

Patterson unbuttoned his coat in the warmth of the Sumners' sitting room. No music played this morning; the wind tugging at the slates on the old house, the gulls crying, the sea, restless and dangerous, provided the background sounds. "But he doesn't," he said. "I think you knew he was wanted for murder."

F.D. smiled. "Hardly," he said. "I knew he was in trouble when he came to me that night. He was frightened. I was leaving for the States that week, and he wanted to come with me. The only problem was that he wanted me to pay his fare, and he wanted to travel as Reginald Howard Maxwell." F.D. grinned. "Years before the method was popularised," he said. "But then, Howard is a conman."

"So," said Patterson, leaning back, apparently relaxed, "in what way has he crossed you, Mr. Derwent?"

"He's the one who was with Wanda on Friday afternoon," said F.D. "I knew it had to have been him—I put it to him, and he admitted it."

"And that bothers you?"

"Of course it bothers me! Wouldn't it bother you if he had been sleeping with your wife?"

Patterson took out his pipe. "Do you mind?" he asked.

"Go ahead," said F.D.

Patterson crushed the slice of tobacco in the palm of his hand. "And as soon as he told you, you rang me and told me about his criminal past?"

F.D. shook his head, and got up. "Drink?" he asked.

"I'll have a small whisky, thank you."

F.D. picked up the bottle. "Last time you wouldn't have a drink with me," he said. "Want anything in it?"

"No," said Patterson. "Last time I thought you had killed Barbara Slaney."

F.D. handed him his drink. "Not any more?"

"The tape checks out."

"So you no longer imagine I murdered Wanda in a jealous rage, and did Barbara in to keep her quiet?" He poured his own, splashing soda into it. "Or—what was your next try? That I planned it all in advance and tried to frame your wee lassie?"

Patterson sipped the whisky. "Good stuff," he said. "No, I no longer think that. I think you were blackmailing Howard Maxwell into doing whatever you required of him, but that's got nothing to do with me. I know you used threatening and abusive behaviour towards Barbara Slaney, and I believe that you frightened her into doing whatever you required of *her*. But she ended up killing herself, so that'll get me nowhere. In short, Mr. Derwent, I think you are possibly the nastiest piece of work I have ever come across. But this is a very decent whisky, and I suspect, therefore, that it is Mr. Sumner's. So I don't mind drinking it."

F.D. sat down, smiling. "I didn't ring you straight away yesterday," he said. "I told Maxwell he had twenty minutes to get here and explain what the business in London was all about, or I would phone the police. But in fact," he said, picking up his glass, "I waited for almost an hour and a half. He failed to take advantage of that."

Patterson nodded. "I hadn't noticed this generosity of spirit before, Mr. Derwent," he said.

"I take it he's given you the slip again?"

"Well, we've found his car. It was abandoned in the town. Would you have any idea where he might have gone?"

164

"No—should I have?"

"No. But you were the last person to speak to him before he took off." He finished his whisky, and got up. "I'll see myself out."

"Hang on," said F.D.

Patterson turned reluctantly.

"I might not have been the last person to speak to him," said F.D. "Maxwell said there was someone at his door, and he might be held up. At the time, I thought he was stalling, but perhaps there was."

"Perhaps," said Patterson, and he walked to the door.

"And Patterson," said F.D.

"Yes?" Patterson sighed; he didn't turn round this time.

"It *is* my whisky."

They were bored: hanging around a street corner, kicking their feet. Three of them, about ten years old, with spiky hair and dirty faces.

Across the road, people boarded a coach for a scenic tour of the area. Its exhaust vibrated as it sat by the pavement, sending clouds of diesel fumes drifting across the street.

"We could go on the bus," said one.

"Away. That's for the visitors."

"Who says?"

They looked at one another.

"Where's it going?"

"Just round," said the first.

"How much is it?"

"I don't know."

"I've no money."

"Neither've I."

The coach was half full. It sat shuddering at the stop for a few more minutes, then pulled away with a final puff of diesel.

"Half term," said one, dispiritedly, looking at the rainclouds gathering once more over the lowering hills.

"Better than school," said another, sliding down the wall, landing with a bump.

165

"We could go and see where that woman was killed," suggested the third.

"They won't let you near the place," said the voice from the pavement.

"Come on and we'll watch the filming," suggested the first.

"Nothing was happening yesterday."

"It was dark! Anyway, we saw her from *Stones*," said the proposer.

"So you say."

"We did!"

"I never saw her."

"We might see Barry Strong."

"Ach, they're stupid, these."

"I think they're good."

"No one ever gets killed!"

"Come on and we'll see if they're filming."

His persistence met with eventual success, as he knew it would. They ran off, pushing one another off the pavement, getting angry hoots from cars.

". . . and here at home, police investigating the murder of Wanda Derwent, wife of Hollywood director Frank Derwent, are joining forces with Scotland Yard in the search for another member of the film community who has gone missing. Mrs. Derwent was found dead on Sunday, in the cottage she was renting in Ardcraig to use as an office for her work on a book she was writing. The man the police wish to interview is known as Reginald Howard Maxwell, who is a business partner of Mr. Derwent, as well as his assistant director on the film being made here on the west coast. Lindsey Rannoch of our Ardcraig newsroom reports . . ."

The wild coast, the cave. A shot of the cottage.

"It was in this holiday cottage on Sunday that police, acting on information received from a local private investigator, found the body of forty-year-old Wanda Derwent."

Shots of the shore, the harbour wall.

"Mrs. Derwent had accompanied her husband to Scot-

*land in order to put the finishing touches to a book she was
writing about the British in Hollywood, and in order to work
undisturbed, it was to this cottage that fitness fanatic Wanda
Derwent would jog the five or so miles from Highcliff, the
house that she and her husband were renting from superstar
Phil Sumner, who is currently touring the United States and
Canada with his group Restless Bodies.''*

Pictures of the Mercedes being hauled out of the sea, water
pouring out of it.

*"It was on Friday of last week that Mrs. Derwent's car
was found half-submerged in the sea, containing the body of
nineteen-year-old Barbara Slaney, one of the actresses in the
production. Foul play has not been ruled out, and Mrs. Derwent is also believed to have died on Friday. Police say that
they are working on the assumption that the two incidents
are connected, but that they are keeping an open mind.''*

Mark Ingram sat alone, looking up with a lacklustre eye
as Patterson joined him.

*"Police are anxious to trace anyone who may have seen
Mrs. Derwent or Miss Slaney on Friday afternoon. Earlier
today, I spoke to Chief Superintendent Calum Shaw of . . .''*

"Mr. Ingram," said Patterson, by way of greeting, and
sat down beside him.

"Not guilty," said Mark.

Patterson smiled. "Of what?" he asked.

"Ah," said Mark. "That's a trick question."

*". . . we now know to be a man known to us as Ronald
Neve, who is wanted in connection with the murder of a
police officer in Balham, London, in 1963.''*

Mark's mouth opened as he stared at the screen.

"What are you drinking?" Patterson reached into his
pocket for his wallet, which seemed to be proving elusive.

"Put it away," Mark said, without taking his eyes from
the television. He tapped the bell, and ordered two doubles
when the girl appeared.

*". . . We wish to question Howard Maxwell, as he calls
himself, in connection with both of these deaths and the killing of the police officer in 1963.''*

167

"I'm on duty, Mr. Ingram," said Patterson, as their drinks arrived, picking his up, none the less.

"Mark." He held out his hand to the Superintendent. "Howard?" he said incredulously. "Murdering a *policeman*?"

"Hugh." Patterson shook hands. "Yes," he said. "Well, he didn't pull the trigger. But he was there, which is and was the same thing. His accomplice was hanged."

Mark poured his previous drink into his new one, still bewildered. "But—how? I mean—how come he . . . ?"

"He had fixed himself up with a false passport, and a new identity," said Patterson. "Believing that the raid would come off, and he could leave Britain a rich man. As it was, it all went wrong, but he got away with it until now." He shrugged. "He's escaped hanging, at any rate."

"So how . . . ?" Mark was at a loss for words, but he didn't need many.

"A little bird," said Patterson.

Mark stared at him. "Not Wanda? She didn't find out about him, did she?"

"She could have," said Patterson. "She certainly could have."

Mark nodded slowly, still shocked.

"Mr. Maxwell suddenly decided to go to London," said Patterson. "He says he went in Mrs. Derwent's place, but that seems more than unlikely, in view of the circumstances. He did go, though. He flew to Glasgow from here, then took the London flight, and stayed overnight, returning on Saturday morning. Sunday, he was at the location for the filming of the stunt until we discovered Mrs. Derwent's body. From then, as far as anyone knows, he was in his room until approximately seven o'clock on Monday evening, when he took a phone call from Mr. Derwent. No one seems to have seen him since."

Mark took a sip of whisky. "I saw him leave," he said.

"When?"

"Just after seven. I was here." He smiled. "Propping up

the bar, as usual," he said. "You can see through to reception from here—look."

He slid off the stool, and Patterson took his place, frowning, nodding.

"Did he have a suitcase or anything?"

"No," said Mark, resuming his seat. "But have you spoken to Sue? She might know a bit more. She was with him."

"Good. Right, I'll . . ." Patterson hesitated. "I'll get someone to have a word with her." He sat down again.

"But I was there when he was told about Wanda," said Mark. "He seemed . . . well, genuinely upset."

"Tell me something, Mark," Patterson said.

"Are you supposed to be on first name terms with the suspects?" Mark asked.

"Are you a suspect?" asked Patterson.

"I was told yesterday by her own husband that I had every reason to kill her," said Mark. "I suppose I did, when you come to think of it. And your Detective Constable Tate seems to find me highly suspicious."

"What reason did you have to kill Mrs. Derwent?"

Mark smiled, and looked at Patterson over the rim of his glass. "You haven't read the manuscript of her book," he said.

"There wasn't one. Just tapes. I haven't listened to them yet."

"You should."

"I will." Patterson took a drink.

"So—what did you want me to tell you?" asked Mark.

"How are you on gossip?" Patterson asked.

"I hear it," said Mark.

"Your ex-wife," said Patterson. "Any rumours there?"

Mark offered him a cigarette, and he refused. "I'm a pipe man," he said. "Thank you."

"No rumours about Wanda," said Mark, lighting his own. "Not as far as I know. Did you have anyone in mind?"

"Howard Maxwell," said Patterson, with a nod towards the television, where a photograph of Howard was being shown.

169

"Detectives from Scotland Yard are travelling up to Ard-craig to liaise with local police." She paused, and the photograph turned into a middle-aged man with long hair. *"Phil Sumner, whose house the Derwents were using during their stay in Ardcraig, said in Philadelphia today that he was 'devastated' by the news."*

The photograph went, and the newsreader reappeared, her expression rearranged. *"Local education chiefs say that schools in the region will be badly hit by government plans to . . ."*

Mark cocked his head a little. "He and Wanda have been working together on her book," he said. "Not out of the question, I'd say. In fact, his reaction to her death was . . . well—he certainly could have been involved with her." Mark finished his drink, and put down the empty glass. "But pinning it on Howard would solve a lot of problems, wouldn't it?" he said.

"I'm not trying to pin it on anyone!" said Patterson angrily.

"Oh, I wasn't talking about you," said Mark.

"Who, then?"

Mark looked at him. "Who do you think?" he asked. "Who else? Who wanted rid of both Barbara and Wanda? The rest of us were all here, except for Howard. But where was F.D., Hugh?"

Patterson sighed. "Everything he tells us checks out," he said.

"But where *was* he?"

"All right. He says he was supposed to be meeting Barbara, but she didn't turn up."

"And you believe him?"

"I didn't." Patterson drained his glass. "But the way things are going . . ." He stood up. "Maybe I'm barking up the wrong tree altogether," he said. "Maybe Barbara was with Mrs. Derwent, and some local loony attacked them. She got away in Mrs. Derwent's car, but had an accident."

Mark shook his head. "You don't believe that," he said.

170

"I'm running out of suspects," said Patterson. "My boss thinks it was Maxwell."

"Yes, well . . ." Mark rang the bell. "You listen to the tapes, Hugh. You'll have more suspects than you know what to do with."

The gentle waves came to the shore, falling short of their previous mark, and the cave entrance was once more accessible. Sue Quentin pulled her coat more tightly round her in the quickening breeze, and looked at her watch.

Just after one o'clock. She sighed, and turned slowly away from the sea, walking towards the ring of trailers.

"Well?" said Patterson, his mouth still full of his last piece of meat pie. "What do you think?"

Baxter negotiated the door with two steaming mugs, and kicked it shut. "To be honest, sir," he said, "I think it looks as though it must have been Maxwell." He put down the mug, and looked at the musical box, as it produced three notes in quite rapid succession. "That's going quite fast," he observed.

Patterson peered at it. "Good," he said, and picked up his mug. "I was trying to work out Barbara Slaney's involvement in all of this."

Baxter sat down, and looked expectantly at the Superintendent.

"Ronald Neve," said Patterson. "He was a petty criminal, Baxter. A confidence trickster. He wasn't violent." He shook his head slightly, and blew on his tea.

Baxter bit into a biscuit.

"He dabbled with acting. He was good enough for Derwent to give him a part in a play he was putting on."

"I suppose most conmen are," said Baxter.

"Meanwhile, in the hope of getting even more money, he got himself involved with a real crook, and it all went wrong. The Met picked up the other one, and they soon knew all about Ronald Neve, but he had simply disappeared."

"Gone to the States with Derwent," said Baxter.

171

Patterson nodded. "And he went straight, in a manner of speaking. He probably cooks F.D.'s books for him, and he practically procures young women for him, but he has led an officially blameless life since he was twenty-four years old." He took out his pipe and searched his pockets for his tobacco pouch. "Derwent knew, of course. That's why Maxwell did his bidding, however demeaning it might be." He struck a match. "But suppose, Baxter, just suppose Wanda Derwent found out?" he said. "What would a conman do?"

Baxter's mouth was full of biscuit.

"I'll tell you. He would ingratiate himself with her." He got the pipe going to his satisfaction, and let the match burn itself out in the ashtray. "He'd known her for twenty years—all of a sudden, she means so much to him that he won't let her go to London for some film in case there's a bit of trouble?"

Baxter swallowed his biscuit. "It can happen, sir," he said. "Someone you've known for years. Taken for granted, just thought of as a friend. Suddenly, you—"

Patterson had a broad grin on his face, and Baxter went slightly pink. "It didn't happen to me," he said. "It happened to my father, though. He'd known my mother fifteen years. She was forty when they married. I think they were the happiest couple I've known."

"You'll have to excuse my cynical view of the world," said Patterson. "But to get back to my supposition . . ." He puffed his pipe, and sat back. "If she knew, he had to get her on his side. The last thing he would want her to do would be go to London, and maybe dig up some more dirt on him. A wrong word . . ." He shook his head. "He didn't go to pick up any film," he said. "Run the risk of being seen by some old crony who wanted to make a bob or two by informing on him? He wouldn't dare leave the airport in case he got spotted. He just wanted to make sure *she* didn't go, that's all." He leant forward. "But a conman wouldn't murder her," he said. "He would trick her. Tell her it was going to be dangerous, offer to go instead. Flatter her. That's how conmen work."

Baxter frowned.

"And then there's Barbara. What do we know about her? One-parent family, eldest of a number of half brothers and sisters, mother with a succession of men friends, at least one of whom abused her. Runs away to London when she's thirteen, and I think we can guess how she made her living."

Baxter opened his mouth, but Patterson continued before he could speak.

"She gets involved in some sleazy club act, and drifts into acting." He smiled. "I expect if you can make the punters think you're enjoying it, you can play Lady Macbeth any day."

Baxter's frown grew deeper. "Sir," he said.

"Yes, Baxter?"

"Sir, you don't know that she was a prostitute—I presume that's what you mean."

Patterson puffed on his pipe. "It's a baseless, prejudiced assumption," he said. "She might have been the chairperson of ICI for all I know, but she didn't have a National Insurance number until she got the part in the soap opera, so I don't think she was. Girls of thirteen don't have very many career choices, Baxter. Child prostitution is just another return to Victorian values."

Baxter looked at the biscuits, and had another.

"All right, we'll stick to facts. Barbara discovers she's got talent—she gets parts. She can afford a flat for herself and her boyfriend. And when she got the part in this film, she gave him as her next of kin—called him her husband." He sucked at his pipe, and took it out of his mouth, frowning at it. "Some no-hoper junkie jail-bird is the closest friend she's got on this earth, Baxter. Her mother hadn't seen her for over five years—she didn't even know she was in that soap opera."

"It was only shown in some regions," said Baxter, slightly mutinously. "Sir."

"And our friend Howard 'introduces' her to Derwent, who's got money wall to wall. She sees a better way of life, and she wants it." He struck a match. "And," he said, between puffs, "can you blame her?"

173

Baxter munched, shaking his head.

"She thinks she can supplant Mrs. Derwent, but it doesn't work like that. Derwent's got too much to lose. So she plays on that—tries blackmail, but even that doesn't work. She puts up with all kinds of abuse from Derwent, because she's desperate to get on to the gravy train. He threatened to have her beaten up, Baxter—and I think when Derwent threatens, he means it. And she calmly made him believe that she had destroyed that tape, when she had it all the time."

"I still don't really see . . ."

The door opened and Patterson and Baxter stood up as Chief Superintendent Shaw came in.

"What the hell's going on with these film people, Patterson?"

"Constable Baxter and I have been airing some possibilities, sir," said Patterson, laying the pipe down in the ashtray with a resigned expression.

The Chief Super glanced at Baxter, and looked less than impressed. "I don't want Scotland Yard charging up here like the cavalry to solve this little local difficulty for us, Patterson," he said. "I want Maxwell. Do you need more CID back-up? We can just about spare a couple more."

Patterson shook his head. "We've got more police officers than I can count crawling all over this," he said. He picked up a sheaf of paper. "Writing reports, getting statements, making enquiries . . ." He smiled grimly. "Looking for clues," he said. "Constable Baxter and I will manage with the strength we've got."

Shaw looked at Baxter again. "I think Baxter should be getting back to his normal duties," he said. "We're having to organise cover for him. I'll get you a DC from—"

"I don't want another DC, sir," said Patterson. "I want Baxter. He knows the area."

"Leave us, would you?" said Shaw to Baxter.

"Sir."

Shaw waited until the door closed. "Sit down, Hugh, and get off your high horse, for God's sake. Local knowledge has got damn all to do with this."

174

"Probably," said Patterson, sitting down. "But I seem to remember someone saying we were keeping an open mind."

Shaw snorted.

"I was the beat man here once," said Patterson. "The local bobby patrolling a rural area. The job consists of dealing with petty theft and poachers, bored kids and drunk and disorderlies, out-of-date tax discs and speeding tourists. Nothing like this has ever happened here before, and it will never happen again. So why make poor Baxter miss out and send in some DC who thinks he knows it all?"

"Wouldn't experience in CID investigation be a bit more useful to you?"

"We've got a dozen experienced CID officers working on it as it is." He smiled. "Come on, Calum. Let Baxter have something to tell his grandchildren."

"All right," said Shaw, shaking his head. "But I want to be at the briefing tomorrow. Where are you holding it, by the way?"

"The church hall," said Patterson. "The film people were using it, but they've halted work of course, so we've taken it over."

"I want to make it very clear to everyone that this is big. The people being questioned are famous, and the media are making the most of it."

"Don't we know it?" said Patterson. "We'll need traffic lights here if we get any more estate cars and Range Rovers piling in with their camera crews."

"Right. So practically the entire civilised world will be watching to see how we handle this. And so far . . ."

"So far, we haven't the foggiest notion what's going on," said Patterson. "Blackmail, infidelity, murder, suicide . . ." He tapped his pen on the blotter. "Are we doing anything about Derwent's harbouring a criminal?" he asked.

"That's up to Scotland Yard," said Shaw. He frowned at the musical box as it doggedly produced notes. "I'm not concerned with whether or not Derwent knew who Maxwell was. I doubt anyone can prove it anyway."

"He told me he did!"

"That's not what he told the Yard, though. And you didn't caution him, didn't have a witness. I can't believe you were that stupid, Hugh."

"God damn it, I'm investigating his wife's murder, not something that happened over a quarter of a century ago! You don't expect to need witnesses and cautions! He just told me!"

"It may have happened over a quarter of a century ago, but it's *why* Mrs. Derwent was murdered," said Shaw. "Derwent said that his wife told him last week. She had some contact in London who told her—that's why Maxwell had to stop her going."

"Maybe," said Patterson. "It doesn't mean he murdered her."

Shaw sighed. "I know you don't like Derwent, but he's been very candid about his relationship with the girl, and his wife. It hardly shows him in a good light, but he hasn't shirked the truth. And *he* hasn't skipped, has he? *He* isn't using an assumed identity, and *he* isn't wanted for a previous murder into the bargain!"

"Saying I don't like him is something of an understatement," said Patterson. Then he frowned, thinking about something. "Calum, could I put a forensic team into the Sumner house?"

Shaw frowned. "What for?"

"To look for traces of barbiturates."

"Now what are you saying?"

"I don't think Maxwell is a murderer, sir. I've got a theory that I'd rather keep to myself until I speak to wee Eddie Anderson again."

Shaw agreed to the forensic team, and left. Baxter came in, after knocking on the door.

"Don't knock, Baxter, it's your office."

"Am I still on the enquiry, sir?"

"You are." Patterson picked up the phone. "Get me wee Eddie, would you, son?" He held his hand over the mouthpiece and smiled. "We're going to do some detecting, Baxter," he said, then took his hand away. "Eddie!" he said. "Can you do me a favour?"

They ran along the top of the cliffs, their legs whipped by the long grass, racing one another into the strengthening wind blowing across the sand.

The one in the lead stopped. "There's nobody there," he said, disappointed.

The cove beneath was deserted: no scaffolding, no cameras, no lights, no actors. The trailers sat, pulled round in a circle like a wagon train, still and silent. Inside the circle, the wind was broken, their voices deadened by the vehicles. They hid behind tyres taller than they were, suddenly appearing, arms outstretched, hands clasped together, making little explosions in their throats as they attempted to gun one another down.

One drew back, rolling under one of the trailers, dodging the phantom bullets that tore into the ground beside him, and crept along on his stomach before emerging, triumphantly, silently, behind the other two, who ran off despite his holding them at fingerpoint.

He was on his own when the trailer door opened; she looked at him, puzzled, for a moment. "You shouldn't be playing here," she said, her voice friendly enough, as she climbed down and locked the door.

For a moment, he stood uncertainly in the middle of the grass, watching her walk away. Then he ran back out to where the other two were continuing their gunfight. "I've seen her too!" he shouted.

They stopped and turned. "What?"

"That woman from the telly."

"No, you've not!"

"I have so."

"You have not, you have not!"

They whooped and rode imaginary horses; they bumped and slid down the slope to the sand. They took off their shoes and socks and paddled in the grey waves, splashing one another.

A hotel-room key, a car key. Two Yale keys. One was pushed into the lock, and wouldn't turn. The other one was pushed home.

"A lot of things puzzle me," said Patterson, as he unlocked the door of Wanda Derwent's cottage.

Baxter's face suggested that a lot more things puzzled him, not least of which was his superior.

"Miss Slaney's key," the Superintendent said, removing it from the lock. "Derwent said she had it, and she did."

"He seems to have told the truth about most things, sir," said Baxter earnestly, and a little gloomily.

Patterson grunted. "It's all right, Baxter," he said. "I've been convinced that I was wrong about him. But a lot of things puzzle me, all the same. Why would Barbara Slaney bring Wanda Derwent all the way back here to listen to the tape?" he asked. "She'd been in the Sumner house—she must have known there was a hi-fi. But even if she didn't, she had one of these personal stereo things. You've got one. Everyone's got one. You can't move for them. Why bring her back here to listen to it, Baxter?"

Baxter shrugged. "Sir," he said.

"And why was Barbara Slaney driving Wanda Derwent's car, Baxter?"

"Well, I said, sir. She might have—"

"She might have done away with herself in a Mercedes as a final gesture," said Patterson. "Right. Where was the car when she got into it?"

Baxter frowned. "Eddie saw it outside the Sumner house," he said. "So did that witness."

"So Barbara leaves here, and goes to the house—what? To see Derwent?"

"Maybe," said Baxter guardedly. "He says she was supposed to be meeting him. Maybe she got mixed up about where, with being tipsy."

The sky turned slate-grey. Long trails of cloud moved across it, and the sea grew restless. Patterson and Baxter still stood on the doorstep, not entering the cottage.

"How did she get there?"

Baxter deemed it wiser not to attempt an answer.

"Did she drive? But her car wasn't found there, was it? It was found back here." He indicated the clump of bushes. "In there, to be precise," he said.

Baxter's face cleared. "Mrs. Derwent's car was *here*!" he said.

"It should have been, Baxter. It should have been."

Baxter looked petrified.

"Jogging," said Patterson. "That's discipline, Baxter. Keeping fit. Watching your weight." He tapped Baxter's belt buckle, on the last hole. "Running a set distance each day. Ten miles. Five there, five back. That's a stiff regime, isn't it?"

Baxter nodded.

"But she looked good on it, wouldn't you say?" He took his pipe out. "Half her age."

"Yes, sir. I saw the photograph of her. She was lovely." Baxter looked sad.

"But she had done her jogging for Friday. So if she came back here to meet Maxwell, how would she get here? She would have showered, changed. She'd hardly go jogging back, would she? She would take the car."

"Yes," said Baxter, decidedly. "She would."

"But it was Barbara Slaney who was in her car. And the skid marks show that it was being driven from the Sumner place *towards* the cottages—not the other way round."

Eddie Anderson's car drew up, and Patterson smiled. "Eddie," he said, as he got out. "I'm glad you could make it."

Eddie closed the car door and positively strode up to where they stood on the cottage doorstep.

"Right, Eddie," said Patterson. "Show us where you parked when you were watching Mrs. Derwent."

Eddie pointed to the clearing in the bracken. "I always parked there," he said. "But when I came back after lunch on Friday, that pink car was there."

179

"And did Barbara Slaney know that that was where you parked?"

"Yes. She was with Mr. Derwent when they showed me what they wanted me to do. I told them that's where I'd park."

Patterson nodded. "And when you couldn't get back in there on Friday—where did you park then?"

"Down there." Eddie pointed down the row of houses to the other end. "It's the only other place you can park without being seen."

"Show us," said Patterson, leading the way back down the path to Eddie's car. He got in the front; Baxter sat in the back as Eddie drove off slowly, carefully, past the police car, down towards the last house.

"I backed in behind there," said Eddie.

"Do it, Eddie, do it."

Eddie backed the car in, then pushed its nose out from the side of the house.

"That's it," said Eddie. "I watched from here."

"You saw her leave," said Patterson.

"Oh, yes. At three o'clock."

"And what did you do?" Patterson was looking out of the window, not at Eddie.

The bleak sky held grey-edged clouds, underlit by a sudden shaft of sun.

"I phoned Mr. Derwent, and told him she'd left."

Patterson turned to him. "Did he ever tell you why he wanted you to do that?" he asked.

"No. At first, it wasn't him I had to ring. It was the girl." Eddie narrowed his eyes a little. "There was something going on there, if you ask me. I mean, he paid me, but she was the one who hired me, if you see what I mean."

Patterson looked at Baxter.

"I mean, she told me what I had to do and all that. And she said to ring her—he just said I had to do whatever she wanted. But I think they fell out," he said.

"What made you think that?"

"Well, I rang her on the Tuesday . . ."

Patterson held up a hand. "Which Tuesday?"

Eddie opened the glove compartment, and drew out his Filofax. "Two weeks ago," he said. "This is Tuesday, isn't it? Two weeks ago. Tuesday the twenty-fourth of April. Anyway, I rang her as usual, and she said she didn't think there was any point me ringing her any more. I said that Mr. Derwent paid my bill, and I would carry on doing it, and she said that I'd better see Mr. Derwent about that." He closed the notebook. "It was her tone of voice, you know? I don't think they were on speaking terms."

Patterson nodded. "That checks with what Derwent said," he said to Baxter. "Again," he added, his voice irritated.

"So I carried on ringing her until I did see him, on the Sunday. That's when he would pay me. And he said to carry on, but to ring him, because . . ." He opened the notebook again, like a police officer giving evidence in court. " 'I like knowing where my wife is. It gives me a distinct advantage,' " he read. "That's what he said."

Again, Patterson and Baxter exchanged glances.

"And once you had rung him the following Friday, what happened then?" asked Patterson.

"I followed her."

"But she had already left."

"I watched her from the phone box. Then I went back to the car. She jogged along the beach, and I drove along the road. That's what I always did."

"Was she ever out of your sight?" asked Patterson.

"No."

"Not even when you went back to your car from the phone box?"

"If I'd been where I usually parked she would have been out of sight for a second or two. But on Friday she wasn't out of sight at all. I was going the same way as her when I went back to the car."

Patterson looked out at the threatening weather. "So from the moment she left the cottage, till the moment she went into the Sumner place, she was never out of your sight?"

"Till the moment she went in the *door*," said Eddie. "Oh,

181

I had to duck down when she passed the car to go down these steps." He pointed at them as he spoke. "That's all."

The hills, dark shades of green, were losing themselves in the mist of rain as it advanced across the loch.

"Did she always go straight home?" asked Baxter.

"Now and then she went to the Lodge first, and I had to be careful that she didn't see me."

"Do you think she ever did see you?"

Eddie gave the question serious consideration. "No," he said eventually.

"But following her home every night," Baxter persisted. "Her on foot and you in a car. Did she not notice you creeping along the road like that?"

"If you're down on the sand, you can't really see what's on the cliff top, can you?"

"Let's find out," said Patterson. "Go on, Baxter," he said. "You be Mrs. Derwent. Go and jog along the beach."

"Me, sir?"

Patterson smiled, and Baxter sighed, opening the car door. "How far, sir?" he asked.

"Until I tell you."

Baxter looked horrified.

"It'll do you no harm, Baxter!"

The wind blew the clouds through the sunlight; shadows chased over the ground, swift and furtive, as Baxter's burly figure jogged uncomfortably across the road.

Patterson got out of the car, and crossed to the phone box; he watched Baxter as he went down the steps, and began the journey towards the Sumner house. He left the phone box, watching all the time, and got back into the car.

"Right, Eddie," he said.

The car moved slowly along the cliff road, its windscreen wipers working as the rain came on.

"It didn't rain on Friday," said Eddie, earnestly. "I had a clearer view of her than this."

"It rained twice," said Patterson. "Early on, and then a downpour at midnight."

"Oh, I know that," said Eddie. "But it didn't start until

182

seven. It was as clear as a bell when I was following her home. I didn't lose sight of her, Mr. Patterson. Not once."

"No," said Patterson. "Good man."

The hills disappeared as sea and sky became one grey mass, and the panting, perspiring Baxter, cap held in his hand, lumbered along the beach, Eddie's car crawling along above him.

Patterson nodded after a few minutes, and told Eddie to stop. He got out, and looked down with a grin. "All right, Baxter!" he shouted. "You can come up now!"

Baxter stopped thankfully, then looked at the sheer cliff face. "How, sir?" he shouted.

"Jog back again, Baxter!" Patterson said, as the rain began in earnest. "Jog back again!"

Their wet feet were covered with sand as they sat on the beach, and the rain grew too hard to ignore.

"Will we see if we can get into one of the caravans?"

"We'd get caught."

"Who by?"

"That woman might come back."

"You never saw her!"

"I *did*! She was in a caravan."

"It's not right, anyway." The referee, a firm decision, bringing the argument to a close.

The other two subsided, and all three looked at one another.

"Will we explore the cave?"

"Yes! Come on and we'll explore the cave!"

"Explore! It's only a wee hole in the rock." He tried to sound as authoritative as before, but the confidence was gone now that he no longer occupied the moral high ground.

"You're scared."

"I'm not scared! But you can get caught in there if the tide comes in."

"You're scared, you're scared." The chant was taken up by the other. They danced barefoot in the wet sand. "You're scared, you're scared, you're scared."

Baxter got back to the steps, and stood at the bottom catching his breath before tackling them. When he made it to the top, Patterson stood in the rain, shaking his head.

"I'm going to put you on a fitness regime, Baxter," he said. "What if you had to chase someone?"

Baxter couldn't reply.

"A gentle jog for what—half a mile altogether? Look at you, man! Mrs. Derwent did ten miles a day!" He looked Baxter up and down. "My God, Baxter, I could beat you in a sprint, and I'm giving you twenty years. No more biscuits, no more sugar in your tea—weight training, running—we'll have you up to ten miles a day in no time."

Baxter looked appalled, but couldn't muster enough breath to protest.

"Well, Eddie's gone," said Patterson. "A happy man, Baxter. A happy man. I couldn't tell him."

Baxter frowned. "I . . ." He tried to take a deep breath. "I couldn't see the car," he gasped. "And . . ." He puffed. "And there's never any other traffic along here," he said in a rush before he had to breathe again. "I think he's right—no one would see him." He panted with the effort of getting the words out.

"I'm sure he is. But we've all been wrong about one thing, Baxter."

Baxter looked along the wet road, as though it might tell him something, then looked back at Patterson, who smiled.

"Wanda Derwent didn't come back to meet her lover or listen to a tape or anything else," said Patterson.

"No, sir?"

"No." Patterson looked along the road to the cottage. "Because Wanda Derwent never *left*," he said.

CHAPTER TEN

THE SAND WAS POCK-MARKED WITH THE HARD, fast rain as the boys stood looking at the cave.

"I'm *not* scared." He took a step towards the mouth, and stopped. "You come in with me," he said.

They looked at one another.

"Come on! If you're so clever."

All three walked slowly, reluctantly, up to the entrance.

"Hello-o."

The word echoed, and they laughed nervously. The laughter echoed, and their eyes were afraid.

"Go on, then."

They pushed one another, their voices echoing back at them.

"I'm not staying out here getting soaked," said one, resolutely stepping into the narrow mouth. "Come *on*."

"Come *on*," said the echo. "Come *on* . . . come *on* . . . come *on* . . ."

They walked through the rain back to the cottage.

"Think about it, Baxter. Mrs. Derwent's car pointing the wrong way, Eddie having to park further away because Barbara Slaney's car was in his place, Barbara Slaney's shoulder bag still being at the cottage . . ."

Baxter thought, and was given more clues.

185

"Mrs. Derwent's carry-all in the car—only Barbara Slaney's prints in the car . . ."

Baxter thought some more.

"She and Derwent were here just after one," said Patterson. "Derwent left, but she didn't. She stayed, Baxter. And she got rid of Mrs. Derwent once and for all. That's why she had the canvas bag instead of her own. She put her own clothes in it, and then she put on the jogging suit, and left. Illusion, Baxter. Film folk know all about illusion. Eddie saw what he expected to see. A tall, slim blonde in a bright blue jogging suit."

Baxter nodded, his worried frown gradually disappearing. "Right enough, she looked like Mrs. Derwent," he said.

"Derwent's type," said Patterson. "And she was never that close to Eddie except for when she had to pass his car, and of course *he* was the one who didn't want to be seen, so he ducked down at the only time he could have got a good look at her."

"But—" Baxter began.

"She got to the Sumner house, and got in with Wanda Derwent's keys. She left again the minute Eddie was on his way, and drove off in Mrs. Derwent's car—the only person to drive it, you said that yourself. But she had to wait until the time was right. It had to look as though Wanda Derwent had gone back—for something she had forgotten, or whatever. She had to wait, in case anyone saw the car on its way. It had to look right."

Once again, Baxter's frown appeared.

"Spit it out, Baxter," said Patterson.

"But the doctor says Mrs. Derwent was with a man before she died." Baxter opened the cottage door for Patterson.

"Of course she was," said Baxter. "Maxwell. Just before lunch. And she died within two hours."

"But Barbara Slaney wasn't here when Miss Quentin came to see Mrs. Derwent," Baxter said, shaking the rain from his coat, and closing the door.

"She didn't *see* her," said Patterson. "That doesn't mean

186

she wasn't here." He smiled. "Go out again, Baxter, count to ten, and come in."

Baxter looked unenthusiastically at the driving rain, and pulled on his coat again. He stood on the doorstep, rain pounding down, obediently counting to ten, then opened the door to an apparently empty room.

Slowly, the cupboard door swung open, and Patterson stood amongst the brooms and meters. "This was a larder, Baxter," he said. "Look. It's ventilated. You could stay in here for a week if you had to. Forensic went over it with a fine tooth comb—you tell them I want the results fast." He came out. "Barbara Slaney waited until Mrs. Derwent got up to go, came out, picked up the mirror . . ." He shrugged, leaving the sentence unfinished.

"What would be the point of it all, sir? Making it look as though it happened later wasn't going to do her any good?"

"No. But it was going to do Derwent a lot of harm. Especially when she produced whatever story she had in mind about what had happened. She left that tape to incriminate Derwent, not the other way round. She wanted us to think that she and Derwent had been surprised by Mrs. Derwent, and that Derwent killed her. That's what she would have told us. She assumed, like I did, that Derwent had got rid of his copy of the tape, and that we wouldn't believe his story about the blackmail. Luckily for him, he hadn't."

"So she had to go to the Sumner house, and drive the car back, to make it look as though it had all happened after Derwent left the Lodge," said Baxter.

"Which she made sure he would, because she had arranged to meet him." Patterson closed the cupboard door. "She had to drive the car away from the house, because Wanda was supposed to be away to the airport in it, and she couldn't leave it there. So she drove it into the woods, and stayed with it, ready to take it to the cottage. But I think Barbara was panicking, now that she had time to think about what she was doing. And what did Barbara do when she panicked?"

"She took those pills," said Baxter. "But they were sleeping pills," he said. "She'd hardly want to sleep."

"I don't think she wanted just to sleep. The windscreen wipers were going on the car—I'll check it out, but in the meantime I'll take Eddie's word for it that the rain didn't start until seven. Which tallies with when the car was seen in the woods. That means that from when she left the cottage, there was at least four hours before she came back. Why would she wait that long?"

Baxter shook his head.

"I think she did try to kill herself. She panicked, and just wanted to finish it all. She took the stuff out of the capsules to make it work quicker, and she had to have somewhere to do that—there was nothing in the car to open them up, and she'd need water or something to take them. That's why I wanted Forensics to go over the Sumner house, because I think she took the stuff there, and went back to the car to await her fate. But there weren't enough to kill her. Enough to knock her out for a couple of hours, the doctor said. After that she would be able to be roused, but she would be confused and disoriented. I think something woke her."

"The dog, sir. Mr. Watson's dog barked at the car."

Patterson beamed. "And she remembered what she had intended doing, or maybe she was just trying to find her way home, or get help. But when she drove the car, she was still smashed out of her skull, and she drove over a cliff." He took out his pipe. "If she had gone through with it, she would have left Mrs. Derwent's car at the cottage, picked up her own bag, left the canvas bag, and driven off in her own car. The picture would have been complete."

"But how was Derwent's being suspected going to benefit her?" asked Baxter.

"Because she could condemn or save him. And she could name her price."

"Maxwell was just an innocent bystander?"

Patterson nodded. "On this occasion. But he made the

mistake of telling Derwent about himself and Wanda, and he knew that he'd have to get out fast."

Baxter looked out of the window as he thought. "But if she was leaving to go home," he said, "why would she be wearing her jacket? She would put on her jogging suit, not her—" He frowned a little, trying to make out the movement in the distance through the rain-streaked window. He opened it, letting in a blast of wind and rain, and gradually the moving shapes defined themselves into three little boys, running pell-mell towards the police car.

"What's up with them?" he asked, leaving Patterson in the cottage as he went to investigate. Drops of water bounced off the dark blue of his uniform overcoat as he walked to the car, and watched them through the teeming rain.

They came up, faces flushed, legs pounding.

"Hey, hey—where's the fire?" he said, as they almost cannoned into him.

"There's a body," one of them gasped. "There's a body!" He pointed back towards the beach. "In the cave!"

"Is that right?" Baxter looked down the rain-soaked shoreline. "Just the one, is it?" he asked.

"There's a *body*, mister, honest!"

Baxter smiled. "I think Ardcraig's had enough bodies for one week," he said. "Away home, the three of you. You're getting soaked. You shouldn't be playing near that cave anyway. You've let your imagination run away with you."

"There's a *body*! In the cave, honest!"

"What sort of a body?" he asked, with a heavy sigh.

"A man."

"A man?" Baxter crouched down to be on the boy's level.

"He's been battered!" said one of the others.

Baxter frowned. "Has he?" he said, looking round as Patterson came down the path.

"Battered to *death*," said the original spokesman.

"OK," said Baxter, taking off his cap and putting it comically on the youngster's bare head. He stood up, and glanced at Patterson, who had got into the car.

He held the door open for the boys, who piled into the back seat, then got in himself, fastening his seat-belt.

"You show us the body," he said, starting the car.

The sheet was removed.

"Is this the man you knew as Reginald Howard Maxwell, Mr. Derwent?"

F.D. nodded, looking a little shocked. "What . . ." He looked up. "What the hell *happened* to him?" he asked. "He looks as though he's been run over by a tank."

"A tank would have done less damage, Mr. Derwent," said the doctor. "The sea did that."

F.D. was escorted out by Baxter, and the doctor looked at Patterson. "I'll start on this one tomorrow," he said. "How long are you planning on keeping me here?"

Patterson grunted. "How do you think I feel?" he asked.

"Better than him," said the doctor, with a nod towards the body. "Well," he said. "I suggest that we make the best of a bad job. You and your wife must come to the Hamilton for dinner with me tonight."

"Oh, there's no need for you to invite—"

"Nonsense. I don't think it'll measure up, but I'm sure Mrs. Patterson would welcome the break."

"That's very kind of you," said Patterson. "I'll give her a ring." He looked at Maxwell's body. "I don't suppose you can tell me anything now?" he said.

"It looks as though he drowned," said the doctor. "But I can't be a hundred per cent sure of that until I open him up. And I'm still working on your last one, so don't expect miracles."

Patterson closed his eyes. "Don't remind me," he said.

"Mr. Derwent seems to have been doing more than his fair share of identifying corpses," said the doctor. "And, as I told him, the sea did the damage to this one—after death, I'm pretty sure, but I'll confirm that. The tide carried him into the cave—his body would have been flung on to the rocks."

"All of the damage?"

"I'll tell you for sure once I've examined him. But they all look like post-mortem injuries, yes."

"Suicide?"

The doctor shrugged.

Maxwell's room was neat and tidy; the manageress explained that they had used the master key to get in to clean it.

"Never mind," said Patterson. "I didn't expect we'd find much in here anyway."

"What are you looking for?" she asked.

"I don't know," said Patterson, with a candour that took her by surprise.

"Mr. Maxwell left something in the safe," she said. "Do you think you might want that?"

Patterson nodded. "I think I might want anything," he said. "Lead us to the safe, Mrs. Macdonald."

"Oh, Helen, please," she said, coquettishly, and went downstairs ahead of him. "It's some sort of a briefcase," she said. "One of those slim ones. It's an old one."

Patterson looked just a little smug. "And I think I know what's in it," he said to Baxter.

Baxter looked enquiringly at him.

"Two and a half thousand pounds, Baxter," he said. "Taken on a round trip to London."

They followed Helen Macdonald into the room behind reception.

"Won't be two ticks," she said. "I just have to get hold of the key."

Patterson grunted, and waited, listening to the radio programme being broadcast through the Lodge while the safe key was found.

"Now, Robbie . . . who had a number one hit in 1974 with a cover version of this song about a dying man? This is the original, mind. We want to know who had the number one hit in 1974 with a cover version . . ."

Patterson smiled. "I know," he said.

Mrs. Macdonald found the key and opened the safe, pulling out an old burgundy document case, offering it to Patterson, who waved it smilingly on to Baxter.

"Open it, Baxter," he said. "Let's see what's in it."

Baxter had a little trouble with the zip, but he finally got it to move, and withdrew a round, silver-coloured can, which was labelled *Meg and Ivy at Rhyl*.

"Looks like some sort of film, sir," he said, not trying too hard to keep the amusement out of his voice.

"Thanks," said Patterson, a touch put out. "I'll . . ." He searched his pockets for a pen. "I'll give you a receipt, Mrs. Macdonald." He smiled. "Helen," he amended, and looked at Baxter. "I don't think it needs two of us here, Baxter," he said. "You go home and get something to eat, eh? I've got an appointment tonight, so maybe you can go back to the station? These wee boys are coming in to make statements at about eight."

He handed Mrs. Macdonald her receipt, and took Baxter aside, speaking quietly. "Talk to them separately," he said. "Find out what they've seen up there—one of them said they played there quite a lot. See if they've ever seen anything odd going on. But separately, mind—if you talk to them together they'll egg each other on."

"Yes, sir."

Baxter went off, and Patterson made a little sigh of relief. He put the can of film back in the document case and zipped it up.

"Would you care for a wee dram?" she asked, eyebrows arching.

Patterson put the case under his arm, nodding. "That's very kind," he said. "But I'm running a bit late, I'm afraid."

Mrs. Macdonald watched him leave, a disappointed woman.

"Oh, bad luck, Robbie! It was Terry Jacks—see, you remember now, don't you? Four out of five. Close, close, but you just miss out on the LRS Record Quest sweatshirt and mug. Never mind! We'll send you a car sticker to amaze your friends! Well, that was bad luck for Robbie Chapelton there

192

in Lochhead. The national news at eight, but we've a wee while yet to enjoy the sounds. How about this one from the sixties, when we all had flowers in our hair, and now we haven't even got the hair . . .''

The nasal would-be mid-Atlantic tones gave way to music, and Mark Ingram looked up to see John Landers standing beside him.

"Er . . . have you seen Sue?" asked Landers.

"Nope." Mark took a deep gulp of whisky. "I've seen some people," he said, the words slurring. "The Apeman's been here, to say that filming's starting again tomorrow morning. Not one to be put off by a spot of murder, our F.D. He's been here, too, but he didn't stay. And some others. They've put their heads round the door and thought, 'There's Ingram, pissed out of his mind,' and gone into the other bar." He twisted round, almost falling off the barstool. "See? I am alone." He smiled. "So you are excused."

Landers sat down. "I'll stay," he said. He ordered a beer when Mark got his next double. "You look like you could use company," he said. "Who's the Apeman?"

"Stuart. Elevated in view of Howard's demise. Doesn't hang about, doesn't F.D. Instant promotion." He smiled sourly. "Maybe Stuart did it, crazed by the heady thought of moving up to assistant director," he said. "Do you suppose he's got to find a replacement for Barbara? I mean in her non-acting capacity?"

"Why's he called the Apeman?" asked Landers.

Sue Quentin walked slowly through the emptying streets, gleaming with reflected light. Shop-keepers knocked the rain from their awnings and pulled them back, closing up for the night. She watched one small boy run with practised ease from one side of a long window to the other, unhooking the padlocks, leaving them ready on the ground, then shinning up one of the uprights to pull himself on to the metal grid, flexing his knees to jerk it down over the plate glass with his body weight. Then back along the padlocks, snapping them shut, while his father rolled down the door shutter, making it secure. Together, they got into the car that sat outside and drove off.

She stood outside the closed shop and watched as the car made its way home through the rainy night and the traffic. When its rear lights could no longer be distinguished from the others, she moved on.

Patterson pulled up outside the cottage, and switched off the engine and the lights. There was silence, except for the wind and the dark, heaving sea; darkness except for a dozen stars shining through the drifting clouds. He walked quietly, almost stealthily up the path, and let himself into the cottage.

His eye on the door, like a burglar, he used torchlight to find his way across the room to the desk, opened the drawer, and pulled out the slim files. He sorted through them quickly, drawing one out; he gave another glance at the door before replacing the rest of the files, closing the drawer, extinguishing the torch, and leaving. The door clicked shut, and he walked quickly back down the path, and drove off towards the tiny station normally manned by Baxter.

THIS STATION IS CLOSED BETWEEN 6:00 P.M. AND 8:00 A.M. the notice on the door read. ENQUIRIES TO ARDCRAIG POLICE STATION, EMERGENCIES DIAL 999.

He unlocked the door, and allowed himself the luxury of a light as he removed two sheets of paper from the file, tearing them up and putting the pieces in his pocket. He deposited the file in the desk in the office, looked at the clock, and raised his eyes to heaven.

Light out, door locked, and he was back in his car, driving fast into the empty, quiet town, his car engine sounding like an intrusion. It took a while to find a space in the Hamilton's tiny car park; he swore under his breath as he shunted backwards and forwards to try to park in a space not large enough. A group of people came out, calling noisily to one another. He waited for them to get into their cars and leave.

"Come on, come *on*," he said, his fingers drumming on the steering wheel.

194

At last, he got the space, parked, and went into the hotel where his wife had at least found the doctor.

"I must apologise," he said. "Traffic. You'd hardly credit it, would you?"

The tough voice sang tender words to a solo piano accompaniment. Knowing she was loved might just be all she needed to know. The music faded, and the jingle played. *"Keep abreast with LRS . . . LRS national news!"* Urgent music heralded the newsreader. *"LRS News at Eight with Norma Reay."*

"Why don't you go and enjoy yourself somewhere?" Mark asked.

"A night of fierce shelling in Beirut has left . . ."

John Landers smiled. "Maybe I felt like some company too," he said.

"Company?" said Mark. "The company has gone, John. It's like *Ten Little Niggers*—who's going to be next? You— me? Where *is* Sue?"

"Don't talk like that!"

"No. Sorry."

". . . this is the third tragedy to hit the production since filming started in April of this year. Mr. Maxwell was being sought by . . ."

"Put that thing *off*!" roared Mark, and somewhere, someone obeyed. "And let's have some service here!"

"How long had he been in the water?" asked Patterson, as he picked up his knife and fork.

His wife shot a look at him, which he ignored.

"I'd hazard a guess if you can tell me when high tide was," said the doctor, cutting into his steak.

"Elevenish," said Patterson.

"And the boys found him at about two o'clock, they think?"

Patterson nodded.

"Well, from the state of the—"

"Do you think," said Mrs. Patterson, "that it would be asking too much for this not to be discussed at the table?"

"I do beg your pardon," said the doctor.

"Och, ignore her. When?"

"I'll be able to be more accurate when I've done a proper examination," he said, with a slightly nervous look at Mrs. Patterson. "But I'd say over twelve hours—maybe nearer twenty-four."

"So yesterday evening would be a fair enough assumption—until further notice?"

"Oh, I think yesterday evening's probably all you'll end up with."

"Right," said Mrs. Patterson. "Now you know that, can we just eat this meal in peace?"

"Yes, dear," said Patterson, and pushed his chair from the table. "I just have to make a quick phone call, that's all."

"The woman in *Stones*?" queried Baxter, snaking a look at the office clock.

"Whatsername," said the boy, helpfully.

"He means—" began the child's mother.

Baxter held up a hand. "Let him tell me," he said gently.

"Oh, here, maybe he was going to attack her too," she said. "And she just—"

Baxter frowned slightly.

"She's the boss," supplied the child. "You know. She's got a diamond place."

"Susan Quentin?" asked Baxter, raising his voice a little as the rain began to lash the window.

The boy looked blank and the phone rang. "Excuse me," said Baxter, picking it up.

"Oh, hello, sir. Are you not supposed to be—? Oh, I see. Yes. Yes. Oh, right. Yes, right, I will." He pulled open the drawer and took out a notepad. "Yes," he said, writing down the times. "Got that. Yes, sir." He replaced the phone, and made to close the drawer, but his eye was caught on a file labelled SUSAN QUENTIN. Frowning, he pulled it out. The picture of her posing in front of Cartier fell out, and he smiled, picking it up and showing it to the child.

"Is that her, Terry?" he asked.

"Yes. The one that's got the diamond place," he said, clearly now realising that he was speaking to an idiot.

"And she was in one of the caravans at the location just before you and the others found the body?"

"Mr. Baxter, it's getting awful late. It's after nine o'clock. Can he not tell you this in the morning? He got an awful fright, finding that man."

"I'll be finished with him in no time, Mrs. Callaghan." He smiled. "Were you the only one who saw her, Terry?"

He nodded. "They didn't believe me," he said. "Just because I didn't see her yesterday. They said I was making it up. But she was there. She told me not to play there."

Baxter licked his lips slightly. "Yesterday?" he said. "Did the others see her yesterday, then?"

"*Said* they did." Terry was skeptical.

"And were you with them?"

"I was hiding. I was hiding today as well, but—"

"What time yesterday?"

He shrugged.

"Same time as today?"

"No. It was dark."

Mrs. Callaghan aimed an ineffectual slap at her son's shoulder. "What have I told you about playing up at that cliff in the dark?" she demanded.

"About this time of night?"

"No," he said scornfully, before his mother could protest at the implication. "About half past seven. They sometimes film then. They let you watch if you keep quiet."

"But they weren't filming yesterday, were they?"

"No."

Baxter nodded, and let the Callaghans go. Then he phoned his wife, apologised, and pulled on his coat.

* * *

The girl appeared, and served Mark yet another. Landers sipped beer and watched as Mark addressed the glass, weighing it up, like a golfer considering a shot.

"Do you have a problem with alcohol?" he asked.

"No." Mark knocked the whisky back. "See? No problem at all." He coughed, and fumbled for his cigarettes. "I'm not an alcoholic," he said. "But then, I'd say that if I was, wouldn't I?"

"I guess."

"I get drunk. Not the same thing. Quite different. I don't have to drink. I choose to."

"And you could choose not to?"

"Sure. Why would I, though? You don't have to stay here and watch."

"That's OK."

"No." Mark tried to get up, and thought better of it. "It's the legs," he said. "They don't work. So I can't leave and I just have to drink more."

His eyes went past Landers to where Simon Waterford stood in the doorway. He looked unsteadily at him. "Is it Friday already?" he asked.

"No."

"Shouldn't you be south of the border? Don't you have a proper job during the week?"

"I heard about Wanda on the news," said Simon. "I thought you might . . ." He tailed off. "I came up as soon as I could."

"And have you heard about Howard?" Mark thumped the bell. "Have you heard about Howard on the news? Howard who isn't Howard—Howard who isn't anyone any more?" With a smile, Mark offered his empty glass to the girl, and she looked worriedly at John, who indicated that she might as well give him more.

"And whatever my friends are having," said Mark.

The wind brought high waves crashing down on the rocks beneath as Sue Quentin, too close to the edge of the cliff for safety, stood and watched, drenched by rain and spray. The sea roared, inching up the cliff face.

Her foot moved tentatively even closer to the edge, and she closed her eyes. Wind swirled round her, tugging at her. She sank to her knees, sitting on her ankles, and clenched her fists round clumps of long grass, pulling them out. Her body swayed as her hands came up, and the grass was whipped away. She lifted herself from her ankles, leaning out over the edge, eyes screwed shut, but the wind had dropped, and she opened her eyes to the dark surging sea. She threw her head back, shouting something that couldn't be heard over the pounding waves, bringing her fists down with all her force on the ground.

"She's out at the moment," said the girl.

Baxter looked a little nonplussed. "When are you expecting her back?" he asked.

"I don't think she said."

Baxter wiped rain from his face. "I'd better wait."

"Here?" she said. "I don't think Mrs. Macdonald would like that very much. A policeman in the foyer. It sounds like Moscow."

"Thanks a lot."

"You know what I mean! Anyway, you're soaking wet. Come on through and get dry. Would you like some supper?"

Baxter looked wistfully into the cosy back room. "Yes," he said. "But . . ." He shook his head. "No, I ought to stay here. Watch for her coming back."

"She's either going to come back or she isn't," the girl pointed out. "If she sees you sitting there she might turn round and go away again."

"That's true," said Baxter, cheered.

The bell rang from the bar.

"Just go through," she said. "I'll be back in a minute—that's just to top up Mark Ingram. And I'll get the kitchen to bring you something to eat."

* * *

"What the hell's going on?" Simon asked. The question was directed at the sober one of his companions, but he didn't get the chance to reply.

"God knows," said Mark, offering up his empty glass to the girl, who exchanged it for the double she had already poured and then went back to reception. "Or F.D.," said Mark. "Same thing. Isn't it? Same thing. God and F.D. He's invited us here to bump us off, one by one."

"John?" Simon's tone held a plea for rational comment.

"Don't ask me," said Landers. "They don't know that anyone killed Howard. Maybe he just couldn't face what was going to happen."

"Balls," said Mark. "What *was* going to happen? Then, they would have hanged him just for being in the same street as the guy who pulled the trigger, but now? What was going to happen to him twenty-seven years after the event? The courts aren't so blood-thirsty now. Even the police don't think he knew this other guy was carrying a gun. What was going to happen to him? I'll tell you. Prison—maybe. But he's an American citizen now. So . . . maybe not. And how long for? A couple of years. Maybe. He's ah—he *was* a nice guy. A jury would have liked him. He didn't kill himself. You mark my words, he didn't kill himself."

Simon drew a breath, but Mark hadn't finished.

"And—and do you know *how* he got found out? Mm? Do you? Because he told F.D. that he'd slept with Wanda, that's how. F.D. was here, bragging about it. No one took advantage of him and got away with it, et cetera, et cetera. Who knew that better than John the Baptist, eh?"

Simon and John exchanged baffled looks.

"So why did he admit it? I'll tell you. Because he was tired of jumping when F.D. said jump. He was serious about Wanda—so he told the truth. It couldn't hurt her any more— F.D. couldn't hurt her. So he told the truth. But he didn't kill himself."

"What are the police doing?" asked Simon, when he could get a word in.

Landers opened his mouth.

"What you'd expect," said Mark, running the words together. "They're crawling all over Howard's room now. They're asking questions." He stubbed out his cigarette. "They're waiting to talk to poor Sue because I saw her leave with Maxwell yesterday. I saw that cop arriving. He's gone in the back with the receptionist, but I saw him. I know why he's here."

"I don't think we head the popularity poll," Landers said, when Mark had subsided into silence. "Especially not with the Lodge. Bringing all this with us."

"One by one," said Mark. "One by one." He picked up his glass, and looked at Simon through the amber liquid. "They don't like it, because they don't know who'll be next," he said. "They don't know who to trust. Neither do you."

"Oh, for God's—"

"Maybe I'm a mad axeman," said Mark, cheerfully, and passed out, neatly, his head resting on the bar.

"Asking Dr. Dalziel about dead bodies when he's trying to eat his dinner! He didn't invite us there so that he could carry on working."

Patterson slowed down as the rain grew wilder. "Toby didn't mind," he said. "You're the one who minds."

"I should think so! Who wants to hear about someone's organs when they're eating? And turning up half an hour late—traffic! There's never any traffic in Ardcraig in the evening—the man's not daft, Hugh!"

"Oh, give it a rest," he said, tiredly.

She didn't. "And getting up from the table to make a phone call—honestly, Hugh, you've got no idea."

He sighed, loudly. "Baxter was going to be talking to those kids," he said. "They play up there all the time. I wanted him to know what times were relevant. I've got a murder enquiry, remember. That's more important than a dinner date."

"Well, if you were listening to the man you know that he said he could have gone into the sea anywhere along that stretch of coast," she said. "The current would have carried him towards the cave anyway."

Patterson slowed down to negotiate a flood, and drove out of it, testing his brakes gingerly before speaking again. "They go up there to play," he said. "You can see for miles along the coast from there."

"And have you got poor Laurence working all hours too?"

Patterson sighed. "I don't tell you how to run the house, do I?"

John tiptoed across the room and opened the bedroom door as quietly as he could.

"You're not going?" said the voice from the bed. "We could have a party."

"Yes," he said, smiling. "I'm going."

"Simon?" Mark asked, his eyes barely open. "You'll stay, won't you?"

Simon sighed a little. "Yes," he said, looking at John. "I'll stay."

John lifted a hand in salute, and let himself quietly out, closing the door with some relief, only to find himself looking at Sue, mascara streaked down her face, her hair dripping, her face white.

"What's happened?" he asked, alarmed.

"I got caught in the rain," she said, her voice light and airy, as she passed him.

"Don't give me that!" He was angry; he went after her, and caught her arm, forcing her to turn and look at him. "Where have you been?" he said. "I've been worried about you!"

She didn't seem to take that in for a moment. She frowned slightly.

"Where have you *been*?" he asked again.

"What do you mean, you were worried about me?"

"What do you think I mean?"

She looked up at him. "I was trying to . . ." She didn't finish the sentence.

"Trying to what?" he demanded.

"Throw myself in the sea, just like Howard."

"What?" Landers was horrified. He looked down the corridor as heavy footsteps came upstairs, and looked at her. "It's the police," he said. "Mark says they're waiting for you."

She closed her eyes, and her shoulders drooped. "Oh, no," she said. "I can't talk to them now."

John stood for an agonised second, still holding her arm, hearing the footsteps. He looked at the shadow of the peaked cap on the stair wall, and looked back at Sue. Then he swallowed and pushed her back along the corridor.

"My room," he mouthed at her, then put a finger to his lips.

"Key," she mouthed back, as the heavy tread grew closer and more laboured.

"It's open." He motioned to her to get in, sprinted back along the corridor, and was walking towards his room again as Baxter reached the top of the steep steps, out of breath.

"Good evening," said Landers.

"Evening," said Baxter, and stopped at Sue Quentin's door, knocking quietly. "Would you know if she's back, sir?" he asked.

John shook his head. "Sorry," he said, opening his own door. "I've just come up."

"Only we thought we heard the front door a few minutes ago," said Baxter.

"Ah. That would probably have been Mr. Waterford leaving," said Landers.

"Oh." Baxter sighed. "Well, I'll wait a bit longer downstairs," he said. "Goodnight, sir."

"Goodnight," said Landers, going into his room.

Mrs. Patterson murmured a little in her sleep, and turned over, waking herself up. "Are you still at it?" she said, sitting up.

Patterson glanced at her, and removed the headphones, putting them round his neck. "What did you say?" he asked.

"It's quarter to three!" she said, her hand on the alarm clock.

"Don't worry," he said. "Go back to sleep."

"I can't sleep properly with the light on."

He switched it off. "I can listen in the dark," he said.

"Oh, Hugh! I wish you'd do your work in working hours like everyone else!"

He grunted in the darkness. "No such thing as working hours," he said. "Mark Ingram was right about these tapes." He sighed, rubbing his eyes. "Mrs. Derwent was a very bitter lady," he added. "And she was making herself a lot of enemies."

She sat up. "Hugh Robert Patterson," she said. "You have been impossible all night. What's wrong?"

"Nothing. Go back to sleep."

"What's *wrong*, Hugh?"

Patterson unhooked the headphones from his neck and put the Walkman on the table by the bed. "How would you feel if I got the sack?" he asked.

She put on the light and looked at him. "Why would you get the sack?" she asked.

He inspected some minute blemish on the palm of his hand, and half smiled. "I destroyed some evidence tonight," he said.

"Why would you do that?" she asked quietly.

"It was two letters," he said. "They seemed to me to be surplus to requirements. They concern an item which may possibly constitute a motive for murder—but since we have the item in our possession, we hardly need bits of paper telling us what it is." He looked at her for the first time. "Or it has nothing to do with it," he said. "In which case the letter drawing people's attention to it would hurt someone unnecessarily."

"Susan Quentin," she said.

He nodded.

She thought for a moment. "Do I have anything else to worry about as far as she's concerned?" she asked. "Apart from your getting the sack over her?"

He smiled, shaking his head.

"Then I hope you're clever enough not to get the sack," she said.

"So do I." He smiled again. "Morag," he said. "Seeing as you're awake . . ."

"It's far too late," she said. "You've got your work in the morning."

He smiled, putting his arm round her. "Baxter isn't going to give me a hundred lines," he said.

"At least one of us has to be crazy."

Sue Quentin looked up at the ornate ceiling, lit by the orange light from the street lamp on the estate road which ran below the window.

Landers didn't reply, but he wasn't asleep. He smiled, and twisted a strand of her hair in his fingers.

"My room doesn't have a light shining into it," she said. "You should complain."

"I like it," he said. "It's like a night light."

She smiled. "Do you need a night light?" she asked.

"Doesn't everyone, sometimes?"

Sue sighed.

"Why does one of us have to be crazy?" he asked.

"A one-night stand? With someone old enough to be your mother? If you're not crazy, then I am."

"My mother's fifteen years older than you," he said.

Shadows shifted in the room as the wind moved the branches of the trees in and out of the path of the light.

"Is that what it is?" he asked. "A one-night stand?"

"Isn't it?"

"I don't know," he said. "I didn't plan for it to happen. But now it has . . ."

She sat up on one elbow and looked down at him. "You *plan*," she said, "to get married in the fall. You've told us often enough."

"No," he said. "Not any more."

Sue's eyes widened slightly. "Not because of this," she said quickly.

"No." He took her hand in his. "When we got back here on Friday, there was a letter waiting for me." He smiled, and sighed. "And it really did begin Dear John," he said. "She was going to tell me before I left the States, but she thought that wouldn't be fair, since I would be concerned

205

about this big part in the movie, so she waited. But she wanted me to know before I got home.''

Sue nodded slowly. "So that's why I'm here," she said.

"No," he said quietly. "I don't expect you to believe that, but it's true. You see, I tried to feel angry and hurt and cheated and all the stuff you're supposed to feel, but I didn't. I just felt relieved."

"It was Barbara you were looking for," Sue reminded him gently.

"I wanted to ask her advice," he said. "About you."

She frowned a little.

"She knew how I felt about you. But I didn't think I could go back on my commitments." He smiled. "She thought *that* was crazy."

"But I had no—"

"That's why I was so bad at the love scene," he said. "They say you shouldn't have any real emotional involvement, don't they? Anyway, I wanted to ask her what she thought you'd do if I told you. When she wasn't there, and you were on your own . . . I tried to get up the courage, but—"

"But what?"

"I thought you'd laugh at me."

She looked at him for a long time. "Oh, John," she said. "If we go on seeing each other, everyone will laugh at you. They'll call you Mr. Quentin the Fourth and make jokes about pacifiers and diapers—you don't know what they're like."

He squeezed her hand. "Oh, I won't mind that if you don't," he said. "I don't care who laughs, as long as you take me seriously." He kissed her. "Everyone who's anyone has a toy boy," he said, with a smile.

"They're not usually international film stars," she pointed out. "The press will have a field day."

"No—they're usually gold-diggers," he said. "I think I start from a better position."

She lay back down. "Like I said," she murmured, "at least one of us is crazy."

CHAPTER ELEVEN

MARK INGRAM OPENED HIS EYES TO DAYLIGHT, looked at Simon Waterford, and closed them again.

"I'm going to stop getting drunk," he said.

"Because you keep waking up with me?"

Mark sighed. "Yes," he said, and pulled his legs out of bed, reaching over to where his clothes were neatly folded on the chair. "What happened this time?"

"Nothing," said Simon.

"I mean," said Mark, pulling on his clothes, "how come you're here?"

Simon sat up. "You really don't remember?" he asked.

Mark looked at himself in the mirror and shuddered. "I remember talking to John," he said. "Maybe I remember you being there. I don't know."

"You passed out. John and I got you upstairs."

Mark pushed his shirt into his trousers. "Look," he said, "you're not obliged to put me to bed. You're not obliged to stay with me."

"I stay because you ask me to," said Simon.

"I ask because I'm drunk!"

Simon shook his head. "You ask because you're lonely," he said.

"I'm *drunk* because I'm lonely. I ask because I'm drunk." Mark sat heavily on the bed. "Simon, I like you. You're a nice guy." He turned to look at him. "But all we have in common is that we're both gay. And I . . ." He turned away. "I'm sorry," he said. "I've had a rough week."

Simon smiled. "A bit of an understatement," he said.

"Yes." Mark pushed himself off the bed.

"Would you mind if I got a room here?" Simon asked.

Mark shrugged. "They've got one or two to spare," he said. "I'll see you downstairs."

Sue Quentin smoked nervously, without a cigarette holder, at the breakfast table. Her nails were unpolished, her face naked of make-up. She had a croissant that she wasn't eating, and a pot of coffee that she was emptying. She poured the last of it into her cup, and asked for another.

John Landers pushed a kipper about his plate. "Do you think Derwent will join us?" he asked. "He stayed here last night."

"Please God he doesn't," said Sue.

Landers nodded solemnly, and ate some kipper. "Do you think Mark should join AA or something?" he asked.

She exhaled smoke, shaking her head.

"He passed *out*," said Landers.

"Mark's frightened," said Sue.

"Of what?"

She smiled a little sadly. "Everything," she said, stubbing out her cigarette.

"Are you all right?"

"No," she said. "I'm frightened too."

He ate some more kipper. "Why don't you tell me what it is you're frightened of?" he asked.

She didn't answer.

"Why didn't you wake me this morning?"

"I didn't want to disturb you." Her coffee arrived; she poured herself another cup, strong and black.

"I don't get it," he said. "Why are we behaving like strangers?"

"Because that's what we are."

He dropped his fork on to his plate. "No!" he protested. "Last night, you—"

"Last night was last night." She nodded at the window. "That's the cold light of day."

He dropped his eyes from hers. "You don't think you can feel the same about me," he said.

She lit another cigarette. "Of course I could," she said. "You're the first man for years who has genuinely cared for me. It would be easy."

"Well?"

"I don't want you to get hurt."

He leant over. "Do you think those cretins who write garbage in the papers can *hurt* me?" he whispered fiercely.

"I can hurt you."

"How?" he demanded.

She stubbed out her cigarette, barely started, and lit another. "I could humiliate you," she said. "And that would be the worst thing anyone could do to you. I know you, John. I know you much, much better than you think I do."

Landers frowned, then saw Mark, unshaven, unkempt, his shirt hanging out a little at the front.

"Don't look at me like a puppy, please, John," he said. "You'll be pleased to hear that I am not going to get drunk any more as from today."

"Good," said Landers, unconvinced.

"My bathroom isn't free, or I would have made more of an attempt to look human," he said. He smiled at Sue. "You should leave off the warpaint more often, Sue. You're even lovelier without it."

"You are," said John. "It's true."

She managed a smile, as the waitress took Mark's order.

"I'll have the full English breakfast this morning, Winnie," said Mark.

John looked worried again. "Are you sure?" he said. "You had an awful lot to drink last night."

"I'm sure," said Mark. "Today is the first day of the rest of my life, and I am going to start it with the full English breakfast." He smiled. "Then I'm going to have a bath, and shave and dress, and try to remember who I am."

"Do you think," said a voice from behind him, "you

could spare me a few minutes of your time when you've done all that?''

Mark twisted round to see Superintendent Patterson. "Hugh," he said. "What a pleasant surprise. Or am I being arrested?''

"No, nothing like that," said Patterson. "But I would like to talk to you—would that be all right? I might take up a fair bit of your time, I'm afraid."

Mark saw his eyes go past him, to Sue. He glanced over; she was smoking, drinking coffee, not looking at anyone.

"Miss Quentin," Patterson said. "I'm glad you're here. My constable tried to have a word with you last night—we were both a bit worried that you hadn't returned to the Lodge."

"No need," said Sue.

"Obviously not," said Patterson. "Will you be available later for a wee chat with the Detective Constable?"

"We're filming this morning," she said.

"Will it be all right if he comes to see you there?" he asked.

She nodded. "We're filming at some disused church," she said. "But it's quite close to the trailers—he can see me between takes, I suppose."

"This morning will be fine for me," said Mark. "I've got all the time in the world."

"I'll give you a couple of hours to organise the first day of the rest of your life," said Patterson. "I'll be back to pick you up."

"Good," said Mark. "What brings you here at the crack of dawn anyway?"

Patterson smiled. "I was up before the wife," he said. "Mrs. Macdonald very kindly offered to feed me."

"What an admission. You can't have breakfast if your wife isn't up?"

"She won't even tell me how the cooker works," he said, and looked at Landers. "Are *you* married, Mr. Landers?"

"No," he said.

210

"But he's to be married in the fall, isn't that right, John?" said Mark.

Mark looked at Sue. "Yes," he said. "Sue and I are to be married in the fall."

Patterson's mouth fell open, Mark beamed, and John looked defiantly at Sue, who got up and left the dining room.

"I think your technique needs some—" Mark began.

John didn't listen. He got up and ran after her, following her out of the Lodge, into the garden where watery sunlight was breaking through the clouds.

"Go away," she said, as he caught up with her.

"No."

She turned. "Why did you have to say that?"

"Because I'm going to make it come true," he said.

"Don't say it to anyone else. Do you understand? They won't repeat it. Just don't say it to anyone else."

He smiled, shaking his head. "I want everyone to know," he said.

"I *mean* it!"

He caught her shoulders. "Are you ashamed of me?" he asked.

She closed her eyes.

"You said you loved me," he said.

"We were making love," she snapped. "What else do you say?"

He let her go. "I don't believe it was like that," he said.

"Just promise me that you won't tell anyone else that we're getting married," she said.

"All right." He put his head to one side. "Does that mean we are?" he asked.

She shook her head. "One step at a time," she said.

The water splashed into the basin as the doctor washed; he shook his hands and pulled a paper towel from the dispenser. "Drugs and alcohol," he said. "But died by drowning. Just like Slaney."

"*Just* like her?" asked Patterson.

211

"Exactly like her. Right down to the sleeping pills minus their capsules."

"According to young Landers, they were Barbara's pills," said Patterson.

"But you didn't find the bottle in her possession, did you? Or anywhere else."

"No—but the lab's just confirmed that there were traces of barbiturates on the worktop in the Sumners' kitchen, not to mention Barbara Slaney's fingerprints on the back door."

"So how did Maxwell get hold of them if they were hers?"

"Are you saying *he* killed Barbara?"

The doctor shrugged. "Well, it wasn't the other way around," he said. "Anyway," he carried on, shepherding Patterson to the Perspex doors, "we don't have to stay in here."

In the more welcoming surroundings of the empty day room, Patterson was given a plastic cup of machine coffee, and some more detail.

"What about Maxwell himself? Suicide?"

"Well," said the doctor. "There are a number of reasons to wonder about it being suicide. One is that you don't take sleeping pills in order to jump off a cliff—the two actions are totally incompatible. On the one hand, you're trying to slip out of the world peacefully, and on the other you're ending it all with a flamboyant gesture."

Patterson nodded agreement.

"Two is that I can't see why he would park his car in the town, and then go all the way back to the cliff to do himself in."

"No," said Patterson. "I was having a bit of difficulty with that."

"And the other is—we can't find his glasses."

"What?"

"I asked your lot to look in his room. We've searched the car. They're not in any of his pockets. The case was, but his glasses weren't in it."

Patterson frowned. "Couldn't they have come off in the sea?"

212

"Almost certainly did, Hugh." The doctor smiled. "It's a sweeping generalisation, and nothing like as compelling as the first two reasons, but the fact is that suicides tend to remove their glasses before they jump."

"Do they?" Patterson smiled.

"Oh, yes. You see, suicide is something people prepare for. They don't just see a cliff edge and think, 'There's the edge of a cliff, I'll throw myself over,' they get themselves ready. And people who wear glasses tend to take them off and put them away. He obviously kept his in a case in his pocket, and they're not there."

Patterson filled his pipe. "Are you seriously asking me to believe that Maxwell murdered Barbara—in the Sumner house, no less—and then was murdered himself by someone else altogether?"

"I would say that that is a possibility that shouldn't be dismissed," said the doctor.

"But Landers told me they were Barbara's own pills," said Patterson again, frowning. "Why would he say that if they weren't? How would he know about them at all if they were Maxwell's?"

"Maybe you shouldn't accept what he says as gospel. He might have an interest to protect."

"Landers? What connection could he have with any of it?"

"I don't know. But if I were you, I'd start looking long and hard for that pill bottle."

"It'll be at the bottom of the sea, if someone's bumping people off with the contents," said Patterson. He struck a match and puffed silently for a few moments. "Anything to confirm that it *was* Maxwell who was with Mrs. Derwent before she died?" he asked, almost as though the question was of no importance.

"I've sent off samples," said the doctor. "But it'll be a couple of days before we know."

"In the good old days you could hazard an opinion," said Patterson.

"Sometimes. Only sometimes. If the circumstances were

right. Which in this case they aren't. In the good old days, I'd have told you that I had an idea. Now, you'll know for sure by the weekend.'' He paused. ''Maxwell saw her just before lunch, didn't he?'' he asked. ''If it was him,'' he went on, without waiting for confirmation, ''she has to have been killed almost immediately after she came back from lunch.''

''The jacket,'' said Patterson, his eyes widening slightly.

''What?''

''Baxter wanted to know why she was wearing her jacket. If she had just come back from lunch, then—'' He broke off, almost flustered. ''But perhaps it wasn't Maxwell who was with her,'' he said quickly. ''And who's to say it wasn't Landers, if we're looking for his interest in the matter?'' he muttered, almost to himself. ''He seems to prefer the more mature woman.''

The doctor sorted out change and went to the other machine. ''Do you want a biscuit, or something?'' he asked.

''No, thanks.'' Patterson stared into space as he worked something out. Whatever it was seemed to depress him; he shook his head, arguing with himself.

The doctor pressed buttons, and nothing happened. ''Come on, you bitch,'' he said to the machine, pressing the buttons again.

Blue sky, now. Long folds of white clouds. Patterson gave a long sigh as he smoked.

''Oh, I think we'll find it was Maxwell she was with, all right,'' said the doctor, as something clunked into the reservoir. He took it out. ''It's not what I wanted,'' he said. ''But I suppose it's better than nothing.'' He sat down. ''There's the private detective's report, for one thing. And Derwent says Maxwell confessed to him, doesn't he?''

Patterson puffed smoke. ''He could be lying,'' he said.

''Why would he want to do that?''

''If he's involved.''

The doctor unwrapped his chocolate bar. ''You mean if he murdered him?''

''It's a possibility that shouldn't be dismissed,'' said Patterson, with a half smile.

214

"Not if your switch theory's right, it isn't—and I think we'll find that it is. Anyway, why would he make up something that gave him a motive?"

"I'm just saying he could be lying. We've only got his word for it. For a lot of things, come to that." He took his pipe out of his mouth, and looked at it a little sadly. "Someone murdered Mrs. Derwent," he said. "There's no doubt at all about that."

"Why have you written Maxwell off just because someone's done him in?" the doctor asked. "Barbara Slaney could have decoyed away the detective to let Maxwell meet Mrs. Derwent in secret."

Patterson shook his head. "I doubt that Barbara was helping Mrs. Derwent to have an affair," he said. "She wanted her out of the way, remember."

"So did Maxwell. Maybe he and Barbara Slaney were in cahoots," persisted the doctor.

Patterson smiled. "Maybe," he said. "But I don't believe he killed Wanda Derwent, whatever Shaw thinks. And you don't think he killed himself, so . . ." He shrugged. "I'm looking for a murderer still," he said.

"What makes you so certain one person did them all? If Maxwell did kill Mrs. Derwent he might have felt it necessary to get rid of Barbara before she told the police what her role in the affair was. Then he goes to London and comes back next morning. He's interviewed by the police, and he has to work on the Sunday, all before Mrs. Derwent is even found. I can imagine he might have felt the need for sleeping pills. He'd asked not to be disturbed, hadn't he, when Derwent rang him? So say he'd taken the stuff by then. If someone happened along just at that moment, whoever that was might well have taken advantage of his dulled reactions."

"Derwent says someone did happen along," said Patterson, dully.

"Well?"

"He's a liar. I'm sure of it."

"All you've found out shows that he's telling the truth."

"So Maxwell's murder is a coincidence?" Patterson looked scornfully at the doctor.

"Who's talking about coincidence? It could all have the same root cause. You sound like a man who doesn't want to go the way the evidence is pointing," he said.

"I think it does all have the same root cause," said Patterson, heavily. "But I don't believe Howard Maxwell killed Wanda Derwent."

"Why?"

"Because he went to London to collect a film," he said.

"Eh?"

"London was a very dangerous place for Maxwell to go," said Patterson. "Anyone could have seen him, informed on him. He knew that. If he'd been establishing an alibi, or getting away from the scene of the crime, he'd have chosen anywhere on this earth but London."

"Ugh, this is disgusting." The doctor took another bite. "Then why *did* he go to London?" he asked, with his mouth full. "If it was so dangerous?"

"Because there was going to be trouble, and Mrs. Derwent didn't have his street wisdom," said Patterson. "He was afraid she would get hurt." He tapped his pipe out in the ashtray. "He risked his freedom for her. And he risked it again when he told Derwent that he and Wanda had been lovers. He didn't murder her." He stood up. "It might sound corny," he said, "but I think Mr. Maxwell had discovered a new set of values."

"It does." The doctor finished his chocolate bar and screwed up the paper, lobbing it neatly into the bin. "And look where it got him."

"He was tired of running." Patterson picked up his cup and dropped it into the bin. "Could someone have given him the drugs in a drink without his noticing?" he asked.

The doctor pulled a face. "Yes," he said. "Not in a vintage wine, I shouldn't think. But in plonk or an average whisky, or a cup of strong coffee—you'd just think it was a bit bitter."

"Right," said Patterson.

216

"Is something falling into place?"

"I think I'm getting there," said Patterson, grimly. "I hope I'm not, though. As you say, I don't like the way the evidence is pointing."

The film was threaded into the projector.

"It's old film," said Mark. "I can't guarantee the quality."

"Label's new," said Patterson gruffly.

"So it is," said Mark, squinting down at the can. "How clever of you to notice."

"It's my job to notice."

"Don't the police have access to film projectors?"

"They do." Patterson pulled the thick curtain across the first window. "Is that all right?" he asked. "Can you still see what you're doing?"

"Yes, but don't do the other one yet." Mark worked for a moment or two. "What made you pick on me?" he asked.

Patterson walked to the other window. "A little bird told me that you know everything there is to know about film. You can do any job in the business, from operating the camera to operating the projector, she said. You've even got a little cinema in your London *pied-à-terre* to show—what are they called?—out-takes?"

Mark smiled. "Do I detect disapproval?" he asked. "I like to have a London base."

"No, no," said Patterson. "Nice work, if you can get it. Which do you regard as home? London or Los Angeles?"

"Why?"

"I'm interested."

"Los Angeles," he said, then looked up at him. "So how come you know everything about me all of a sudden?" He gave a grim little smile. "Of course," he said. "Wanda. You have listened to the tapes now, I take it."

"I have. Mrs. Derwent said that you've been film-struck since you were five years old," said Patterson.

"It's true."

"Have you ever thought of directing?"

217

Mark smiled. "Are you suggesting that once everyone knows I'm gay, I'll be finished as an actor?"

Patterson looked surprised. "I can think of a good many actors it hasn't finished," he said.

Mark lit a cigarette. "Maybe they were better than me," he said.

"Maybe they were."

"Anyway, why am I doing this?" He addressed himself once more to the projector.

"Because I'd like to take an unofficial look at this film," said Patterson.

"Oh." Mark screwed his eyes' up against the smoke from the cigarette that hung from the corner of his mouth. "That's it," he said, standing back. "Are Meg and Ivy friends of yours?"

"Maybe," said Patterson, pulling across the next curtain. Ingram's cigarette glowed red, and Patterson used it as a beacon to guide him back behind the projector. "Let's see it, then," he said.

The strong light from the projector lit their faces as it beamed on to the screen and back again.

Mark smiled a little as the grainy black and white images appeared. *"Bondage Maidens?"* he said, and cast an amused glance at Patterson.

Patterson's face was serious and still, a slight frown drawing his brows together as he watched. The light flickered and danced, and his eyes stared fixedly ahead.

Ingram watched him for some time, then turned his attention to what was happening on the screen. Shadows danced on his face as he watched, smiling a little. "Meg and Ivy had a high old time at Rhyl," he observed, after some minutes, and looked again at Patterson.

His face was set, taut. No reaction to what he was seeing; just determined concentration.

Ingram looked back at the activities unfolding before Patterson's intense gaze. "Strong stuff," he said. "Considering the vintage. Look at this one. He's really giving—" He broke off. "Good God, that's *Sue*!" he said.

"Switch it off," said Patterson, his voice harsh.

Mark blinked a little at the screen, too startled to do anything but stare.

"Switch it *off*!"

He turned to Patterson, and looked at him; then obeyed, and they were plunged in darkness and silence. After a moment, he pushed past the Superintendent to the curtain, pulling it back, his face angry. "Why did you want me to see that?" he demanded.

Patterson sat down. "I didn't," he said wearily. "I just didn't want anyone else to see it."

Mark pointed at the blank screen. "When did she make it?" he asked.

Patterson sighed. "Twenty-five years ago," he said.

"What the hell are you doing with it? How did—" He slapped his head. "Wanda," he said. "This is Wanda's doing, right? That's what's been making Sue so unhappy."

Patterson didn't answer.

"I still don't see why you've got it," said Mark.

"Isn't it all becoming obvious?"

Mark frowned, then he shook his head in disbelief. "Oh, no, no, no," he said. "You can't think that Sue *killed* Wanda because of it."

Patterson looked defeated. "Can't I?" he asked.

"Look, how could it have been Sue? Wanda Derwent left the cottage and went home. You said so. Sue was back at the Lodge by then!"

Patterson shook his head. "Barbara Slaney left the cottage," he said. "Not Mrs. Derwent. Someone who answered her general description, someone wearing her clothes, in the distance, mostly back view. Who can tell the difference?"

"And you're saying that Sue was a *party* to this?" shouted Mark. "Don't confuse the character she plays on TV with Sue herself!"

"And don't you be so patronising!" shouted Patterson. "I know Sue! I know what that . . . that garbage being dragged out into the open would do to her! Apart from anything else

219

the networks would drop her like a hot brick, and you know it!''

Mark's anger subsided. He dropped his cigarette on the floor and stood on it, then lit another as he looked at Patterson. ''If you know her,'' he said, ''then you know she isn't capable of it.''

Patterson sighed. ''I only know one person that I could imagine being capable of it,'' he said.

''Well then?'' said Mark.

''He's telling the truth.'' Patterson shrugged. ''Can you get the film off the projector for me?'' he asked.

Mark complied. ''He may be being economical with the truth,'' he said.

''It's beginning to look more and more as though Mrs. Derwent died when she came back from lunch,'' said Patterson gloomily.

Mark put the film back in the can and handed it to him. ''How did Wanda find out about it?'' he asked.

''I don't know.'' Patterson put the can back in the document case and zipped it up, then looked at it. ''This is old, too,'' he said. ''Someone's carried that about for years.''

''Mm,'' said Mark, not really paying attention.

''And yet Derwent didn't seem to recognise it,'' said Patterson. ''That's a bit odd, don't you think?''

''Is it?''

''Well, if Mrs. Patterson had been using one of these for years and years, I'd know,'' he said.

Mark looked interested. ''Yes,'' he said. ''I suppose you would.''

''So how come he's saying he didn't get that good a look at it, as though he had never seen it before?'' Patterson sat down, holding the case on his knee. ''Unless . . .''

''What?'' said Mark urgently. ''What? Come on, tell me.''

''Supposing Derwent wanted to get hold of the film? He *sent* Maxwell to London—that would explain why he went, even though it was so dangerous for him to be there.''

''What would Derwent want it for?'' asked Mark.

''I don't know! But it did seem that he sounded as though

he'd never seen this case before. It's hardly likely, is it? He must have done it. Supposing he's trying to distance himself from it, now that people are getting killed?''

"It seems a bit of a long shot," said Mark, then grinned. "If you'll excuse the film terminology."

"I know," sighed Patterson. "But Derwent's lying about this case for some reason. And if I can just prove that he's lying about something, I'll feel a whole lot better."

The road along the coast was fringed with pale sand and blue, white-frothed sea. The hills, lush and green in the morning sunlight, had a smattering of walkers on them; some paused to watch the film crew as they worked on the old church.

A gardener put the finishing touches to the mown grass, emptying the clippings on to the huge pile of cut grass that lay on the other side of the wall, while someone swept more loose grass from the now-revealed pathway. White-painted stones were off-loaded from a pick-up, and laid along the broken edges of the path, up to the church door, where the last coat of varnish was being applied, and the rusty hinges painted black. Fake stone steps were put in place, and the rubble of the old ones wheelbarrowed out of sight, along with the sledgehammer.

The canvas was removed from the pick-up to reveal polystyrene headstones, of various types and apparent ages, which were artistically set into the grass. The odd one had a bouquet of nylon and silk summer flowers placed on the grass in front of it.

John Landers, Sue Quentin and Sheila Drage, dressed in church-going Victorian clothes, stood talking together as F.D. discussed the shot with Len Charles and Clive Oliver. No one looked particularly happy, except F.D., who watched the industry going on around him with considerable satisfaction, throwing out thank-yous and compliments as people passed.

One of the onlookers, a man with longish hair and a leather jacket, shook his head in some amusement, and got back into the Range Rover.

221

"Crazy," he said.

"It's not three days since they found his wife," said the woman.

The man shrugged, and put the car in gear, driving slowly down the narrow, steep road to the town. "No one ever accused Frank Derwent of being over-sentimental," he said.

"I'd like to think," she said, "that if I get found strangled, you might take a bit longer getting back into the groove."

He smiled. "I'd throw myself on your funeral pyre," he said.

"I know life goes on, but he looks as though nothing's happened. Three people have died!"

"Please miss, it wasnae me," he said.

She laughed. "Just drop me in the town," she said. "I won't make you come shopping."

"Do you want me to wait for you?"

"No. You go back. I'll get a taxi."

He dropped her in the town, and the gleaming Range Rover headed back out, through winding country roads still being repaired after the flood damage, to the long, straight cliff road, and the big house that stood alone, with its magnificent backdrop looking like the Mediterranean today. He frowned as he drove through the gates, and slowed the car to a stop, continuing on foot, up to the car which sat in the driveway. He looked curiously into it, his eyebrows rising as he saw the document case in the rear seat. He looked up, and walked slowly towards the house.

Cautiously, noiselessly, he approached the front door which stood ajar, and peered into the hallway. Through the open door to the sitting room, he could see movement, a shadow.

He took a breath and went in. "Did you want something, pal?" he asked.

Patterson whirled round from the safe.

"You'll not find anything there," he said. "I don't leave it unlocked when there's anything in it." He looked at Patterson with some amusement. "You don't look like my idea of a burglar, I must say," he said.

222

"Ah," said Patterson. "You must be Mr. Sumner."

"And who must you be?" Sumner advanced on him. "Come to read the meter?"

"Patterson," he said, reaching for his identity card. "Ardcraig Police. Superintendent Hugh Patterson." He showed him the card.

"Aw, for Christ's sake! Can you not leave folk alone? I gave all that up years ago. You'll not find anything here—the wife wouldn't stand for it."

"What? Oh, no. No, that's not why I'm here," said Patterson. "I didn't even know you were back, Mr. Sumner. I thought Mr. Derwent was still here."

"Well, he's not. We got back yesterday, and he moved out last night. He's filming at the old kirk—" He frowned. "Is it to do with his wife?" he asked.

"Well," said Patterson, "yes. Only . . . well, I'll be straight with you, Mr. Sumner. I'm here without a search warrant."

"How did you get in?"

"Mrs. Derwent's key," said Patterson, with a shrug.

"So what are you looking for?"

Patterson sighed. "I don't know," he said. "You can report me for this, you know."

Sumner smiled. "You're a bit old to be a rebel, aren't you? You must be my age, at least."

Patterson nodded. "Older," he admitted. "I never got round to rebellion when I was young," he said.

"Oh, I'll not report you, unless you beat me up." Sumner sat down. "The wife was just saying that she didn't much like Frank Derwent's attitude to all this," he said.

"To anything, really," said Patterson.

"That's true enough. Do you think he did it or what?"

Patterson shrugged. "Yes," he admitted, sitting down. "The only problem is that I've proved he couldn't have."

"That's a wee bit tricky, right enough."

"I'll be honest with you, Mr. Sumner. I've no proof at all that he had anything to do with it, and the plain truth is that he probably didn't. But . . ."

"But he's a nasty sod," said Sumner, with a smile.

Patterson smiled back.

"The wife went bananas when I told her I was letting him borrow the house. But I'd rather somebody was in it, you know what I mean? I've got some good stuff here. It was all over the papers that me and the band were doing a farewell tour. Next thing, this Howard Maxwell gets on to me about it, says he's got some tart lined up for Derwent, and the house would be just the job." He looked slightly guilty. "I had a laugh to myself when I heard his wife was going with him," he said. "It's not very funny now, is it?"

"No. And I suppose I'm being very unprofessional, but I thought if I could have a look round here, there might be something. Anything. But . . ." He shook his head.

"Well if there was anything, it'll be gone. The wife's cleaned the place from top to bottom. She didn't think much of the Derwents' housekeeping."

"Glasses," Patterson said. "She didn't find any glasses, did she?"

"Glasses?"

"A man's spectacles. That was what I hoped I might find."

"No joy?"

"None."

"Have you tried down the sides of the chairs? That's where mine are always going."

Patterson smiled. "Yours?" he said.

"Oh, sure. I wear contacts on stage, but, ach, I'd just as soon wear glasses at home. I'm wearing contacts today, though—I didn't want all our summer visitors seeing me in my specs."

Patterson laughed. "Anyway," he said, "I've tried down the sides of the chairs." He thought for a moment. "Maxwell was vain about his glasses," he said. "But I don't suppose he'd take them off to impress Derwent."

"No," agreed Sumner. "Well, maybe the briefcase'll have prints or something. If that's the sort of thing you're after."

Patterson looked blank.

"You've got my old briefcase," Sumner said. "In the back of your car."

Patterson's face fell. "The burgundy one?" he said. "The old document case?"

Sumner shrugged. "Whatever you want to call it," he said. "It's all right, I don't mind. You can do what you like with it."

Patterson sighed again. "It's yours," he said.

"Did you not get it from the study?"

"No," said Patterson.

"Oh." Sumner looked up at him, baffled.

"I got it," said Patterson, "from the safe at the Lodge, where it had been deposited by Mr. Maxwell."

"What was Maxwell doing with it?"

"It's a long story. I'll make sure you get it back in due course."

"Fine."

Patterson sighed. "So that's why Derwent had never seen it," he said, and stood up. "I suppose you can positively identify it as yours?" he asked, a note of desperation in his voice.

"I should think I can. I carried all my arrangements in that case for years."

Patterson looked surprised. "You read music?" he said.

"Yes," said Sumner, his voice bored. "I read music. And I've got a certificate that says I can teach the piano, so I've always got something to fall back on."

Patterson smiled, then sighed. "Right," he said. "Now I'm going to have to start barking up the right tree, whether I want to or not." He turned to go, then turned back. "Tell me something," he said, pointing to the bottle on the drinks table. "Is that your whisky?"

"No," said Sumner. "It must be Derwent's. I keep a bottle somewhere, for visitors, but to tell you the truth," he said, lowering his voice, "I can't stand the stuff."

A different pullover. "David O'Connor," he said, politely. "Do you remember me from the other day?"

225

"Oh, yes," she said, rising to a smile.

"Could I have a word?" he asked.

"Yes," she said. "Mr. Patterson told me to expect you. But I've told you all I can about Wanda."

He came in and sat on the chair by the dressing table. "This isn't about Mrs. Derwent," he said. "Well, not directly. We understand that you saw Mr. Maxwell before he left the Lodge on Monday evening."

Sue looked up at him sharply, then her shoulders drooped a little. "Yes," she said. "Are you sure you've got that right about Howard?"

He nodded. "It was a long time ago," he said. "People change."

She looked thoughtful. "No," she said. "I don't think he had changed. But violence doesn't seem right."

"Well, I don't think he knew there was going to be any violence."

"I suppose we've all done things we'd rather we hadn't," she said, sitting down.

He looked a little disapproving. "We don't all rob security firms and shoot policemen," he said.

"No," she agreed. "Even I haven't done that."

"Can you tell me what time you saw Mr. Maxwell?"

She moved her shoulders a little. "After seven some time," she said.

"Were you in his room?"

"No. I went to his room, but he shouted that he was on the phone. Then he came out, pulling on his jacket, saying he was in a hurry and couldn't stop."

"Did he tell you where he was going?"

"To see F.D., he said."

"Did he indicate that he might not be coming back?"

"No. He said he had only twenty minutes to get there—I've no idea why. I asked if something had happened, but he didn't really answer."

The trailer grew dark as the clouds blocked the sun once more, and she put on the light.

"Is it always like this in May?" she asked.

He smiled. "No," he said. "Sometimes we have glorious weather in May. Or so my father tells me," he added, with a smile. "Yes, it's always a bit unpredictable."

"It was lovely five minutes ago," she said. "How do you ever know what it's going to do next? It's m—" She broke off. "I was going to say it was murder trying to film," she said. "Not a very good choice of words."

He looked at her sympathetically, then smiled. "Weather lore," he said. "So as you know what to expect." He got up and went to the window, motioning to her to join him. "See that wee island in the distance?" he asked, pointing over the sea.

"Oh, yes," she said. "I hadn't noticed it before."

"Well, they say that if you can see it, it's going to rain," he said. "And if you can't see it, it is raining."

She smiled.

"Sue! You're wanted." Stuart opened the door. "F.D. wants to do your close-ups," he said. "John's been hauled off by the cops, so I'll be reading his—oh, sorry! I didn't know you had someone with you."

"This is Detective Constable O'Connor." She introduced him with a hint of defiance. "Stuart Dundas," she said. "Affectionately known as Apeman since an orang-utan took a fancy to him in Borneo."

O'Connor laughed. "I'll not take up any more of your time, Miss Quentin," he said. "Thank you."

The musical box movement refused to turn; Baxter sat, sifting through reports, as Patterson spoke to John Landers.

"So you see," he said, "the evidence now suggests that the murder in fact took place between two and three o'clock on Friday afternoon. So now, we'd like to know what everyone was doing then. As it happens we already know where Miss Quentin and Mr. Ingram were, but perhaps you wouldn't mind giving us an account of your movements, Mr. Landers?"

"I was at the Lodge," said Landers. "The whole time. We had this reception . . ."

"Yes," said Patterson. "I know about that." He looked at the pad in front of him. "Mr. Derwent said that he wasn't sure that you were there *all* the time."

"What?" Landers shook his head. "He kept dragging people over to meet me—and I was not in the mood! Of course I was there."

Patterson sat up a little. "He said that you asked for some time out."

Landers nodded. "Well, yes, yes I did. I—I wanted to stop smiling for ten minutes. But I didn't leave. I just took a walk in the grounds."

Patterson sat back again and stroked his beard. "Why weren't you in the mood?" he asked.

Landers looked at him, a little bewildered. "Well, I don't see what it has to do with anything, but I had just had a letter from my fiancée breaking off the engagement."

"Really?" said Patterson.

Landers stared at him. "Yes, really!" he said. "Do you want to see it or something?"

Patterson moved the fly round with the point of his pen. "No," he said. "Not particularly." He looked up. "Your fiancée was very quickly replaced in your affections," he said.

Landers frowned. "You seem a little hostile," he said. "Any particular reason?"

"Hostile, Mr. Landers?"

Landers didn't bother to explain. "Anyway," he said. "You're wrong about Barbara."

Patterson abandoned the musical box. "In which respect?" he asked.

"Barbara didn't hide in any closet."

Patterson raised an eyebrow. "The evidence says she did," he said. "Her prints were found on the inside of the door—her handbag was in there. Minute fibres which match the clothes she was wearing were found inside the cupboard."

The musical box sounded one note. Landers looked at it,

and back at Patterson. "She may have put her things in there," he said. "But she didn't go in after them. I told you what she was like about the cave scene, and that cave is a whole hell of a lot bigger than any closet I ever saw!"

"Needs must, when the devil drives," said Patterson.

Landers stared at him. "Excuse me?"

"Desperate people can make themselves do almost anything," said Patterson.

"Not that. If you don't believe me, ask Marcia Upjohn."

Patterson looked over his invisible glasses. "Marcia Who?" he queried.

"Upjohn," shouted Landers, his patience giving out. "She told me that Barbara was really panicking when she was in the cave. And that Derwent made her do the whole thing again just to keep her in there longer. She said she was a nervous wreck when she got out."

A tiny frown crossed Patterson's brow.

"I mean, from what you're saying, she'd have had to stay in there for almost an hour—she couldn't have *done* that."

Patterson put a finger to his lips, tapping it thoughtfully against his mouth.

"She was claustrophobic," said Landers. "Ask anyone who knew her."

"Yes," said Patterson. "I know that. And you must realise what that means. That's why you were so keen to tell me that they were Barbara's sleeping pills."

He frowned. "They were! Look, am I a suspect or something? Why have I been brought here? Why would I want to hurt Mrs. Derwent?"

"I'm sure you had no reason to hurt her," said Patterson, once again pushing the mechanism round with his pen, almost as though his interest in the conversation was minimal. "But you might have wanted to help someone else."

"To murder someone?"

"To cover up her involvement in a murder." Patterson took out of the drawer a small, brown plastic bottle. "Do you know what this is?" he asked.

Landers frowned, and shook his head.

"You should," said Patterson. "It was found in your room, which we searched this morning in the presence of the manageress, Mrs. Macdonald."

Landers looked more closely. Inside, the two remaining capsules could just be seen. He lifted his eyes to Patterson's. "Are they Barbara's pills?" he asked. "I never saw the bottle."

"It's the bottle of sleeping capsules that you told me belonged to Barbara Slaney, yes," said Patterson. "What were they doing in your room?"

"I've no idea! Why were you searching my room?"

"We were searching everyone's room, Mr. Landers. Looking for this. And we found it in your room."

"Someone must have put it there!"

Patterson nodded slowly. "So—who's been in your room, Mr. Landers?"

Landers didn't speak.

Patterson's face was serious. "It's all right, Mr. Landers," he said. "I think I can guess."

Landers got up slowly. "No," he said.

"You never saw the bottle, because Barbara never had it. They weren't her pills. She'd just been given some, that's all."

"No!" Landers turned and walked quickly out of the room.

Patterson watched him go, then turned to Baxter. "Why is this photograph of Miss Quentin on the desk, Baxter?" he asked curtly.

"Oh, sorry, sir. I forgot to put it back. It was in the file in the drawer."

"What were you doing in the drawer?" he snapped.

Baxter looked at him. "It's my desk, sir," he said stolidly.

"So it is," said Patterson. "Sorry."

"Sir, have you seen this?" Baxter held out a sheet of paper. "It's Constable O'Connor's interview with Miss Quentin. Maxwell was on the phone to Derwent when she got to his room."

Patterson took it from his hand and read it through, shaking his head.

"Derwent told the truth about that too, sir," he said.

"I know he told the truth about that!"

"Sorry, sir."

Patterson removed the file from the drawer, and put the photograph in it. "Damn Derwent," he said. "Telling the truth seems to be the only principle the bloody man's got."

That afternoon, Patterson drove to the cottage. He replaced the file and locked the door, looking across at the trailers in the distance. He frowned and tried to make out the figure which could just be seen on the high point of the cliff. Then his brow cleared, and, alarmed, he ran to the car.

He drove fast along the road, pulling into the car park, running across the grass to where the waves thundered on to the rocks, sending spray high into the air, and over Sue. Below her the cave entrance had disappeared.

She reacted to the hand on her elbow, but she didn't take her eyes from the crashing waves.

"You're getting wet," said Patterson.

She didn't reply.

"So am I," he said, and pulled her gently away from the edge.

She looked at him bleakly. "How did you know I was here?" she asked.

"Educated guess. The boys saw you here twice." He frowned. "Why?" he asked. "What is there to do here?"

"Killing myself," she said. "But I don't have the nerve."

Patterson smiled. "Thank God for that," he said, raising his voice against the roar of the sea. "My superiors are a bit upset about the number of bodies as it is."

She walked away from the edge, towards the circle of trailers. "I think the problem is that I don't *want* to kill myself," she said. "I want to live. I want to be happy."

Patterson made a disbelieving noise. "With that boy? How old is he?" he asked.

"Does it matter?"

231

"Of course it matters! You are deluding yourself if you think you can be happy with a boy nearly twenty years younger than you!"

She smiled, but there was no warmth, no humour. "I can try," she said.

"You were in his room last night. Did you leave a bottle of sleeping pills there? Did you think we wouldn't search his room?"

"Sleeping pills? I don't touch the things. You know I don't like anything like that."

"I don't know you any more."

She shrugged, and walked away again.

"You can tell me your conversation with Maxwell now," he said, calling after her. "I've seen it. As much of it as I had to. I know why you wanted to catch Maxwell before he left."

She stopped walking.

He didn't speak; he stood still as she turned to face him.

"The police have got it?" she said, her voice flat.

"Yes."

She nodded. "Then you're right," she said. "I won't find happiness with John any more than I could with you."

"What does that mean?" He went up to her.

"There's something about strait-laced men that attracts me," she said. "But it gets in the way now and then." There were tears in her eyes. "It'll hurt him," she said.

"Why, Sue?" he asked. "Why in God's name did you make a film like that?"

She turned away. "I fell for the oldest line in the book," she said. " 'I can get you into pictures.' "

The sea battered the rocks as the wind pulled at their clothes, and whipped Sue's hair back from her face.

"But once you saw the set-up, you must have known what sort of films they made!"

"I was shocked. I told them so. Then they told me how much they would pay me to do it."

Patterson was almost pushed off balance by the wind. "Money?" he said incredulously.

232

"Well, what did you suppose, Hugh? Art?" The Glasgow accent, so long held down, was coming back.

"But I was earning money!"

"Yes! *You* were earning money. I wasn't." She turned away, out of the wind.

"Oh, no," he said, catching her arm. "You're not walking away." He turned her round to face him. "What did you need money for?"

"Everything! Clothes, make-up—a car. I needed a car."

"I'd have given you the money!"

She laughed. "You! Hugh, you're a lovely man, but you're as close as a dead heat, and you always have been."

He looked stung, and let her go.

"You know something? As a multiple of my weekly income, I have never been made a better offer since. For a few hours' work."

The spray was drenching them once more; Patterson grabbed her arm and walked until they were in the lee of the nearest trailer.

"Work?" he repeated.

She leant against the trailer and closed her eyes. "When it was happening," she said, "I knew I couldn't go back to you. You were so . . ." She shook her head and opened her eyes. "I couldn't go back and let you make love to me." She looked away. "I just couldn't," she said. "I loved you."

He stepped back a little. "Barbara Slaney told you about it, I take it," he said.

"No. An old acquaintance wrote and told me just before we came here. He said someone had got hold of it and was going to make a video of it to put on the black market." She put her hand to her mouth as tears threatened again. "So what did I do? I went to Howard. Howard would know what to do, I thought. But Howard said there was nothing he could do." She gave a bitter smile.

"Go on," he said.

"There's nothing much more to tell. I didn't know Howard had told Wanda. I just hoped against hope that it was all some sort of hoax. And then Barbara told me on Friday that

233

she had seen Wanda's file on me. Something to do with some film I made once. She thought I ought to know. When I saw Wanda, she told me Howard was leaving for London. He was picking up the film. She needed it for proof that what she had written in the book was true.'' She blinked away the tears. ''*I* could have bought it! If she had got hold of it, I could have! But Howard wasn't in love with me, so that was my hard luck.'' She shook her head. ''Oh, he said he didn't think he'd done anything that bad. It would all come out as soon as the video hit the clubs and the strip joints anyway— he was just letting Wanda steal a march on the tabloids. He didn't know she would try to get hold of the film.''

''When did he say that?''

''On Monday, on his way to F.D.'s.''

''You went with him?''

''No. I said I had to talk to him, and he said he had to get to F.D.'s. If I wanted to talk, I'd have to talk in the car. So I did. He said he didn't give a damn what happened to the film. He dropped me here and said he'd pick me up on his way back. But he never came.''

''How come he never got to Derwent's?''

''I don't know! What makes you so sure that he didn't?''

''Because Derwent had no earthly reason to kill the man! You did. Maxwell had the film—and that was your motive for killing Wanda Derwent. What did you do when you got here, Sue? Invite him into your trailer for a drink or two? If he was out of the way, you could get the film back, was that it? Keep your future secure? Money? Like before?''

She stared at him. ''What? My God, is that what you think? He was going to *give* me the film! Wanda was dead— he had no use for it. He said to wait for him at the trailers, and he'd take me back to the Lodge and get it for me, but he didn't turn up. I haven't killed anyone! Certainly not Howard—if I'd had to wrap him in cotton wool to keep him alive, I would have!'' Her eyes searched his for a moment. ''He wasn't in my trailer—he was in too much of a hurry to get to F.D.'s!''

Patterson looked at her. "I want to believe you," he said. "I really want to."

The trailer door suddenly swung open, and they looked up, startled.

"Very touching," said F.D., smiling. "Very touching indeed."

CHAPTER TWELVE

THE EMPTY GLASS WENT DOWN ON THE BAR, AND a hand punched the bell. The girl appeared and produced a double whisky.

"That's my role," said Mark Ingram, arriving at Patterson's elbow. "You're never paying for it yourself, are you?" he said, as Patterson pushed a note over the bar.

"Don't you start! I am not tight-fisted. What are you having?"

Mark smiled. "I'll have a wee dram," he said, in a quite creditable Scottish accent, and sat down. "You've been conspicuous by your absence the last few days, Hugh," he said.

"Nothing much to do."

"Shouldn't you be keeping a clear head for solving all these murders and suspicious deaths?"

"I'm turning the case over to someone else."

Mark's face fell. "You haven't done it yet, have you?"

"No. But I'm going to."

"You can't do that! You know as well as I do that Sue couldn't possibly—"

Patterson held up a hand, stopping Mark in mid-flow. "Let's sit at a table," he said, walking down the empty room to the end furthest from the bar.

Mark followed, drink in hand, and sat down.

"You don't understand," Patterson said quietly. "I have no choice in the matter. I've been taken off the investigation.

It's only thanks to an old friendship that I've not been suspended pending an enquiry into my conduct of the case. And that might still happen once they know about the film.''

Mark blinked at him.

"Mr. Derwent," said Patterson, heavily. "He told my boss that I was personally involved with one of the people being investigated.''

"How on earth did he know?''

Patterson smiled, without humour. "Sue and I played a scene right under his trailer window," he said. "He really does work in his trailer. That was another thing I didn't believe.''

Mark nodded. "And you got hauled off the case just because of that?''

"No," said Patterson. "Shaw's fair. He waited until today. *Then* I got hauled off the case.''

"What's so special about today?''

"Yesterday we were told that someone else had been in Maxwell's car. Probably a woman, perhaps more than one person. But I did nothing about that, though I knew perfectly well who had been in Maxwell's car. And this morning we got positive confirmation that it was Maxwell who was with Wanda Derwent before she died." He shook his head. "My last hope that Derwent was lying went up in smoke.''

"I thought you already knew that," said Mark.

"Yes, I suppose. It was wishful thinking.''

"What difference does it make who was with her?''

"The fact that it *was* Maxwell means that Wanda Derwent died just after lunch, and I was right. She didn't leave the cottage at all. And what did I do? Nothing.''

Mark frowned. "What should you have done?" he asked.

"I should have brought Sue in for questioning. Which is what Shaw did. Because at the very least, Wanda Derwent was dead when Sue went there that afternoon. I think that she found Wanda Derwent dead, and she knew that Barbara had done it, and kept quiet. The only alternative is that they did it between them—and that's what my boss believes happened. I doubt very much that he'll be able to prove it, even once he knows about the film.''

"Sue isn't capable of it!"

"Frightened people are capable of anything," muttered Patterson. "Sue could get talked *into* anything. She got talked into that bloody film, didn't she?" he said in a fierce whisper, with a jerk of his head towards the general direction of the church hall.

Mark rubbed his eyes, and shook his head, as though he was trying to clear it. "God, I preferred being drunk," he said.

"Barbara Slaney was in the cottage at lunchtime. She waits, she plays Mrs. Derwent the tape, tells her all about what her husband has been up to. Then Sue comes, and they do the job between them. Sue leaves. A few minutes later, Barbara leaves, wearing Mrs. Derwent's jogging suit. A murder committed right in front of a witness, and no one any the wiser. That's what the official thinking is now."

"But why? Why would she do a thing like that?"

"In Barbara's case, to remove an obstacle to the good life, or to get even with Derwent—whichever. In Sue's case . . . to stop Wanda going to London to get this film, which would ruin her career. Only she didn't know that Maxwell had offered to go in Wanda's place."

"Then what?" asked Mark, his voice flat.

"Then Barbara panics. Kills herself, either by accident or design, and leaves Sue holding the baby. Worse—Maxwell's got the film. She presumably thought that if she got rid of him, she could get her hands on the film. Only Maxwell had put it in the Lodge safe."

"You don't believe she did that," said Mark. "Or you'd have given your boss the film by now."

"I don't want to believe it. But I know what it's beginning to look like. She didn't tell anyone she'd seen Maxwell, and she was less than straight with young O'Connor about what she did when she finally did have to admit that she saw him. And I know how easy it would be for me to make things less bad for her. God knows, I've already tried. Shaw's not pre-

238

pared to run that risk." He sighed. "And come to that," he said, "neither am I."

Mark sipped his drink. "I thought you wanted to nail Derwent," he said.

"Derwent had nothing to do with this." Patterson filled his pipe. "More's the pity."

"The chips just fell sweetly for him, did they?" Ingram bent his head to get a light from Patterson's match as he lit his pipe. "He gets rid of a blackmailing mistress and a grasping wife, thanks to Sue?"

"Look—whoever murdered Wanda Derwent, it wasn't her husband. The last thing he'd want would be to make it look as though it happened hours later. And as for Maxwell—what motive could he possibly have had for murdering him? Blackmailers don't very often murder their victims. And he took—or was given—an overdose of the same pills as Barbara took or was given. Pills that turned up in Landers' room the day after Sue spent the night there."

"So what happens now?"

"I hand everything over to Shaw when he comes back on Monday. He's off for the weekend somewhere."

"So who's in charge in the meantime?"

"It's being co-ordinated at headquarters." He smiled. "I suppose Baxter is the man on the spot," he said, looking at his watch. "As from about now."

"Do you have to hand over everything?" asked Mark.

"Everything."

"You don't need to give him that film, do you? It'll only get you into trouble—and you said yourself it won't help them with Sue."

"Of course I have to give him it. I got it from the Lodge safe—it's evidence. I can't just hang on to it."

"You could lose it."

Patterson shook his head. "I've already broken enough rules," he said. "And these people are still operating their dirty little business. They have to be stopped too, remember. You can't pick and choose which crimes to overlook—and that's just what I'm in danger of doing."

"But what good's that film going to do? It was made years ago! Dragging it into the open won't help solve crimes *or* prevent them! All it'll do is make damn sure Sue loses whatever chance of happiness she has."

"With that boy! Don't make me laugh!"

"Who are you to decide what will make her happy? You know your problem? You're jealous!"

Patterson stared at him. "Don't be—" he began, then stuck his pipe in his mouth while he thought about it.

"And what's the big deal about some porno merchants?"

"You think what they were into twenty-five years ago," said Patterson, "and you'll know the sort of stuff they'll be churning out today. Little girls like Barbara Slaney—kids who run away to the city. Twelve, thirteen—younger. They *have* to be stopped. They don't know we're on to them, and they want that film back. It's bait. And I've got to hand it over." He looked at Mark. "I shouldn't have hung on to it in the first place. And I shouldn't have told you all that the other day, and I shouldn't have told you any of this now."

Mark smiled. "I know." He finished his drink. "But we've still got the weekend, right?"

Patterson gave him an old-fashioned look. "I'm not officially concerned with this investigation any more," he said.

"Good. Make that your last, Hugh," he said. "And meet me in the church hall after lunch."

Patterson looked at his drink and sighed. "What for?" he asked.

"Another film show." Mark stood up, and almost bumped into Simon Waterford.

"Oh, sorry, Simon. Can't stop. Too busy." He smiled. "Have you been here all along, or is it Friday again?"

"It's Friday," said Simon. "But yes, I've been here all along."

"Have you? You've been keeping a low profile. See you later."

Simon watched him leave, and sat down disconsolately. "Lager," he said, with uncharacteristic terseness when the girl appeared.

240

Patterson paid for it, then got up. "I'm afraid I have to go too," he said. "Mrs. Patterson will have my dinner ready." He walked towards the door, then turned back. "But if you want some advice, son," he said, "I'd play harder to get, if I were you."

The curtains were drawn; one of the lights was on. In front of the blank screen, Mark sat on a high-backed chair, the solitary light acting as a spotlight. He didn't speak as Patterson moved towards him in the gloom.

Patterson opened his mouth.

Mark put a finger to his lips, and indicated that Patterson should sit. Then he reached for a metal waste bin which he placed at his feet. All the movements were studied, theatrical. He smiled, and shot his cuffs, then Patterson watched as he produced a cigarette from thin air, and dropped it in the bin, immediately producing another, which followed it. Over and over again.

"Voilà!" he said, the cigarette between his lips. He stood up, holding up the empty bin with one hand, producing a lighter with the other, and lit the cigarette. He sat down again in a cloud of blue smoke.

Patterson clapped sardonically. "Nice," he said. "But can you juggle?"

"You know what makes that trick work?" asked Mark.

"You're going to tell me," Patterson replied, taking out his pipe.

"Persistence of vision," he said. "Nice phrase, isn't it? Persistence of vision." He savoured each syllable. "It's a trick our eyes play on us. The retina retains images after they've gone. If another one comes along quickly enough, it joins them together." He smiled. "You see the cigarette about to fall into the bin, and another appear. For an instant, you can see two cigarettes, then just one again. Your logic tells you that the first must have gone into the bin. It's an illusion."

Patterson crumbled tobacco in his hand.

"You've seen it dozens of times. You know there's only

241

one cigarette. But your eyes play the same trick on you, every time. You can't prevent it. Persistence of vision." He got up, walking down the edge of the chairs to the projector. "It's how all this works," he said, patting the projector. "You think you see someone walk across the room, but you don't. You see a series of still photographs shown quickly enough one after the other, to give the *illusion* of someone walking across a room. It's all illusion, Hugh."

"I might not have known what it was called," Patterson said, filling his pipe. "But you're not telling me anything else I didn't know."

"But what it's called is important," said Mark.

"I was promised a film show."

"And you shall have one," said Mark. "I've been working very hard on your behalf. It's taken two days."

Patterson took off his coat, the unlit pipe in the corner of his mouth. "Why would you do that?" he said.

"Because I like you," said Mark, and he smiled. "But that's my problem."

"It certainly is." Patterson sat down again.

"It always has been." Mark opened up the projector. "I might have come out of the closet a long time ago if I had thought there was any real point. But I find men like you and John Landers attractive." He smiled quickly. "I obviously have the same taste as Sue," he said.

Patterson lit the gloom as he applied a match to his pipe. "Maybe you're just afraid to start something you'd actually have to finish," he said.

Mark looked away. He tapped the projector. "What I'm going to show you are the rushes," he said. "Normally, they're shown in the order of shooting—no continuity. But I've sorted them out into something like the order they'll appear in when the film's shown."

Patterson sucked his pipe, nodding.

"It won't be anything like the final version," warned Mark. "But it'll give you an idea." He lit another cigarette. "But before I start, I'll set the scene. So that you know what it's all about."

Patterson frowned. "I don't see where this is going to get us," he said.

"Samuel Rogerson is a young Bostonian Christian missionary," said Mark, ignoring him. "He's sent to convert the heathens on some South Sea island, and while he's there, he sees a native girl swimming naked in a lake. This so unhinges him that he resigns from the mission, using his wife's health as an excuse, and takes her home to Britain. Leo March—that's who I play—is a friend of Sophia Rogerson's father. He arranges for Samuel and Sophia to come to Scotland, where the bracing air should do Sophia good. They are staying at the home of Letitia Lovelace, the widow of a wealthy engineer. She has a private beach, which is where most of the action takes place. Lovelace had been a stage-door Johnny; Letitia had been on the stage—a showgirl. Leo has an understanding with her."

"Right, I've got that," said Patterson, still puzzled.

"The film opens with Samuel being sentenced to death for murdering his wife," said Mark. "The story is told in flashback. March was a witness for the prosecution, because he saw a lot of what went on. But he is convinced that Letitia, on whose evidence the jury placed a great deal of weight, is lying." He walked to the light switch. "Letitia tells her story again, and we can see that she's telling the truth. Little flashes of the scenes surrounding Sophia's death are shown; it's an odd thing, you know, but cinema audiences expect the pictures to tell the truth. You show a flashback, it had better be what really happened, or they'll want their money back."

Patterson grunted.

"So we *see* what happened, in flashbacks, and they bear her out. She was there, watching and listening, when Sophia asked Samuel why he didn't come to her room any more. Samuel says it's her health; she isn't strong enough. She says she feels fine, and tells Samuel that she misses making love. This shocks Samuel rigid; he reacts violently, and she runs away into the cave. Letitia overhears this conversation that you're about to see."

243

He switched out the light, and the gloom of the cave scene barely lit the room.

John Landers, stiff and correct, looked angrily at the camera. "You came here without assistance," he said coldly. "You can leave without it."

Off screen, Stella muttered Sophia's response. "I can't."

"You must seek God's help."

"It isn't God's help I need, it's yours."

Landers' face grew thunderous. "Blasphemy! Blasphemy, too!" He stepped back. "This is all a direct result of . . ."

"She's stuck in the mud," said Mark, as the scene went on, John Landers' voice echoing in the empty hall. "And Samuel leaves her there."

Landers turned and walked away from the camera.

"She's begging him to help her," said Mark. "But he walks away."

He put on the light again. "Letitia was on the cliff top— she heard it all. So do we. We even see it. We know that that's what happened."

He sat down. "It goes on like that," he said. "Scenes are shown that prove that he ran naked into the sea and swam in it as the tide rushed into the cave, drowning his wife, and then he came out and raped Letitia." He smiled. "March was rock climbing," he said. "He's on a peak, at a much higher vantage point than anyone else. He sees a lot of it happen, but he's powerless to do anything about it."

"All this is very interesting, but—"

"The lower crane shots are Leo's point of view," said Mark. "He can see the cliff top, and the shore line. He can't see the cave. But he saw Rogerson walking and talking with Letitia. Saw him suddenly strip off and run into the sea, swimming about as the tide came in. He saw him come out again and rape her. He couldn't do anything except climb to the top and run to Letitia's aid. When he gets there, Letitia tells him the rest. He's in your position," he said. "He has to listen to what someone is telling him, and piece together what happened from that and from what he knows to be the truth. But he still thinks she's lying, so he persists."

244

"Persistence of vision," said Patterson, his pipe clenched in his teeth.

"Yes," said Mark. "Each time, as the day of execution gets closer, he breaks her down further, and he gets a bit more—each time, we see a bit more of what happened. But it still all proves that Letitia's telling the truth. Until the final Sunday, when the whole sequence is shown. All the pieces of information that have already been given are there—the same shots, the same pieces of film. But this time, we're shown the pieces in between."

Patterson grunted. "No one's going to show me the pieces in between," he said.

"No," agreed Mark. "But watch it anyway. It took me a long time to sort it all out." He switched off the light.

"All right," said Patterson, as pipe smoke drifted and curled in the beam of light.

Samuel walking from the cave, and waiting; the sea, still harmless, lapping the shore. On the cliff, Letitia watching. Coming down to him, talking to him. Samuel pouring out his troubles to her; she is kind, and sympathetic, walking with him, leading him up the slope, along the cliff. She confesses her love for him.

It was a long, intense screen. Patterson looked round, a hint of pride in his eyes. "She always could act," he said. "She's wasting her time in that American thing."

Mark smiled. "F.D. was at his very worst then," he said. "It took almost a week to do that scene. It will be intercut with shots of Sophia, who isn't trapped at all, in the cave."

The screen went blank, and the next clip came on.

Samuel, jumping up, running to the edge, seeing the water running fast into the cave. Running down the slope, tearing his clothes off, trying desperately to reach the cave, but being hauled back by the undertow until he had to give up. Turning, swimming back. Standing with the water buffeting his body, striding out.

Mark smiled again, and sighed wistfully again.

Letitia, watching. Not moving. Waiting.

An overhead shot of the apparent struggle.

245

The close-up. Letitia, helping him push her clothing out of the way.

An overhead shot of the rape.

Sophia, removing her dress, climbing the rocks.

The close-up of Samuel and Letitia; Letitia turning her head away in apparent disgust, seeing Sophia.

Sophia's point of view. Letitia is smiling.

Sophia, going back down the rocks, back into the cave.

The screen went blank.

"Ice cream, chocolate, drinks on sticks," said Mark, switching on all the lights with a sweep of his hand down the switches. "It's all too late; Samuel dies on the gallows at eight o'clock the next morning."

"So what's all that supposed to prove to me?" Patterson twisted round to look at Mark.

Mark smiled. "Simon wants it to prove his contention that women choose subordination. It's safer. They can call all the shots, and pull all the strings, and the men take the blame. Sophia was never trapped; she gives herself even more freedom when she removes the dress, but she goes back into the cave when she realises that freedom isn't all it's cracked up to be, and that you have to cope with unpleasant reality. Letitia is simply doing what she'd been doing all her life— manipulating a man. Only Samuel is out there, naked and vulnerable."

Patterson expelled smoke. "Do you agree?" he asked.

"No," said Mark. "But then, I like women."

"And Simon doesn't?"

He shook his head. "I don't think so," he said. "And F.D. hates them. That's why he was so keen to do this film."

"Do you want me to arrest Derwent because he's made a film that might be offensive to women?"

"No. This is by way of being an illustrated lecture." Mark pulled back the curtains, to reveal grey, fast-moving clouds, and left the lights on in the gloomy afternoon.

Patterson smiled. "All right," he said. "Fire away."

Mark got up, and walked around as he spoke. "You didn't see anything like that, of course," he said. "That is the essence of illusion. It forces you to believe something that isn't true. A good illusionist can make you believe what he wants you to believe." He sat down, and leant forward eagerly. "Sue wasn't raped by John—Barbara didn't climb a cliff face. I wasn't there at all most of the time, never mind witnessing it from a peak that doesn't even exist. It's all an illusion."

"I've known that this crime was a set-up from the very beginning," said Patterson. "I was wrong about who set it up, that's all."

"You had persistence of vision to start with," he said. "You were convinced it was F.D." He sat back. "F.D.'s an illusionist," he said. "That's his job. And he's good at it."

Patterson got up and fetched the waste paper bin, tapping out his pipe on the edge. He shook his head. "Look," he said, "I don't like the man any better than you do. But the plain fact is that this particular illusion didn't benefit Derwent at all. Someone wants me to think it was him. Because someone tried very hard to make me believe that Wanda Derwent left that cottage and came back."

Mark smiled. "But that *isn't* what you believe, is it?" he said.

Patterson stopped tapping the pipe.

"A good illusionist makes you believe what he *wants* you to believe," Mark repeated. "And you believe that Wanda never left the cottage."

Patterson straightened up, his voice sounding less than definite when he spoke. "We've proved that," he said.

"Have you? How many people did you see in the clips of film I've just shown?" asked Mark.

Patterson smiled. "Sorry, Mark," he said. "That won't work. I saw five people."

Mark raised his eyebrows. "Did you?"

"I saw young Landers. And I know that he's a fantastic swimmer, so I'm assuming he did his own stunts. And I saw Barbara Slaney." He was counting them off on his fingers. "I saw the stunt woman who stood in for Barbara," he said.

"That's three."

"I saw Sue," said Patterson. "And I saw someone else playing Letitia. In the overhead shots of the love scene, and the rape scene."

Mark looked crestfallen. "Someone told you," he said.

"No one told me, Mark. I *know* Sue. I know how she stands, how she holds her head, how she walks. I know how she *looks*—and that wasn't her." He put his pipe away. "I grant you it'll fool people who don't know her," he said. "But it didn't fool me."

Mark sat back, and smiled. "The private detective knew Wanda," he said. "He'd spent weeks watching her. Every day. He watched her come out of the cottage, and jog down to the beach. Five days a week for over a month. Hours of his life were spent just watching Wanda. How she moved, how she walked, how she *jogged*. Five miles, Hugh—anyone not used to it . . ."

Patterson sat down. He looked at Mark, at the projector, at the blank screen.

"Everyone's telling the truth," Mark said, in a quiet voice. "Except F.D."

"But he *is*," said Patterson, his eyes far away, as he thought it through. "Everything I've found out confirms it."

"Everything confirmed what Letitia was saying, too," said Mark. "Persistence of vision, Hugh, that's what you need."

"Why would he murder Maxwell?" Patterson asked. "I can see why getting rid of his wife and Barbara would help him, but Maxwell? Because he made love to his wife?"

"You must be joking," said Mark.

Patterson nodded, frowning. Then his face cleared, and he stared at Mark. "Of *course* it was because he made love to his wife!" he shouted. "I owe Phil Sumner a drink," he said, smiling.

Mark looked mystified. "Come on," he said. "You'll have to explain that."

"No," said Patterson. "Not yet. I still have to prove it. I have to make him lie." He thought for a moment. "Are you involved in the filming?" he asked.

"No."

"Oh, good. In that case, could you do me a wee favour, do you think?"

John Landers stopped on his way into the lounge bar, and looked at Patterson, who was talking to Simon Waterford. Sue sat alone, as usual. He turned to leave again, then changed his mind, and went up to the bar, hitting the bell.

The girl arrived, and gave him a Coke.

"Mr. Landers," said Patterson, by way of greeting.

"Superintendent."

"See? I told you you'd get the hang of it, sir."

"How are you, John?" asked Simon, a little bewildered.

"I'm fine," said Landers, picking up his drink and turning away.

"I owe you an apology," said Patterson. "I was being hostile. Put it down to . . ." He puffed out his cheeks. "My lost youth," he concluded. "That'll do."

Landers turned to look at him. "You still suspect Sue of Mrs. Derwent's murder," he said, his voice low. "She told me. She's been answering questions all day."

Patterson shrugged his shoulders a little. "Not me," he said.

"Well, I don't care," said Landers. "I don't care if she did. Understand?"

"Oh, yes," said Patterson, putting his pipe in his mouth. "I understand."

Mark appeared, carrying a weekend bag. "I'm off," he said to Patterson. "Taxi's here."

Simon looked up. "You—you're going away?" he asked.

"Just for the night. I'll be back tomorrow." Mark glanced at Patterson, then back at Simon. "To what Patterson calls my *pied-à-terre*," he said, and smiled his Barry Strong smile. "Would you like to come?"

It was Simon's turn to look at Patterson. "No," he said. "No, thank you." He got up and left the bar.

Mark put down his case. "Well," he said, startled.

Patterson smiled.

"I don't know what you're grinning at. I took your advice, didn't I?"

"Sort of," said Patterson. "But then, so did Simon."

John frowned as Mark made an exasperated noise, picked up his case and left.

"Are you matchmaking?" he asked Patterson.

"Far be it from me to interfere in other people's business," said Patterson.

John took his drink to where Sue sat. "I don't get him," he said, with a glance in Patterson's direction as he sat down.

Sue looked over to where Patterson stood at the bar, and smiled. "That's because you're so like him," she said, a little sadly.

"Hugh—I'm beginning to think that tape does something for you," said Mrs. Patterson, raising her voice.

Patterson removed the headphones, put down the pen with which he was listing something, and stretched the cord towards her. "I'm not listening to the naughty bit," he said. "It's music. Listen."

She listened to the mellifluous sound of a guitar, lazy and quiet. " 'Albatross,' " she said. "I like that."

"There's got to be something," he said. "This isn't Barbara Slaney's copy of the tape. If she had wanted Mrs. Derwent to listen to the tape, she'd have gone to see her in the open, not sneaked in when her back was turned. And if she had wanted to do the woman in, she'd hardly leave evidence of her presence on the cassette player."

"But didn't you say it had her prints on it?" she asked.

"Oh, it's her tape all right. I just don't think it's her copy of *the* tape, if you see what I mean."

"I think so. But how can you prove that? Anyway, if he is lying, how do you know he didn't just frighten her into giving him her copy?"

Patterson smiled. "I don't think Barbara was that easy to frighten," he said. "And as to your other objection, I can't prove it. Yet." He looked up. "This bloke that plays the old hits. When's he on?"

"On the local radio, you mean? Duncan Whatsisname?"

"That's him."

"Sunday mornings," she said. "I think he's on from eleven till half past twelve—it'll be in tomorrow's paper, though. Which will be here any minute," she said, shouting again as the headphones were clamped to ears once more. "I'm going to bed."

Baxter jumped to his feet. "Good morning, sir," he said.

"Relax," said Patterson.

"Sir, I wasn't expecting you."

"No," said Patterson, sitting on the spare desk. "I'm not supposed to be here." He smiled. "But I just wanted a wee look at young Landers' statement. The first one—you know, the one he made the Sunday we found Mrs. Derwent's body."

"Sir, I'm not supposed to discuss the case with you. Or give you access to the papers."

"Oh." Patterson looked penitent. "Sorry."

Baxter looked up without raising his head. "I haven't told anyone about that film, sir. Or the file."

Patterson smiled, shaking his head. "You do whatever you think you should, Baxter," he said. "Don't put your head on the chopping block for me. I'm retiring soon—you're not."

"I don't think they had any right to take you off it, sir," said Baxter.

"Oh, I think maybe they did."

He lifted his head. "Why did they, sir?" he asked.

Patterson thought for a moment. "They thought that I might be biased," he said.

"Because you think Derwent did it?"

"Not really," said Patterson. "Why, do you think he did it?"

"I'm sure he did." Baxter opened the drawer and began looking through papers.

"What makes you think that?"

"He's so . . . so *smug*, sir. As if he was putting one over on us." He extracted two sheets of paper, and laid them on

251

the desk. "And I never thought I'd say this about anyone," he said, "but I think he's evil. And they didn't say I couldn't make you a cup of tea, sir," he said, getting up. "I'll be a minute or two, if you don't mind waiting."

Patterson smiled as he left, and picked up John Landers' statement, nodding as he read. Then he reached over the desk, opened the drawer, took the cassette from his pocket, and dropped it back into the drawer, sliding it shut.

"Don't put my name in the pot," he called through to Baxter on his way out. "And thanks, son. I owe you a drink."

"Running order?" Duncan Jameson squeezed past the typist's desk to get to a filing cabinet. "What day?" he asked.

"That's the problem," said Patterson. "I don't know."

Jameson closed the filing drawer. "I'm not a miracle worker, Mr. Patterson," he said. "Is this police business?"

"Er . . . no, not exactly. I'm doing some research." He took the handwritten list from his pocket. "What I've got is the running order of records played on one of your programmes from a few minutes into the programme. I want to know if you can tell me what day that was. It would be in the last seven or eight weeks."

"Oh," said Jameson, taking the sheet from him, and scanning it. "We don't keep scripts for very long, I'm afraid." He smiled. "Och, this is easy. It was just the other day. Hang on." He delved into the filing cabinet. "Here it is," he said. "A fortnight ago."

Patterson beamed. "Sunday the twenty-ninth of April. You're sure?" he said.

"You can have a copy of the script if you like," said Jameson. "Complete with all my off-the-cuff ad libs."

"Thank you, Mr. Jameson," said Patterson warmly. "I owe you a drink."

"Hugh, I haven't even unpacked, and I get the impression that we are in some way breaking the law by being here," said Mark. "Don't you want—?"

"All in good time," said Patterson, ushering him into the cottage. "That can wait. This is urgent."

"We're not supposed to be here, are we?" said Mark.

"I'm not supposed to have Wanda Derwent's keys," said Patterson, going over to the cassette player. "But I have."

Mark sighed.

"Now—this," said Patterson, producing a cassette from his pocket, "is a cassette that I recorded yesterday." He looked slightly coy. "It's me reciting 'To a Mouse,' actually," he said, putting it in the left-hand deck.

Mark nodded a little doubtfully.

"And this," he said, producing another cassette, "is blank." He inserted it in the right-hand deck. "Now—if I pause this one, and press play, and press record on *this* one . . ."

"Wee, sleekit, coorin', tim'rous beastie, O, what a panic's in thy breastie! Thou need na . . ."

With some reluctance he turned down the sound. "I want everything as it was," he explained to Mark. "She was copying it without sound."

"Best way," said Mark.

Patterson looked injured. "Now," he said. "You've to do a bit of acting for me."

"Always pleased to be of service," said Mark.

"You turn up the sound, and realise that what you're listening to horrifies you."

Mark nodded seriously. "That might be difficult," he said.

"So you stop the left-hand tape, and take it out. And you shout—ask me what the hell I'm doing. Then I stop the other tape. OK?"

"OK."

"Oh—wait. He said she had it on double speed. I'd better do that in case it makes a difference."

The tape was solemnly re-run, high-speed dubbing selected, and the process begun again.

Mark turned up the sound after a few moments.

". . . truly sorry Man's dominion has broke nature'ssocil union,an'justifiesthatillopinion,whichmakesthee—"

Mark switched off the left-hand tape, removing it. "What the hell?" he roared. "Just what the hell do you think you're doing?"

Patterson looked round as the words echoed, then stopped the other tape.

"Now," he said. "Let's see." He ran his tape back, and played it.

". . . social union, an' justifies that ill opinion, which makes thee—" There was the far-away sound of the tape being pulled from the deck, then Mark, loud and clear. *"What the hell? Just what the hell do you think you're doing?"*

Patterson smiled. "That's what should be on Barbara Slaney's copy of the tape," he said.

Mark sighed. "He'll just say that he shouted after she'd taken it out," he said. "You'd need her copy, and . . ." He shrugged. "I think she must have destroyed it. F.D. threatening you isn't something you take lightly, you know. He never says anything if he doesn't mean it."

Patterson took out his tape and put it in his pocket. "Keep it," he said, when Mark tried to give him his. "It'll be a wee souvenir."

Mark looked at it. "Gee," he said. "Thanks."

"One more favour," said Patterson.

Mark swallowed. "Can I go to prison for any of this?" he asked.

"If anyone ever found out, you might, but this is quite safe." Patterson smiled, and took an envelope from Wanda's desk. "Would you address that to yourself, please?" he asked.

"To myself," repeated Mark.

Patterson nodded.

"I feel as though you're suddenly going to say that I've just furnished you with conclusive proof that I murdered every last one of them," said Mark, writing his name and address, and handing it to Patterson.

Patterson looked at it. "Los Angeles," he said.

"It's where I live."

"Quite," said Patterson, his smile growing even broader. "Quite."

"Now," said Mark. "As to the other matter?"

"Yes, indeed. Let's get on with that—oh."

"What now?"

"Well, this is what you really could go to prison for, so perhaps you'd rather . . ."

"As you say, Superintendent. Let's get on with it."

"Good man, Mark. I owe you a drink."

"As it happens," said Mark, following him to the door, "you owe me several!"

F.D. ordered a martini. "Where are all our fellow guests?" he asked Mark, who sat in his usual place, his hand protectively round his glass.

"Dead, mostly," said Mark.

"Oh, you mustn't dwell on these things, Mark," said F.D.

"I have to admire you," said Mark, looking at him unsteadily. "You don't dwell on these things, do you, F.D.? I mean, you've lost—you've lost . . ." He looked at his hand, the fingers spread. "Your wife," he said, touching his thumb. "Your mistress," he went on, ticking off his forefinger. "*And* your best friend." He shook his head. "And you're carrying on. That's wonderful, F.D. That's wonderful."

"Can I get you another?" said F.D.

"No need, F.D., no need. These are on Mr. Patterson." He smiled. "And besides, I've promised not to get drunk."

F.D. smiled. "I think you've already broken your promise," he said.

"All right," said Mark. "One more—just one." He smiled. "It's Saturday night, isn't it?"

"It is," said F.D. "Another for Mr. Ingram," he told the girl, as his drink arrived.

Simon Waterford came in. "I thought you weren't going to get drunk again," he said.

"See?" said Mark. "I have a nursemaid. Two. Two. The other one will be here any minute. I'm not drunk, Simon. Not yet. Look—I can walk. Watch." He eased himself off the stool, and took a step, catching the edge of the bar as he stumbled. "Oops," he said, giggling, and sat down again. "It's the legs," he said. "I'm all right. I'm celebrating."

"What are you celebrating?"

"Ah." Mark touched his nose.

"For the last time," Sue said, as she and John Landers came into the bar. "I didn't leave anything in your room!"

"Then how the hell did it get there?"

"How should I know?" She looked malevolently at F.D. "Ask him."

"I'm asking you. I want to *know*, Sue. Don't you understand? I just want to know what it's all about."

"And I don't? *I'm* the one who has been questioned, not you!"

"Not by your friend Hugh, though," said Landers. "Oh, no. He still thinks he owns you, you know that?" He ordered a beer and a gin and tonic from the girl, who hadn't left this time. She watched with frank interest as the row developed.

"They've taken him off the case," Landers went on. "He was all for pinning it on me—anyone. Anything to protect you."

F.D. smiled a little into his martini.

"No, no," said Mark. "Don't—don't start accusing one another. That—that's just what he wants, right, F.D.?"

"What who wants, Mark?" asked F.D., frowning slightly.

"You," said Mark, wagging a finger at him. "You. You want everyone to suspect everyone else." He looked round. "Like *Ten Little Niggers*," he said. "Told you so."

Landers sighed. "What are you talking about?" he said.

"Ten Little Niggers," explained Mark, patiently. "Oh—you call it *Ten Little Indians*, I think. But it's all going to be over soon."

"I seriously think you should join AA, Mark," said Landers.

Mark frowned. "Me?" he said, looking puzzled. "But I don't drive. Not here, anyway. I mean, I wouldn't mind driving *here*, but not in London. So I don't . . . no point."

"What?" said Landers.

Simon smiled. "AA is a motoring organisation," he explained. "Its a joke."

"Very amusing," said Landers.

"And how was London?" asked Simon.

"You wouldn't come. So I'm not going to tell you."

Simon sighed.

"Another one of these," said Mark. "In there," he said, pushing his still untouched drink across the bar. "On Mr. Patterson—you are making a note, aren't you? He said he owed me a drink and I'm getting drunk on him." He turned to Sue. "How about that?" he said. "Hugh is footing the bill—is that or is that not a turn up for the books?"

"You'll be lucky," said Sue.

"Oh, no. I'm owed a drink. I was on a mission." He smiled. "Just like Barry Strong. I was on a mission."

The girl topped his drink.

"Well?" said Mark. "Isn't anyone curious?"

"No," said Landers.

"Well, you should be. You're going to benefit. So is Sue."

"Don't you think you've had enough, Mark?" said Simon.

"A mission. To nail this bastard." He jerked a thumb at F.D.

F.D. finished his drink. "And how were you going to do that?" he asked quietly.

"I've done it, F.D. I've done it. You'll see. You'll find out, soon enough."

F.D. shook his head, and pushed away his empty glass. "I wish you joy of him," he said to Simon, and left.

"You'll see," said Mark, raising his voice slightly. "You'll all see."

No one spoke; the girl perceived that the show was over, and left.

There was a moment of silence as they looked at one another.

"Cut," said Simon, with a shy smile. "You were all bloody marvellous."

257

Mark grinned. "It was the script," he said. "We couldn't go wrong, could we—"

He turned to see tears running down Sue's face.

"Hey—he's gone. We can stop now."

She sniffed. "I never knew I had such good friends," she said.

"Why wouldn't you?" asked John, giving her a squeeze. "Come on."

"Thank you," she said, kissing Mark and Simon, and allowing herself to be led away.

Mark looked at Simon. "How was I?"

"Not bad," said Simon. "A bit over the top—you don't slur as much as that when you're really stewed."

"Don't I?" asked Mark, interested. Then he looked alarmed. "But it fooled him, didn't it?"

Simon smiled. "It would fool anyone who hadn't shared an empty bar with you for hours on end," he said.

"F.D. has certainly never done that," said Mark. "But will it *work*?"

"That's up to Patterson now," said Simon. "He's nothing if not unconventional, your tame policeman."

Mark smiled. "I think it's the first time he's been unconventional in his life," he said.

"Well," said Mark, getting up. "I think I'll go up now too."

Mark looked at the enormous whisky in front of him, and rang the bell.

The girl appeared, her hand automatically picking up a glass, and going to the optic.

"Will you do me a favor?" asked Mark.

"Yes, of course," she said.

"What's your name?" he asked. "You've served me a hundred drinks and I don't know your name."

"Belinda Mason," she said, a little shyly.

"Well, Belinda, will you pour that down the nearest sink?"

Belinda happily took it away, and Mark looked at Simon. "F.D. might smell a rat," he said. "If I didn't need to be taken to bed."

"You're right," said Simon. "I hadn't thought of that."

Mark smiled. A genuine smile. "And besides," he said, "I think I do."

CHAPTER THIRTEEN

CHURCH BELLS WERE RINGING SOMEWHERE IN THE town as F.D. got out of his car and went into the tiny police station.

"I'm told Constable Baxter would like to see me," he said to the young policeman on the desk.

"Oh, yes, Mr. Derwent. Would you like to go through? He's in the office."

F.D. strode towards the office, knocked, and opened the door to find Constable Baxter behind the main desk. He looked round the door; Superintendent Patterson sat at the smaller table, the musical box in his hands.

"I understood that you had been removed from this enquiry," he said to Patterson. "In view of your relationship with Susan Quentin."

Baxter's mouth fell open, and he stared at Patterson.

Patterson smiled. "I have," he said.

"Then you are no longer conducting the investigation, and I don't have to answer your questions."

"I'm not conducting it," said Patterson. "Constable Baxter is."

F.D. turned to Baxter. "What sort of nonsense is this?"

"I would like to have a word with you concerning the deaths of Wanda Derwent, Barbara Slaney and the man known to you as Reginald Howard Maxwell," said Baxter, having got over his shock at F.D.'s revelation. "You're not obliged to say anything, but anything you do say will be taken down in writing, and may be given in evidence.''

"Reading me my rights?'' said F.D., amused.

"I have reason to believe that you may be implicated in the deaths of all of these people, Mr. Derwent,'' said Baxter, with a quick glance at Patterson.

Patterson nodded slightly.

"Charges may be brought against you, and you are entitled to have a lawyer present.''

"Well,'' said F.D., sitting down. "Let's see if I need one, shall we? I've a feeling that there could possibly be some irregularities of procedure involved here.''

Baxter cleared his throat, and glanced down at the paper on his desk. "We'll start with the day Miss Slaney died,'' he said. "Friday the fourth of May. You told us that you engineered the row on the set . . . .''

John Landers and Mark Ingram got into Howard's car. They drove off, Howard hooting as they passed F.D., who waved as they left. He walked through the circle of empty trailers, across to Barbara's, opened the door, and went in.

"You kept her there for quite a while, according to your statement to Superintendent Patterson,'' said Baxter. "Long enough to make her understand that it wasn't a good idea to cross you.''

He stood at the door of Barbara's trailer, looking out at the empty site. "I think you've had enough,'' he said. "I'll get your clothes.''

He walked quickly away, as Barbara's trailer door banged shut behind him, and he smiled, climbing into his own trailer, where he poured a cup of coffee and took a brown bottle from his pocket.

"Hold on,'' said F.D. "Where am I supposed to have got hold of pills?''

"The previous Sunday," said Baxter. "Sunday the twenty-ninth of April. You went to Miss Slaney's hotel room . . ."

He went into the bathroom, emptied the linen basket, and separated the garments with his foot. Then he opened the cabinet door, scanning the shelves as he removed the larger jars and smashed them into the bath. He found the pills, and put them in his pocket, then systematically smashed everything else.

He came out, and looked at Barbara, who sat hunched up on the bed as the music played. Then he pulled on his driving gloves.

"You were still wearing them," said Baxter, "when you took the tape."

"What tape?"

"The tape of the Duncan Jameson show for the twenty-ninth of April," said Baxter. "Miss Slaney collected his programmes—every week. You told us that yourself. She doesn't have that one."

"Perhaps she missed it."

"No. I'll come to that later." Baxter paused. "Mr. Landers helped Miss Slaney clear up," said Baxter. "But he had never seen the bottle for her sleeping capsules before Mr. Patterson showed it to him. He should have: it was plastic—it wouldn't have got broken. He didn't see it, because you had taken it. You planned all this, Mr. Derwent."

He emptied their contents into the paper cup, then broke more into the brandy, putting back its cork and turning it one way and then the other like a milk-bottle. He crossed back to Barbara's trailer, and tried to open the door, but it was stuck. Finally, she opened it.

"The drugs would have made Miss Slaney drowsy quite quickly, according to the pathologist," Baxter said. "And the amount she took would have made her difficult to rouse for about two hours or so."

F.D. walked towards the cottage as Barbara came out of the little clump of bushes. She walked slowly towards him. He had to put his arm round her when they went up the narrow pathway, as Barbara stumbled against him.

Inside, he closed the door; she stumbled again, laughing at herself. He poured brandy into one of the paper cups. She thought it was a game as he lifted the glass to her lips; she drank it, giggling. He put his arms round her, taking her bag, removing her keys, giving her more to drink. She laughed, and kissed him, but he wasn't interested in that, as he pulled her towards the cupboard, reaching out with one hand to open it.

The mirror on the open door reflected the window, the corner of the desk; she was giggling still, protesting laughingly as he threw her bag into the cupboard. Her hand struck the bottle as he tried to push her in after it, and she grabbed the desk, laughing at his grunting attempts to pull her away. The bottle rolled along the floor, bumping into the pulled-out plug.

He looked at his watch, and his hand went round her neck. Her grip loosened as she finally lost consciousness; he pushed her in, slamming the door, seeing his own face, flushed with exertion. He locked the cupboard, pocketed the key, then smoothed his hair, and left.

Wanda's desk was reflected in the mirror once more.

"How ridiculous."

Baxter shot another look at Patterson, who closed his eyes in a brief nod of encouragement.

"There is evidence of Miss Slaney's presence in that cupboard, Mr. Derwent, and she was claustrophobic. She didn't go in there of her own accord. Her fingerprints bear out what I've just described. Her bruises do too."

F.D. smiled broadly, and watched Patterson, who got up and pulled down the blind on the spring sunshine.

"All right," he said. "I've drugged Barbara and locked her in a cupboard—then what did I do?"

"You went to the reception at the Lodge," said Baxter.

263

"You made quite a thing of Miss Slaney's non-appearance; you were angry, apparently. But by your own admission, you had got her drunk; much too drunk to drive. It seems unlikely that you would want her there, meeting the public, in that state."

F.D. turned to Patterson, who had resumed his seat at the table. "I think I detect your style in the constable's script, Patterson," he said.

Patterson picked up the musical box, and started doing something that made it churn out notes one after the other in slow procession. *Soh. Me. Doh. Te.*

"You left after you got the usual call to say that your wife had gone home . . ." Baxter went on.

He arrived at the cottage on foot, and pulled on his driving gloves before taking Barbara's key ring from his pocket, and letting himself in. He took one tape, and put it on the left-hand deck, and another on the right-hand. He pressed high-speed dub, then re-enacted his movements up to the moment that he pulled the original out. Then he stopped the other tape, and left it.

". . . and you made a second copy of the original recording of your . . ." he paused. "Your sexual encounter with Miss Slaney," he said.

"Pure Patterson," said F.D. "Let me give you some advice, Superintendent," he said. "Always bear the actor in mind when you write a script. If he's not comfortable with a line, it shows."

"At about five o'clock," said Baxter stolidly, "you went out again . . ."

The cottage door opened, and F.D. looked round before he came out, walking quickly to the telephone box, dialling a number, talking animatedly when he got a reply.

". . . to call your wife before she left for the airport, bringing her to the cottage on some pretext. A break-in, a

264

fire—something that would make her believe her tapes and files were in danger." Baxter paused again. "She came immediately, of course," he said.

The Mercedes pulled up outside the cottage, and Wanda Derwent got out, running up the path to the door, pushing it open, going in. There was a flash as the mirror caught the light, and she fell to the ground.

"Then you released Miss Slaney. Left undisturbed, she would have slept for about eight hours, but something woke her after four. You, Mr. Derwent. She would have been confused, and disoriented, according to the doctor."

He opened the cupboard, and pulled Barbara to her feet. She was barely conscious as he walked her across the room, out to the Mercedes. He opened the door, and pushed her into the passenger seat, then got into the driving seat, still wearing the gloves. With Barbara slumped beside him, he cleaned every surface that Wanda might have touched, then drove to the Sumner house, leaving the car parked in the woodland beside it.

He reappeared with Wanda's carry-all, and ran back to the car. The rain came on as he drove fast towards the cottages; he put on the windscreen wipers, and drove along the cliff road, turning the wheels suddenly as he braked at the edge of the cliff. He pulled on the hand brake, leaving the car in gear, and pulled the unconscious Barbara into the driving seat, putting her hands on the wheel, on the gear lever, the door.

He got out, leaning into the car across her, and her hand beneath his, he released the hand brake, jumping back, slamming the door as the car slowly moved.

"You let gravity do the rest. You put Miss Slaney's keys back in the ignition of her car, went back to the location, where you had left your car, and where I saw you, at half past seven."

"And why have I done all this?"

"Because you wanted them both dead, mainly," said Baxter.

"Ah—an ad lib."

Baxter looked down. "You knew that taken in conjunction with the evidence we would find at the cottage, we would be forced to the conclusion that it was Miss Slaney who had left, and who was bringing the car to the cottage when she met with an accident. That would alter our conception of the time of the murder to a time when you were very definitely at the Lodge."

"But now you no longer conclude that?"

"On the Monday, you learned that someone had made love to your wife shortly before she died," Baxter went on.

"Ah—my wife makes love, I see. I merely have sexual encounters."

"I think that's about right," said Baxter.

F.D. smiled.

"You knew that if it was shortly before she died, then it must have happened after she had left the cottage, and that whoever it was *knew* that she had left. He had to be got rid of before the impersonation story was advanced. You knew that it had to be Mr. Maxwell from Eddie's reports to you. So, you forced him to go to the Sumner house. You gave him a deadline. Twenty minutes. And he got there in twenty minutes, or you would have rung Mr. Patterson then, Mr. Derwent. You never make threats you don't intend to carry out. So why make an exception for Maxwell? Because you had to confirm that it was he, and only he, who knew Mrs. Derwent had left the cottage. And then you had to get him drowsy, and biddable, and take him for a walk down Mr. Sumner's garden."

"This is all supposition," said F.D. "And nonsense. Maxwell was with Wanda before lunch. She died shortly after she was with him. Which means that she died shortly after lunchtime."

"If you're trying to turn a snag into an advantage, Mr. Derwent, you're wasting your time," said Baxter.

266

"He was with her before lunch—the private detective will confirm that."

"Mr. Maxwell went to see your wife just before lunch—of course he did," said Baxter carefully. "But what went on between them then is not the issue. The fact is that your wife left at three o'clock and went back to the house, Mr. Derwent."

F.D. stiffened slightly. The musical box continued to churn out notes at a funereal pace. "Fact?" he said. "Pure supposition."

"Mr. Maxwell went to London to purchase a film on your wife's behalf. She had left the money in the safe at the Sumner house—you told us that yourself, Mr. Derwent. She must have gone home to give him it. And that being so, they must have made love then—and what took place at the cottage earlier in the day had absolutely no bearing on the matter."

"Who says she had to give him the money? Maybe he used his own money."

"And the money that had been in the safe? What happened to it, Mr. Derwent?"

"How the hell should I know? I don't have to prove anything. It's not there now—but that doesn't prove that Wanda came back."

"The money was in a burgundy document case. The film which we recovered from the safe at the Lodge—left there by Mr. Maxwell—was in the same case."

F.D. shook his head. "Do you have this case?" he asked.

"Yes, sir." Baxter got up and opened a cabinet, taking out the case, now in a large polythene bag. "This is it, sir," he said.

"It's a different case," said F.D., hardly looking at it.

"I don't think so, sir."

"I'm telling you it is. And since I'm the only person who saw the one Wanda had, you are in no position to argue with me."

"But I am, sir. It's Mr. Sumner's case. He has identified it, sir, and the only way it ended up in the Lodge safe is if

267

your wife gave it to Mr. Maxwell. She was simply borrowing it, sir.''

F.D.'s face went blank for a second, then he smiled. ''Well done, Baxter! I really am most grateful to you for your hard work. You could have gone off on the wrong track altogether but for that. Obviously, my wife did indeed leave the cottage, and clearly, she must have been murdered after that. I have to admire your industry, constable.''

''On the Tuesday, we found traces of barbiturates in the kitchen of the Sumner house. You left them there when you doped Maxwell's drink. And we'll find them in your trailer too.''

''You'll need a search warrant,'' said F.D. ''And you're not going to get one with this rigmarole. Of course you found traces of pills in the kitchen! She killed my wife, she drove her car back to the Sumner house—the bag happened still to be in it. She let herself in, and made her pathetic suicide attempt. It didn't work, and she drove off again, over the edge of the cliff. You found her fingerprints, didn't you? What more do you need?''

''Yes, but then she had been in your kitchen, hadn't she? You told the Superintendent. When she first attempted to blackmail you. Her prints were found on the door jamb— only an enthusiastic house-keeper like Mrs. Sumner cleans that very often. If Mrs. Sumner had come back a few hours earlier, we wouldn't have found them. But we did.'' Baxter cleared his throat. ''On Tuesday evening, you moved out of the Sumner house and back to the Lodge. On Wednesday morning, you left the pill bottle in Mr. Landers' room. That wasn't a deliberate choice; he doesn't lock his room—I noticed that on Tuesday night when I was there. It was simply the first one you could get into.''

''Well, it was an interesting story, and someone has a vivid imagination, but it does not prove that I murdered my wife.''

''We found Miss Slaney's fingerprints on the hand brake, the steering wheel, the gear lever and the door of your wife's car, sir. No prints anywhere else. Not your wife's, not any-one's.''

"Doesn't that prove that she was the only one in the car?''

"So who switched on the windscreen wipers?''

F.D. stared blankly at him.

"Someone did.''

"All right, someone was in it with her. Someone who wanted rid of her. Maxwell. They cooked it up between them. Getting rid of Wanda, and framing me with that tape.''

Te. Lah. Soh.

"But it wasn't Miss Slaney's copy of the tape.''

"Only she and I had copies. And the Superintendent here has proved that it wasn't mine. Your nonsense about my making a second copy isn't worth discussing.''

"You made the second copy on to the tape you took from Barbara Slaney. Over a programme that wasn't broadcast until that Sunday morning—the programme that she always taped.''

Lah. Soh. Me. Doh.

"Do you think you could stop that?'' F.D. snapped, turning to Patterson.

"Oh, is it annoying you?'' asked Patterson. "You see, I think it's almost completely wound down,'' he said. "I find that if I turn the key with very gentle pressure, it makes the mechanism turn. Of course, you mustn't push too hard, or the key just comes out altogether—and that doesn't help at all.''

F.D. looked at Baxter. "She obviously made a second copy herself,'' he said. "Isn't that the blackmailer's trick? She could have made any number of copies—that Sunday or any other time.''

"No, she couldn't, Mr. Derwent,'' Baxter went on. "You see, where you went wrong was that you really did think you had frightened her into destroying that tape. Because you're a bully, and most people give in to bullies. So when she told you—after you had ripped apart her hotel room and threatened her with physical violence—that she had taped over it, you believed her. But every now and then bullies meet people

269

who stand up to them. Barbara stood up to you. She hadn't destroyed it, Mr. Derwent.''

Derwent frowned slightly, then rallied. ''The blackmailer as folk-heroine,'' he said. ''It's an unusual concept.'' He smiled again. ''But of course she hadn't destroyed it. Isn't that what I told you? Or have I lost the place?'' He smiled. ''Or were you just *hoping* I'd lose the place, Constable Baxter?''

''It's what you told us, Mr. Derwent, but it isn't what you believed. You believed she had destroyed it.''

F.D. smiled.

''But she told you she had sent it to herself. And she had.'' He picked up Barbara's keys. ''You shouldn't have left these in the ignition,'' he said. ''Anyone could have stolen the car. And got into your wife's cottage . . . and into Miss Slaney's London flat, come to that.''

F.D. blinked a little.

Baxter removed a polythene package from the drawer. ''This was picked up yesterday. Would you like to hear it?''

F.D.'s face was devoid of expression. He shook his head.

''Where the tape stops, there's a bit of shouting,'' said Baxter. ''Of course, the microphone was open all the time.''

F.D. stared at him, at the package, as he laid it on the desk.

''You saw her put the tape in the post box,'' said Baxter. ''And I think you'll agree that if it was lying unopened in an empty flat ever since, then the only person in the world who could have made that second copy is you, Mr. Derwent. And that leaves you with an awful lot of explaining to do.''

F.D. nodded slowly. ''You seem to know it all,'' he said. ''But—as I've had occasion to point out before—knowing and proving are two different things.'' Without warning, he lunged across the desk, grabbing the package. He dropped it on the floor and ground his heel into it. He looked up. ''Now prove it,'' he said.

Te. Lah. Soh. Patterson put down the musical box and looked at Baxter, tutting. ''Malicious damage,'' he said. ''Wouldn't you say, Baxter?''

270

"Definitely, sir."

"I think you should charge him, Baxter, and then take him to Ardcraig police station. He might do further damage if we were to let him go. And that means we'll have him under lock and key until we can charge him with his wife's murder."

"Oh, no," said F.D. "Ingram had no authority to enter Barbara Slaney's flat, Patterson. He had no right to remove anything. Now perhaps if you could have produced the evidence, your boss might have gone along with it—cooked the books to cover you. But I've destroyed it for real this time, and you have nothing to show for your friend's spot of burglary. So Chief Superintendent Shaw won't be best pleased, will he?"

Patterson raised an eyebrow.

"So if I were you," F.D. went on, "I'd forget all about the malicious damage charge, and any ideas of search warrants. In fact—if you want to keep your jobs, I'd forget that this conversation ever took place. And if you want to keep your friend Ingram out of prison, I'd forget you ever saw that tape."

"What's Mark Ingram got to do with anything?" asked Patterson, looking vague.

F.D. scooped up the package, tore it open, and produced the mangled tape. "*He* picked this up," he said. "You couldn't go without risking your job, so you sent him. But I was forewarned, Patterson, by your drunken friend—and I've destroyed the only piece of real evidence you had against me."

"That?" said F.D. "No, no. That's—that was," he amended, slightly sadly, "a snatch of a rather nice recording I made of 'To a Mouse' by Robert Burns—Mr. Ingram thinks very highly of it. As for his trip to London, I asked him to do some shopping for me." He picked up a Harrods bag, and smiled. "You are remembering," he went on, without drawing a breath, "that anything you say will be given in evidence?"

271

Soh lah te doh, said the musical box, triumphantly, all by itself.

"What if that tape *hadn't* been at her flat?" said Mrs. Patterson.

"I'd have been for the high jump," said Patterson, comfortably. "But it was. It was a calculated risk. I felt I had got to know that wee girl, and I had."

"Hugh, how could you?"

"I played a hunch. I was right. I couldn't ruin everything by finding out beforehand—like the man said, I would have been breaking the law, and anyway, it would have been inadmissible evidence." He smiled. "As it is, it is going to keep him in custody long enough for us to search that trailer, and nail him." He pushed away his breakfast plate, and stretched. "You can't do away with three people and leave no traces," he said. "And we'll find them now that we know what we're looking for."

"I hope you're not thinking of making a habit of this," she said. "I'm kind of depending on that pension, you know." She looked seriously at him. "She must mean an awful lot to you," she said, shaking her head.

"She meant a lot to me," he said. "And she had nothing whatever to do with any of it. If Derwent had been allowed to get away with it she wouldn't even have got a trial to prove her innocence—she'd just have been suspected of it for the rest of her life. And I couldn't let that happen." He looked at her under his eyebrows. "Could I?"

"I didn't marry a rebel," she said.

"No." He picked up the Harrods bag. "And I didn't marry a film star," he said. "Thank God." He smiled at her. "I don't know about you, but I have never for one second regretted that I took you for my awful wedded life." He delved into the bag and produced a bottle of perfume. "A wee minding," he said.

She smiled.

"I've got to go and meet a man from the Vice Squad," he said, kissing her on the cheek. "See you later."

272

* * *

"He probably just wants to apologise to you for all the hassle," said Landers.

Sue smiled a little weakly. "Yes," she said. "Probably."

"Come on," he said, ducking his head to look at her. "I thought you'd be so relieved when they got Derwent."

"I was. I am, but—"

"But what?"

She sighed. "Nothing. You needn't have come, you know."

"Of course I had to! Look—I don't know what you're so worried about. It's over."

"Yes," she said. "Of course it is."

They went into the little station, and sat in the only two seats provided. As they waited, a large man came in, and stood at the desk.

"Vic Simpson," he said. "To see your Super." He turned as Patterson came out of his office.

"Here it is, Sergeant," said Patterson. "I expect the label is a bit misleading."

The man laughed and took the can of film. "Have you not watched it, sir?" he asked.

Sue closed her eyes.

"No—when would I find time with three suspicious deaths to sort out?"

"Sorry, sir."

Patterson smiled. "Anyway, there's no need to watch it," he said. "You just spread the word that *Meg and Ivy* is available, and I guarantee they'll come crawling out of their sewer for it. They're very keen to get hold of it, for some reason."

"I think we'll have a wee look at it all the same, sir," he said, and went off.

"Sue," said Patterson. "Come through."

Landers got to his feet.

"You wait here," said Sue. "I won't be long."

He looked uncertainly from her to Patterson and sat down again.

Sue went into the office ahead of him; Patterson closed the

273

door. "Oh, well," he said. "It should give them a laugh, anyway."

She didn't speak as he sat behind the desk and smiled up at her.

"They'll find," he said, "that Mr. Maxwell and Mrs. Derwent were the victims of a hoax. All that's on the film is a few . . . out-takes, is it, you call them?"

Sue stared at him, then sank into the chair. "You know perfectly well that's what you call them," she said, when she could speak.

"Doesn't matter what's on it," he said. "It's what these jokers *think* is on it that matters. They're hardly going to be in a position to lodge a complaint." He reached down and picked up the Harrods bag. "A wedding present," he said. "From Mr. Ingram and myself."

She took the bag, and smiled at him, swallowing.

"Only I'd not bother telling the groom about it," he said. "He wouldn't care if you'd massacred half of Ardcraig, but that . . ." He shook his head. "It'll take him twenty-five years to see that in perspective," he said.

"I don't know how to thank you," she said.

"I don't want you to." He stood up. "Just try and be happy, eh?"

"I'll try."

He opened the door for her, and Landers jumped to his feet.

"Oh, John. Could you go back to the Lodge and wait for me?" she said. "There's something I have to do." She hurried past him, out of the police station.

Landers shrugged, and turned to leave.

"Oh, Mr. Landers," said Patterson. He jerked his head. "Come here a minute," he said.

Landers went into the office.

"Listen," said Patterson. He placed the musical box proudly in the centre of the desk, released the catch on the movement, and the fly spun into a blur.

"Looks like a tiny little disc when it does that," said Landers.

Patterson beamed. "You know what makes you see it like a disc?" he said as the soft notes of the poignant little French tune began.

Doh te lah soh me doh te . . .

"No," said Landers.

"Persistence of vision, son. Persistence of vision."

Lah soh me doh lah soh . . .

Life blossomed, like the rose, over and over, slower and slower and slower.

Cast

Movie Idol	Mark Ingram
Film Director	Frank Derwent
Wife	Wanda
Soap Queen	Susan Quentin
Bimbo Starlet	Barbara Slaney
Juvenile Lead	John Landers
Right-Hand Man (Real Name)	Reginald Howard Maxwell (Ronald Neve)
Script Writer	Simon Waterford
High-Ranking Policeman	Hugh Robert Patterson
Local Bobby	Laurence Baxter
Chief Superintendent	Calum Shaw
Detective Constable #1	DC O'Connor
Detective Constable #2	DC Tate
Civilian Photographer	Chris Philips
Fingerprint Man	Fergus Masson
Young Policeman	Yankee Papa
Enquiry Agent	Eddie Anderson
Mrs. Patterson	Morag
The Witness	Tommy Watson
The Doctor	Toby Dalziel
Third Child	Terry Callaghan
Vice Squad Sergeant	Vic Simpson
Hotel Manageress	Helen Macdonald
Waitress	Winnie
Barmaid	Belinda Mason
Reception Guest	Rose Gillies
Local Dignitary	Lady Duncan
Pop Star	Phil Sumner
The Wife	Thelma Wilson
Rock Band	Restless Bodies
Heavy	Harry
Minder	Mo

Contact	Colin
Junkie Boyfriend	Jez Bryce

And the Royal Burgh and people of Ardcraig

Lighting Cameraman	Leonard Charles
Second Assistant Director	Stuart ''Apeman'' Dundas
Script Supervisor	Stella Swift
Key Grip	Kevin Gilbert
Make-Up	Marcia Upjohn
Camera Operator	Clive Oliver
Stunt Double	Sheila Drage
Sound Engineer	Steve Ellis
Film Editor	Fiona Egerton
The Critical Success	Three Clear Sundays
Leading Lady	Letitia Lovelace
Leading Man	Leo March
Supporting Roles	Samuel Rogerson
	Sophia Rogerson
Smash Movie	Strong Medicine
British Spy	Barry Strong
Kiddies' Hour	Know How
Movie Programme	Matinee Performance
Gossip Columnist	Gussie Christiansen
Estranged Wife	Elise Wyatt
Talk Show	Trade Secrets
Chat Show Host	Charlie S. Hall
Local Radio Station	LRS
Disc Jockey	Duncan Jameson
News Reader	Norma Reay
Local Reporter	Lindsey Rannoch
Radio Quiz	Record Quest
Radio Contestant	Robbie Chapelton
Soap	Stones
Blue Movie	Bondage Maidens
The Paperback	The Polson Bunch

Tchaikovsky
Swan Lake, Op. 20:
Swan Theme, Pas de Deux Act II;
Hungarian Dance (Czardas) Act III

Steinman/Meatloaf
Two out of Three Ain't Bad

Jones
I Want to Know What Love Is

Blackwell/Presley
Don't Be Cruel

Bloom/Gade
Jealousy

E Morricone
Theme from the Life and Times of David Lloyd George
(Chi Mai)

Lennon/McCartney
Ob-La-Di, Ob-La-Da

Green
Albatross

Richard Strauss
Also sprach Zarathustra
(Tondichtung fur grosses Orchester op. 30):
Von den Hinterweltlern

de Burgh
Lady in Red

Moroder/Whitlock
Take My Breath Away

Diamond/Lyle
I Should Have Known Better

Mozart
Serenade No. 13 in G Major, K 525 (''Eine Kleine Nachtmusik''):
Allegro—Romanze—Menuetto & Trio Rondo

Endsley
Singing the Blues

McKuen/Brel
Seasons in the Sun

Philips/Adler
San Francisco (Wear some flowers in your hair)

Mann/Weil/Snow
All I Need to Know

Louiguy/Piaf
La Vie En Rose

Sue Quentin stood on the cliff as the tide came surging in; gulls swooped and cried, waves crashed, spray showered over her. Slowly, she reached into the dark green bag and drew out the can of film, pausing for a moment before launching it into the bright, spring air.

And she laughed with sheer relief, her arm outstretched, her past a silver disc against the blue, cloudless sky.

About the Author

Jill McGown is also the author of *A Perfect Match, An Evil Hour, The Stalking Horse, Murder at the Old Vicarage,* and *Gone to Her Death.* She lives in Colby, England.

Murder and Mystery

from . . .

JILL McGOWN